First published 2011 by Complete & Total Asskicking Books
London, UK

Copyright © Michael Stephen Fuchs

The right of Michael Stephen Fuchs to be identified as the author of this work has been asserted by him in accordance with the Copyright, Designs and Patents Act 1988.

This is a work of fiction. Names, characters, places, and incidents either are the product of the author's imagination or are used fictitiously. Any resemblance to actual persons, living or dead, events, or locales is entirely coincidental.

All rights reserved. No part of this publication may be reproduced, stored in or introduced into a retrieval system, or transmitted, in any form, or by any other means (electronic, mechanical, photocopying, recording or otherwise) without the prior written permission of the author. Any person who does any unauthorized act in relation to this publication may be liable to criminal prosecution and civil claims for damages.

ISBN: 1522785574

ISBN-13: 9781522785576

"I am not a man, I am dynamite."
- Friedrich Nietzsche,
Ecce Homo

TERRORIST SAFEHOUSE
DEARBORN, MICHIGAN
21:12:14 EST 05 APR

The keyboard has a lot of blood on it but then again so does almost everything, including Mike Brown. He doesn't really know why he's sitting at this keyboard. There's been a gunfight and it ended so few heartbeats ago that reports still ring in his ears, sulfur stench closes his throat, and most of the blood on the floor hasn't even properly pooled yet.

Mike figures he should probably go around and see if anybody is still alive, anybody he could help maybe. But he somehow knows there isn't. The only things left alive in that little white crackerbox house, out in the shitbird suburbs of Dearborn, Michigan, are him – and the computer that sits on the desk before him.

The machine has got an outsize flat-panel display, which is bleeding a cool glow out onto the still-warm bodies and all the hot smoke. That's the only light. Dusk has fallen outside and shutters cover the windows anyway.

Glancing down at his fingers, which are poised over the keyboard, Mike notices a smear of blood on his forearm. *Christ*, he thinks, *there's blood on everything*. There really shouldn't be blood on him. Mike Brown is a techie – a twiddler of bits and manipulator of abstract symbols. True, he works for a federal agency where people sometimes carry guns. And, yeah, the boundaries between the bit-twiddlers and the trigger-pullers have gotten a little porous in the last few years.

Nonetheless, Mike is nursing this feeling that he should really be 600 miles away in a swivel chair, slinging code and monitoring signals intelligence. Or, at most, directing trigger-pullers on the radio. He shouldn't be sitting in a house full of dead people. He should never have found himself fifteen feet away from a balls-out gunfight. And he shouldn't have blood on his arm.

And on his eyeglasses. Somehow he missed that. He removes them and regards the fine crimson spray – bright arterial-red, probably from way deep inside somebody – then wipes them on his shirt. He puts them back on his face and refocuses on the room. He tries to get his head around what he is seeing.

Like somebody whose car has been towed, walking around in a circle, seeing perfectly well that there's no car there, but not believing.

Scattered on the floor, on a sofa, in a doorway, slumped against a wall, out on the front porch, are a half-dozen very nice sheriff's deputies. Also, an indeterminate number of hajjis, also arrayed in awkward poses. "Hajjis" is how one of the sheriff's deputies described them, in the approximately four seconds he'd had to radio in. Mike forgave him the crude racial profiling, given circumstances.

They're dark-skinned guys, and they'd been shouting in some language not English. Mike guessed they looked Middle Eastern. And they were just armed to the nines and blazing away like goddamn crazy sons of bitches.

And now they are gone. All of them have decamped, or died trying. No surrenders, no survivors. Just this one computer. And Mike Brown.

With that many guns going off, that rapidly, in quarters that close, Mike would not have expected every single one to miss him. He is deeply surprised to find himself having dropped completely unscathed through this meat grinder. For a few seconds there, he'd figured that was his last few seconds. He'd been on the front porch, and grabbing floor, and he hadn't been armed himself. But, still.

Here's the thing. This thing is this. Typically when Mike would go out to serve a warrant on a house he's identified as the physical source of some computer security breaches – some annoying and clever but, you know, basically parryable hacker attacks – when he went to serve a warrant on some hackers, he didn't expect to get shot at. Yeah, he went out with sheriffs. And, yeah, the sheriffs had guns.

But one didn't, in one's heart of hearts, expect to end up getting blasted into the next jurisdiction by a bunch of ferocious guys with assault rifles. Much more typically, he'd be interrupting an online porn masturbation session by some post-adolescent script kiddie with delusions of hacker grandeur.

And Mike could tell you something else – there but for the grace of God. Those geeky kids are Mike without the advanced degree and the federal ID.

So, Mike doesn't know why he sat down at that bloody keyboard and logged in. But this act would set the pattern for the next year of his life. Soon, Mike will get so jaded about typing on blood-spattered keyboards that he hardly notices it. He'll carry hankies.

But on this first day, he's a little vacant, a bit blank in affect. So much so that when the cavalry arrives a few minutes later – in the form of probably the entire Detroit metro area SWAT establishment – he doesn't remember to put up his hands and move real slow.

The SWAT guys could conceivably have shot him, yeah. But probably not.

Because another thing Mike Brown is very shortly to learn? He's going to learn that those SWAT guys are big pussies. Just huge, enormous pussies. And so were those poor dead sheriff's deputies, and so are the FBI (including their fabled Hostage Rescue Team), and so are regular military, and so are most workaday special operations units – and especially so are even the most heavily armed and vicious hajjis you can even dig up.

You know who *aren't* pussies?

Mike Brown will tell you who aren't pussies.

D-BOYS

MICHAEL
STEPHEN
FUCHS

U.S. DEPARTMENT OF HOMELAND SECURITY
ARLINGTON, VIRGINIA
06:02:55 EST 06 APR

"No. Definitely not."

This isn't Mike speaking.

"Sir, let me suggest—"

"Shut up. You shut up, too. You – speak."

These aren't Mike speaking, either. Mike isn't speaking. He's sitting. He's sitting and trying to look blameless, until and if somebody calls on him.

"It's like I said. This is what we've been looking for, because we've known it was on its way in."

This is the closest thing to Mike speaking. This is Mike's boss – James Niewendyke, who is Director of the Information Security Directorate of the United States Department of Homeland Security. That is where Mike works.

"For, call it five years now, we've known this was coming in, and it was more or less undodgeable." James Niewendyke is addressing two generals, an admiral, two undersecretaries of defense, the Director of the FBI, three unidentified guys, and two guys with their faces actually fuzzed out on the overhead video links. Also around the real physical table are a handful of high-level DHS guys and a colonel.

"Why now?" This is one of the undersecretaries. "Why not before now?"

"Because, before now, the guys who had the chops to get into critical systems didn't have any desire to break anything when they got there. And the guys who really want to hurt us didn't have the chops." James Niewendyke takes his glasses off and rubs them with his tie. "But it was always inevitable that some of the geeks would eventually get angry – Kevin Mitnick with a grievance. Or some of the real assholes would get smart – al-Zarqawi with skills."

"Which is it?" This is one of the generals.

"It's the second thing."

"So these are Islamist bad guys?"

"Our early forensics say yes, they're Islamist bad guys."

"So then this is just AQO." This is one of the military guys, an Air Force colonel, from the new Cyber Warfare Command, and in the actual room. He is referring to al Qaeda Online, so-called. "We know this crew, we know what they're doing." Mike knows this Air Force colonel fancies himself a cyberterror expert – but Mike is pretty sure he couldn't reliably find his own asshole with road flares and spelunking gear. Mike figures he'll let his boss point up that issue.

"No," his boss says, with an aspect of thin patience. "You know what they've *been* doing. AQ web sites, jihadi-prop videos, bomb soup. These things spring up, you run D-DOS attacks, you shut down the servers. Maybe you send SAD or SOF out to get them, when you can find them."

"We also shut down guys running attacks."

"You shut down guys *planning* attacks – planning real physical incidents using online comms. And over here we spend all our time chasing hackers around the block – all-American kids who want a screenshot of the Treasury intranet for their desktop. So that's you working serious bad guys fucking around online. And us working fuck-ups doing serious stuff online. But what I'm saying is that now we've got the real deal – opponents who are heart-attack serious, and who are probing drop-dead serious targets in the information infrastructure. *And who are getting in.*"

"How serious?" This is the other undersecretary.

"DOE. Nuke labs. They only got in for a few minutes. But they got in."

"And you're so sure they're real bad guys?"

"Mike." James looks down and across at the patch of desk beneath the younger man's chin. "How many probes or successful breaches of tier one through four systems in the NII have you caught in these three years?"

Mike looks up and tries to make his face, his voice, like his boss's. "All in? About fourteen hundred."

"On how many of those have you gotten a grid reference and sent out a team, or gone yourself?"

"A hundred and twelve."

"How may of those targets have shot us up when we got there?"

"Domestic or foreign?" This is just Mike stalling.

"All in."

"One. The one tonight."

"How many of that team came home?"

"None. Well, me."

James pins the overhead monitors in turn. "Let me tell you what we've got. We've got a domestic intrusion cell that we caught in some very interior systems – specifically, the Department of Energy's Nuclear Test Labs in Idaho Falls. They were about six keystrokes from about ten thousand pages of classified docs on reactors, materials – and weapons. We got lucky and—"

"How classified?"

"So classified they wouldn't tell me. The classification level is classified." No one can tell if he's joking, so nobody says anything.

"We got lucky and they tripped an alarm. The intrusion was extremely well-disguised. But our Mr. Brown here traced it. When we go out to get these guys, with local law enforcement, we end up in an eight-second, thousand-round shootout. We kill two of them, two or three escape out the back door – and our whole team goes down. All the forensics so far say they're AQ."

"And Mr. Brown here can trace them?"

"He's an A resource. That's why we took the risk of putting him out on the firing line."

"*Put him back.*"

Mike thinks even James is looking a little tired now. They've all been up for hours. "Mike isn't officially a field operative," Jim says. "He's not trained for CQB."

"You're going to need tech in the field." This is the other general. "Someone onsite to capture data while it's still actionable."

"That's why we send him out. Sometimes. But there are limits to wha—"

"Get him the tactical support he needs, but get him back out there."

One of the undersecretaries says, "Why don't we get him onto a team that's already out there? TF145? They've taken down some heavily wired safehouses in CENTCOM AO."

"No. Not the Task Force. We need a bunch of Rangers shooting everything up with SAWs like we need colostomy bags. This is finesse work."

After a beat of silence – the staccato energy of the room seems to be ticking down – one of the guys on video link speaks. He hasn't made a peep before this. And he doesn't have a face.

"There's Dick Havering's team."

The general stares out the monitor, straight through the room. "Okay, then. Get them tasked. Jim, we're going to put your boy with some boys in the CAG. That alright with you?"

"Sir."

And with that and nothing more, the general disappears and the room lights come up. Mike sees James eyeing him as chairs scrape floor.

* * *

Mike walks beside and just behind his boss now, their footfalls echoing down a sterile hallway with no visible end.

"Okay, I'll bite. Who's this Dick guy?"

"Check your go-bag," James says. "You'll want a shock laptop, tricked out with your sharp-edged stuff. And probably a rugged handheld. And clothes for extremes of climate."

"Where am I going?" Mike is getting the sense these questions don't hold a lot of interest for the other man. "Am I going to get shot at again?"

Jim blinks noncommittally. "I wouldn't worry too much about that."

"Oh, yeah? Why not?" Mike is starting to feel himself sag behind his eyes. He checks his watch and it's six-thirty in the morning. He hasn't slept since two nights previous – the night before the shootout, which was now last night. While off in his head, Mike realizes the other has stopped at an intersection of empty corridors.

"A bag for how long?"

"Call it indefinitely. Also pick someone to support you from see-woc." CWOC, the CyberWar Ops Center, had been the tactical heart of ISD, ever since things picked up on that front of the GWOT (Global War on Terror).

"Someone who?"

"I'd go with Fred. Or maybe Dharmesh."

Mike's red-rimmed eyes open fractionally. "I can have Dharmesh?"

"You can have part of Dharmesh. Let's call it two-fifths of Dharmesh."

Mike knows that if he is being offered nearly half of the Big D, this is a serious deal. Dharmesh is more in demand around ISD than coffee.

"Get some sleep while you can," James says. "And drive safely." This makes Mike think his stock has gone up. The department obviously wants him getting killed doing something smart, rather than something stupid.

James pats Mike's shoulder once, then turns right, leaving him where he stands. Mike tries to remember the way out of the building from there.

ON INTERSTATE 395
FAIRFAX, VIRGINIA
08:06:22 EST 06 APR

Forty minutes later, Mike rolls it off the beltway, under a sopping blanket of morning sky, and into his complex. This is a generic development in Fairfax, Virginia, the suburbs southwest of D.C. He picked it out on a two-day interview trip – at which time he'd figured both the job and the apartment would be temporary situations. Now, five years later, he still hasn't adapted to either the traffic or the weather.

He lets himself in, drops his coat on the couch, and lays himself down beside it. He knows he should go to bed, but can't find the energy. Instead, he takes his glasses off and peers through them at the muddy morning light leaking in through the picture window. To his dull amazement and horror, there's still a faint reddish smear in the corner of one of the lenses, and on the black plastic frame.

He tries to remember how he got here.

Ten years earlier, in the spring of 2001, he'd graduated from Columbia University in New York, with a BS in computer science. He'd managed to pay for this mostly by means of a partial ROTC scholarship, with the understanding that afterward he would serve a sporadic six years in the Army Reserve – one weekend a month and two weeks a year of playing soldier. He spent the summer after graduation backpacking around Europe – and then going through Army Basic Training at Fort Knox, in Louisville, Kentucky. He then went to work, as one did in those days, for an Internet start-up – in his case, a start-up in Manhattan's Silicon Alley. His start date was the 3rd of September, 2001.

Eight days later, two things changed: the tech economy downturn, which had already begun to accelerate, became catastrophic in New York; and the Army started calling up reserve units for active duty. Worried about losing his job, and horrified by the prospect of having to play soldier for real, Mike applied to a PhD program back at Columbia. He also didn't mind going back uptown again. From his briefly occupied office in the Flatiron District, he had been able to hear, and feel, the twin towers hit the ground.

Four years later, in the spring of 2006, when Mike became Dr. Brown, the tech economy had stabilized, and lower Manhattan had resumed normal life. But Afghanistan and Iraq had done neither. Army Reserve units were still serving 15-month deployments in theater, with no end in sight. Mike, still unable to think of himself as cannon fodder, cut a deal: he used his degree and skills to wangle himself a position at Homeland Security, as an alternative to going to war.

But it wasn't really an alternative to going to war. It was just war in a chair. But, before last night, it had at least been, if not a quiet front, one without live fire.

Now, on his couch, stunned, Mike thinks perhaps this was always inevitable – only a matter of time until he found himself staring down the wrong end of sparking gun barrels. He should have known, when they first started asking him to go out with these warrant teams. They'd wanted someone on the ground with one foot in the networks. And because he'd had military training, however rudimentary, he'd been cleared for fieldwork.

Before the field trips started, it had been all digital thrust and parry, info-security work and white-hat hacking, with a tinge of high stakes. Because he knew his shit, and because he wasn't shy about making it obvious, he'd quickly become one of the go-to guys in guarding the so-called National Information Infrastructure. Up until now, for the most part, he'd been defending it from the types of all-American computer geeks who had always made up the ranks of the hacker elite.

But he'd also been shoring up the defenses – in anticipation of the next great wave of attacks to come. And now it had – and as best as Mike could interpret from his boss's cryptic comments, he might not being seeing his desk again for some time. It was going to be fieldwork for the duration, and he couldn't guess what field, and he could only wonder who he'd be sharing it with.

With his last pulse of strength, Mike places his glasses safely on the coffee table and slumps sideways onto his coat. He curls himself up into it, and into what does not prove to be, alas, a dreamless sleep.

UNMARKED MILITARY COMPOUND
NEAR FORT BRAGG, NORTH CAROLINA
08:38:52 EST 06 APR

At the same moment Mike Brown is surrendering consciousness, Colonel Richard E. "Dick" Havering is pacing the narrow aisles of his Tactical Operations Center. He wears khaki fatigues with no insignia, Oakley assault boots, a stiff brush of grey hair, wire-rimmed glasses, and a wireless audio headset. He is commanding eight men and four women, all of whom stand or sit at glowing consoles arrayed around the room. But he is speaking to a man in a cave in the mountains of central Asia.

"How we doin', Bo Peep?"

"The complex is down. It's being cleared now." This, the answering voice, speaks out into the room with no perceptible static or delay. *"Only four rooms, but deep as hell."*

"Anybody get hurt?"

"No real people – except for one of the blocking force guys, who ate some shrapnel when a grenade took a funny roll. And he was only down as long as it took him to wrap it up with his Iraqi flag bandana."

"Bad guys?"

"Two tangos down, two coming out."

"What's the haul?"

"Two machines, which we're duping the drives, and BT's trying to see who they've been talking to from here. Also a weapons cache – small arms and man-portable air. Nothing to put in a parade."

"Okay, Sergeant. You bring 'em home. And have a good 'un."

As Havering pulls off his headset, a female non-com touches him on the shoulder. He looks over the shoulder at her.

"General Buster for you," she says.

"What channel?" he asks, turning away and bringing the device back to his ear.

She taps him again and points to the other end of the room. Behind thick glass stands a thick man with two stars on each shoulder.

"Whoah hoah," Havering whispers, impressed, and strides across the room.

* * *

"What's the good word, top?"

Sergeant Major Eric Rheinhardt, call sign Little Bo Peep, looks over his shoulder, 8000 miles away. He's standing on a 300-meter cliff edge, which overlooks a valley winding amidst snow-blanketed ridges. He folds down the antenna on his satphone and turns back to face the mouth of the cave complex, and the person poking out of it.

"Clean up, pack up. Exfil in twenty."

"Back to the FOB?"

"Back to the Ranch."

"Nice. I'm freezing my nuts off up here."

Rheinhardt smiles. "Ali, you really don't have to take every opportunity to remind us of your enormous package."

"Roger that, top." Sergeant First Class Aaliyah Khamsi smiles in return. She slings her rifle – which is nearly identical in height to her – hitches a thumb in her tactical rig, and disappears back down the hole.

A dog barks in the distance. Rheinhardt calls after her, "Oh, and have one of the Rangers go get Mac."

Rheinhardt turns back to face the valley. He pulls a palmtop from his duty belt to look up today's code for a helo pickup. He reflects that he spends most of his time these days inserting via helicopter onto frozen mountaintops, or belly crawling through baking wadis. And trying to remember passwords.

The last sunlight glints blindingly off the snow on the ridgelines.

COMMANDER'S OFFICE
MILITARY COMPOUND AT BRAGG
09:00:02 EST 06 APR

"General." Colonel Havering now sits behind his spare desk, with the senior man opposite. He neither offers nor invites pleasantries. He knows general staff officers will blow that smoke up your ass if they're in the mood, or suck it right back out if they're not.

"What's that new team of yours up to, Dick?"

Havering squints slightly and leans back. "The usual stuff. Grenade-throwing contests in caves. Packet sniffing."

General Bobby "Buster" Dilbeck eyes the other man. "That one of your high-tech geegaws?"

"Packet sniffing? That's one of our high-tech things."

"How's all that going for you?"

"Like a five-finger prostate exam."

"That bad, huh? Matter of fighting for the missions, or fighting for the support?"

"Bit of both. The guys who know what's going on won't talk to us. And the guys who know what they're doing won't take the time to teach us anything."

"I thought your boys already knew how to do everything. Jump from 40,000 feet in scuba gear. Make a headshot a mile out. Speak Farsi. Take apart computers in the dark."

"That's an image we like to keep up. But the cyberwar space is pretty deep, and moving fast. It's a tough river to swim in without some help."

"CIA?"

"Won't talk to us much, not outside the Task Forces. Turf. And trying to have a debate with those guys is just hammer-throwing at ten yards."

"How about the Activity?"

"Heh. Everyone knows they don't exist, Bobby." Both men smile. "If they did, they're still stretched too thin – providing SIGINT for north of ten thousand SOF worldwide… Delta, DEVGRU, and everybody else. They don't have time for a lot of handholding."

"Cyber Warfare Command?"

"The Air Force? Please. They took two years just deciding where to put their building. We've read the reports of their constituent electronic-warfare groups. Of course, those guys are done doing anything useful now that they've been put under one big, stupid roof."

Both men nod and regard each other. "Tell me again why you're fighting so hard for these kind of jobs. And why you're putting the time in to learn all this stuff."

Havering nods and picks up a pencil. "General, everyone's trying to learn this stuff. Even if they don't quite know why – or how important it is. See, the thing is: so-called military experts generally only understand future technologies *in the current military context*. But the trick is seeing the technologies in the new battlespace *being created* by the technology."

"Dick, I'm an old infantryman. Put it in simple terms for me."

"Okay. In the run-up to World War Two, the Germans listened to Mansfield, who was a proponent of rapid, armored warfare. The French mainly ignored de Gaulle."

Dilbeck nods. "They got that one wrong. They didn't see the tanks coming."

"Oh, no. Monsieur General Fuckhat can see the tanks coming." Havering taps his pencil. "He sees that they can drive over open ground, he sees that rifles and machine guns can't touch 'em. He can even imagine more powerful tanks, with longer range and better armor. What he *doesn't* see, unless he thinks a lot harder and deeper about it, is *roads*."

"He doesn't see roads?"

"He doesn't consider that the same technology that gave rise to the tank also spawned a whole new network of paved roads. The roads weren't built by the military – they were built by civil society. But that doesn't matter a sweet rat's. They're there. And the result is that society has uploaded its entire stock of important things, things that need defending, to a new battlespace."

The General shifts in his chair, thoughts crossing his puffy yet lined face. "A new network."

"Right. And in May of 1940, largely inferior but faster German armored divisions poked a hole in the French line, swarmed onto the road network, and hauled ass to Calais. The French had all these plans to fight in the rail network, but the Germans went ahead and fought on the road network – which was much superior in mobility and communications. France was *lebensraum* in three weeks."

"So you're saying we don't want to get our backsides handed to us when the bad guys swarm over the new network and take our important stuff."

"No, we do not. The lesson, General, is that the soldiers have to fight where the war is. And the war will go where the people are, and where the valuable things are. In 1914 they were on the rail lines. In 1940 they were on roads." Havering lets the other man finish for him.

"And now they're online." The General looks off at the corner of the room. Havering figures the point of the visit is coming now. "Well, okay, that all sounded so good I'm going to go ahead and give you one of these jobs you're always asking for." When Havering still looks skeptical, he adds, "The squeaky wheel gets the grease."

"That's true," Havering says. "But who the fuck wants grease?"

Dilbeck laughs. "Don't worry. The job also comes with a resource. Computer guy from Homeland Security."

Havering looks carefully noncommittal. "Is this the kind of help I've been asking for?"

"Not on purpose. But it might be on accident. He's a civilian employee of DHS – one with a very pointy head. Caught some hackers busting into something important – something with isotopes on it. When he went out with some locals to get 'em, the cops all got shot, and the hackers all got away."

Havering stops tapping his pencil.

"We now know these 'hackers' were AQ. And we don't know whether or not they've got some buddies still out there somewhere. Pentagon wants to put this guy with you – he'll be the brain, and you'll be the muscle. Where's your team?"

"Inbound. Ten hours."

"Your guy will be here about the same time. Make him feel to home. He'll tell you what he knows, and you tell him what you can do. Then we'll see if you can go out and make some things happen."

POPE AIR FORCE BASE
NEAR FORT BRAGG, NORTH CAROLINA
19:08:02 EST 06 APR

Mike Brown is shivering and bouncing on the metal bench in the back of a C-130 Hercules turboprop cargo plane as it touches down, like a skyscraper sliding into home plate. The in-flight meal sucked, there was no movie, and now the landing feels lethal.

After he'd woken from his couch coma, but before the car picked him up to take him to the flight, Mike spent some time trying to figure out what the hell was happening to him. He wasn't supposed to be able to get a transcript of the meeting from that morning, but he did, and he spent the afternoon expanding acronyms.

The first thing he learned was that CAG was the Combat Applications Group – which was the current preferred opaque term for what used to officially be called the First Special Forces Operational Detachment-*Delta*. Reading this caused his blood to run cold, though he'd also felt a thin ribbon of excitement in the wash of fear.

He couldn't find out anything about Dick Havering, from any data source, public or private. It was, as they say, above his pay grade.

Then he'd logged into the DHS net from home to update his files with the latest forensics from the site in Michigan, and to touch base with Dharmesh. Big D hadn't had time for him then, but they'd swapped mail and agreed to hook up when Mike got where he was going.

Which is now. A loadmaster starts opening the rear doors and lowering the ramp before the plane stops rolling, and Mike slings his puffy trekking bag and his rock-hard electronics case and clambers down onto the tarmac. Lights twinkle on too many things to make out, some moving and some buildings, and the very last purple light of the day settles on a featureless horizon.

A few ground-crew guys are moving around the plane, but no one takes notice of Mike, so he hitches his bags up and heads off toward the nearest largest bunch of lights. Two jet fighters come out of nowhere and flash over his head in one second. When he levels out his gaze again, a man is trotting toward him, backlit by the building. He comes up fast, slows, then puts his hand out.

"Dr. Brown? I'm Sergeant Roque." He's wearing khakis and an untucked blue button-down over a white t-shirt. His black eyes are steady, but his face boyish. "I'm going to take you out to the compound. Jeep's just there. Good flight?"

Mike lets him take one of his bags and follows alongside.

"Not bad," he says, eyeing the civilian clothes. "Sergeant…?"

"Call me Javier."

"Mike."

As they settle in the vehicle, he hands Mike a badge on a chain. "You'll need this to get anywhere, including the head. It's already keyed to your biometrics. Other than that, I'm going to get you settled and get you anything you need before your briefing."

"Who's briefing me?"

"No one. You're briefing us."

"Oh." They drive through a security gate without stopping and turn onto a ring road. "When?"

Javier's eyes dart to his watch, which looks heavy and high-tech. "Forty-five minutes."

Mike snorts. "What, can't manage anything sooner?"

"We would," Javier says, twisting his head at the neck and nodding at another building-sized airplane skidding to earth behind them. "But the team's just getting in now."

Open-mouthed, eyes tearing in the breeze, Mike looks over his shoulder at the plane rumbling over the tarmac, and the lights and shrieking recede behind them.

* * *

"Let me get you a DWEP key, for your laptop," Javier says, placing Mike's other bag on a bunk. They are in a tiny single room, and Mike is already clunking his hardened laptop on the desk and firing it up.

"No need," Mike says. "Free wireless is everywhere – if you happen to be in a position to task satellites."

Javier smiles at him. He's leaning on the doorframe, which doesn't make Mike think immediately of military posture. "That must be very convenient," he says. "However, you may find the roof in here interferes with your link-up." Mike is finding exactly that – his machine, his phone, and his handheld are getting nothing to talk to. "Not much electromagnetism goes in or out of the building."

Javier hands him a USB device with a card and thumbprint reader on the end. "This will get you on the local network. If you give me your phone, I can have that re-locked to internal GSM." Mike hands it over. "Meanwhile you can use the desk phone, if you swipe your card and print in." He bounces Mike's phone in his palm. "Need anything else for now? Okay, I'll come back for you here in thirty minutes." As he closes the door on himself, he adds, "Have a good 'un."

Mike shakes his head to clear it. Seeing that his machine is now online and into the DHS VPN, he picks up the desk phone and dials CWOC.

* * *

Back at DHS, James Niewendyke leans over Dharmesh Patel's back and breathes warmly on his ear hairs. Dharmesh no longer notices this.

"Break it down for me. What did we get from the safe-house in Michigan?"

Dharmesh is typing at paper-crumpling speed, and doesn't slow while he speaks. "We got two machines blown with small charges. Those are toast. We've got a third that took a bullet to the hard drive."

"What can we get off that?"

"Anything on any sectors not actually carried away by the bullet. But it's taking time to pull the data off, and longer to piece it back together. With every Nth sector missing, it's kind of like trying to read—" and he flips to a text window and types:

```
Tel ou mthr 'l pckhe u a egh.
```

"Hilarious. But what actionable intel have you got for me – right now?"

"Related to the nuke labs hack? Nothing so far. But it looks like that's not all these guys were into. For starters, it appears the user of this machine was running the Bank of America web site."

"Oh was he, now?

"Okay – something that looks an awful lot like the B of A site."

"Gotcha. A phishing attack. They get anything?"

"About a hundred and eighty thousand dollars."

Niewendyke whistles. "Nice. That'll finance one or two spectacular terror attacks. Good work."

"Gets better. Because, naturally, I broke into the host where they have their fake bank site. And I've determined that there's another machine that's definitely also been accessing it. That one lives in London."

"Got the address?"

Dharmesh sighs. "Gimme a second. British Telecom are bastards."

"That's why you get paid the big bucks. Keep at it. Mike have what you've got so far?"

"It's in mail. And I'm expecting his—" at which his phone rings and he grabs for it "—call now."

1ST SFOD-D COMPOUND
NEAR FORT BRAGG, NORTH CAROLINA
19:56:52 EST 06 APR

Mike is just getting off the phone with Dharmesh when the door of his new little room knocks. He opens it, finding not Javier, but a grizzled colonel in tan fatigues. The man hands Mike back his phone.

"Hi, Mike," he says. "I'm Dick Havering. Welcome to the Ranch. Follow me."

Mike twists around to log out, then pulls the door shut behind him. He figures he must look bewildered, because the man adds, "Not my name for it. Predates me." Havering looks sidelong at him. "What, you didn't watch *Bonanza* growing up?"

"A little before my time," Mike ventures.

The two fast-walk down a stretch of hallway together, passing a number of secure doors, and a handful of other people. Some are soldiers in fatigues, others are men in civilian clothes. A couple of the latter look to Mike a bit like urban cowboys – lanky, boots and jeans, the odd moustache.

"What do you know about the Unit, Mike?"

"Just what I see in the movies."

"Well, most of that's true. Except for the Chuck Norris shit. Couldn't get the motorcycles with the rocket launchers. Know anything about F Squadron?"

"From what I've read, you only have A, B, and C."

"We've got a couple more besides that now, which you won't have read about. But it ain't like Dick Marcinko with his SEAL Team Six. Claimed it would fool the Soviets into thinking three, four, and five were already deployed. But everyone knows he just thought it sounded cool." Havering's eyes crinkle.

He pauses to swipe and print through a doorway – not holding the door for Mike, but making him swipe and print, too.

"F is new, and not up to operational strength yet. It's sort of my personal attempt to up-tech, while we've got the breathing room for it. You're going to be working with Alpha team, commanded by Sergeant Major Rheinhardt. Sergeant Roque, who you met, is also on that team, and he's gonna look after you personally." He pauses at another doorway. "We're through here." This time he holds the door.

* * *

"Folks, this here's Mike Brown, PhD. He's one of those info-sec guys from Homeland Security, and he's got some real good intel for us." Mike has the sense this good-ole-boy routine is a bit of a put-on. "Try not to ask any stupid questions."

Mike steps up to the front of the room. Behind him is a whiteboard, a digital whiteboard, and a large LCD. He's not using any of them, just talking. He's also trying to figure out which of three aspects of the people sitting before him is most jarring.

First, there's the fact that – aside from Javier Roque, who is seated with the others, and nods at him – they all look like they just stepped off the set of *The Dirty Dozen*. None are showered, all streaked with dirt – and what might be smoke or soot. All wear desert camouflage fatigues, with more or less tactical rigging festooned about them. All but one wear sidearms.

The second thing is that one of them is a girl. She's dark-skinned with wildly curly black hair and sits with one camouflaged knee up and her chin on it, looking a lot more relaxed about being there than Mike is.

Third is that one of them is a dog. It looks to Mike like maybe a beagle, except about twice the size of a normal beagle. It lies on the floor alongside the five chairs with people in them, chin on paws, holding Mike's gaze.

Mike swallows and says, "Hi." He realizes he's got nothing to shuffle or cue up, so he just jumps in. "Okay. Two nights ago we identified an intrusion into some highly secure computer systems within the Department of Energy. We then sent out a warrant team based on the grid reference we got. The team, uh—"

One of the four sitting men, the largest, raises a hand politely. Mike points at him. He says, "We already got that briefing on the plane."

"Right. Sorry. Um, okay. Since then, we've ID'd the two suspects who were killed. They're both German nationals of Saudi descent, Wahabbi Muslim of course, computer science degrees from the University of Heidelberg, with student visas for PhD programs at the University of Michigan – which they stopped turning up for six months ago."

While Mike pauses, the large man says, "Yeah, we got that, too."

Havering, behind and beside, says, "Mike, I think what we need right now is the computer forensics. What you've dug up from what you found at the site."

"Right. Okay. First is that, in addition to the hack into our systems, they were also running a phishing attack – probably to finance their operation. What this means is they were sending out a lot of email telling people to log into what they would think was a major bank's web site, but was really a fake site they set up themselves—"

Another of the sitting men raises his hand. He's leaner and shorter, with glasses and a ball cap and, Mike notices, a couple of pens in his shirt pocket. "Sir, with respect, we know what a phishing attack is."

"Okay," Mike says, nodding. "Do you know what it means if they were phishing with a D-DOS attack from a botnet of a thousand zombies? Sergeant—"

"McDonough. Sir, it means they'd hijacked a large number of individual PCs by infecting them with malicious code. They then used these zombie PCs to launch a distributed denial of service attack, overwhelming the real bank site with HTTP requests, causing it to go down. The phishing mail they sent out, most likely from the same zombies, will have said that the real bank site was down and the recipients should use the alternate site. When users went to it and logged in, their usernames and passwords were captured and their accounts emptied of funds. Sir."

Mike arches his eyebrows and nods. "That pretty much covers it."

The man taps another pen on a pad, where Mike sees he is taking notes. "How'd they hijack the PCs?" he asks.

"We don't know yet. There are a hundred ways to hijack that many machines – as long as there are millions of people out there who don't upgrade their anti-virus software, don't use anti-spyware, and haven't upgraded Windows in ten years. Home computers are hijacked and zombified all the time."

The man regards Mike through his glasses. "But surely you could locate some of the zombified machines – from the bank's records of the compromised accounts?"

Mike arches his eyebrows. "Yes. Yeah, my team did just that. And they've tasked the FBI to send some guys out to pick up a few."

The man in the hat smiles. "As soon as their busy schedules permit, no doubt. Have you figured out where the money went?"

"Through a domestic account first – and then somewhere offshore, we think. We haven't gotten to the bottom of it yet."

"Were they working alone, son?" This from the colonel, sounding not quite impatient, but intent.

"Almost definitely not. All of the funds disappeared *after* we took down the safehouse in Michigan."

"Do you have anything like a lead on their buddies?"

"I think so. We've traced a second location that was also accessing the back-end of the phishing site. It could really only be the same people."

"Where?"

Mike looks down at his phone, and writes on the whiteboard. "At this address in North London."

"*Righty*, then," the colonel says. "Wheels up in thirty."

And with this, everyone in the room, including the dog, spontaneously gets up and files out. Mike looks around, with his mouth still open. He sees that Javier is stepping toward him – and he feels a hand on his elbow. It's the colonel.

"How long have you had that address?"

"Only ten minutes." Mike feels like he's fucked up already.

"It's okay," Javier says, steering him toward the door. "We'll finish the briefing in the air."

POPE AFB
NEAR FORT BRAGG, NORTH CAROLINA
20:45:00 EST 06 APR

Mike is now bouncing on the seat of a C-17 Globemaster – a larger, jet-powered, much faster, and slightly less noisy aircraft – this time taking off. The four men and one woman from the briefing sit strapped in around him, Javier at his side.

"Can we just go and raid a house in the UK?" Mike asks, nearly shouting over the engines.

"Shouldn't be a problem," Javier says. "We've got friends there."

As the plane nears cruising altitude, the others in the group unstrap, set up a folding table, and start booting up laptops on it. At the same time, Mike's phone rings. He pulls it out of his jacket pocket and sees that GSM (it's quad-band) plus SATCOM (it's that, too) are both working again. The call is from CWOC.

"Mike Brown," he says.

"Hey, it's Dharmesh. Update for you. We made some progress on running down the funds. Like I told you, all of it went straight into a domestic account. We woke up a judge and got a warrant for that, but the money was already gone."

"Track it from there?"

"Yeah. Went from there into a PayPal account. However, that one was registered overseas, and those assholes at PayPal won't honor our warrant."

"Let me guess," says Mike, unbuckling and stretching his back. "You took a peek anyway."

"Yes and no. I tried the usual stuff to break directly into the account in question. But these guys are good enough to be in the eight percent of the general public with unguessable, uncrackable passwords."

"I guess that's not a big surprise." Mike sees Javier get up and join the others round the table, where they all pore over things.

"However, PayPal security hasn't gotten a whole lot better since that huge intrusion whenever it was. I was able to get into their UK mirror and read some front-end web server log files. I still can't tell you what that account was doing, but I'm pretty sure I can tell you who was using it – it's the same computer as the one accessing the bank phishing site. The same machine in London."

"No shit?"

"Pretty much no shit. I can't be totally sure, but it'd be a big coincidence. Now, I've been trying to get into this machine myself, get a keylogger or something in place. No luck. But if we can get someone out there in person, get possession of the physical box quickly, we can maybe fish out the footprint of the PayPal credentials. And then find out what they've done with the money."

"I think we can get someone there. Me."

"No shit?"

"No shit. I'm currently roughly right over your head, in another military transport – and then heading out over the Atlantic." He realizes he's being gestured at from the table. "Gotta run. Thanks, man."

"No problem. Try not to get shot at anymore."

* * *

"You didn't mention it was a mosque." This is one of the men in the grimy uniforms, one who hasn't spoken before. But he seems to Mike to have the bearing of a leader. He immediately hits Mike with this comment when he comes over.

"I didn't mention what's a mosque?"

"The quote address in London unquote."

Mike has no response to this. He didn't know himself.

"I hate mosques," the very big guy says. "They've always got so much goddamned ammo in mosques. Plus half the time they're wired to blow."

The first man exhales. He looks at Javier and says, "You want to introduce everyone?"

Javier puts his hand on Mike's shoulder and says, "You all know Mike. Mike, this is Sergeant Major Eric Rheinhardt, who commands the team. This," he says, pointing to the big man, who has wavy hair and a moustache, both dirty blonde, "is Master Sergeant Johnson."

The man puts out his hand and mangles Mike's. "Call me BJ." Mike smells chewing tobacco on his breath, and sees that his eyes have been crinkled by the sun (or possibly habitual laughter).

"This is Sergeant First Class Aaliyah Khamsi."

"Ali." She takes his hand, incrementally less painfully.

"And you've kind of met Staff Sergeant Tim McDonough. Under the table there is Mr. MacSnuggles, AKA Mac, AKA Nutmuncher." Mike ducks down and regards the giant mutant beagle.

"Hello, Mac," Mike says. "Do you like flying on planes?"

"Don't talk baby talk to Mac," the woman says. "He'll bite your nuts off if he thinks you're patronizing him."

"Hence the nickname," says Javier.

* * *

Mike and Javier return to their bench after an initial planning session at the table.

"Is everyone in this outfit a sergeant?" Mike asks.

"Operators are all senior non-coms, so yes," Javier says. "Of course, the Unit has officers – you met Colonel Havering, for instance. But they rarely go out on small-unit ops like this one."

Mike nods. "And you say you've got friends in London – who presumably will keep us from getting nicked by Scotland Yard? Or MI5, I guess."

"Colleagues of ours. We do some cross-training with them."

"Spend a lot of time over there?" Mike asks.

"London these days is effectively the political and media capital of the Middle East. Which pretty much makes it the radical Islamist capital, too. Hezbollah, Hamas, the Algerians, the Egyptians – by which I mean the Muslim Brotherhood – they're all there. Anybody who's anybody."

"Why there?"

"For one thing, it's a financial and transport hub. For another, the immigration and asylum policies. Britain is very liberal about letting people in. And they're bound by an EU rule that you can't be deported back to a country where you're subject to capital punishment. Abu Hamza, the guy with the hook hands, got to hang out in London for years, preaching death to the infidels every day, because he was under a death sentence himself in Yemen."

Javier is in uniform now, and Mike looks down at the sergeant's stripes on his shoulder. He has to deal with military guys occasionally, almost all of them at a much higher rank – and those guys never seem half this knowledgeable. Mike feels a little at sea. These aren't grunts. That much is already blindingly obvious.

* * *

Stirring him from his reverie, a hand touches Mike on the knee. It's Sergeant McDonough. The one with the pens in his pocket.

"Have you seen these guys before?" he asks, just above the engine roar.

"No. I haven't."

The man takes a seat on Mike's other side. "Nothing like them?" Javier gets up now and rejoins the group at the table.

"In terms of cyber attacks from overseas, so far it's mainly been limited to stuff like web site defacement. Sites will get hacked and covered with pro-Palestinian slogans, denouncements of the occupation of Iraq, that kind of thing."

"Who's responsible for that?"

"There's one group called USG, the Unix Security Guard. They're mainly Egyptians, Moroccans, some guys from the Muslim former Soviet Republics. Another called FBH – the Federal Bureau of Hacking. They're out of Pakistan."

McDonough nods. "Well, sounds like they've got a sense of humor. So that pretty much rules out al Qaeda affiliation."

"Pretty much," Mike says. "They're kids. Geeks like me, just on the wrong side."

"What about AQ and affiliates? What are they doing online?"

"I sometimes do some work with guys at the Air Force Cyber Warfare Command, working what they call al Qaeda Online – AQO. They've been active for a while, but so far their antics are even less impressive than web site hacking."

"Like what?"

"Same kind of stuff everyone else does online, really – except their interests are jihad and mayhem. Trading bomb-making tips. Posting head-hacking videos. Occasionally coordinating training, or sometimes even attacks, via message boards."

"What do you do in those cases?"

"Usually, we'll break in – bring the server down, trash the file system. We grab the logs, to see who's been accessing the materials, bulk up the terrorist watch lists. In some cases, we'll leave it all running and lay sniffers, to keep tabs on users in real time."

"What if you can't break in?"

"Then we'll put pressure on the web provider to pull the plug. If they won't play ball, then we do it ourselves – usually with denial of service attacks. If worse comes to worst, we go there and get them. Well, *we* don't go. We pass it all on to CIA. After that, some of these guys who were posting suddenly stop posting. I get the impression the Agency's tactical unit, the Special Activities Division, has been busy."

The other man pauses before answering. "Not just S-A-D."

Mike arches an eyebrow.

"Sometimes SAD is up to a snatch job, and sometimes they are not."

"So you're saying we've been working on opposite sides of the same jobs? Sergeant McDonough?"

"Call me Tim."

"Some call you… Tim?"

"Yeah, I get that a lot."

"How long have you been doing this kind of work?"

"Three years ago we took down a safe house in Pakistan. It was an al Qaeda facility – and it was devoted solely to training people for computer hacking and cyber warfare. Intel guys called it a 'cyber academy'. This AQ cell had gathered a lot of information on the automated systems that control U.S. infrastructure. Dams and power grids, that kind of thing. Colonel Havering considered it a wake-up call. That's when he started putting together the new squadron."

"You know, now that you mention it… a couple of years ago, there was a D-DOS attack on nine of the thirteen root DNS servers. That was a pretty major ding to the Internet infrastructure. I think that was my boss's wake-up call, when he started putting together my team." Mike leans back. "But I don't think guys like us are brought on to think – just to twiddle the bits."

"That's actually my radio call sign," Tim says. "Bit Twiddler, or BT." Mike laughs aloud at this. "Don't misunderstand. I do a lot of tech stuff. But there's no one in the Unit who wouldn't be in the Unit anyway – who hasn't been through Selection. And our job continues to be much of what it's always been – kicking doors, moving and shooting well, blowing things up. It's just that there's an increasing IT component to figuring out where to go to do the shooting – and in making sense of what we find when we get there."

Mike chews on this. "So are you a soldier or an IT guy?"

"Well… I suppose it depends how much weight you put on the degree."

"What degree?"

A shadow falls on Mike and he sees Javier is back. "Come on," he says, offering Mike a hand up and toward the rear. "Gotta get you kitted out."

* * *

By an equipment bay in the back of the plane, Javier sizes Mike up then digs into a locker and hands him a set of black, full-body overalls.

"This is a Nomex and liquid Kevlar assault suit," he says. "The Nomex means you won't burn, and the Kevlar means you can't be stabbed or shot – well, except with something, you know, really big. Like, crew-served."

As he pulls the garment on over his shoes Mike says, "I take it you're proposing I go in with you."

"You can stay outside while we do the takedown. But the bad guys don't always go where you want them, or stay where you put them." He smiles the boyish smile again. "And you'd be amazed at the unlikely things that can blow up on you."

TARGET BUILDING
NORTH LONDON, UNITED KINGDOM
05:22:17 GMT 07 APR

Mike is standing in a dark alley wearing a radio headset clipped to his ear. Javier gave him this after the jumpsuit, but before their final briefing, and touchdown. He's cut out of the internal team chatter, though, so the device is silent, and there's little other sound in the alley. Mike pulls at the seams of his garment and listens for anything, anything at all in the near-black foreign night.

He's alone. Time is dragging. Finally, he imagines he hears a faint crack from above and around the corner. Then some kind of noise from inside the building. And then gunfire, good and loud – and it doesn't let up even slightly, for what Mike imagines is at least thirty seconds.

And then the wall next to him explodes outward, showering him with stone rubble and dust. He hits the deck, not voluntarily, covering up his head with his shaking hands. Something is on fire. He hopes it isn't him.

* * *

Not quite two hours before, the plane had landed at the RAF station at Hereford. They were met there by a British soldier and a helicopter. The British soldier was called Nigel. His uniform, like that of the Americans, had no insignia. Mike figured he was SAS, which would make sense of the cross-training comments.

"Welcome to Blighty!" Nigel had shouted over the whine of the engine and the shriek of the blades as they'd lifted off from the same tarmac they'd just set down on. After a quick introduction, he handed Mike a headset and asked, through the mic, "You come here to slot some jihadis for us?"

Mike positioned his own mic. "Javier told me you've got some. I thought the big problems with radical Muslim immigrants were on the continent."

"Well, yes and no. France actually has this Jacobean tradition of suppressing violence. They bloody well do mosque surveillance and make no apologies. If the French are convinced you're up to no good, you'll be deported at best – and at worst you'll be found floating in the river. What we need are more people fished out of the Thames with fingers missing – both to send a message, and as a concrete tactic." He gazed wistfully out over the black hills, presumably toward their destination – London. "What this town really needs is a good right-wing death squad."

Mike looked at the American team loading weapons around him – and wondered if they were it.

On their last few minutes in the air, Javier tapped him on the shoulder. At that point, the glinting, humming body of London was beginning to spread out beneath them. One of the crew chiefs gave them the two-minute warning. Into his headset, Javier said:

"A combat insertion by helo is an amazing feeling – the roar of the engines, ground blasting by below, wind trying to pull you out the door, the adrenaline. It's almost worth the high probability of becoming charred meat waffles."

* * *

Mike peeks out from underneath his gloves and the rubble, wincing from the pain in his head. Flames from somewhere are illuminating the alley now – including two figures who tumble into it from the ragged breach in the wall, ten yards away. They're both wearing black, or maybe they're just back-lit, and both carry Russian assault rifles. Before Mike can try to burrow further into the ground, they spare one glance in his direction and then take off in the opposite one.

A second later two more figures follow – these holding the big, tan assault rifles Mike recognizes from the unloading of the plane (but didn't recognize otherwise). One takes a knee and covers the far end of the alley, while the other comes to Mike. It's Javier. He pulls Mike to his feet.

"You okay?" His voice sounds muffled, but Mike can make it out. He nods vigorously. "I told you things blow up!"

With that, firing erupts up and down the alley – from the far end, and from a few feet away where the kneeling man opens up in return. Mike sees that it's the big guy, Sergeant Johnson, triggering off a series of stark, staccato, perfectly spaced rifle reports. They feel huge and heavy in between the close, stone walls. Feeling incoming fire – on nearby surfaces, in the air around him – Mike throws himself up against the opposite wall.

Javier promptly pulls him back. "Good place to get shot, Mike. Bullets follow walls." Later, he'd explain that they skim the surface, sometimes skipping along for hundreds of yards.

But now, Johnson is advancing down the alley, rifle to his shoulder, quick-walking smoothly and firing steadily. Squatting in the middle of the alley, with Javier beside him, Mike can see the gunmen at the far end break cover and retreat in panic. Both are instantly shot and go down. Later,

Mike would learn that Delta operators are trained always to be closing with their opponents – always keeping the initiative, always being aggressive.

Mike is watching Johnson flip over the two bodies when the wall explodes again – even closer this time. Mike goes down with Javier on top of him, and half the wall on top of them both.

Lying prone, trying to breathe, he hears his phone's text beep go off. It's been squeezed or blasted out of his pocket, by the explosion or the rubble, and lies now in front of his face. The message preview – which is also the whole message – appears on the lit screen six inches in front of his nose.

```
From: Niewendyke, James (DHS ISD)
Hey Mike - How are those D-boys treating
you? Jim
```

Mike coughs, raising dust. Behind the cloud, he sees Sergeant "Uncle BJ" Johnson returning from his grim errand.

"What I tell you?" he says. "*What* did I tell you? Goddamned fucking mosques."

INTERIOR OF TARGET BUILDING
NORTH LONDON, UNITED KINGDOM
05:32:47 GMT 07 APR

Mike is sitting in another safehouse – this time a *safehouse of God*. He's in a basement, at one of two machines on a table, arrayed opposite each other.

Two of the D-boys stand at the entrances to the room. Another, Tim, sits opposite Mike, working at the other machine. Sergeant Rheinhardt, the leader, is outside conferring with Nigel – presumably regarding how many seconds they've got until the Metropolitan Police arrive. The last, the D-girl, is still somewhere on a nearby rooftop.

And, this time, making a change for Mike, all the bad guys, and none of the good guys, are dead.

But no one seems all that happy about it.

"Not *one*?" Rheinhardt asked after they cleared the basement complex.

"We've swept everything," Javier said. "Sorry, top."

"How could you kill everybody?"

"I think they knew we were coming. That one there was typing with one hand and shooting with the other."

The one in question had been at the station Mike is currently occupying, which is why Mike is typing on another keyboard with blood on it. But Mike's too focused on doing his bit of the job to notice or care. He really doesn't want to get it wrong – not after the heart-stopping bits the others have done.

Rheinhardt steps back into the room. Mike looks up and can see the Brit over his shoulder, looking like he's shifting his weight from foot to foot.

"Out of time," Rheinhardt says. "Pop the drives. Exfil in two." As he exits again, he can be heard to mutter, "Since the fucking drives are all we've got to interrogate."

Mike pulls his multi-tool from his belt and begins unscrewing the back of the CPU. Hearing a groaning sound, he looks around his monitor and sees that Tim has levered his open with a knife. He feels something on his left arm. Sergeant Johnson has unsheathed, and is handing him, a knife the size of a baby.

"Don't cut yourself off," he says, grinning beneath his moustache, and beneath his lightweight, black, hockey-style tactical helmet.

With his first attempt at the Delta style of cracking a case, Mike actually does slice his thumb. Moving smartly away from his machine, Tim looks across and says, "Don't worry, man. Fingers grow back."

Mike looks up in surprise. "They do?"

The others laugh aloud from their corners of the room.

***

Javier has his arm around Mike's shoulder, ducking him back into the helicopter, up on an adjacent rooftop. The last one onboard is Aaliyah – with the dog. And with her Aaliyah-sized rifle, which she is carrying with both hands while she runs, Mac trotting alongside.

"Do you always leave her out here by herself?" Mike shouts over the engines, taking his seat. Javier straps him in, hands him a headset, and seats his own. "When we take down a building, she's generally on overwatch. Ideally, we'd have a two-man team – one sniper, one spotter. However, with the operational tempo and number of deployments since 2001, things are a little tight. Like they used to say in Texas: one riot, one ranger. And she's pretty safe out there with Mac. I'd rather have him for security, than a spotter."

"I didn't think they let women in Delta – much less dogs."

"We don't officially let women in. But, unofficially, she's not just *in* Delta – she's the best sniper in the Unit. Well, definitely best with a first shot – on some of the bigger weapons, she gets tired. But, then again, she only ever needs a second shot for a second target."

The chopper lifts off and Mike's eyes sting as he follows the plumes of smoke from the mosque. The fire is dimming, and the knot of emergency vehicles out front becoming visible, in the first morning light.

Mike shakes his head. "I'm really not sure I'm going to be up to this."

"You'll get there," Javier says. "Don't worry, I'll see that you do."

Mike regards Javier dully. "That can't be in your job description."

"Actually, it's exactly my job description right now. The thing is, the more you know, the less likely you are to get in the way – or to do something stupid and get somebody killed. Plus the more useful you'll be. The game is knowledge, *mi hermano nuevo*. And we'll be learning from you, too."

"I hope I've got something useful to teach," Mike says.

"*Ojalá*, Mike. God willing."

Mike puts his head against the vibrating wall and closes his eyes.

BRITISH ARMY COMPLEX
NEAR HEREFORD, UNITED KINGDOM
06:42:21 GMT 07 APR

Mike is sitting alongside Tim again, this time in a computer lab in a less explicitly religious building. They've been hustled straight there under the blades of the helo, hot hard drives clutched in their hands.

Plus one other piece of hardware. Still stinging from the ribbing of the cadre members, trying his best to laugh along, and get along, something had tugged at the corner of Mike's brain as the others tried to hustle him out the door.

"Wait," he said forcefully, stopping at the vestibule, amusing no one with the delay. "There's something else." He needed a good five seconds of standing still looking at nothing before he knew what it was. Shaking the hand from his arm, he darted back into the basement room, looped a strand of blue network cable from one of the PCs and followed it to, not so much a closet, as a dirty panel in the wall. Levering it open, he'd found his prize: "Network router," he said, stripping it of cables and tucking it under his arm.

Now he sits plugging it into a British Army-issue PC, via USB cable.

Beside him, Tim is seating a drive in a new machine the more pedestrian way this time, with the screwdriver on his multi-tool. Looking sidelong, Mike can see it's the sort of elaborate Leatherman that inspires shame and envy in guys with keychain pen knives. Every one of them, Mike has noticed, has a Leatherman in a belt pouch.

Since the first helicopter ride, Tim has also been wearing a pair of wrap-around eyeglasses, rather than his previous, black-framed, geeky ones. These have an elastic band and foam inserts – nearly goggles, but more rock star. He catches Mike checking him out.

Taking a screw out of his mouth, he says, "Most guys in the Unit get their eyes fixed if they need it. But I figured there was no point in giving myself the option of not having full-time ballistic eye protection." He slaps the cover back on the PC. "As you saw, there's often a lot of shit flying around."

"Javier warned me about things blowing up."

"Like the machines at your first safehouse, right? How about this one? Is it booting for you?"

"Yeah."

"What do you see?"

"Gimme a second."

"Time is the one thing we've almost never got around here."

* * *

In the next building over, Rheinhardt is having his asshole chewed by Nigel.

"That's your idea of a nice quiet snatch job, is it?"

Rheinhardt clenches his teeth and looks out of the corner of his eyes. Across the room, Johnson is lying on a couch with his boots on the next couch, reading the *Daily Mail*. He says aloud, "Hey, they finally convicted that guy who was planning to behead a Muslim British soldier last year. Says here the sumbitch was on twenty thousand pounds a year benefit payments." He looks over at Nigel. "You guys are paying for your own destruction, you know that?"

"It's cheaper than paying for your mum," Nigel answers.

Ignoring all this, Rheinhardt says, "They had a pretty good idea we were coming, Nige."

"How?"

"Unknown. They may have just lost contact with their cell in Michigan. And went on high alert after that."

"Like I do with your mother," Johnson says, "whenever she starts pawing at me. Hey – it's the incredible exploding IT guy." He's looking over his newspaper now, where Mike, with Tim, has appeared in the doorway.

"They knew we were coming?" Mike asks.

"You tell us," says Eric. "You're the hacker hunter."

"They're not hackers," Mike says. "They're vidders. And, in any case, these weren't the guys we're looking for."

***

The full group is in the computer lab now, with both machines booted up. Mike has placed his phone on the table, on speaker with Dharmesh in D.C.

"I've ghosted the drives and am sending them up now," he says, speaking toward the phone. "But I can already tell you three things about what they were doing with these machines. One is, the money definitely went through them."

"How do you know?" Rheinhardt asks.

"Because, as my colleague Dharmesh predicted, by getting the physical box, I was able to get the PayPal credentials, and get into their account. All the money, nearly two hundred thousand dollars, went in. And then it went back out shortly before we got there."

"Where to?"

"A currency trader. FV Exchange, Ltd."

"Good. Into what currency?"

Mike pauses and keeps his expression neutral. "Warbucks."

Nobody says anything, until finally Johnson quips, "What's that – the replacement since the dollar won't get out of the toilet?"

"And since Iraq," says Javier, "is still swallowing two billion a week?"

Mike scratches his head and eyes the floor. "It's a virtual currency. A game currency." Nobody says anything again. "And that's the second thing I know. These guys are gamers. Both of these boxes have AfterWar installed."

"So what," says Javier. "Who doesn't play video games? Why do you think the Predator drone pilots are so good? Or Green Berets out on ATVs painting targets with lasers for smart bombs? Everyone in the Army under the rank of colonel was raised on video games. The GWOT is the world's first first-person shooter war."

Mike pauses and resets. "Fair enough. But there's a third thing. There's almost *nothing* else on these boxes. Just the game. And I don't think these are your guys. Not the guys who hacked the nuclear test labs."

"How do you know?" asks Rheinhardt forcefully, "And do you know it for sure?"

Mike pauses. "No. I can't be sure. But the fact that there's nothing very interesting on these machines probably means no one was doing anything interesting with them. A good hacker needs a set of tools."

"He could have them on removable media," Tim ventures.

"That's true. He could. But there's another thing. The router I grabbed. It's got a proxy server installed on it. I can't tell for sure, because its records have been scrubbed… But I'm pretty sure the London safehouse was just a front. A digital front. They've been proxying all their hacks through there – so if they got caught, the authorities would come not to them, but here."

"And to the shooters guarding this place," Johnson adds.

"Yes," Mike says. "They could easily have just been muscle – guarding the storefront."

Rheinhardt raises an eyebrow. "You said the router was scrubbed. What does that mean?"

"Scrubbed, cleaned, wiped of all records and data – exactly four hours and twenty minutes before we walked in their door. What I'm hoping is it was scrubbed on the cheap, with off-the-shelf utilities – and we'll still be able to dig out something from the deeper residue. I'm sending it home for that purpose – along with the PC drives. But, right now, just about the only thing on these boxes – in terms of software, records of network traffic, data files – is the game client."

"And PayPal," says Rheinhardt.

"And that. As I said, somebody had logged into PayPal, not long before we walked in the door, which is why I was able to follow them in. And you can see right here—" and he swivels a monitor up, with a browser window, "—where the money went. 'FV' is *First Virtual Traders Limited*. That's who converted the U.S. dollars they stole into Warbucks."

"Okay, I was at Virginia Military Institute while you assholes were playing video games," Rheinhardt says. "What does that even mean?"

Mike takes a breath. "Every currency in every major online game has a real-world exchange rate. You can buy and sell virtual currencies, virtual weapons, and characters on real-world exchanges. Like eBay."

"And how exactly does a seller *ship* that?"

"Generally, after payment is made, the buyer arranges to meet the seller in the game, and hands over the goods. And that's the other bad news." Mike flips to another window – the game console. "I was also able to follow them into the game, with those credentials, too. And this character doesn't have a penny."

"Okay. So he handed off the money to someone. Who?"

"I don't know." Mike looks away. "And I don't know if there's even any way to find out."

"So it's gone then," Rheinhardt says. "It's been laundered."

"Something a lot like that."

Johnson rouses himself. "So you're saying all that money disappeared into a fucking video game?"

"Not just a video game. A massively multiplayer first-person shooter." Mike looks around at the group, and isn't seeing a lot of sympathy for this line of explanation. "A synthetic world," he adds.

"Well," drawls Johnson, "that gets me up to about 8.6 on my Beats-the-Shit-Out-Of-Me-O-Meter. Time for a pint." He looks at Nigel. "That chippy still there on the main drag? Not leaving England without some of that."

"You've got two hours until wheels up," Rheinhardt says, checking his watch.

"Right, then," Nigel says, "Uncle BJ and me are off."

Rheinhardt pins Mike, and then Tim, with his unamused eye.

"So you're saying that A) this was a front operation for the real hacking cell; B) they've made the money go bye-bye; and C) as of this moment, you've got no leads on either the hackers or the funds."

Mike eyes floor. Tim says, "That pretty much nails it."

Rheinhardt exhales. "What we need, guys, is actionable intel. What I need you to do is trace the real financial networks underlying this. And I need real SIGINT telling us what these guys' plans are. And, most importantly, I need a grid reference so we can go mop up the rest of the cells in this network. And then their buddies and bosses, all the way up to al-Zawahiri. And then we can all go home."

Mike looks up from the floor and parts his lips.

Rheinhardt cuts him off. "And you need to do all this before that money gets used for something bad. And before these assholes hack into something important. And before they make something really picturesque blow up. Am I clear?"

Mike nods. He meekly picks up his phone and heads for the exit.

Rheinhardt leans on one of the tables, and looks at Tim. "Does this guy know what he's doing?"

"Yeah," Tim says. "He's clued up. Just a little rattled, I think."

Javier says, "The ground's still out from under him, with the two contacts he's been in. He doesn't have the background or training for it."

"Well, you take care of him, and start getting him the training he needs. And you put the ground back under him as necessary."

"Roger that, top."

"And you," Rheinhardt says to Tim, "make sure we're not being led down some garden path into bithead heaven. This morning might have gone much worse than it did."

BRITISH ARMY COMPLEX
NEAR HEREFORD, UNITED KINGDOM
07:23:12 GMT 07 APR

Mike lies on the grass in a patch of sunlight outside the building. He can still smell explosive residue on his clothes, probably in his hair. He keeps his head tilted off the ground, holding the blocky satphone to his ear.

"The guy in charge here, Sergeant Rheinhardt. He thinks these guys knew we were coming."

"Oh, yeah?" says Dharmesh, from five hours earlier in the day.

"I got shot at again," Mike says. "Plus blown up. Twice."

"Shit. Sorry, man. You okay?"

"Yeah, fine. Anyway, Rheinhardt thinks it was because they didn't hear from the cell in Michigan, and they figured we'd be coming for them next. Now, do you think that's it, Dharmesh? D?" Dharmesh doesn't say anything. "Tell me about that keylogger you tried to put in."

"Okay," Dharmesh says. "They may have caught me trying to break in."

"May have? Or did?"

"I'm looking at this stuff you sent," Dharmesh says. As usual, his machine-gun typing in the background has not slowed as he carries on the conversation. "It's possible they detected my intrusion attempt."

"Great. That's great. If these guys find out I nearly got them killed, I'm going to wake up with a grenade rolling into my tent, like *Platoon*."

Dharmesh sighs. "I didn't disguise it as carefully as I might have. I just didn't expect that level of sophistication from guys like these."

"Guys like what? Dark-skinned guys? You're a dark-skinned guy."

"Gimme a break. I just didn't expect it."

"Well, start expecting more, and worse. And why don't you bail us out now by digging up some leads, something actionable, off of those drives."

"I'll do it, Mike. Meantime, try not to get fragged."

Mike rings off and lets his head fall back.

* * *

He wakes up when Javier's shadow passes over his face. He's got the beagle with him. They both sit as Mike stirs and pushes himself up on his elbows.

"How's the head?" Javier asks.

"Still ringing. But okay."

The dog comes up and sticks his face two inches from Mike's, sniffing at narrow intervals, his eyes darting fractionally as he subjects Mike to some kind of intimate, close-range scanning process. Mike leans back, but the dog follows, maintaining distance.

"Does he bite?"

"You have no idea," Javier laughs. "But don't worry, he's just sizing you up. If Mac likes you, the rest of us will. He's the best judge of character in the team."

"So, what, do you have him for bomb-sniffing or something?"

Javier seats a pair of Oakley shades against the sun. "He can do that, yes. Plus drug-sniffing – and also suspect takedown, perimeter security, and fugitive tracking. He's been to every one of the military and spec-ops K-9 schools. And first in his class in every one."

Mike looks back to the dog, who is still sizing him up. He imagines he can see a distinct, probing intelligence behind the dog's eyes.

"So he always goes out with you on operations?"

"At this point, I don't think anybody'd be real enthusiastic about going out without him. How do you think we stay alive at night? The same way our ancestors did. Humans can't hear very well, we can't see in the dark at all, and our sense of smell isn't directional."

"So if someone tries to sneak up on you, he barks?"

"Most of the time, that would be counterproductive. Typically he'll just wake one of us up and tell him. Or he'll take down enemy personnel himself if he needs to."

"How?"

"His signature tactic is to go for the genitals. The beauty of that is, the bad guy will usually get a hand down there to block – and Mac will get both the hand and the nuts in one mouthful. And I challenge you to design a better technique for disabling an opponent." Javier is smiling underneath the sunglasses. Mac has rejoined him now and lies in the grass, rolling over for a tummy rub.

Mike shakes his head. "What was that doggie sweater he was wearing?"

"Nomex and liquid Kevlar – just like yours."

"What is *liquid* Kevlar?"

"Regular body armor, to be effective, needs about thirty to forty layers of Kevlar fabric stuck together, which is extremely bulky and heavy. Ours is just a few layers, but soaked in a shear-thickening fluid – a liquid with nano-particles suspended in it. It moves very supplely – but when it's hit by a bullet or other projectile, it locks together into a solid lattice and becomes impenetrable."

"Does it work as well as regular Kevlar?"

"It's about as good against bullets – and a little better against knives and explosives. But it's light enough and flexible to cover your arms and legs, which regular body armor is not. You'll appreciate that when the IED goes off underneath your vehicle."

"I guess so. So why don't all soldiers have it?"

"Because, at least for now, it's pretty much unbelievably expensive."

"Huh. I guess it's nice your superiors care so much about your well-being."

"It's not so much that they care about our tender hides. It's more protection of investment – because we cost even more than the suits. It's about eight hundred thousand dollars to put an operator through OTC, the Operator Training Course – and that's just the first six months. It only adds up after that."

Mike lets himself fall back in the grass, and allows a few beats to go by in silence. He feels the sun on his skin. "Can I ask you something?"

"Sure. Hit me."

Mike closes his eyes from the sunlight. "These guys. The people we've been fighting all these years now. I don't understand it."

"Okay," Javier says. "What don't you understand?"

"Anything. Any of it. I don't know what these people are about. What they're thinking. I don't know what they want." He exhales. "And mainly I don't understand why so many worlds have to be turned upside down because of it."

Javier nods respectfully. "It's certainly not the world we would have chosen for ourselves. Someone once said to Wittgenstein, 'Life is so hard.' And Wittgenstein said – 'Compared to what?'"

Mike laughs grimly. "But couldn't there be some other way? The War on Terror has now gone on longer than World War Two. Does it go on forever? These people who are blowing things up. I mean, obviously, they must want something, right? They must have grievances. Couldn't their grievances be placated in some way?"

Mike realizes another shadow has fallen upon him. Slitting his eyes open, he sees it's Aaliyah, standing between him and the sun. Blindingly backlit, dazzling, she speaks down in answer.

"They most certainly do have grievances. They're aggrieved whenever they see a woman in public with her face uncovered. They're aggrieved whenever a gay man or woman gets to live life without being stoned to death. Whenever anyone freely casts a ballot, or lives under a democratic government, in a secular society. When a woman chooses her own husband, or whether or not to get pregnant." She kneels down closer, and Mike can see she's wearing sunglasses as well. "Whenever anybody refuses to bend the knee."

She scruffs Mac around the ears. "Come on, Mac," she says. "Let's get you ready to fly." The two of them rise and walk away.

Mike looks at Javier. "I'm sorry… I didn't mean to…"

"It's okay," Javier says. "You're going to be pretty close to events on the ground while you're with us. And you may see some things that change your political views. You're definitely going to see *something* along the way…"

BRITISH ARMY COMPLEX
NEAR HEREFORD, UNITED KINGDOM
07:55:54 GMT 07 APR

Mike is back in the computer lab, alone this time. His screen shows a desolate urban scene, and the barrel of a weapon. A strip at the bottom of the window contains readouts of weapons, ammo, health, and armor, a 360-degree radar display, and other heads-up graphics. His point of view is advancing down a detailed three-dimensional alley. The sound of gunfire fills his headphones. By the time he turns, he's dead and on the ground.

His phone, on the table beside the keyboard, rings and vibrates. He takes off the headphones and picks it up. "Yeah."

"Hey." It's Dharmesh. "Good news or bad news?"

"Good news."

"Those zombies that were behind the D-DOS attacks and the phishing scam? I found out the source of the infection. It's that goddamned game."

"AfterWar?"

"Yeah. Those zombie PCs were infected when they downloaded a mod for the game – a weapon patch."

"How do you know?"

"Working with the bank security guys, I traced a few hundred of the attackers, then sent the FBI out to pick up a dozen or so of them. They've all got AfterWar installed, and they've all got the same custom gun. And the malicious code is definitely in the weapon mod."

"Clever," Mike says. "And the bad news?"

"That's all I've got. That's it. I've rubbed down to the bone on the drive images you sent. And there's nothing there. Those machines, and the router, have been *cleaned*. Network-wise, there's no evidence of them having talked to anything. Not Google. Not weather-dot-com. The only thing I can tell they've been talking to is PayPal – and an AfterWar game server, and only because they were doing it when you got there."

"So the trail ends here."

"No. The trail just goes into the game."

"Rheinhardt's going to *love* that. And, anyway, I'm in the game myself right now. And I just keep getting killed."

"Have you played before?"

"I've played plenty of games like it. But not exactly like it. On the one hand, it's a shooter, so it's constant action. But it's also a role-playing game, persistent – so all these guys who have been playing for, I don't know, years, have got characters with experience and weapons I don't have. Not to mention a lot of friends. Anyway, I'm not trying to play. I'm just trying to see where the damned money went."

"Any luck?"

"None. The character I've hijacked, who originally had the money, must have handed it off to someone – then got killed, and respawned at his army's marshalling point, a hundred miles away. He could have given it to anyone. And, at least so far, I have no way to figure out who or where."

"I'll take a look on the game server end and see what I can do. But I've got one other thing for you, if you want it."

"What?"

"These Delta guys you're with. I've got some background on them. Delta operators don't have regular military records.

When they join the Unit, their files disappear. Technically, they're not even in the Army anymore."

"But you got something anyway."

"I got a little something. Want to hear it?"

"Yeah. Hit me."

"Tim McDonough, for starters. He's got a freakin' PhD in computer science."

"Holy shit. He said something about a degree. Where from?"

"Duke University. He got it mostly at night, while on active duty. He already had a bachelors in CS, from Georgia Tech, when he joined the Army."

"Why'd he join the Army, then?"

"Don't know. But he's been in constant study and training since. All of these guys have. They're all airborne qualified, Rheinhardt's studied at the Army War College. Taken together, they've been to most of the Army's top schools: Infantry, Intelligence, Ranger School, NBC Course – now the CBRN Course, since dirty bombs became all the rage." Dharmesh is obviously reading off a list on a screen now. "Jungle Warfare Course, Mountain Warfare, Air Assault School, Defense Language Institute, Pathfinder Course, Combat Medic Advanced Skills Training, SERE School, JFK Special Warfare Center… And Aaliyah Khamsi: she's completed sniper school, extended counter-sniper training – and, before that, the rotary wing aviator course. She was a freakin' helicopter pilot in a previous life."

"How is it possible she's here in the first place? I didn't think women were allowed in any combat roles, never mind special forces."

"Okay. Check this out. She was born and raised in Somalia. At age 16, she flees to the U.S."

"Fleeing what?"

"Civil war, violence, a society in collapse. Also – arranged marriage, servitude, day-and-night Koranic study. Occasional abuse. The usual fun shit you get as a woman in some traditional Islamic societies."

"Hmm."

"So she comes to the U.S., gets political asylum, falsifies her name and date of birth so her family can't find her. Then she goes and gets a BA in political science at Cal Berkeley – and then enlists. She's accepted into pilot training, flies *Apache helicopters* in Afghanistan and Iraq. Shot down twice, walks away with minor injuries both times. Then three years ago, JSOC – the Joint Special Operations Command, Delta's parent unit – rings her up because they need a fluent Somali speaker for a mission. And they need a girl. She's about the only such creature in the whole Army."

"Why Somali?"

"After we kicked al Qaeda out of Afghanistan, they started scoping out Somalia as a new location for terror training bases. So our SOF sets up across the border in Djibouti to counter them. There were, let's call it, some cross-border activities. But, anyway, what they had in mind was wildly dangerous, and they couldn't just order a regular Army soldier to do it. And so Khamsi only agrees to participate if they *guarantee her a spot in Delta Selection*. So they said okay – nobody thinking she'd pass in a billion years."

"But she passes, anyway. How tough is it?"

"Dude. Put it this way. In her Selection class, somebody sneaked in a Navy SEAL incognito. It was some kind of a bet between an Army general and a Navy admiral. This guy had already been through BUD/S, the SEAL course, which itself has like an eighty percent failure rate. He's got years in the field in combat zones and in counter-terrorism. He fails out of Delta Selection – *in the second week*. Aaliyah Khamsi passes."

"Damn."

"Yeah. And this Johnson guy. You won't *believe* the operations he's seen."

"For instance?"

"Well… remember those photos of SOF guys pulling Saddam Hussein out of his hidey hole? With their faces blacked out? Go look again."

"Fuck me."

"He's also at least partially to thank for the fact that Hussein's psychopathic sons, Uday and Qusay, are rotting in hell, as they should be, instead of still raping and torturing people. And as for Rheinhardt—"

"Brown." Mike spins on his chair. Rheinhardt is standing in the doorway.

"Gotta go," Mike says and snaps the phone shut.

"Anything?"

"Um. Well, no. These machines have been totally wiped. I'm trying to use the game now to track dow—"

"Okay. Pack up. We're flying as scheduled. You've got forty minutes." He pauses and regards Mike. "The Colonel was hoping we might get something else actionable in Europe, Africa, or the Mideast, so we could stay and operate out of here. But since you didn't, we're packing it in for now and going home."

As he turns and leaves, he adds, "Also, I haven't had a shower since before you and I met…"

1ST SFOD-D COMPOUND
NEAR FORT BRAGG, NORTH CAROLINA
14:15:33 EST 07 APR

Back at the Ranch, there's a knock at Mike's door. When he opens it, it's Javier. They both still have wet hair from the showers. They've only been back on the ground an hour.

"Gotta minute? Something I want to show you."

"Sure." Mike locks his screen and follows.

They exit the building where Mike is billeted and emerge onto the paths that thread the isolated compound. Their route takes them by the front gate.

"I noticed the rose garden on the way in," Mike says. "Didn't seem like the kind of image you'd project here."

"The guys who first formed the Unit planted it," Javier says. "One of their numerous gifts to us. They fertilized it with five truckloads of sludge from a local sewage plant. We've never had to refertilize it, and the roses always come up."

"You guys don't do things by halves, do you?"

Javier smiles. "Though, it might be noted that Uncle BJ has laid down some organic matter here more than once on his way back from the bars."

Mike muses. "Sergeant Johnson… *Uncle BJ*. What does the B stand for?"

"Big."

"Big Johnson. That's evocative." The two loop back toward the center of the complex. "One thing I've noticed, actually. He seems like the exception. I would have expected to find a lot of enormous, professional wrestler-sized guys here. But no one else on our team—" both Mike and Javier smile, catching him using the first person plural "—is bigger than normal. And almost nobody I see walking around is, either."

Javier shoves his hands in his pockets. "Huge guys don't often make it through Selection. The common wisdom is that size is irrelevant, so huge guys make it in about the same proportion as everyone else. And there are of course a lot fewer huge guys than normal-sized guys. Personally, I think all that bulk just slows you down – it's more weight you have to drag through mud or sand or water. Or up the mountain."

"Is that what Delta Selection is like? Dragging yourself up mountains?"

"To a fair extent. Guys are invited to try out for a variety of reasons: past assignments, schools attended, foreign languages, tech skills – plus exemplary service records. But when they get here, Selection consists of a lot of PT tests, psychological tests – and, mainly, cross-country navigation, all of that in the mountains in, let's call it, an almost adjacent state."

"I hear it's pretty ball-breaking."

"Yeah, well… the culmination of the final Stress Phase is a 40-mile overnight march, carrying a 70-pound rucksack." They've come now to the door of a very large, warehouse-like structure, and pause at the entrance. "But it's not about the distance, and it's not about the weight. It's not even really about being physically tough. It's about intelligence and toughness of mind – having an insuperable mind. The only people who pass Selection are the ones who don't have any quit in them. Guys who may break a leg or have a heart attack – and would probably figure out a way to finish, anyway – but will never voluntarily pack it in."

"How many people pass?"

"One hundred and eighty three of the best soldiers in the entire Army were invited to the first full Delta Selection. Twelve of them were still standing at the end, and joined the Unit."

"Jesus," Mike says.

"And at seven percent, that was the highest pass rate since, or ever."

Javier swipes and prints the door and holds it open for Mike.

* * *

"And even all these normal-sized guys," Mike says. "They're not very sinister-looking. Not as, you know, badassed as I'd expect. And they're not that muscular. I'd figure you guys would be lifting a lot of weights."

Javier smiles genially. The two sit side by side on a full-length sofa now, in a large living room. There are end tables, a bookshelf, and floor lamps. Jarringly, there are also life-sized manikins of gun-wielding terrorists. Some have headscarves, some Budweiser ball caps. They carry more or less huge rifles and pistols and one or two hold terrified manikin hostages in front of them. The lighting is dim.

"As far as being sinister… the more you work with people here, the more you'll be struck by their simple professionalism. We're here to do some fairly serious work, and the stakes are high. So there's very little hot-dogging or cowboy stuff – the guys who are like that generally just aren't good enough at their jobs, or serious enough about the work."

"That guy we passed in the hallway just now, for instance – with the conservative haircut, the khakis, and the clunky glasses. Is he an operator?"

"Twelve years in."

"I mean, that guy looks like, I don't know, an ice cream salesman."

"Yeah, it's a funny thing. A Delta guy might look like an ice cream salesman – but when he drives away in the van, everyone in the neighborhood is dead, including the dogs, which never barked." Javier shifts on his seat slightly and checks his watch.

"And as for muscles, we don't have a ton of free time, which means a limited amount of gym time. Our PT focuses on cardio. It's true that running out of wind could get you into trouble. But in combat, we don't prevail by physical strength. We prevail through surprise, speed, violence of action – and the perfection of our training as a team."

As Mike nods in acknowledgement, the room explodes utterly.

Mike is vaguely aware that the door, which they'd closed, has gone away. Searing light and noise blossom in the center of the room, in mid-air, and hit him like a punch in the face. At the same time – everything happens at once – bodies spill in, radiating outward in orthogonal directions, too many and too fast to track, and ribbons of fire pour off them. Mike feels the overpressure of expanding air as supersonic rounds pass in front of his face. There's too much to track, and Mike's attention is fatally divided, and it's overpowering and awesome like a force of nature, and it's over already anyway.

When Mike restarts his breathing, there are four men in black in the room – one in the back corner, one in the opposite corner near the door, and one on each side of the doorway. And none of the bad guy manikins have any heads. Most of them have also been shot several times in the chest.

"Heya, Ryan," Javier says. Mike sees that he hasn't moved – his arm still draped genially on the top of the couch. "Appreciate it, guys."

"No probs," the man in the back corner says, clearing and holstering his weapon. A single round ejects and tinkles onto the floor.

"Welcome to the Shooting House," Javier says to Mike. "AKA the House of Horrors." In a mock aside, he adds, "These guys suck, actually. Our team makes them look like a bunch of drunken duck hunters…"

Mike coughs dryly, as unseen fans suck the smoke out of the room.

* * *

"Delta was formed in 1977, because a variety of terrorist groups were on the rise and increasingly targeting Americans. And the U.S. didn't have a significant counter-terror or hostage rescue resource. Although we were modeled on the British SAS, our founders still more or less had to figure everything out from scratch, and build it all from the ground up."

The two are sitting now on a bench outside the Shooting House. Javier has gotten Mike a cold drink, to relubricate his throat.

"What exactly did you have to figure out?"

"Taking down rooms and rescuing the hostages inside, while killing all the bad guys, like you saw just now. Perfectly, every single time. If we couldn't do it perfectly, and ended up killing hostages, there'd be no point – it would be easier and cheaper to call in air strike and level the building."

Mike nods and takes that in.

"Shooting perfectly, from every range, while moving, while in awkward positions, in the dark, in the air. With pistols, with submachine guns, with sniper rifles. Retaking hijacked aircraft. Which is even harder than it looks, by the way."

"How do you do it?"

"You always start the same way – by learning everything there is to know. Location of fuel and oxygen lines. Operation and breaching of the outside doors. How to open locked cockpit and bathroom doors. We actually compiled the specs on every commercial passenger plane in the world: height off the ground, how to disable emergency slides, location of emergency lighting switches, fire extinguishers. We figured out that airplane seats are tough and offer good protection from gunfire and shrapnel. And that cockpit glass doesn't, after all, alter the trajectory of bullets."

"How'd you figure that out?"

"We bought a bunch of cockpit glass and had our snipers shoot the shit out of it. Then we trained as ground crews, learning every role and getting comfortable on the tarmac: driving baggage trucks, refueling, operating the SST."

"The SST?"

"The shit-sucking truck."

"*That* sounds like fun."

"Well, some of it's fun. We learn offensive driving – how to spin out another vehicle, how to punch through roadblocks. We do cat burglar and escape artist type stuff: scaling buildings, opening every kind of window and door lock, getting out of handcuffs. We can get into a locked vehicle and start it up about as quickly as you can with the keys. There's explosives training – blowing up bridges, railroads, safes. Destroying vehicles, or whole houses. With military explosives, or with fertilizer and motor oil from the hardware store."

"That sounds like angry redneck terrorist school."

"Yeah, it turns out you have to become a pretty good terrorist if you want to be a top-notch counter-terrorist. We also learn the tradecraft of spies: dead drops, pickups, surveillance and counter-surveillance."

"Where from?"

"We bring in instructors from The Farm, the CIA's training camp in Virginia – or we go there and take the courses ourselves."

"I heard that, actually. That you've all been to all the top schools."

"The schools are just the baseline. We also train regularly with the SAS, the Australian SASR, German GSG-9, Israeli Sayeret Maktal. We study at the FBI Academy, with the CIA, the State Department, FAA, ATF, the U.S. Marshals Service. Our snipers train the Secret Service snipers – and they teach us executive protection."

"Do you have to do that, as well? Bodyguard work?"

"Not so much these days. But we used to have pretty regular assignments protecting ambassadors in some of the world's great shitholes. Occasionally you'll still see a Delta guy on CNN, babysitting a general or the secretary of defense around Baghdad or Kabul."

"Sounds like you do it all."

"Funnily, there's always something new. Last few years, we've been spending a lot of time with NEST, the Nuclear Emergency Search Teams, on counter-proliferation, on security at nuclear installations."

Mike leans back and looks thoughtful. "You're not telling me all this for nothing, are you? And I'm not here by accident."

"No. I said there's always something new to learn, Mike. But the pace is accelerating. Now it's spoofing, session hijacking, port scanning. Cryptography and cryptology. RFID skimming. And a lot of such mysterious tech stuff Tim's always talking about and trying to get us to understand. We need more help to keep up."

Mike nods and looks around. "Okay, fine. But why did you… do *that* to me? In there?" He tosses his head at the building behind them.

"Two reasons. One, you need to understand our capabilities. You have to have total faith in what we can do, so you can concentrate on your job. Second, you simply have to get more used to kinetic operations. Combat, in a word. You're probably going to be seeing more of it, and we need you to be able to function at a high level when you're in the middle of it."

"Well, stuff like this should toughen me up."

"Yeah. But we're not just going to toughen you up. We're going to train you up. Learning's always a two-way street, my friend."

"How do you mean?"

"You'll see. We'll get started soon, but after the briefing. C'mon, everyone's gonna be on telepresence in fifteen."

DELTA TELEPRESENCE FACILITY
NEAR FORT BRAGG, NORTH CAROLINA
15:30:00 EST 07 APR

"This is an after-action briefing for the London safehouse takedown op of 07 April." Sergeant Tim McDonough is standing at the front of a small conference room. The other members of Alpha team – Khamsi, Rheinhardt, and Roque – plus Mike, are seated around a boat-shaped table. James Niewendyke and Dharmesh are seated at another table, on an enormous screen on the wall. And Colonel Dick Havering is holding up a wall, looking like he's got too many things to do to sit down.

Tim continues: "The Colonel's already got our written after-action report from the air, and Mike's DHS colleagues have gotten a civilianized version. The main purpose today is to review the intel assets we gained from the op – and to assess and analyze implications and next steps. Mike starts."

Tim sits and Mike stands.

"Okay. The good news is, unlike in Michigan, we were able to take the onsite machines undamaged. I guess we came in too quickly for them to blow them up this time. The bad news is, the machines had almost nothing on them. And an elaborate proxy server on the router we found makes me think that the real hackers, the ones who orchestrated the attack on the nuke labs, are somewhere else completely. That this was just a front."

"How do you know?" Havering says, from near the door. "Maybe there is no rest of the group. Maybe you killed 'em all and that's that."

"Well, the money definitely went to somebody," Mike says.

"Well, you killed four of 'em, anyway," Havering says. "Maybe one of 'em was your master hacker."

"I don't think so."

"Or maybe he was one of the two got killed in Michigan."

"Or maybe he's on the other side of the world in a mud hut, or a Saudi royal palace." Mike feels that Havering is intentionally putting obstacles in his path. And all he's got to scale them with is his intuition. No hard data.

"Huh. Well, that's six less we have to kill, anyway," Havering says. "Now – what's this horseshit about the money disappeared into some damn video game?"

Mike draws breath. "Both machines had the client for a game called AfterWar. It's a massively multiplayer online first-person shooter. It's fast-moving and combat-oriented. But it's persistent, like what we call a morpeg – a Massively Multiplayer Online Role-Playing Game. One result of this is it's got a widely traded game currency – so it was very easy for the suspects to turn the funds into that currency, pick it up in the game from the broker, and then pass it off to someone else. Someone who could be physically on the other side of the world, and who we may never be able to track."

"And why exactly," Havering drawls, "do we give a shit? In case they buy some magic spells or something with it?"

"Okay, first of all," Mike says, "it's not a fantasy game. It's sort of a post-apocalyptic war game. You've got three enormous armies, each consisting of hundreds of thousands of players, taking part in large-scale maneuvers and combat for control of the earth. It's got some slightly futuristic weapons and vehicles, but it's basically realistic and based on existing or planned technology."

"Mike," says Niewendyke, deadpan, from Virginia, from out of the screen, "I don't think the Colonel gives a shit what kind of a game it is."

Mike blinks once. "Okay, fine. But our enemies probably do give a shit. And the Colonel may decide he wants to start giving a shit when he finds out what they can do in this game." He turns to face Havering directly.

"The first thing you've got to understand is that these are not just games anymore. Many people, including sociologists, have started calling them 'synthetic worlds'. And this is for the good reason that tens of millions of people are living an increasing portion of their lives there. Their friends are there. Their activities are there. And, increasingly, their valuable belongings are there."

With this, Havering starts to drop his dismissive expression and look more interested. Gaining confidence, Mike goes on.

"The economies of some of these worlds are bigger than the GDPs of many small countries. You've got people setting up businesses inside the games, and earning very decent livings. You've got sweatshops in the third world where people sit all day earning in-game money, or making in-game goods, and then trading them for real money. The currency and goods trade alone is worth billions. And the thing to realize is that gold pieces in Ultima Online or World of Warcraft are not *like* money. They *are* money. They've got an exchange rate, and they're completely fungible."

Havering still looks slightly skeptical. Mike says, "Anything with a market value is by definition valuable to everybody.

AfterWar Warbucks may not be useful to Colonel Havering. And I don't personally give a shit about Andy Warhol's soup can paintings, either. But it doesn't matter, because other people do, so the value is real, and absolute."

"Okay," Havering says. "Tell me this. Has anybody here ever seen terrorists moving money this way?"

"Not us," says Tim.

"We haven't, either," says Niewendyke, out of the wall. "It wasn't even on our radar. But, then again, we've had an enormous amount of success shutting down traditional terrorist financial networks – intercepting and confiscating funds, pressuring overseas banks to close suspect accounts, taking down front organizations. It's probably not that surprising they found a workaround – a totally new way to move money. Someplace we wouldn't be looking for it."

"Well. Those cocksuckers," Havering says. He, and everyone, let the word hang. "Do you have any way to track this money now?"

"Not yet," Mike says.

Niewendyke leans into the screen. "What I'm more interested in is: do you have anything connecting the game to the intrusion at the nuke labs?"

"No," Mike says.

"Not yet," says Dharmesh. "We're working on it."

"Does *anybody*," Havering says, "have *any* information on any other members of this group? For instance where the hell they are?"

"No," Mike says. "The only trail we have leads into the game."

"And can you follow that?"

Mike hesitates. "Not so far. But I've got some ideas ab—"

"Alright then," Havering says, waving this off. "The trail's gone cold. Maybe we got 'em all already, and maybe we didn't. Maybe they'll pop up again – if they do, we'll go out and kill 'em again." He turns to the screen. "I think what we'd all really like is for your man to stay seconded with us for the time being – at least another week or two. That okay by you folks?"

"That should be fine," Niewendyke says. "But Mike – you and I have a chat after this. Your day job hasn't gone away."

Havering turns back to Mike. "You can spend some of your time chasing virtual bad guys around this game of yours if you want. But you also spend part of your day working with Sergeant McDonough. I want to see some knowledge and technology transfer. When you leave here, you don't leave us empty-handed."

He looks to Javier. "And I understand you've got some training lined up for Mike, too. We don't sit on our asses around here. And all of you," he gestures to the rest of the team, "are behind on all kinds of shit. Try and catch up." On his way out the door, he adds, "Sergeant Major Rheinhardt, come find me later."

1ST SFOD-D COMPOUND
NEAR FORT BRAGG, NORTH CAROLINA
17:30:00 EST 07 APR

"You're going to enjoy this, I think," Javier says.

The two are back outside – this time heading to the outdoor target/close quarters combat range. Mike can see it coming up – a row of covered stalls and static and motorized targets covering half the area. And what looks like a medium-sized shanty town on the other. Intermittent gunfire rises in volume as they approach.

"We've got a variety of just-in-time, accelerated combat arms training programs for people who come work with us. Everything from a two-hour session on how to fasten your helmet chinstrap and when to duck – to three months on marksmanship, explosives, infiltration, jump school…"

"How much of that will I get?"

"I'm going to start you on a one-week deal. We'll see how much time we have, and how much you get through."

They reach the stalls. Three are occupied by men firing handguns. They take an open one on the far left.

"You know I've already been through Army Basic Training?"

"Yeah. But don't worry about that. First thing we'll do is unlearn you all the crap they taught you there."

* * *

"So what did you get for me out of all that mess in London, Eric?" Havering says. He's sitting behind his desk, Rheinhardt before it.

"A big, flaming bag of shit. Basically. Sir."

"Yeah, that's about what I thought."

The door knocks, Havering nods, and Rheinhardt reaches around behind him to open it. It's Sergeant McDonough.

"What now, Tim," Havering says.

Tim takes off his black cap and steps in. "It's about that video game… *horseshit*, Colonel. I didn't want to bring it up with the DHS personnel, but there might be more to it, and I want to run some thoughts by you."

"Sit."

* * *

"This is an H&K USP," Javier says, opening a hard plastic case on the table of the stall. "The Heckler & Koch Universal Service Pistol. And it's yours to keep."

"Wow," Mike says.

"One thing we've got plenty of is guns. In Basic, you qualified on the M9, right? The first thing you should know is that Delta operators carry forty-fives. Gear is very personal for Delta guys – and the handgun is the tool he relies on more than anything else."

"Why the forty-five? Isn't that a little, I don't know, World War Two?"

"New doesn't mean better, Mike. There's just no substitute for the stopping power, accuracy, and reliability of the .45. It's also got a very low muzzle velocity compared to

9mm – so slow you can sometimes see it going, or coming. But this also means it generally won't pass through seats, walls, or opponents. This is important when your job is to kill the bad guys while keeping the regular people alive. The gun's tough to master – but, like most great tools, once you do, you'll never go back."

"I saw .45s on a few hips," Mike says. "They didn't look military issue."

"Operators have complete latitude in their choice of sidearm, and people are very fond of their personal guns. We've all got at least two and most have custom-built models based on the original Colt 1911 frame – the Wilson CQB or Wilson Combat, Les Baer, Colt National Match. Vickers Tactical. And every gun we shoot is 'accurized' by Delta gunsmiths – the loose-fitting parts in mass-produced weapons are replaced by custom-built pieces with closer tolerances, specialized trigger mechanisms, better sights. They polish and hand-fit the gas cylinder and piston to improve operation and reduce carbon buildup. Sometimes better barrels are added, bedded into the forearms with a special fiberglass compound."

"Nice."

"Yes, nice. But, remember – it's still always the violinist, never the violin."

* * *

"It's what else they might be doing with this game," Tim says, "that's got me worried."

Havering eyes McDonough. "Shoot."

"Okay. At this point, almost everyone in this building has trained on some type of video game at one point or another. Year before last, the Army set up a whole project office for games, housed within TRADOC. There are the big, large-screen, stand-alone systems for training and test-firing of expensive weapons systems. There are also PC-based games that allow unit combat exercises, from the squad to the company level. Like America's Army."

"Isn't that that recruiting video game?" asks Havering.

"Originally, yes. It's a military first-person shooter the Army built as a recruiting tool – but it was so realistic that we started using it as a training tool for our own soldiers. Do you know CROWS?"

"Isn't that the robot gun," says Rheinhardt, "they're putting on Humvees?"

"Pretty close. It's a top-mounted heavy machine gun or grenade launcher, but it's actually fired from inside the vehicle, using a video screen, with thermal viewing and zoom – and *an actual joystick*."

"Too many sniper and IED casualties in Iraq," Rheinhardt says, "from guys standing up in the turret with their faces hanging out. Right?"

"Exactly," says Tim. "But the punchline is that they added it to the America's Army game not long after. And *then we started using America's Army to train soldiers on it*, before they deployed. So now we're using a video game – to train personnel on what is essentially also a video game-controlled weapons system."

"Video game war," mutters Havering.

Tim pauses a beat, holding the colonel's gaze. "Yes. And the first take-home is that video games have become an invaluable tool in our training. But the next thing to understand is that these same tools can be used by the bad guys as well. The emergence of realistic, open-source military games has basically turned the whole world into a giant military research lab."

Neither of the other men speak. Tim goes on.

"The behavior of both the weapons and the environments can be extremely true to life. Players learn how to use AKs, and RPGs, and explosives. They can learn how to employ them in urban environments. If there's a superior command and control system, or better tactics, or weapons combination – they find them. And the people playing these games – whether they're good guys, bad guys, or indifferent – abandon stupid practices faster than big slow organizations doing old-style training."

"So you're saying," says Havering, "we're going to lose the war to video gamers."

Tim takes his glasses off and rubs the bridge of his nose.

* * *

Mike inserts a magazine into the butt of the pistol, checks the safety, and racks the slide. "If these custom forty-fives are so great, how come I get the stock H&K?"

Javier smiles. "For one thing, those guns can cost upwards of $5,000. We all get stipends to buy our own, but you don't. For another, the H&K has a twelve-round capacity, versus seven or eight for the old-style forty-fives."

"And you don't think I can hit with seven or eight…"

"Don't take it personally. Anyway, when an op goes well, there will be little if any shooting. However, if it goes sour, a situation can quickly develop where the first side to run out of ammo loses."

Mike pinches a pair of foam plugs into his ears. "Okay. What do I need to know?"

Javier nods, and seats his own earplugs. "Okay. The first thing we're going to do is unteach you use of the gun sights. That's why many soldiers, and almost all police, miss so badly when they get into a gunfight. They've trained looking at their sights. But when they get into a confrontation, they naturally look at their opponent. So, instead, we're going to teach you 'instinctive fire'. Raise your weapon and fire a doubletap at the target at twenty-five yards."

Mike raises his gun and fires, then fires again.

"No – faster. Bring the gun up faster – and don't squeeze the trigger. Slap at it – at just the right time to hit the target."

Mike fires twice again.

"Too far apart – both in space and time. Faster."

Mike triggers off two quickly – but they fall on opposite sides of the human-shaped silhouette target.

"Now tighter. It's not a doubletap until you can put two shots into an eye socket-sized area from twenty-five yards."

Mike fires three more sets of two, watching the groupings tighten up, then stops to reload. "Eye sockets, huh?"

"That was good," Javier says. "I said eye socket-*sized*. In real life, it doesn't necessarily have to be an eye socket. Not necessarily!"

Mike drops his slide forward and goes again.

* * *

"It's not as simple as losing to video gamers," Tim says. "As you've said yourself, Colonel, the history of military strategy is the history of development of technology – and of *ideas*. Military ideas have to do with application of force in certain environments. But now we've got these extremely realistic *virtual* environments – ones that can perfectly model real-world environments. And staying ahead in tactics, training, and skills becomes more difficult when the enemy has got these tools – and can practice all day and all night with our weapons on our terrain."

Tim puts his glasses back on. "Basically, open-source games are another source of asymmetry."

"Gimme some concrete examples," Havering says.

"Okay. In virtual space, a terrorist can figure out the ideal position for launching an RPG at a jetliner. This is a lot harder to practice in real life, where trial-and-error often draws attention. The same applies to any type of terror attack: How do we get in? Where do we strongpoint? What are the sight lines? Where would an explosion have maximum effect? Look outside: How many shooters would you need to hold the building against assaulters?"

Havering nods. "And we may be the next assaulters through the door."

* * *

"Good," Javier says again, while Mike reloads magazines.

"My thumb's starting to bleed," Mike says.

"Before we're done, the webbing between your thumb and forefinger will be wrecked. You can always tell a Delta guy by the huge permanent callus there. Comes from putting out maybe a million rounds in a career here."

Mike seats another magazine and steps forward.

"No. Now we get out of the booth. You'll learn to shoot while walking: left and right, backwards and forwards. And then on the run – always closing, always being aggressive."

"Okay," Mike says, stepping around. "I didn't realize I had so much left to learn about shooting."

"Delta means change, Mike." And as he begins firing, again, Javier adds under the noise, "And as Rilke nearly said – A whole constellation of events must align for one human being to successfully kill or incapacitate another…"

U.S. DEPARTMENT OF HOMELAND SECURITY
ARLINGTON, VIRGINIA
08:52:01 EST 08 APR

"Jesus, Patel – all you do is parcel out your time in twenty-minute increments like some goddamned high-priced Hollywood lawyer. And now I see we're paying you to sit here and fuck around."

Dharmesh doesn't even turn to face Jim Niewendyke. He's in the middle of a firefight, and he's talking to Mike on a Bluetooth headset. "Yeah, that's Jim," he says. "No, I'll explain it to him later. Watch your left. Covering fire. Left!" On the screen,

```
Dharmesh is squatting and leaning around
the side of a rusty barrel, squeezing
off single rounds with an M4 carbine. He
pauses to load up a 40mm HE round in his
underslung M203 grenade launcher. "Fire
in the hole," he says, as he whumps it
off.
    On the opposite side of the street, in
an inset doorway, Mike steps back under
cover. He hears the explosion and sees
splinters and dust settle out on the main
street. Leaning around again, he sights
in on the balcony where he's been trading
fire with some ChiCom infantry. But the
balcony doesn't exist anymore.
```

```
"Nice," he says, running across the
street to link back up.
```

Ninety minutes earlier, after installing the game on his laptop, and after logging in using the username and password of one of the people they'd killed in London, and after having been repeatedly gunned down, Mike rang up Dharmesh for fire support. Dharmesh grabbed the game, created a character, and took transport to where Mike was, all in about a half an hour.

Mike's headset beeps. "Hold on," he says, and flips channels. "Mike Brown."

"Mike, it's Javier." Mike can hear what sounds like a jet engine in the background. "Listen, I can't make our two o'clock. Uncle BJ's going to come get you instead, and take you through it. Okay?"

"No problem. I'll see you soon, though?"

The engine noise revs up, almost drowning out Javier. "*Ojalá*, Mike. *Ojalá*."

Mike flips back and says, "I'm back."

"You know," Dharmesh says, "if you create a new character and we form a proper squad, we can do voice comms inside the game, instead of on the phone."

"I know," Mike says. He's learned enough by now to know that AfterWar is a team-based game, and almost all effective game play happens in squads – who are in turn part of platoons, companies, battalions, brigades, and divisions, those finally making up the three great armies in the war. "But I want to stay on as this guy. I don't how yet, but I'm still hoping it will lead me to something."

```
The two advance down the street now,
swiveling to cover the doorways on either
side. A waterfowl-like aircraft comes
roaring over the row of buildings to the
left. It's got ChiCom markings, and imme-
diately opens up on Mike and Dharmesh
with a door-mounted minigun. They're
caught in the open, and dead in seconds.
```

"I've gotta go, anyway," Mike says. "I've got real guns to shoot."

"No problem," Dharmesh says. "And my suspect's here."

* * *

"This is the SCAR," Sergeant Johnson says, ramming a magazine home and pushing on the charging rod. "SOF Combat Assault Rifle. Very new. Made by SOF *for* SOF. This one's chambered in 5.56mm. Mine's 7.62. No, you can't use mine, and no you don't get to keep this one."

Mike admires it. "It's the gun I wish I could get my hands on in the game," he says. In real life, it's the intimidating, tan assault rifle with the retractable stock that he'd seen the team using in London. It's also the gun that, in its simulated virtual version, had been used to shoot him up all afternoon by more experienced players in AfterWar.

"What game?" Johnson says. "The one those bozos in London were playing? How'd they get our gun?"

"It showed up in the game over a year ago."

"Jesus. I got mine *less* than a year ago."

"I think they can design a game version of a gun from specs – before a new weapon is actually in production."

The two of them are back at the range, this time in the shanty town – which is a dynamic training environment with programmable moving and pop-up targets. Johnson is wearing faded jeans, cowboy boots, a flannel button-down that doesn't really conceal his well-muscled torso, and a Harley-Davidson bandana sweeping back his dirty blond locks.

"Well, good luck to you in the game. In real life, you're not going to get one, either. But I've been told to make sure you know how to use the weapon. You never know when there might be a bunch of them lying on the ground, and no one left to shoot them but you."

Mike finds it very hard to imagine the Delta operators getting hurt – and this shows in his expression.

"We walk side by side with death every day," Johnson says, catching that look. "Sooner or later, it turns its face to each of us." He places the rifle on a table in front of them and changes tone. "The SCAR is Belgian. It's beyond reliable – it will fire totally lubeless. No more clearing jams in the middle of firefights because another goddamned sandstorm blew up."

Mike remembers what Dharmesh told him about Johnson and Iraq.

"It's fully SOPMOD-compatible – the front rail will hold all the accessories the M4 did: optical, point, and holographic sights, IR illuminators and pointers, and laser rangefinders and markers. But, for now, I'm just going to teach you how to shoot the damned thing – with the good old iron sights. And after that, maybe with the HDS – the holographic diffraction sight, which is what most of us mount most of the time. Now pick up the weapon, and make it unsafe."

Mike complies.

* * *

"Where'd you get the gun?" Dharmesh asks the terrified young man on the other side of the desk in the DHS interrogation room. Dharmesh isn't particularly intimidating, but the two FBI agents by the door are. They are the ones who picked up the guy's computer, at Dharmesh's direction – and then went back shortly afterward to pick up the guy himself.

"I don't know," the guy says, shifting on his chair. "From a weapons dealer in the game. A friend of mine had one, and he told me where to get it."

Dharmesh spins a laptop around. "*Show me.*" On the screen is a large-scale map of the AfterWar world. The man points. "Definitely in the northern theater. Somewhere in the northern theater. One of the cities. This one, I think."

"Take the cuffs off him," Dharmesh says around him to the FBI guys. Facing forward again, he intones, "*Take me there.*"

* * *

Mike stands at the corner of a building with the rifle tucked into his shoulder, elbow extended, one eye closed, squinting down the sights. Fifty meters away stands the facade of another building – two stories tall, with six windows and a door. Cut-out figures with weapons pop up, scroll by, and then disappear again. Mike swivels in two dimensions, firing single shots and quick groupings at the cardboard opponents.

His magazine goes dry, he drops it on the ground, and pulls another one from a belt pouch. He seats it, charges the weapon, and then sprints headlong to the next firing position. Finding no more targets appearing, he looks behind him and sees that Johnson is waving him back to the control table.

"Good," he says. "Now give it here." He produces a black-framed square of glass, and begins mounting it to the top of the rifle. "This is the HDS – holographic diffraction sight. It's the same basic tech as the heads-up display in a stealth fighter." He finishes attaching it and switches it on. "Here, you can see you've got a red holographic aiming dot of one minute of angle – and a wider targeting ring around it that's 65 MOA. As you can also see, the viewing area is big – thirty-five degrees off-axis peripheral, so it doesn't obscure your target, and lets you see what's going on around it. It's got thirty levels of brightness, so you can use it in all conditions, including at night with NVDs. It's also low-power consumption – the only thing worse than having to remember to turn off your damned sights is realizing you forgot to turn them back on when you need them."

Mike shoulders the rifle, looks through the sight, and fiddles with the brightness control.

"And unlike earlier models," Johnson says, "it's all passive, with no muzzle-side signature, so it doesn't show up in *opposing* NVDs. The optical surfaces are flat with an anti-reflective coating. Look through it from the side – the reticule is on target at any angle. It even works when shattered. Magic, huh?"

Mike nods in agreement. "Magic hologram."

"Yeah, all that's cool. But the reason we like it is simple: target acquisition. It's fast as hell. You can keep both eyes open, keep moving, keep situational awareness – and acquire, sight, and engage a target in a fraction of a second. Now – get back out there and show me something."

***

"You're sure the game is the source of the zombie virus?" Jim Niewendyke has pulled Dharmesh aside, after he left the interrogation room. He'd been watching on closed circuit, and now wants a moment – while the young gamer is getting set up at a machine.

"Pretty sure," Dharmesh says. "It was smart, it deleted itself after it sent the phishing mail and did the D-DOS attack. But every one of the zombie machines we picked up had AfterWar installed – and also has this particular weapon mod. When I picked it apart, I couldn't find any trace of the virus. But I did find traces of it on this guy's drive, on sectors that hadn't been overwritten yet. And it got installed at the same time as the weapon patch. Downloading the weapon patch definitely caused the zombie, and powered the attacks."

Jim squints deeply. "Okay. So these guys are using this video game to hijack thousands of PCs and use them as platforms for cyber attacks."

"Exactly. And they're doing it by designing a new weapon that's kick-ass enough that a lot of people want to pay for it, and download it."

"Okay, since we know this, now all we've got to do is find the source of the gun. Who designed it, who's distributing it."

"Yeah. But the source is in the game. I've got to go look for it there."

"No," Jim says. "The source is some real assholes in the world somewhere. We need to go find *them*. Then we send Mike and his D-boys to go get them."

"Yes and no," Dharmesh says. "I'm telling you that the place these people are operating is *inside* this game. And that may really be the only place we can go after them. It's definitely where I've got to start."

* * *

Mike pulls his last magazine out of the rifle and makes his way back – stooping to pick up empty mags from the ground where he dropped them. He has progressively gotten faster and more accurate in the last few go-rounds – particularly as he got the hang of the holographic sight.

"This thing rocks," Mike says, as he lays the empty magazines and the rifle back on the table.

"Yeah, the latest tools are great," Johnson says. "But always remember – the most powerful thing in the world is the human being. People are at the heart of everything we do here. If we're training right, then our guys will be the most dangerous guys on any battlefield – even if they're armed with studded clubs and longbows."

Mike doesn't respond, but just takes this in. He believes it.

"Good job today," Johnson says. "Gotta make tracks now. I'm late."

"What," Mike says, grinning, "is there a motorcycle rally on?"

Johnson looks up unsmilingly from under his Harley bandana. "No. Parent-teacher conference."

Mike understands the man to be joking – but he finds neither of them to be laughing, as they briskly pack up.

"Hit the showers," Johnson says, hefting the rifle case and turning to leave. "You stink."

DELTA SHOWERS
NEAR FORT BRAGG, NORTH CAROLINA
11:44:54 EST 08 APR

"Didn't realize you were such a skinny son of a bitch," Johnson says. To Mike's horror, as he is stepping out of a shower stall, there's Johnson – and Sergeant Rheinhardt as well, both shaving. "What do you weigh, like a buck twenty-five – soaking wet, with a hard-on?"

Mike pauses one second before falling for this. "You do realize nobody weighs any more or less with a hard-on…"

Johnson flicks a look at Mike's groin. "I can see where maybe you don't…" Sure enough, it was a set-up. Johnson cackles, and Rheinhardt smiles deeply under his shave cream, neither moving his face too much. Mike wraps a towel around himself and hastily exits. "Have a good 'un," he hears echoing behind him.

Back in his room, he's got a date with Dharmesh in a war-torn city. He's early, so he

```
slips into town by himself, and goes pok-
ing around. He's still in the rough loca-
tion where he first experienced AfterWar,
using the terrorist's character, and
where he's still got a feeling he may find
something useful. He's got headphones
in, so when a voice speaks aloud, he can
tell it's behind him. He spins around,
```

backing up a step and preparing to strafe to one side or the other.

Before him is a player in a Eurabian uniform, like Mike wears – but also wearing a green headband. He's holding a large combat shotgun, but angled downward. The figure steps closer, still talking – and the volume of his voice rises in Mike's ears with proximity.

Only he's not speaking English. He's speaking Arabic, Mike is pretty sure – and he's speaking it increasingly intently. Mike has got his mic turned on, but he doesn't dare speak. The other player is clearly asking something of him.

In excited Arabic.

When Mike still doesn't respond, the figure backs away. When Mike follows, the other snaps the shotgun to his shoulder and fires a blast into Mike's chest. His armor prevents it from killing him. But the force knocks him over and, before he can react, the man is standing over him, and fires again.

Mike, dead, watches the figure run away, from his prone position on the ground.

"Okay, who the hell was that?" Mike says aloud. "And how does he know who I am?" But he's actually got a pretty good idea. He's just met the enemy.

***

"Who the hell's this?" Mike says. Dharmesh has finally appeared, at the south side of the Eurabian Marshalling Point. And he's got another guy in tow. When Mike places his cursor over the new guy, his name appears in heads-up as "TheDude." Panning slightly, he sees that Dharmesh is going, unsurprisingly, as "BigD."

"This is our new best friend," BigD says. They've now formed a squad together – and thus can use in-game communications (instead of the phone). Mike sees from his heads-up that TheDude has been patched in to their squad net. "His was one of the zombie machines, and he's now here with us in the office, courtesy of our friends at the Bureau. Moreover, he knows where the infecting weapon can be bought – and he's going to take us to it."

"Nice," Mike says. "Lead the way."

"We've got to get transport north," says TheDude.

Traveling around AfterWar is a lot like traveling around the world, but more time-efficient. The three board a northbound train from the depot, headed for a city much closer to the front – one the Eurabian Army has held long-term, and which serves as a launching point for offensives. It has also long served as a place for Eurabian troops bound for the front to pick up interesting new weapons and equipment.

Once they board the train, time conveniently compresses – the train accelerates to implausible speeds and the view out the window turns to blurred motion lines. By this method, the game preserves the realism of a nearly world-sized world, while minimizing boredom. After two minutes of this, they arrive at their destination.

The station sits on the outskirts of town, which itself lies in a depression of the local geography. Led by TheDude, they begin descending – and threading through the streets of what looks like half garrison town, half wild-west mining camp.

"Wait a second," Mike says into his headset mic. "Doesn't buying weapons cost money? My character's broke."

"No problem," says BigD – as the three duck under an awning to get away from what looks like an aerial dogfight kicking off overhead. "I requisitioned a million Warbucks earlier, and picked them up in the game before we met you."

"You put in a purchase req… *for Warbucks?*"

"Well, no, I just put it on the corporate card. Anything under five hundred dollars I can just buy."

"How much is the gun?"

The three avatars make a left – then TheDude reverses course, and the other two scramble to follow.

"When I bought mine, it was two hundred and twenty thousand," says an unfamiliar voice, which Mike takes to be their captive and guide.

"Do you have it now?" asks Mike. "What actually is it?"

"Yeah, I've got it." Mike watches TheDude switch from his standard M4 assault rifle to something with a bigger barrel – and a large drum magazine. "Full-auto twelve-gauge shotgun," he says, triggering off a half-dozen rounds against the nearest wall. "Three hundred rounds a minute, twenty-round magazine."

"Jesus," Mike says. "Does that gun exist in real life?"

"Dunno," says BigD. "Hey, how close are we?"

"Pretty close, I think," says TheDude. "There!"

They're in the very center of the metropolis now. Down the block and across the street is a storefront, which TheDude angles toward, Mike and BigD following.

The door is open – but out front stand two Eurabian infantry. Judging from their weapons and armor, they look to Mike to be serious players. They are also both wearing the green headbands. They step forward, blocking the door, as the three approach.

BigD puts his hands up, empty of weapons, in a calming gesture. (Mike makes a mental note to look up the keyboard shortcut for that.) "We just want to buy one of what he's got," BigD says, turning to TheDude.

Ten minutes later, the three are safely back out of town, approaching the station again – BigD holding his auto shotgun.

"Okay, so what does this get us?" Mike asks.

"It gets us the weapon mod patch, in its original form. Whatever Trojan or virus it lays down I can deconstruct from the original code base – before it deletes anything or modifies itself. Oh shit – you, take the headset off." Mike realizes Dharmesh is talking to the suspect in the physical room. "Can you guys take him back to the holding room? Thanks. Hey, Mike."

"Yeah."

"Having now thought about it for two seconds, I realize we shouldn't actually be having these kinds of conversations

```
inside the game. I haven't even begun to
figure out the security issues around in-
game comms, either text or voice. Gimme
a call on a secure line in a couple of
hours and I'll walk you through whatever
I find."
     "Okay, man. I've got another training
session now anyway."
```

As Mike pulls his headset off, his door knocks. He reaches across to open the door. It's Tim. Tim takes a look at what's on Mike's screen.

"What have you got there?"

"We've got the goods," Mike says. "The gun. And the malicious code."

"You got the guys, too?"

"Not yet. But we know where some of them live."

"Outstanding. Where?"

Mike points at his screen, where the building with the gun shop is still visible way down in the bowels of the city. "That one there. The big, ratty-ass one."

"Great," Tim says. "I'll just get my coat then."

DELTA HEAVY ORDNANCE LOCKER
NEAR FORT BRAGG, NORTH CAROLINA
14:00:30 EST 08 APR

"Demolitions are all about respect for the ordnance – and attention to detail," Tim says. He, and Mike, are in a supply room full of locked lockers. Tim is placing a variety of dangerous-looking objects into a duffel bag. He zips the bag, looks up, and pins Mike's eye. "You handle them like eggs and you check everything three times more than you think you need to. If you don't, you're going to end up as smoky barbeque spread across an entire map grid. Got it?"

"Got it," Mike says.

Tim locks the explosives locker, and the two exit – heading for another outdoors training area, behind the building.

"How is it you're the demo guy for the team – in addition to the tech guy?"

"Everybody's multidisciplinary," Tim says. "Sometimes an entire squadron will deploy for a mission. On one of those, you can do whatever your core specialty is. Most of the time, as you've seen, it's a much smaller group, often just a four- or five-person team. Then everybody wears several hats."

"I heard Aaliyah flies helicopters."

"Yeah. Small planes, too. You'd be surprised how often that comes in handy. Just for one instance, we'd all still be in Nigeria, and dead, if she hadn't stolen a plane and flown us out. And BJ's a hell of a combat medic. If you ever need field surgery, you'd probably rather have him around than your doctor. He can work on you while being shot at – and while wounded himself."

* * *

Dharmesh waltzes into his boss's office.

"Okay, it's official now," Dharmesh says. "I've taken the weapon mod apart, and it's all in there. The code for D-DOS attacks, the code for spamming out the phishing emails – and, most importantly, code for doing *distributed brute force attacks on public key encryption systems*."

"You mean the nuke labs intrusion?" Niewendyke asks.

"Yep. Can't know for sure, but I'd bet my ass that they used all these machines to farm out the task of cracking the PKI encryption at the DOE nuke labs. With enough machines, they can potentially crack some really high-bit crypto. And, if they keep on infecting more, they can keep right on doing it, day and night."

"And just exactly how many machines *do* they have control of?"

"As of this minute… there's absolutely no way to know."

* * *

Mike stands in silence, holding a green cylinder with a pin at the top.

"Okay," Tim says, "you've learned this stuff at Basic, so just show me that you can do a couple of things at once: cook one off, and then toss it to the near far-side of a defilade. As you can see from the label, it's a five-second fuse. Depending on range, five seconds can be plenty of time for your opponent to pick it up and toss it back to you. And you don't want to be in a grenade tossing contest."

Mike nods – and gulps. "Gotcha."

"How much you cook it off of course depends on how far you've got to throw it – and how big your nutsack is. Okay. Aim for about two seconds. I want you to pull the pin, count two-Mississippi, then chuck it over that wall there. You want it to land on the other side – but as close to the wall as possible. Your targets are hiding behind it. Proceed."

Mike tries to call back the muscle memory from Basic Training, nearly ten years ago – then pulls the pin, lets the spoon pop, counts the fastest two-count of his life, and lets it fly. It thunks into the middle of the curving wall and falls to the ground – on their side.

Tim seizes Mike by his collar and pulls him to the ground, behind the reinforced bench which fronts the range. The grenade explodes out beyond it.

Wordlessly, they stand up – and Tim hands him another one.

Mike cooks this one off and sends it sailing as well. This time it clears the wall – by a wide margin – and neither of them has to duck.

"Hey!" Mike says, smiling. "That was better." Tim doesn't respond. "Better's good, right?"

Tim isn't really smiling. "Yeah, better's good," he says, handing over another one. "But good would be better."

* * *

"Fine," says Niewendyke to Dharmesh. "Then we're going to shut down the goddamned game."

"Oh, no, we're not," says Dharmesh. "We can't."

"Oh, yes, we can. You'd be amazed what we can do under the Patriot Act. If this game is being used as a platform for attacks on critical national systems, we can have the directors of the company that runs the game under subpoena in twenty-four hours – and all their servers in an evidence locker quicker than that."

"No company," says Dharmesh, flatly. "No directors. Nobody runs it."

"What kind of bullshit is that?" Niewendyke looks starkly agitated. "Well, the goddamned servers live somewhere. We'll just go and get them."

"The servers live everywhere and nowhere. And they come up and go down all the time – much faster than you can find and track them."

"How is this possible? No company running the game – and a cloud of phantasmagorical game servers?"

"All things are possible. It's a synthetic world. This is the open-source, P2P age. *And it is only just beginning.*"

"You've got some explaining to do, Patel."

"I know. Clear your schedule."

***

"Alright, presumably you also learned to fire an M203 at Basic, yeah?"

"Yeah," Mike says. "But this doesn't look like the 203." He's holding another SCAR assault rifle now – but this one with an underslung grenade launcher.

"It's not," Tim says. "This is the EGLM – Enhanced Grenade Launcher Module. The 203 was fine if you had a direct line of sight target. Or one you could lob something onto, in an arc. What the EGLM allows you to do is engage targets behind cover, with programmable ordnance – by telling the round when to blow up. This is the laser rangefinder. Range that wall – press here."

Mike complies.

"Okay. Now that range is locked in. Now use the buttons here to tell it how much further, or less far, to travel before exploding. It's in meters. Set it for two meters further than the range of the wall." Mike does so. "Now. Pull the weapon into your shoulder. Sight just to the right of the wall. Good. Now fire."

Mike does so, the launcher whumps – and a half-second later an explosion erupts in mid-air beside and past the wall.

"Anybody back behind there," Tim says, " – ground beef."

"Sweet."

"Yeah. Now, fire off a half-dozen of those, then we'll do a little bit with shape charges. And then we'll call it a day."

Mike swings open the breach of the grenade launcher, and loads another round. "What about EOD – explosive ordnance disposal? You said we were going to show me a little about defusing bombs."

Tim exhales heavily. "Well… If we get into a situation where you have to defuse something, then I'm probably dead so it won't be my problem anymore. But if it does come up… it's, uh, generally the blue wire you want to cut."

"The blue wire." Mike's skepticism is poorly disguised.

"Yeah. Generally, the blue wire. Either that will work or it won't. If it doesn't, then it won't be your problem anymore, either."

Mike nods once and goes back to his grenade launcher.

DELTA SNIPER RANGE
NEAR FORT BRAGG, NORTH CAROLINA
17:30:44 EST 08 APR

"Everybody goes through basic sniper training, whether they're going to do this job or not," says Sergeant First Class Aaliyah Khamsi. "This is because we don't want the short-gunners – or you for that matter – getting in our way and screwing up a shot. And you sure don't want us shooting you."

"What are short-gunners?" Mike asks.

"Assaulters, door-kickers. The poor schmucks with the pistols and SMGs who actually have to storm buildings and get shot at and kill people to their faces. Our job as the long-gunners is to do everything we can to tip the odds in favor of the short-gunners before they go in. All from the safety and comfort of a sniper hide."

"Gotcha," Mike says.

The two of them are flat on their bellies on the far back-side of the Delta compound. They're facing down the length of a 2,500-yard firing range, with a variety of targets – many of them placed so far away that they are completely invisible to the naked eye.

"Most of this job actually involves scene observation and intelligence collection, not shooting. All of that intel goes to a central sniper TOC, gets logged into a central schematic – and fed back out to the rest of the team, including into heads-up real-time mapping systems."

"Do you ever actually shoot anybody?"

"It comes up now and again."

Mike pauses before asking, "What is it like?"

Ali pauses herself and looks thoughtful. "It takes someone with a psychological profile in a fairly narrow range to do it. Off to one side, you've got people who might be prone to what we call Munich Massacre syndrome."

Mike looks blank.

"When Palestinian terrorists kidnapped the Israeli athletes at the 1972 Olympics in Munich, German snipers spent days watching them through their sights. Day and night, eating, sleeping, laughing. They kind of got to know them. When the time came to pull the trigger, they couldn't do it."

"I suppose that's understandable."

"Less so if you were one of the Israeli athletes – all of whom the Palestinians ended up murdering."

"Oh."

"On the other side is Texas Tower Syndrome, named after that famous shooting spree at the University of Texas. There's this exhilarating feeling of power being able to reach out and touch someone from hundreds of yards away. And, for some, the temptation to keep finding targets and shooting them goes on after there are no more legitimate targets. Some people just can't stop sniping."

Mike whistles quietly. "Okay. What's in the middle?"

"The Delta sniper. An extremely balanced and sober professional who does a job that needs to be done. But enough philosophy. Down to hardware now."

She pulls the nylon cover off of the (very) long gun that rests between them. Beside it, on a ground mat, there's also a small pile of electronic devices.

***

Staff Sergeant Tim McDonough, now going by "BitTwiddler", holds his eye to another scope. He pans his rifle from side to side – not as smoothly as he might do in real life, but better as he gets the hang of the mouse. He's toggled his scope view so he stays zoomed in – and can adjust the magnification with his up and down arrow keys.

He's lying on an empty hillside on the outskirts of the low-lying town – on the same side as the train station, but far enough to the side that he is not visible to the players getting on and off of transport. From his spot, he has a line of sight to the gun shop in the center of town, just off of the main drag.

He's zoomed in tight on the front door – where Eurabian soldiers have been going in and out for the past half hour. From their uniform markings and insignia – and from the green headbands – all, or almost all, of them are members of the same unit. At extreme zoom, BitTwiddler takes a couple of screenshots of their unit crest, with the idea of looking it up later.

His phone beeps. He'd thought ahead and patched the phone into his headset, along with the game audio and comms – so he's able to reach to his waist and answer without taking his eye from the screen.

"McDonough," he says.

"Rheinhardt. Where are you?"

"Mike Brown's room," he says. "The guest billets."

"What are you doing? Can you meet me in the Squadron Ready Room?"

"I've sort of been shanghaied into some duty here. Can you come to me?"

"In five."

They both ring off, and Tim smoothly returns his right hand to the mouse.

* * *

"This is the Cheyenne Tactical Intervention Long Range Rifle System," Aaliyah says. "The rifle itself is a .408 caliber, semi-automatic, takedown rifle with a detachable ten-round magazine. This is the M400 – the semi-automatic version of the M200 bolt-action CheyTac. You might have seen the M200 elsewhere, but you haven't seen this one, as it's still in testing and, so far as I know, we're the only ones who have it."

"I'm not sure I have seen it."

"Maybe you haven't. And if someone's shooting at you with it, you probably never will. It holds the world record for best grouping at extreme long distance – three bullets within sixteen inches at 2,321 yards. That's almost a mile and a half."

"Having that kind of range must make your life easier."

"It sure does. Not least because I don't have to sit up here like a swamp creature in one of those ghillie suits. At a mile and a half, I can't be seen even under direct surveillance with powerful binoculars. But the flip side of that coin is that an awful lot can happen to a bullet in flight over such an extreme distance. That's where the rest of the system comes in." She begins pointing out the electronics.

"The heart of it is the advanced ballistics computer. This takes the place of the old sniper trig tables – plus does a whole lot more. Not to mention a lot more quickly, which can make all the difference to my outcomes. The software can run on almost any consumer, hardened, or mil-spec PDA. The input data it needs come from these two other devices." She puts the PDA down and picks up a black cylindrical device.

"This is the Vector IV mil-spec laser rangefinder." She hands it to Mike to play with. "High-end laser rangefinders that can accurately measure distances over two thousand yards are prohibitively expensive for most civilian shooters – and definitely for most of our enemies." Mike puts it back down on the ground cloth.

Ali picks up another small device that looks like a large phone, or small GPS. "This is a Kestrel 4000 meteorological and environmental sensor package. It measures wind speed, air temperature, air pressure, relative humidity, wind chill, and dew point." Mike checks out the screen.

Ali picks up the original PDA again. "Both those sets of data feed directly into the computer, which then corrects for all those variables – plus the type of round in the gun, the rifle barrel twist rate, and any windage settings you have at the gun, at the target, or at the halfway point in between.

Also, it uses your latitude and direction of fire off true north to correct for the Coriolis effect."

Mike looks blank. "I don't know what that is."

"Rotation of the earth. At the equator, your target is moving a thousand miles an hour. Your bullet will *start off* moving at the same speed – but over a flight time that can be up to two and a half seconds, it slows. Your target, assuming his feet are on the ground, does not."

"God, you must not miss much."

"Yeah, it's wonderful technology. On the other hand, for anything inside a thousand yards, I pretty much just take the shot."

"And you still don't miss, do you?"

"No."

* * *

Rheinhardt walks into Mike's room without knocking. He leans over Tim's shoulder and says, "What's all this?"

"I'm on a surveillance op," Tim says.

"It's a good thing I trust you completely at this point. Even when I have no idea what the hell you're doing. Where's Brown?"

"Out on the range with Ali."

"Great. So now he's doing our job and we're doing his."

"You said you wanted him trained up." Tim's eyes have not left the screen.

"Okay. I give up. What are we looking at?"

"A weapons cache, I think," Tim says. "The DHS guys figured out that the zombie machines behind the attacks, including the nuclear site hack, were infected by a game modification – a weapon patch. And the weapon can be got at *that* building there." He bumps his zoom up and pans across the avatars at the building entrance.

"So, what – we have to take the building down and secure the weapons?"

"Actually, yes, we may have to do that. But, then again, I'm not sure taking the building would get us what we need. We, or the DHS guy, has already bought one of the guns and has the malicious code. I think what we need is to find out where the guys playing these characters are in real life."

Rheinhardt pauses a very sarcastic beat. "Do ya *think*?"

"Well, boss, all I can tell you is I've got eyes on them right now. If you've got a better play, you just tell me to run it."

Rheinhardt exhales. "Well… Havering said from day one that we're here to fight in a new battlespace. Maybe this is it."

"Maybe this is it."

* * *

Mike squeezes off a last large-caliber round and feels the bolt of the rifle lock back. He takes his eye from the scope and looks to his side, where Ali is peering through a spotting scope mounted on a short tripod.

"Outstanding," she says. "That's all ten on target at six hundred yards."

"And that target's man-sized?"

"Yes. Almost any one of those would have been a killing shot."

Mike rolls on his side and onto his elbow. Ali sits up, cross-legged. The two regard each other.

"I heard you studied political science," Mike says.

Aaliyah eyes him carefully. "You have a lot of little electronic birds in your world, don't you?"

Mike smiles. "I was just wondering why you chose that field."

"Well, I wanted to try and understand why some political systems result in very negative outcomes—"

"Like Somalia."

"Like Somalia. And why other political systems result in very positive outcomes. Like the U.S. And Western Europe."

"I also heard you used to be Muslim."

"I still am, in some ways."

"Back in England… I didn't mean to give offense…"

"You didn't offend me, Mike. No more than does most of the liberal establishment, or the so-called Orientalist academics, or the mainstream media. You hear it from many corners."

"Hear what?"

"That religion of peace stuff – and that the West, through its imperialism, or its colonialism, or its economic oppression, has brought terrorism upon itself. But the thing you find is that none of these people have ever actually sat down and read the Qu'rân – much less the Hadith. If they had, they'd understand that when bin Laden kills people and then quotes Muhammad in justification of the act, he isn't perverting Islam. He's merely following the script."

"So you're saying Islam is inherently violent?"

"Yes and no. There's much in the Qu'rân that's noble and reasonable, and in some ways ahead of its time. And there are hundreds of millions of Muslim men and women who have no desire to impose their values on anyone – much less hurt anybody. But they're doing that in spite of, or at best in ignorance of, some of the fundamental dictates of Islam."

"Dictates like what?"

"Like those that state that the faith should be expanded by the sword, and that infidels should be made to submit – or be struck down – wherever they can be found. And that women are the 'tillage' of men."

"I didn't know any of that."

"The church of multiculturalism won't allow you to know it – or, if you do know it, to say anything about it. In multicultural, postmodern society, it's become almost completely forbidden to make any value judgments whatsoever about any other culture or belief system. There's this almost perfect blindness to bad ideas – even when they come crashing through your office wall, reciting suras. But the fact remains that the ideology of Islam has real problems – in its compatibility with modernity and democracy, with its treatment of women as property, with its vilification of Jews and gays. The terrorism is just the one manifestation that's impossible to ignore."

"Maybe you should be a religious reformer."

Aaliyah looks out to the horizon at the edge of the sniping range. "God knows, if any system of thought has ever been in need of an Enlightenment-style reform – or a Voltaire-style skewering – it's Islam."

Mike tries to follow Ali's distant gaze. But she snaps back to close range and says, "But as much fun as that would be, my job is just to shoot jihadis in the head – before they can blow up innocent people."

"And imagine their surprise when you do it from a mile and a half away."

"Yes. And which, come to consider it, is sort of fun in its own way."

Mike smiles. He pauses before asking, "Do you believe in God?"

"Yes, of course – in the one true God. And Darwin is his only prophet."

* * *

```
"BitTwiddler."
   Tim doesn't quite jump, but he does
look rapidly from side to side when
someone speaks his call sign out loud.
Swiveling his mouse instead of his head
he sees another avatar standing above
and behind him on the otherwise deserted
AfterWar hillside.
   "It's, uh, BigD," the avatar says,
sheepishly using his new call sign.
"Mike's colleague."
   "Right," BitTwiddler says.
   "But we can't talk here. Hang on."
   Tim's phone beeps and he smoothly
switches channels again.
   "What I can do for you, BigD?"
BitTwiddler is still prone on the ground
with his rifle, but swiveling to look up
at the other player standing beside him.
   "Mike told me where you'd be. Listen,
I don't know how much he told you about
recent developments. But we need to do
```

another video conference. Everybody. And ASAP."

"You couldn't have just called to tell me that?"

"Yeah. But I wanted to see what was going on in here. Anything happening?"

Tim pauses – considering what this DHS guy needs to know, tactically. He decides that, at least for the moment, he is their intel lifeline, and has to be looped in.

"A lot of foot mobiles going in and out of the target building. Almost all from the same unit. About a platoon's worth have come up to the station and taken transport."

"You didn't follow them?"

"Couldn't both follow them and keep eyes on the building."

"Hmm," BigD says. "Maybe we need more bodies in here." And then his head explodes.

AfterWar having both a very realistic physics model and a pretty decent physiology model, much of the contents of BigD's virtual cranium splashes onto and around BitTwiddler.

"Oh, hell," he mutters, tasting his first AfterWar gore. But he quickly puts his eye back to the scope and pans around the target house. Nothing on the door,

```
nothing on the street…and then he thinks
to look to the rooftop. A heartbeat too
late.
   His crosshair lands on an opposite
number – another scope, nearly a (game)
mile away. He can just make out the top
of the head above it, and the prone body
lying behind. The muzzle flashes. Tim's
scope goes black, his avatar rolls on his
back – and white contrails in the blue
sky fill the screen. He's dead.
```

"Wow," Rheinhardt say. "That's a brisk kick to the swingers."

"No kidding," says Tim, still squinting at the screen.

"Maybe you need to put in some range time with Ali yourself."

"Not funny, Sarge. Now these guys know they're being watched."

"Or maybe they were just playing a video game, and enjoyed smoking some newbie sniper."

Tim nods a couple of times at the screen. "Maybe you're right. But I think we'd be making a mistake to count on that."

* * *

Aaliyah's phone beeps and she pulls it smoothly from her belt.

"This is Bette Noire," she says. "Roger that. Brown's with me. There in ten."

Mike watches her as she replaces her phone. "*Bette Noire…?*"

Aaliyah looks slightly defensive. "My call sign. Bit of a pun. In French."

"I see. And a bit of a play on skin color?"

"Okay, that too. Hey, if you can't laugh at race…"

As they pack up the rifle system and begin to trot back, he says, "I thought you didn't use call signs at the compound?"

"We don't use them indoors." She tosses her head at the sky. "Since the end of the Cold War, most of the satellites up there are ours. But not all of them."

The two figures, one pale, one dusky, approach the rows of buildings as the sun begins to set and flashes light and long shadows behind them.

DELTA TELEPRESENCE FACILITY
NEAR FORT BRAGG, NORTH CAROLINA
20:20:04 EST 08 APR

The physical conference room fills up as before, but this time Dharmesh sits alone behind the table on the screen on the wall.

"Where's Jim?" Mike asks, taking a seat.

"Prior commitment."

"He couldn't reschedule for this?"

"He's at the White House." Nobody in the room says anything. "Anyway, I already briefed Jim on what I have to tell you."

Colonel Havering is the last in and shuts the door behind him with his back. The others stare up attentively from around the table.

"Alright," Dharmesh says, looking quickly from the camera to something on another screen. He pauses to type for two seconds, then looks back. "I think many of you already heard the most recent big news – that we've traced the source of the nuke lab hack to the game AfterWar. Essentially, these guys are using the game as a platform for attacks. They've created an in-game weapon, one that's popular enough that at least a thousand people have downloaded it. And we have no way to know how many more. By buying the gun, and downloading and installing the code for it, they've infected their computers with a virus that allows these guys – and let's maybe assume for now they they're AQO, or AQ-affiliated – to run distributed denial of service attacks, as well as distributed brute force cracks of highly secure systems."

"So let's shut down the goddamned game," Havering says.

"Funny," Dharmesh says, "that's exactly what my boss said. But it's not going to happen. Not today, and probably not in the lifetime of anybody here."

"Okay. I expect you're going to explain why."

"If this were EverQuest or Second Life or something, no problem. We could go to the company running the game, get an injunction if necessary. And the company would have to clamp down on whatever criminal activity was going on in the game – and also give us the identities of any players who were involved. There'd be a controlling authority, the company that runs the game – and they would be subject to the laws of the country they operate in. Which is usually the U.S."

"So what's so different about this game?"

"No company. No controlling authority. Okay, morpegs – massively multiplayer online games, or synthetic worlds – are almost always created by video game companies. All the big ones have been. But the first thing to notice is that these worlds almost never die, or get shut down. This is because the cost is almost all in building them, not in running them. So sometimes they limp along, with minimal oversight, with maybe only a few thousand players, for years."

"But surely the company still has control?"

"In almost all cases, yes. But they rarely have much incentive to exercise it. There's a political model in these games and it's not democracy. Basically what you get are isolated moments of tyranny embedded in widespread anarchy. The players can do whatever the hell they want within the rules of the game, often for years on end. This is because the cost of running the game, keeping the servers up, is very small. But the cost of having human employees intervene and arbitrate messy disputes is very expensive. Things bash along this way until something gets really out of hand, then the company may eventually step in."

Havering grimaces. "I'd say things have gotten out of hand."

"They have. But AfterWar is different. *The company that designed the game went out of business entirely.* In 2007. But instead of shutting down the game, they handed it over to the community of gamers. They made all the code open-source, and free for use."

Havering looks at Tim. "Open-source game development," he repeats.

"Worldwide military research lab," Tim says, also echoing himself.

Dharmesh nods onscreen. "Open-source, yes. But it's another technology that really changes the rules of the game: P2P. Ever since the Napster crackdown, there's been a move away from centralized client-server systems, and toward peer-to-peer systems – where every computer on the network talks directly to every other computer, rather than a centralized server. In a P2P system, there's no central node to shut down."

Mike squints deeply. "You're not saying AfterWar is P2P? I don't see how that could be possible and still have a shared world. Never mind a shared battlespace."

"That's true," Dharmesh says. "It's not totally P2P. But when they designed the game, they used some aspects of P2P to overcome some longstanding limitations of synthetic worlds. Specifically, the network problem."

There's a beat of silence, and Tim jumps in, speaking to the others around the table. "The complexity of a network is a function of the square of the number of nodes on the network. In this application, that means that as you add more players to a shared space, the complexity of the computation and network traffic increases exponentially."

"Right," says Dharmesh. "This came up in morpegs early on, when they tried to have very large gatherings. Any more than fifty or a hundred players in the same area and the games slowed to a crawl. Because every player had to update every other player on its activities, all routed through the central server."

"And AfterWar overcame this?" Tim asks. "How?"

"Well, they had to overcome it, in order to have these huge set piece battles they had in mind. There were already games where you could have fifty guys fighting fifty other guys – though that often pushed the limits."

"But," Tim interjects, "if they wanted a division of six thousand infantry fighting a couple of armored battalions of a thousand each, that's not quite… sixty-four million relationships that have to be updated in real time."

"Right again," Dharmesh says. "Their trick was only to update players in the game who were in the immediate vicinity of you – and to push that updating out to the clients themselves, peer-to-peer, so the game players' machines talked directly to one another, as necessary. Instead of to the server."

"But that means…" Tim says, "we could in theory get the IP address of players close to us in the game, just by hacking the game client…"

Dharmesh puts his finger in the air. "*Bingo*. But hold that thought. In addition to the peer-to-peer aspect, there's the previously mentioned open-source aspect. This means that anybody can run an AfterWar server. And all kinds of people do. They run on university networks. They run on shared hosts and private co-located servers. They even run on some players' home machines. To set one up, all you have to do is download the source code, compile and install it, start it up – and give your new server the IP address of one other running AfterWar server. After that, they all pretty much run as a cloud. If one goes down, another takes over the geographical area of the world it was responsible for. It shifts all the time. There's no central way to find all the servers. And there's no particularly good way to map geographical areas of the game to physical servers – it maps about like the geography of the Internet to the real globe. That is to say, very loosely."

"I'm finding this a little hard to get down," says Havering. "But assuming there's no way to shut down the game, where does that leave us?"

"There are only two ways to influence or disable a game like this," says Dharmesh. "Or, really, *any software system*. The first is externally, viewing it as a physical system of boxes and wires. But because this one is P2P, and because it's open-source, and mainly because it's distributed, there's no way to attack it – no way to blow it up with a single bomb, or even a lot of bombs. There's no single wire we can cut – or even a thousand wires.

"With that out, the only other way to affect it is *internally* – viewing the system by its own internal logic, and following its own rules. By that I mean, going into the game, as players, and influencing events in this synthetic world by *acting* within the world. *Inside the membrane.*"

"Mike and I have been doing just that, I think," Tim says.

"As has Dharmesh," Mike adds. "But we all keep getting killed."

"Killed by who?" Havering asks.

Tim taps his pencil twice. "The guys we've been watching wear common insignia. I looked it up, and they're part of an AfterWar team that calls itself 'al Buraq'. It's a brigade-sized unit, so maybe that tells us something about their numbers. Anybody know what the name means?" He asks this casually, but looks unwaveringly at Aaliyah.

Holding his gaze, Ali says, "Buraq – Mohammed's horse, upon which he ascended to Paradise, surrounded by angels. In Islamic lore, the event is called the 'miraj' or Night Journey. Buraq is part eagle, part horse – and could gallop in a single stride as far as the eye could see."

Tim nods, still watching Ali. "Well, that fits. Operating within this game allows them to fly around the globe in an instant."

"And to cohere and fight pretty well within it, by the evidence," says Rheinhardt. He looks up to the group. "I watched them counter-snipe Tim right into a hurt locker."

"Hold on a minute, hold on," Havering intones, pulling out his most gobsmacked look, which evidently he'd been keeping in reserve. "Are you trying to tell me now that what you need is *fire support*? In a video game?"

"Yes," Dharmesh says. "That's pretty much what we're saying. And this is where things get weird. Possibly very weird. Look, you only really need two technologies – morpegs, and P2P – to get this state of affairs where a synthetic world essentially has its own sovereignty, or even complete lawlessness, and is protected from external interference by decentralization. And we've had both of these technologies since 2001."

Rheinhardt speaks quietly. "So if what you've got here really is a 'synthetic world'… and the nature of its borders protects it from being attacked externally… but nobody's actually running the show anymore… then what you've got is—"

"Yeah," Tim says. "*A failed state.*"

"Why," says Rheinhardt mournfully, "do I feel like we've been here before…"

"A rogue, failed state," says Havering. "Where our enemies are regrouping and planning new attacks."

"And where," says Dharmesh, "your team may have to go in and get them."

"Heh," says Johnson, rocking back in his chair. "I had a goddamned blast riding around Afghanistan on horseback in 2001. This job just gets more fun all the time."

"Yeah, real fun," says Havering. "So what's our next move? And how much time do we have to make it – before they attack us again?"

With that, every light source in the room – with the exception of the screen of a single laptop on the table – goes black, plunging the room into near-darkness.

For five seconds, by the ghostly light of the LCD, the participants of the now-ended meeting stare around the table at one another – unruffled, though having no idea what's just happened.

All except for Dharmesh – who disappeared from the wall entirely when the video link went dead.

DELTA TELEPRESENCE FACILITY
NEAR FORT BRAGG, NORTH CAROLINA
20:55:51 EST 08 APR

"It's the Southeastern Region Power Grid," Mike says. He's just stepped back into the conference room – the overhead lights of which flickered back to life when the complex generators kicked in, a few seconds after the blackout.

"How much of it?" Havering asks, standing now to his full height.

Mike tries to steady his voice. "All of it. D.C. to the Florida Panhandle. And as far west as Little Rock." His hand hangs limply by his side, holding his phone. He's been in the hall getting a hurried sitrep from Dharmesh, who was doing nine other things at the same time. Now the phone rings again.

Mike shoots a glance around the conference room, then takes the call.

"Brown," he says. "Yeah," he says. "Impossible. Those systems are 1024-bit asymmetrical." He pauses, grimacing and feeling all the eyes in the room upon him. "Do that. Seriously. Yeah. Believe me, the team here will be ready when you are. Right." He closes the phone.

To the room, he says, "It was definitely an attack."

"Well," says Johnson, looking directly at the Colonel, "isn't your timing just a son of a bitch?"

"Seriously," adds Javier, "you couldn't plan shit like that."

"*Children be silent*," Havering says. "What the hell just happened?"

Mike takes a breath. "Someone hacked in and brought down the entire Southeastern power grid, which is run out of Charlotte. And they pulled out enough gears and bellows that it's going to take some time to get it back up."

"How long?"

"We think maybe… four to twelve hours."

"Twelve hours of darkness – on the *entire East Coast?*"

"Well," drawls Johnson, "isn't that just a big flaming bag of shit right on our doorstep."

"*And the location of the attackers?*" says Havering.

"Nothing yet," Mike says. "My whole department, every warm body, is working on finding the source of the attack – and I will be too the second I get back to my machine."

"Gear up," Havering says to the soldiers in the group. "When and if you get a target, take the Gulfstream. Wherever the hell you're going, it'll get you there faster. It's on the ground now, and you can have it until something worse happens." He turns on his heel and exits, muttering.

This time, Mike is part of the rapid but orderly exodus from the room.

* * *

"How long have we got generator power for?" Mike asks Javier, the two of them fast-marching down the corridor.

"Forever. There are two diesel generators out back each the size of your house. I'm not sure how much fuel we keep onsite, but they can truck it in from Pope until the wells run dry."

They reach Mike's door and pause.

"I knew those weren't the real attackers," Mike says. "The ones in London. I knew they weren't the brains behind this."

"We'll get the real brains," Javier says. "And the bodies around them. You just get us a grid reference to go to."

"*Ojalá*," Mike says.

"No, not on this one, Mike. Some things are too important to wait around for God's help. We have to take care of business ourselves."

* * *

Forty minutes later, Mike bursts into the F Squadron Ready Room, his laptop folded under his arm.

"I think I've got them," he says. "Or we *can* get them. But I need help."

The entire team is camped out in the large space, wearing their assault suits, slung with tactical and load-bearing vests and sidearms. Several large, bulky duffel bags – presumably filled with guns, ammunition, explosives, and other D-boy toys – sit piled by the door. Rifles rest against various surfaces. Everyone in the room is either poring over a laptop (Rheinhardt, Tim), reading a book (Aaliyah, Javier), or sleeping (Johnson, the dog). The latter two come awake with Mike's explosive entry, and the others look up.

"What kind of help?" Rheinhardt asks.

"We need to take down a safehouse."

"Then we're your guys," Johnson says, unfolding his bulk from the couch. "Where we goin'?"

"Is there a facility here with at least six PCs in one place? A microlab, or computer training room, or something?"

"Oh, my," says Tim, also standing. "I think I can see where this is headed. Yeah, Mike – next building over." He looks back at the others. "Come on, guys. We're going through the looking glass now."

* * *

"Okay," says Mike, fast-walking backwards in front of the team, moving across the compound in the dark, navigating by the footlights receding before him. "The short version is this: the attack on the power grid was extremely well-disguised. Part of it was brute-forced."

"Using the AfterWar zombies?" Tim asks.

"Yes. At least some of them. But the thing is this: I can't isolate the machine which was the originator of the attack. We were able to get a single source address for the nuke labs hack, which allowed us to find them in Michigan. But, now, all I can figure out for sure is that it's *one* of about *two thousand* IP addresses. All of which have been slinging shit at the power grid systems all evening."

"Two thousand dummies," Tim says. "They've gotten better at camouflaging. Or spoofing."

"I'm afraid that's exactly it. That they're learning. And learning fast."

The group – five people in full tactical gear, one lanky guy in jeans cradling an oversized laptop, and one yawning dog – reach the door of the next building. Tim opens it and leads the group down the hall to a computing lab. Inside are a dozen PCs in three rows. Half are occupied.

"Piss off," rumbles Johnson to the room. "Mission priority."

"Yeah, right," says the man at the closest PC. "I'll prioritize your mission for you, BJ. Just bend right over that table there."

Rheinhardt strides in from behind the others. "Gentlemen," he says. "Piss off."

The man who spoke sobers. "Sergeant Major." Everyone in the room briskly logs off and exits. Mike resumes his explanation.

"Okay. So, the attacker is one of two thousand machines. We can't go knock down two thousand doors. We can't even send locals to knock them down – these things are all over the globe. Some in allied nations, some not. Some God knows where."

"So how do we narrow it down?" asks Tim.

Mike squints. "Who do we know who are likely to be the same guys as the guys running this attack?"

"The guys in the game," Tim says. "In the Eurabian gun store."

"Right," says Mike.

"Hang on," says Rheinhardt. "You're assuming it's the same guys."

"No, we pretty much *know* it's the same guys. We know zombie AfterWar clients were used in *this* attack. We *are* assuming that the actual hack was launched by a machine that's also being used by a player in the game. But it's a decent bet. And anyway it's all we've got."

Tim furrows his brow. "And you said because of the P2P nature of the game, individual clients talk directly to other clients. Which mean *your machine has to have access to the other player's IP address.*"

"*Right*," says Mike. "However, I said, *sometimes*. In normal circumstances, the game runs on a standard client-server model – the players' machines all update the server with what they're doing, and the server updates the world, and the other players. The P2P stuff is just to run battles, where all the connections from the clients to the server and back would be too slow. It only kicks in when there's a many-on-many battle."

Tim looks up over his glasses. "And you want us to give you a battle."

"Just get in a fight with the guys in the gun store." Mike pats his laptop. "I've got a sniffer here which will detect network traffic – and if one of our opponents matches one of the two thousand attackers, we'll know who they are."

"This is a bit of a stretch," Tim says. "I don't think any of us have played this game – and I'm not sure Eric has played any such game."

"It's okay," Mike exhorts. "Just get in there and pick a fight. You don't even have to win."

Johnson snorts. "Now *that's* a stretch." He pushes Mike aside, angling for a machine. "Let me in there and I'll drill you some new cyberterrorist assholes."

"Seriously," says Javier. "I've probably got a thousand hours logged on various shooters. I'm ready to rock."

Mike's phone rings. As he reaches for it, everyone else's phone beeps, within about two seconds.

"Brown. Hey. Oh, *fuck me*…"

Things have just gone from bad to horrifying.

PENNSYLVANIA AVENUE
WASHINGTON, D.C.
20:30:22 EST 08 APR

Jim Niewendyke drives out past the White House guard shack, after passing in his security tokens, and heads west on I Street. He's dodging traffic on his way to the Roosevelt Bridge, which will take him back to DHS in Arlington. It's Friday night and both street and foot traffic are heavy – federal employees and politicians heading out of town for the weekend, revelers heading in, and the ever-present tourists heading in all directions.

Jim looks up in his rearview at the light on top of the Washington Monument, blinking serenely against the purple sky, and enjoys a sense of calm. He's just had a good meeting with the deputy National Security Adviser, and feels proud of what he's done at DHS. So far, on his watch, there have been no successful attacks on the National Information Infrastructure. Lots of threats parried, and many more on the horizon. But no punches landed.

As he's thinking that thought, he realizes the green light he's about to pass beneath has stopped being green. It has stopped being any color. He instinctively moves his foot to the brake pedal and begins slowing – but too late. A throaty *thunk* shakes the cabin from the right side and spins his front end a quarter way around. He's been hit by a car in the cross street.

His first thought is to get his vehicle off the road – but more cars and trucks have moved in to fill up the intersection, one or two others colliding jerkily. All are stopped now and the logjam makes movement impossible. Jim looks over and through the riot of headlights and clocks that there are no lights on behind or around them. No street lights, no buildings lights.

A blackout.

He pulls his phone, not to dial 911, which he already knows will be jammed up – but just to see if he has service. He doesn't, on the GSM channel, but SATCOM is okay. He dials CWOC – either to tell them about what's happened, if this is just one of those things, or to find out from them what's happened, if it's not. Within a few minutes, he's learned that it's not just one of those things.

"Hell," he says aloud into the dim air of the car. "Jinxed myself."

He feels bad abandoning the vehicle and contributing to the chaos, but he has to get back on station. He figures his best bet is the White House helipad. He's not sure he can get cleared to use it, but he knows he can get a bird to come to him there. And if the White House staff won't let it land, they'll direct him to an alternate pad close by. He exits the car and settles into an even jog, straight back the way he came.

He sticks to the street, weaving through stopped cars, rather than the sidewalks, where milling pedestrians move unpredictably. There's no particular sense of panic, but the mood is tense. This is still the age of terror. And the power has been off now for nearly ten minutes.

He angles south toward Lafayette Park. People have been emerging from the Metro here and there along his route – first those in the station concourses, then, presumably, those who were trapped on stopped trains. Now, ahead, he sees a commotion at the Farragut West Metro entrance. Only one thing is clear about the scene from a distance – it is *definitely* a panic of some sort.

He picks up his pace and angles from the street onto the sidewalk, on a vector with a number of uniformed police officers, also moving at a smart trot. He hears shouting now – and crying. And then coughing.

Hunched figures sprawl at the top of the stairs, unable to push past those ahead, crushed by those behind. All are in a frenzy to get out. There's definitely hacking coughing, Jim notes with professional concern; and also, he sees now, vomiting. He'll really have to fight to get closer from this point – at which he realizes it's much the best thing if he doesn't.

He has his own chem-bio suit – back in the trunk of his car.

A thin tendril of panic begins to slither around Jim Niewendyke's chest now, tightening his breath. He has to clench all ten digits and focus on fighting it back down. All around him is a maelstrom of terror and the impulse for flight, and he can't get caught up in it. He has to get back to where he can make himself useful.

Just as he begins to disengage and reverse out of the melee, a woman comes crashing through the barrier of bodies before him. She's more wild creature than human – hair in a frizzy penumbra, clothes torn and clawed, and tears and spittle slicking her face. From closer up, her shirt front appears streaked with vomit, and a dark oval stains her skirt.

The woman twitches and writhes, and then trips headlong – straight into Jim's arms. He can only catch her, his instincts on this too strong to overcome. She looks desperately into his face. Her pupils are so constricted as to be nearly invisible.

Within a second of enveloping her with his arms, Jim can sense the chemical doing the same to him – a tightness in his chest, stark irritation of his eyes, and an instantly runny nose. His professional chagrin at letting this attack get through subsumes into a resigned sense of being a captain going down with the ship.

He lays the woman on the ground as gently as he can and stumbles away. The chest constriction increases dramatically, and breathing for him becomes a battle. When the waves of tremors and dizziness begin to hit him, he considers in a dispassionate way that he will probably soon pass out.

* * *

"The stakes just got raised," says Rheinhardt, snapping his phone shut.

The entire group has just gotten virtually the same news at the same time. Mike's version, however, was personalized.

"My boss is injured," he says.

"What?"

"He was coming from the White House, and was right in the middle of it. He's hurt, how badly I don't know."

"Fucking Tabun gas," says Ali. "Where the hell did they get it?"

"Probably from Syria," says Johnson. "You can just have my entire nutsack if that isn't where Saddam sent his stockpiles before the war."

"You're probably right," Ali says. "Nerve agents don't generally get made in basement labs."

Mike is still staring dully off at nothing.

"Put it aside, Mike," Javier says.

"They used the confusion of the power outage," Mike says. "They used it to pull off the WMD attack. The chemical detectors in the stations must have shut down with the power off. Nobody knew anything until it was too late."

"It's never too late," Javier says. "And if they've got their shit together, they'll hit us again while we're reeling. Wherever they are, we've got to find them. Now."

Johnson stretches his fingers out before him. "Okay, then." He cracks his knuckles aloud. "Let's get in the game."

TARGET BUILDING
N.W. BORDER TOWN, AFTERWAR
02:20:36 AUT 09 APR 2018

Mike peeks out from behind a corner, putting the 4x optical scope to his eye. The doorway of the building is as he remembers it, including the two goons out front. "I'm in position," he says out loud. Since the entire team is in the same room, there's no need for in-game (or any kind of) comms.

"Assault element stacked up," BoPeep says. He, UncleBJ, and J-Dawg (aka Javier) are all lined up in an alley on one side of the building. Their recon has already determined there are no back entrances, nor ground-floor windows.

"Sniper and spotter – eyes on," BetteNoire says. She and BitTwiddler are on a rooftop across and further down the street.

Mike has just led the team on a mad sprint from the train station into the center of the town. Problems which would never occur in real life – lost personnel, drunken running, and accidental discharge of weapons – have plagued them here. Real life is a different country.

But not entirely different. Just before entering the game, Mike received a crash course in planning an "emergency assault."

When a Delta team takes down a building, or a plane, or a train, it endeavors to put together a highly detailed assault plan. However, sometimes just when you're doing your planning, the terrorists decide to start shooting hostages. That's when it's helpful to have a five-minute version of the assault plan, thrown together hastily at the outset. And that's what they've put together here.

Rather, half the team worked on the plan – based on Mike's drawn-from-memory map – while the others installed AfterWar clients, registered new players, and ran through the pro forma training for the Eurabian Army. Mike already had a character, as did Tim. The others had to start from scratch.

All of this was taking precious time.

"Hurry it up," Mike scolded.

"You can't fuck up fast enough to win an engagement, Mike," Javier responded. Everyone in the group was moving quickly – but with perfect control and concentration. Or as perfect control as could be managed, which for the game novices was limited.

Now their game skills are going to be tested under fire.

"I have control," says BetteNoire, from the rooftop. "Three. Two." And with that she fires on the first outside guard. Mike watches his head liquefy through his scope, the rest of the body collapsing below. "One," says BetteNoire. She fires again – but the other guard has already moved, and comes up firing. Her second round sparks off the wall behind him.

Nonetheless, the three-man assault stack comes around the corner as planned – straight into the fire of the surviving guard. All is now confusion and the bark of automatic weapons fire through fuzzy computer speakers. Mike sees the three fanning out to engage the guard – but the leader, BoPeep, almost immediately goes down. UncleBJ also gets hit, but stays on his feet. J-Dawg finally puts the guard down, advancing with his rifle at the shoulder and firing. He moves toward the door.

But it opens before he reaches it – and out of the doorway spill a half-dozen of the Eurabian fighters in the green headscarves, all from the Buraq Battalion. And all armed and firing.

Mike has AfterWar running in a large window – but filling only about 80% of his screen. In a narrow window to the side, he has his local traffic sniffer. This he's rapidly jury-rigged not only to display the IP address of any incoming or outgoing network traffic – which should include any player in the game he's connecting directly with – but also to pattern match it against a file with the 2,000 suspect IPs. A match will flash an alert on his screen.

Two new IPs, those of the guards out front, did come up. But neither was a match on any of the 2,000. And when the half-dozen-strong back-up force spilled out of the building, none of their IPs matched either.

Which means that if their real target is here, he's inside the building. Which it doesn't look good for them getting into at this point.

But as Mike is the designated backup for this assault, he needs to get in the fight himself – and fast.

```
He pauses to flick his M4 onto full-auto.
He knows this is normally a bad idea –
you also can't miss fast enough to win a
gunfight – but things are desperate, and
he's got a lot of targets to engage.

  Mike sees that J-Dawg has gone prone
on the street, and is changing out mags.
BoPeep is still dead, and his body has
flickered and disappeared. He'll be spawn-
ing back at the marshalling point – and of
no use for at least 15 minutes. UncleBJ
has been hit again, and goes down. Mike
can't tell if he's dead.

  He sprints into the street, strafing
around wide to the left to try to get a
flank on the defenders, who have formed an
arc around the door. Two have been gunned
down, Mike doesn't know by whom, leaving
four in the fight. Mike opens up on the
survivors.
```

He immediately finds he is slinging an impossibly large amount of lead. Only when BitTwiddler runs past him does Mike realize he must have dropped down from the rooftop behind him. And BetteNoire is also firing over their heads. He and BitTwiddler storm the doorway together.

In the front of the shop, they find no opposition – for the first quarter of a second. After that, defenders pop up from behind the counter, and from inside a doorway that leads to the back. Mike and BT fire back, but hit nothing. They're completely exposed, and the defenders under cover. They're both cut down in seconds.

Mike turns to see about Javier. From the man's screen, he can see he's wounded and trying to get up. Another defender emerges from the doorway and kills him. Mike flinches involuntarily. That's it. The assaulters are all dead.

"Fuck," says Javier. "These guys are equipped for heavy weather."

"We were outgunned," says Johnson.

But Mike is hardly listening – scrolling, instead through the list of IPs. None of them match, even partially, even by subnet, any on the long list. "*Bastards*," he says.

By the time Tim has stepped up to look over his shoulder, Mike is running traceroutes to each of the IP addresses he did pick up.

"What did you get?" Rheinhardt asks, also hunching over from behind.

"Hang on," Mike says. "I'm finding out where these guys are... Um, nowhere... can't tell... *Pakistan*, I think... ah, PacBell.net. That's definitely Atlanta. One of these assholes is in Atlanta. I've got one in Miami. And... hang on..." The little asterisks of the traceroutes follow Internet paths across the curve of the globe, giving him hostnames at their final destinations. A last one resolves: "Washington D.C."

Mike's phone rings again. "Brown."

The others' phones also beep, once again within about two seconds. Mike merely listens – then squeezes his eyes shut and swallows dryly.

Johnson snaps his phone shut. "Atlanta," he says. "Another Tabun gas attack."

"Mike," Javier says. He grabs Mike's shoulder and shakes it. "*Man up, Mike.*"

DELTA COMPUTER FACILITY
NEAR FORT BRAGG, NORTH CAROLINA
21:52:02 EST 08 APR

Tim grabs Mike's chair and rolls him away from the console. Leaning around him, he jams a keychain USB key into the machine. He copies the list of new IP addresses, yanks the key back, and heads for the door. "I'm in the TOC," he says over his shoulder, seating a Bluetooth headset on his ear. "Brief you en route."

Two seconds later, Rheinhardt's phone rings. He puts it on the table on speaker. Without preamble, Tim speaks into the somber air of the lab.

"We didn't get an IP address hit on the power grid attacker. Fine. But there were two city-on-city matches – both of the WMD attacks – D.C. and Atlanta. Which means we've got players in the game physically in both those cities."

"Could be coincidence," Rheinhardt says.

"Yeah. But it's not." Tim is breathing hard, moving fast – and talking even faster. *"I think they're using the game to C&C the attacks."*

"What?"

"I talked about the game being a training tool. But it's also a comms tool. It's like phone, or instant messaging. In the game, personnel from anywhere can issue and take commands. They can coordinate and share intel, from locations anywhere on the globe. Together only virtually, inside the game."

"Why?" Rheinhardt asks.

"He's right." Mike comes out of his stupor now. "Along with financial networks, we've had good luck shutting down terrorist communications networks. Not even shutting them down so much as *compromising* them. We've got sniffers laid everywhere, in Internet backbones, local hubs. We read email. Satellites and planes pick up cell phone and radio traffic. The NSA can decrypt anything. And the bad guys know it. We've pretty much got every channel covered now."

"Every channel but one," Javier says.

"The cloud of the game," Mike says. "They can communicate in the privacy of a whole other world."

"And the best part for them is," Javier says, "if we try to sniff comms chatter for suspicious activity, what are we going to search for? Stuff about attacks, or explosions, or weapons, or targets? That's everything."

"Jesus," Rheinhardt says.

"Get Colonel Havering in here," Tim says. The others realize he's speaking to someone in the TOC, rather than to them over the open channel. *"Get me FBI in Atlanta, most ricky tick. I want their tactical guy. Jameson, I think. Ditto D.C. and New York. Lisa – you're on me. This is a list of IP addresses. I need an exact grid reference for each—"*

With this, Rheinhardt puts his hand over the phone's speaker, muting McDonough's rodeoing of the TOC personnel. He looks at Mike.

Mike says, "Tim's play is this: he figures we've got to physically take down every node in this game we've virtually fought so far. Every player we encounter in the game could be part of a cell running the WMD attacks. If the game – if that building in the game – is their command and control center… then we have a chance to get to them in real life before they launch more attacks."

"How do we know we've got all the nodes?" Rheinhardt asks.

"We don't," Mike says. "And we definitely don't have the command node – the one that actually launched the cyber attack on the power grid. But any of them we *do* have could represent the physical location of another attacking cell."

"Then we've got to get back into the game," Javier says. "And we've got to do a hell of a lot better. We need to get into the heart of that safehouse. We don't have to kill everybody in it. But we do have to find everybody in it."

"No," Rheinhardt says. "If we kill everyone in it then we destroy their communications network."

"For a little while," Mike says. "Until they can spawn and get back there."

"By that time," says Javier, "… the FBI may be on their doorstep."

"Kill 'em all," Johnson says, clapping his hands and going back to his station.

"I need some training on this shit," Rheinhardt says, sitting down.

"What, you can't shoot an M4?" Javier asks, ribbing. "Can't run a door stack?" His smile melts as he realizes that civilians are even then melting in real chemical attacks in D.C. and Atlanta.

Keeping his game face on – when the mission is in a literal game – seems to be one of the many challenges of this new battlespace.

ONBOARD RAIL TRANSPORT
N.W. PROVINCE, AFTERWAR
03:08:21 AUT 09 APR 2018

"Two words," UncleBJ says. "High fucking explosives."

"Roger that," BitTwiddler says. "I've got two HE canisters. What about the rest of you?"

"That's standard issue," Mike says. "When you respawn."

They're all on the train back to the border town – all except BetteNoire. It was only when the others jumped back in that they realized she was never killed. She kept sniping from the same rooftop, slotting opponents who stuck their heads out the door, until they realized their peril. They then sent a couple of grenades, and a couple of players, up onto the roof after her. By that time she was several rooftops over. And still sniping.

So far, it's she whose real-life skills are looking the most transferable of anyone in the group.

The reason no one else clocked she was still alive was that she had slipped earbuds in, the better to directionally locate in-game threats. Stereo sound, as the rest of the team would soon learn, is a major tactical advantage.

"This time we go in with main force," BoPeep says, as the train decelerates into the station. "Mike – if we blow the door, will it actually blow?"

"Yes," Mike says. "Virtually every structure in the game, aside from some big physical features, like mountains, is subject to the physics model. If you blow it up, it will go away."

"Right. Bettie stays on overwatch. Since there's only one entrance, she can engage any reinforcements coming in behind us. The rest of us go in strong – right behind a second grenade barrage. If we can clear that main room, we'll have a chance to disperse into the building. And gain some depth."

"There's a waist-high counter along two walls," BitTwiddler says. "And a doorway on the third. That's the defilade. Our tosses need to get behind and inside them."

"Roger," the others say in unison.

And then they run the gauntlet of the city again, more efficiently now. As they reach the final approach, BoPeep says, "Sniper sitrep."

"Eyes on, no targets. Infil path is open."

"We go straight in," BoPeep says. Then he stops in the middle of the street to figure out how to bring up a grenade.

When Mike sees their leader has fallen off the group, he goes back. "*Five*," he says. "Your five key is the shortcut for grenades."

```
They place three canisters by the door
without being compromised. They then duck
around the corner - all except UncleBJ, who
sticks out and takes light damage when the
grenades go off.
    "Ouch," he says.
    They then execute a rapid run by the door-
way, each chucking a grenade, then clearing
out for the next man.
    Only when they reverse direction and file
in, rifles at the ready, do they realize how
crappy their grenade-throwing has been. The
area in front of the counter is heavily
scorched and splintered. But the area behind
it is still heavily manned.
    The entire assault force is gunned down
again.
```

The phone on the table comes to life again. It's Tim.

"Did you assault the store again? How'd it go?"

A beat of silence passes before Javier answers: "*Lo mismo – pero peor.*"

Mike looks in confusion to Johnson, who sits beside him.

"The same," Johnson translates. "Only worse."

* * *

"Any new IP addresses?" Tim asks. He's standing at the front of the TOC with his headset on, and a phone in each hand, still wearing his assault gear.

"None," Mike says. *"All of them this time were the same as last time."*

"Roger, out," Tim says and rings off.

He turns and gestures urgently at a woman in tan ACUs, who sits at a nearby console. At the same time he puts one of the phones to his ear.

"Yes," he says. "When are you going? Roger that. Don't keep me in suspense."

To the woman at the console, he says, "The Atlanta team's on station and going in. Get me a sitrep from Miami, RFN."

"Yes, sir, right fucking now." The woman leans into her headset, then covers the mouthpiece. "They're scrambling and inbound. But the station chief is trying to get a fast-track bench warrant before they go in."

"Motherfucker," Tim says. From the expressions of those around him, he doesn't do a lot of cursing. "Patch me straight through… Yeah. The chief. Give him to me." There's a five-second pause.

Tim says, "This is the tactical commander on station with JSOC at Bragg. We have hard intel. You ready for it? Okay. Do you have CNN on? The video of the mass casualties? Okay, I want you to take a piece of masking tape and put it over the news ticker at the bottom of the screen where it says, 'Chemical weapons attacks in Atlanta and Washington.' Now take a magic marker and write 'New chemical weapons attack in Miami. FBI station chief had advance knowledge.' You got that? Yes. Ninety seconds from now will do – if that's your best. Yes, I will hold."

* * *

The four avatars – BoPeep, J-Dawg, UncleBJ, and Mike – are back on the train, commuting into town again.

"This is starting to feel Sisyphean," J-Dawg says.

"Hah," UncleBJ scoffs. "At least Sisyphus got close."

This time they throw everyone into the assault – including BetteNoire. When only winning matters, and death doesn't, overwatch means less.

They modify the plan slightly, tossing their grenades as they each enter the room, then hitting the deck. This time the tosses go where intended. And, at least as critically, BetteNoire takes the lead on the galloping assault through the building. Mike doesn't remember her saying anything about playing video games. But she obviously has the skills. Sniper sims, maybe.

As he sprints down hallways, Mike alternately watches for targets, watches his health declining from the hits he's taking – and watches new IP addresses popping up on his sniffer.

When their assault ends at the back of the building, all are badly wounded, and two dead. The survivors burst into a large warehouse-type space, getting the drop on a large knot of figures in the back

```
corner – all of them Buraq Battalion. But
one of the opponents turns and fires a
shoulder-launched weapon at the invading
group. They freeze, watching the nose
cone of the rocket come into them on
a huge plume of smoke. A second before
Mike and everyone with him dies, his IP
sniffer beeps out loud.

   Meaning one of the players in the room
is their guy – the guy who cracked the
power grid and turned the lights off on
the entire Southeastern United States.
```

"*Owned*, motherfuckers," Mike says, pushing himself back from his keyboard.

DELTA COMPUTER FACILITY
NEAR FORT BRAGG, NORTH CAROLINA
22:50:54 EST 08 APR

"*Grid reference*," Rheinhardt says, standing at Mike's shoulder now.

"Right," Mike mutters. He pulls himself forward again. As the traceroute output scrolls by, with longer delays between each hop, he taps at the tabletop. "*C'mon, c'mon…*"

The traceroute finally finishes.

"I don't know that host. Hold on." He flips to a web browser window and looks it up. "Pakistan," he says. "Western Pakistan, I think, far west. It may take a little while to figure out exactly where." He copies the whole traceroute output into mail and sends it to Dharmesh, then rings him.

"Got it," Dharmesh says, by way of answering the call.

"Get me a location," Mike says.

"Give me five minutes. Call you back."

Mike turns back to Rheinhardt. "Can you get local forces moving now? Before I get you an exact address?"

Rheinhardt shakes his head. "Not locals on this one."

"Why not?"

"We can't trust the locals in Pakistan. It's not Atlanta or Miami. If it were Islamabad or Peshawar, then maybe. *Maybe*. But not up in the mountains, FATA or Baluchistan. On this one, we go in ourselves."

"Isn't time the most important thing?"

"Don't worry, we'll fly fast."

Mike looks to Javier, who says, "The guys in Pakistan may be quarterbacking these attacks. But they're not located in the U.S., so they're not on their way out the door with an aerosol sprayer. We can take the time to do this one right. And, believe me, out there, doing it right means doing it yourself."

* * *

"I'll meet you on the tarmac," Tim says over the phone to Rheinhardt, who with the others is halfway back to the ready room. "And I'll brief you in the air."

Tim leans down for parting words with Lisa.

"We're airborne for Pakistan. Keep an open channel," he says. "Otherwise, you're driving the train for now. Keep comms open to all four cities."

"No, I'm driving the train now," Havering says, appearing and striding across the TOC.

"Here's where we're at—" Tim begins.

"Lisa will tell me where we're at," Havering says. "You get your ass off the ground."

ONBOARD DELTA GULFSTREAM JET
OVER THE ATLANTIC SEABOARD
00:01:03 EST 09 APR

"It's the gun from the game," Mike says. "It's real."

"Yes," says Tim, clearing a cavernous chamber, and seating an enormous drum magazine of 20 twelve-gauge shotgun shells. "Auto Assault 12. We've had a couple of them in the armory for a while. But I haven't been motivated enough to take one out – until just now, for some reason."

"Payback… *is a medevac*," Johnson says, pulling a second drum mag out of a duffel bag. He slides one of the rounds out, twists the base, causing four little fins to click out and into place. "Twenty millimeter grenades, with pop-up stabilizing fins. Useful when you need to blow up every room of a building. From out in the street. In three seconds." He presses the round back in and tosses the drum to Tim, who drops it into a duty bag.

"No blowing up buildings," Rheinhardt says, checking the mags on his two .45 pistols – one in a drop holster on his leg, the other on the front of his chest harness, angled quick-draw style.

Mike starts to get the impression that sometimes checking weapons takes precedence over briefings. Maybe just when they're pissed off. Only when they're all locked and loaded do they take a seat around the tiny table.

All business, Rheinhardt says, "First, McDonough updates us on the fallout from the domestic attacks, and from our response takedowns. Then I'm going to tell you what's going to happen in the foreign takedown we're about to conduct. Go."

"Casualties in Washington and Atlanta were light," Tim says. "Lighter than we had any right to expect. Their timing was a little off – the subways were partially evacuated by the time they launched the chemicals. And their dispersion wasn't great. In chemical attacks, dispersion is everything." He pauses, expressionless.

Ali: "How many?"

"Most recent figure is… forty-two dead in Atlanta, sixty-two in D.C. Times about six injured." He lets that sink in. "Which, actually, is about the same number of dead and injured in U.S. highway crashes – every single day of the year. Just to put it in perspective."

"It's not the numbers," Ali says. "It's the psychological effect."

"Yeah, I wouldn't want to be on the New York Stock Exchange trading floor in the morning," Johnson says. "That's gonna be ugly."

"It's ugly now," Rheinhardt says.

"The numbers are going to get a bit worse," Tim says. "Some who survive the first few days won't survive longer. And a few will suffer long-term, chronic neurological damage."

"How about enemy casualties?" Rheinhardt says.

"All on the scene died in the attacks. They went out with it."

"That's Atlanta and D.C. How about Miami and New Orleans?"

Tim squares himself up. "As you know, we got a grid reference for the attackers in the other two cities, from our raid in the game, before those attacks kicked off. The Miami attempt was thwarted. FBI HRT got there almost exactly as they were coming out the door – tanks and sprayers in hand. Captured their safe house, plus four personnel. They're under interrogation now."

"And New Orleans?"

"Situation unclear. FBI stormed the target location – and found it empty. No weapons, no personnel. And no attacks yet. They're scouring the site for forensics. But the city had already locked down public transport, so maybe that scared them off before they could strike."

"We stopped two attacks," Mike says. "That's something."

"So's a dog turd," says Johnson. "This was one championship screw-up."

Tim shakes his head. "We were in the game, right in front of them, the day before. If we'd known we could get their physical locations from the game, if we'd gone in then, we could have stopped it entirely."

"Instead we waited around for another attack," says Johnson. "And we got one – good and hard."

"We weren't expecting a real attack," Mike says. "Just another hack. Anyway, we still stopped two."

"We stop hundreds," Rheinhardt says, his mouth a hard line. "Every day of the year. The only ones that matter are the ones that get through."

"Nearly ten years," says Ali. "No domestic attacks since 9/11. This doesn't reflect real well on the new administration."

"Speaking of the White House, have we heard anything?" Tim asks.

"The Colonel duly reports that huge flaming bags of shit, in twos and threes, are being launched all up and down the National Command Authority – and, yes, starting at the Oval Office."

Johnson snorts. "So why the hell wasn't the FBI staking out this location?"

"Why not CIA?" says Tim. "Or Interpol? Whose jurisdiction is AfterWar? Domestic or foreign? Are we violating the *Posse Comitatus* act by conducting military ops in the game? Are the enemy personnel on American soil? Are we?"

"Jesus," says Ali. "These games might not only screw with our view of objective reality. They might actually overturn the nation-state system that's been in place since the Peace of Westphalia."

Rheinhardt shakes his head. "As for all that political crap: don't know, don't wanna know; don't care, not gonna care. Our only job now is to take another look for our sacks, and go out and get these people."

"Okay. What's the plan?" Ali says.

Rheinhardt adjusts the screen of his laptop. "This is a non-permissive environment – we do not have clearance or support from Islamabad for the op. No police, no military, no security services."

"Thank fuck for that," Johnson says.

"So we go in alone," Ali says. "And quiet."

Rheinhardt nods. "We are operating in the west of Baluchistan. The physical location of the guy we ID'd in the game, as pinpointed by Mike and his people, is the town of Koh-i Dalmach, about 200 clicks southwest of Quetta, the provincial capital."

"Oh man," Johnson says. "Back to Baluchistan. I shit you not, someday somebody's going to have to deal with Pakistan."

Mike looks to Rheinhardt. "Baluchistan?"

Ali says, "Westernmost province of Pakistan – and its largest, with forty-four percent of the country's landmass. One of the most rugged and remote places in the world - vast deserts, high mountains, and sparsely populated plains. Which is why it's been a favorite hide-out of Taleban, al Qaeda, and other Islamist fighters since Afghanistan fell. Much longer than that, really."

Mike says, "I thought those guys were in Waziristan, the Northwest Province?"

"NWFP and FATA – the Federally Administered Tribal Areas – get all the ink. But Baluchistan is the real dark water. Whenever Islamists feel the heat up in the north, they know they can retreat down amongst the Baluchs. But now they effectively have control of the north. They've immobilized 70,000 Pakistani troops and begun regulating moral life, administering justice, and enforcing their version of Sharia. And Baluchistan looks like next."

"It is next," Rheinhardt says. "Our AO on this one, Koh-i Dalmach – and you're going to love this – was taken over by a force of about 200 Taleban, with supporting AQ elements, three months ago. And it's hardly the first town to fall to them. In this case, they got the police and army barracks, the courts, all the administrative centers. And here's the punch line – there was no popular resistance. Evidently the local population thought it was just groovy. Or not worth getting up in arms about, anyway."

"Biggest province," Ali says. "Fewest schools, lowest literacy rate. Upwards of 80% of the suicide bombers in Afghanistan are recruited in Pakistan. And there's either a nationalist or an Islamist insurgency going in every one of

Baluchistan's thirty districts. Increasingly driven by AQT. The notion of national control by the government there is a joke."

Javier: "Did Zardari respond to the takeover of the town?"

"Yeah. He dropped some bombs, declared victory, and changed the subject."

Johnson: "So this place is, basically, the hornet's nest."

"Pretty much. And a really bad place to lose your shit."

The group absorbs this in silence for a few beats before Rheinhardt goes on.

"Insertion and infiltration are as follows. We're doing a night landing onto the deck of the USS *Theodore Roosevelt*, which is currently cruising in the western Persian Gulf. Once on the boat we load up a Chinook with ATVs – the quiet, tricked-out ones. The helo then puts us down at the western edge of the Central Brahui mountain range, about five miles outside of the town. And we ride in, nice and smooth."

"Why so on the prowl?" Javier asks.

"Because we need to not fucking kill everyone this time," says Rheinhardt. "Since we killed everyone last time, we couldn't ask them if they had any buddies who might be planning domestic chemical weapons attacks."

"The helicopter noise over the mosque," Mike says.

"It gave them thirty seconds warning," Javier says.

"Thirty seconds they're not going to get this time," Rheinhardt says. "I also want people with rubber bullets loaded up this time. Put some in that twelve-gauge fire hose of yours, if you've got 'em." Johnson looks crestfallen, as if that wouldn't be any fun – despite the fact that he's not even carrying the weapon.

Rheinhardt swivels his laptop on the table for the others' view.

"Insertion point is here – a rare flat spot in this part of the Brahui. We travel this route." He traces a finger across the screen. "As you can see, the path through the mountains goes by a couple of small villages. The target is at the end of the line here."

He flips to a video window, presses play, accelerates the speed. "This is satellite imagery, tasked about an hour ago. You can see the bodies moving in and out of the target building – even at this hour. And, in any case, it's dead in the middle of the medina of the old town. Going to be cozy."

"It's a fucking labyrinth," Johnson says, peering at the maze of tiny, curving streets.

"Bring string," Rheinhardt says. "The minotaur is coming out with us."

ONBOARD DELTA GULFSTREAM JET
OVER THE NORTH ATLANTIC
00:03:58 GMT-3 09 APR

An hour later, Mike sits by himself looking out a port-side window.

"Beautiful sight, isn't it?" Javier says, walking up on him. "The moon reflecting on the Atlantic from thirty thousand feet." Javier stands in the narrow aisle, in the back section of the executive jet, where there are regular rows of seats. The front half of the plane, where the briefing occurred, and where the rest of the team still sit, has couches along the sides of the fuselage, and a table in the middle.

"It's a lot better view than out of a C-130."

"It's the upholstery I really appreciate," Javier says. He sits down on it, in the next seat over. "How's your boss? Heard anything?"

"Yeah. He got triaged on the scene and then sent to Bethesda Naval Hospital. They were able to get him atropine pretty quickly. But he's in ragged shape."

"Atropine itself is pretty toxic."

"That's what they told me. The prognosis isn't definite. But right now they think he's going to be okay. They're keeping me posted."

"Glad to hear it." Javier pauses respectfully. "There's one other thing, Mike."

"Yeah?"

"I'm just heard back from the TOC. They sent some other guys into the game, after we left. To have another go at the gun store."

"And?"

"It was empty. Abandoned."

"Makes sense, I guess. It had been compromised."

"Yes. And this also means that right now… the safe house we're taking is the only lead we've got. When we get in there, you've got to make it happen. We'll take care of security. But you've got to execute the online op. You've got to find out if there are any more of them, and if so what they've got planned next. And, most importantly, where they are. Are you ready for that?"

Mike nods. "I think so. We know what we're looking for, it seems like we know what we're doing. It's a good plan. I've got to think we'll be fine."

Javier pauses a heavy beat, holding Mike with a steady and slightly sad eye. "Yeah, well, despite all of these preparations… one lucky shot or one overlooked booby trap can ruin the best laid plans. That's the funny thing about soldiering: one bad afternoon, and your career is over. And, in our jobs, a bad afternoon can have even worse consequences."

Mike holds his gaze quietly. Finally, he says, "Hey, back at the Ranch, Rheinhardt made some noises about not trusting the local authorities. Isn't Pakistan our ally in all this?"

"They are. But it's an uneasy alliance. You'll recall that it was the Pakistanis who created and armed the Taleban in the first place. It was only when Bush made them an offer they couldn't refuse that they switched sides. And there are still an awful lot of guys in their military and security services who have never wavered in their support of the Taleban, the Islamists – and even AQ. It was only Musharraf's, and now Zardari's, decreasingly iron fist that keeps them on side."

"Okay. I can see where we would want to loop them out."

"And even if we could trust them, it's not likely they could help. The central government simply doesn't have control over the areas we're going into. Their forces don't operate there. And, finally, adding to the fun, they've gotten really cool on even allowing *us* to operate there."

"You're saying we don't have permission for this?"

"Much easier to ask for forgiveness. Better still to not get caught – just get in and out. Look, we did a lot of cross-border ops from Afghanistan in the years after 2001. Particularly TF145."

"I heard that designation before. Still don't know what it is."

"Task Force 145. It was one of the SOF joint task forces put together to go after HVTs – high-value targets – in Afghanistan and Iraq. Mullah Omar, bin Laden, Saddam Hussein, that kind of top-shelf bad guy. It's made up of portions of Delta, DEVGRU – AKA Seal Team Six – the 75th Ranger Regiment, and a whole SAS Sabre Squadron. Plus SOF aviators, the Air Force's 24th Special Tactics Squadron, and CIA's paras. Extremely capable operational outfit."

"Was Johnson part of it?"

"I'm not allowed to tell you that. But, yeah." Both men smile. "Anyway, we were doing an awful lot of hunting and killing of AQT – combined al Qaeda and Taleban forces – over the Pakistani border, most of it on a free-fire basis. But in the last year or two Pakistan has come down with delusions of sovereignty – which is particularly funny in Baluchistan, FATA, and NWFP, where they pretty clearly don't have any. We've kept up the drone attacks, as you've probably heard, and which they can't really stop. But they've started taking a really dim view of ground ops on their soil. Which I suppose is fair enough."

"But we're going in anyway."

"Absolutely. Nowadays we either have to ask for advance authorization – or just go in quietly and take our chances. In response to the first WMD attacks on American soil, I think we're pretty happy taking our chances on this one."

"I'm in," Mike says. He lowers his voice slightly and steals a glance toward the front of the plane. "Hey, speaking of Johnson. You remember when you pawned me off on him for rifle training? Before we finished, he said something about having to go to a parent-teacher conference. Was that some kind of a joke? Or a code word for some other covert activity?"

Javier smiles very broadly. "Yeah, it's a code word for mid-point of spring term at the local elementary school. And for once BJ was actually home for it."

"Are you telling me he has a kid?"

"Nope. Two of them. A four-year-old, Nathan, and a seven-year-old, Marissa. And they're both so cute they make you want to stop whatever you're doing and have some kids of your own. Picture a three-foot-tall BJ with angelic blonde hair and missing teeth."

Mike shakes his head. "I find that just about impossible to picture. Heck, I find it hard to imagine him married. What does his wife do?"

"She's a captain in the 82nd Airborne."

"His superior officer…" Mike raises his eyebrows. "But isn't that kind of dangerous? Both of them off fighting the war?"

"She's headquarters staff. Never leaves Bragg. Always there for the kids. Anyway, this isn't the only job that can get you killed. I hate to put it this way, but people got killed yesterday taking the train home from the office."

Mike doesn't respond to this. But his expression darkens. When he speaks, his voice cracks. "I've been thinking about that a lot, actually. I can't seem to *stop* thinking about the people who were hurt and killed yesterday – trapped underground, choking to death, bodies shutting down…" He pauses to try to master his voice, but it only cracks with anger now, rather than sorrow. "God, what the hell is wrong with people? I mean, why would they go so far out of their way to do something like that? To cause such suffering – in people they don't even know?"

"Yeah," Javier says quietly. "You pretty much would think the one rule, if there weren't any other rules we could agree on, would be not to hurt anyone else." He pauses, stretching out his legs beneath the seat ahead of him.

"On the other hand, it's not completely mysterious. I mean, if you had it drilled into you from a very young age that God wants you to convert, or subdue, or kill the unbelievers… that being martyred in the process will earn you a fast-track ticket into Paradise, no waiting around for the end of the world, no board exam before you're allowed in… that you get to bring your seventy favorite friends and family members along with you… And not to forget all the dark-eyed virgins when you get there. There's actually a theory I've heard that suicide bombing is just the most expedient means for some young Muslim men to get a date."

Mike laughs bitterly. "I suppose there are times when I was so desperate to get laid I wanted to blow something up."

He shakes his head. "Okay, it makes sense internally. But I still don't understand why people would teach their children that in the first place. That to kill themselves, and to murder others, is glorious."

Javier's smile melts away before he replies. *"Et in arcadia ego."*

"Meaning?"

"Even here, in Paradise, Death abides. Roughly translated."

The two sit in silence in the near-dark.

A moment later, Mac rises from where he's been lying up front and shakes himself out. He pads silently down the aisle and sits beside their row of seats. Javier reaches down and rubs the dog's head. He then clears his throat quietly.

"A long time ago, Nietzsche made some predictions. Eerily accurate. Of course, he famously said that God was dead – and with no God, there would no longer be any morality. But he also predicted that the next century, the twentieth century, would see unimaginable wars."

Mike turns to face him, their eyes glinting in reflected blackout lights.

"And he said that the century after that… would see an abandonment of all standards whatsoever."

Mike takes a second to absorb that. "Great. So what do we do now?"

Javier sighs. "Stop reading mad, syphilitic Germans, I think."

Mike laughs weakly. "Seriously."

"We do what we can, I guess. Try to stand up for some principles. Try to live according to them. Or die for them, if we have to."

Javier stands up again, patting Mac on the backside. "*Vámonos, Macote*. Let's let Mike get some rack time." The two head for the front – where the others still sit up studying maps, setting comms frequencies, and practicing other minute martial arcana that leave Mike blank, and leave him awed.

1000 YARDS ASTERN OF THE USS THEODORE ROOSEVELT
THE NORTHERN ARABIAN SEA
00:12:55 GMT+6 10 APR

"What kind of friggin' maniacs put a tail-hook on a *Gulfstream jet?*"

Mike is very thoroughly strapped in – including in a chest harness, non-standard on executive jets – but also bloodlessly gripping the armrests and pressing on the legs of the seat in front of him with both feet.

"We do," Javier says, as if that was the stupidest question in the world.

But a single second later Mike blacks out – when their already harrowing descent and deceleration is violently arrested by the steel cable strung across the carrier's landing deck. He comes to almost immediately and his vision unspools from a dilated pinprick. Luckily, he cannot see out the front of the plane from his seat, and it's night-time anyway – or else he'd have to watch as the cable reels out behind them until the plane reaches, and slightly passes, the terminal edge of the deck. Finally, a big fat nothing sits between them and a plunge into the black ocean.

Not releasing the armrests, Mike turns his head to Javier. "And how do we take off again?"

"We don't. But the plane can get up again with a catapult. C'mon."

Mike shakes his head and clutches his bag as he and the others descend the stubby ladder, and then are hustled across the roar and glare and tumult of a working carrier flight deck at night.

"*Welcome to The Big Stick!*" their handler shouts to Rheinhardt, keeping them moving with the energy of a man all too aware that this is a dangerous place for people who don't work there.

That place consists of four acres of flight deck, slick with oil and hydraulic fluid, swarming with hundreds of sailors (average age nineteen), a half a dozen tractors, and fifty aircraft – routinely rocketing from 0 to 150mph in under two seconds. All this on a seagoing vessel longer than the Empire State Building, with a control tower looming 150 feet above it, and on all sides a pitching and yawing steel cliff 100 feet above the surface of the ocean. (Survive the fall and you'll drown in the ship's churning wake, where there's too much air in the water to hold you up, and too much water to catch a breath.)

But the non-Mike members of the group have all been here before and take it in their stride. Mac the badass mutant beagle also seems less fazed by the light and noise and motion than Mike does. But the dog too has been on carriers. Also, he's had a lot more training.

As Mike steps out of a glaring cone of deck lights into shadow, and his eyes begin to adjust, he sees that the ship is surrounded by other bobbing lights, at various distances, in all directions. As he's led through a gangway and down a rough steel staircase, he touches Javier on the shoulder and asks, "How many ships here?"

Over his shoulder, Javier says, "Well, the supercarrier itself… a destroyer squadron, one or two Aegis guided missile cruisers, two or three guided missile destroyers, an oiler and supply ship – and two nuclear submarines cruising around out there somewhere only the Admiral knows where. Plus the carrier air wing, of course – eighty-some planes plus helos. If this ship were a country, it would have the world's fifth or sixth largest air force."

"Jesus," Mike says.

"Yeah," Javier says. "A carrier strike group could single-handedly win a war against pretty much any other country in the world. And, last time I checked, we've got all eleven of the world's carrier strike groups."

"God bless America," Mike says.

* * *

They step through another gangway, down a hallway, and into a briefing room – greyer, steelier, and more cramped, but with the same Spartan and businesslike feel as the ones at the Delta compound.

There are two men in flight suits seated at the table, one making notes on a clipboard, the other sipping a Diet Coke. When Rheinhardt walks in, the one with the can of soda rises. Both men smile and step forward to shake hands.

"Where the heck did you come from?" Rheinhardt asks.

"From going to and fro over the face of the earth," the man answers, "and walking back and forth upon it."

Rheinhardt says to BJ, "Hey, you remember Rick from the 160th."

Their handler, stepping in behind them, says, "Your CO, Havering, managed to get two of your flyers attached to us for your mission. From out of Bagram."

"Thank fuck for that," says Johnson, emphatically.

"We weren't doing too much there," Rick, the pilot, says. "Extracting SEALs from ill-advised firefights up above 8,000 feet."

"Will that flying minivan of yours even get up to 8,000 feet?" Rheinhardt asks.

"Everybody has to take a piss first. Get a haircut."

A newcomer in a Navy officer's uniform steps in through the hatchway. "I see you're acquainted. I'm Commander Lewis. I'm going to be coordinating your mission from the boat here. And we really need to get back on station in the Straits of Hormuz scaring the shit out of the mullahs, so if we could get down to it, gentlemen…"

* * *

Mike is back on deck now – after having been briefed, fed, and allowed to take a shit – and watches equipment being loaded onto the helicopter. He realizes he's come a long way. But people still don't tell him everything – and a lot of people don't tell him anything. He watches, wonderingly, as rated seamen push what look like redneck recreational vehicles up a ramp into the back of the helo. At the same time, in the alternating dark and theatrical light, the D-boys are tossing their large duffels through the side door. Sergeant Major Rheinhardt confers with a man in a yellow jumpsuit, who is holding a clipboard and an enormous flashlight.

Mike is clutching a large knapsack – inside of which nestles his hardened laptop. He needs the backpack to get it with him safely through the mountains.

To whatever waits for him on the other side.

With his free hand, he reaches down to touch the outside of his right thigh. Strapped there is the H&K .45 pistol, his bequest from Javier. It rides in a black nylon drop-leg holster, with Velcro rip-away flap, and a spare magazine pouch on the front. Looped through his belt is another dual magazine pouch. That makes a total of 49 large-caliber bullets upon his person.

These, more than anything else, make him start to feel like an accepted member of this team.

Though, at the same time, he knows that it is the higher-tech, and less sexy, device in his other hand which is going to allow him to make his contribution, if he's going to make one. He is feeling a very strong, urgent desire to contribute.

He is also feeling a very strong desire to survive – which is another reason he's glad for the handgun.

In both directions, guns and gadgets – and despite the rolling of the ship's deck – Mike Brown feels his feet much more firmly beneath him than he did in Michigan, or in London. Then again, on this one, he's about to be a lot farther from home than on either of those occasions – and a lot further from help.

On the other hand, he thinks, acknowledging Javier's gesturing, and sprinting out underneath the whumping rotor blades, *home is where your homies are…*

ONBOARD THE "SHORT BUS"
OVER THE ARABIAN SEA, ONE MILE FROM THE
PAKISTANI COAST
03:15:55 GMT+6 10 APR

The enormous, ungainly, twin-rotor CH-47 Chinook – more graceful in the air than on the ground, but only just – skims the surface of the water, its pug nose angled toward the smooth, black surface of the Arabian Sea. It resembles an enormous sewage tank wearing two large propeller beanies. Or, as the painted lettering under the cockpit glass has it, a school bus for special needs kids. Special Operations Forces kids, in this case.

The slightly darker mass of the land looms before them and in a few seconds the bird crosses the invisible membrane between land and sea. Nearly immediately, the aircraft begins climbing – to surmount, and then settle itself into the nap of, the craggy and forbidding spires of the mountains.

Because it's a bigger, heavier bird, with its doors closed, conversation is possible inside without headphones, just raised voices. Mike soon wishes it weren't.

"Hey!" Mike hails Javier.

"Yeah, man." Javier sidles over to him.

"Back in London, when we were coming down in the helicopter toward the mosque – you said something about 'meat waffles'."

"Yeah. Why do you bring it up now?"

"Because you look nervous as hell. And not just you."

Javier smiles thinly. "It's because of the mountains."

"Not the helicopter?"

"It's because of the helicopter up *in* the mountains. Specifically, *us* in a helicopter in the mountains." Mike looks blank, so Javier leans in close. "I didn't want to bring it up before and scare you. But we really don't like helicopters."

"Why not?"

"Because rotary-wing aircraft have killed more Delta operators than enemy fire and old age – *combined*."

"No shit?"

"None."

With this, Johnson clocks their conversation and sticks his head in, listening at first. Javier says, "Delta's very first mission was to rescue the hostages from the Iranian Embassy in 1980."

Mike nods. "That didn't go too well, as I recall."

"The rescue would have gone fine. We had an outstanding plan of direct action and takedown, and were ready to go. The problem was the helicopters. The Navy insisted on being part of the op, though neither their birds nor their pilots were up to it. When a sandstorm blew in, their pilots freaked out and decided they couldn't go on. When we went to bug out from the staging point in the desert, one of the helos clipped a C-130 and blew itself up – along with the huge fuel bladder inside the plane. Delta guys went streaming out the jump door like a combat jump, inches ahead of an enormous fireball. We almost lost the entire squadron, one of two that existed at the time, in all of ten seconds."

"Holy shit."

"After that, we realized we weren't really a very good counter-terrorist outfit if we couldn't get to where the terrorists were. So we formed our own team of flyers – the 160th SOAR, the Special Operations Aviation Regiment. They're the best fliers in the world – operate in the dark, in the mountains, eight feet off the ground, in hailstorms. They're basically the Delta of helicopter pilots. They've got specially constructed seats to hold their huge brass balls."

"And those are the guys flying this helicopter?"

"Yeah. The lead pilot is Rick, we've flown with him before. I don't know the rest of the crew." Mike has already seen a co-pilot, a navigator, and two crew chiefs in back with them – one of them manning an enormous electric Gatling gun.

"So what's the problem?"

Johnson leans in and speaks now. "It's still dangerous as a motherfucker, that's what. Even with ace pilots flying them, these rickety bastards still go down all the time." He pauses to spit into a plastic water bottle, an improvised spittoon, then continues, warming to his subject.

"In Grenada, Delta was on a helo assault. The intel was crap and there turned out to be a shitload of AA on the ground – all of it shooting like they knew we were coming. They shot those birds up so bad, when they limped back out to sea to put down on a ship, the sailors said they could see the sunlight *through* them when they flared. One crash landed in the forest. Half the guys on that mission got shot in one place or another, or hurt in the crash."

All three of them lurch into one another as the helicopter simultaneously plummets and banks. They are following the nap of the earth, below radar.

When they regain their balance, Javier takes the theme back up. "In Panama, we went in to rescue an American civilian being held hostage. Landed on the roof of a prison, fought our way down three floors, got him out and onto the bird, no problems – but then promptly got shot right out of the sky. So there was this helicopter dragging itself through the streets of Panama City, unable to lift off, half the team wounded. When they finally abandoned the damned thing, one operator went down as if shot. But he'd been clipped on the helmet by a rotor."

Johnson again: "And then there was Desert Storm. Four-man team out Scud-hunting in western Iraq. Came under attack and took a litter-urgent casualty, so they call for exfil. A Black Hawk gets to them, picks them up, heads for home – and promptly flies into a sandstorm and crashes. All hands killed. They would have been better off walking out of the desert. On their hands. With their heads in buckets of shit."

Javier: "And I needn't belabor Somalia. C Squadron goes into the worst part of Mogadishu and successfully grabs a bunch of warlords in broad daylight. Then two Black Hawks get shot down, killing two Delta guys outright – and the team ends up in an all-day, all-night running gun battle trying to get to and secure the two crash sites.

"Two Delta snipers onboard another bird, Gary Gordon and Randy Shughart, volunteer to get put down at the second site, when it becomes clear that help isn't going to get there in time. They saved the life of the pilot. And both got the Congressional Medal of Honor – posthumously."

"I'm sorry," Mike says.

Johnson: "Hey, just one of those things. They knew *exactly* what they were getting into. And they'd still be there holding that crash site today if they hadn't run out of ammo. They just had more opponents than bullets."

"Anyway," Javier says, "from the moment this machine comes off the assembly line, *all it wants to do is kill you*. But until we get teleportation going, this is how we have to insert."

Mike reflects on that for a second. "It's not quite teleportation… but the AfterWar trains are pretty damned fast. And totally safe. Never crash. And you can engage opponents all over the world from the safety of your desk."

"Hey, good point… I think I'm seeing some advantages to fighting in this new battlespace. Where's my mouse?"

The dim red lights in the cabin blink three times. The others look to the front where Rheinhardt is flashing a triptych of fingers. *Three minutes*. The old battlespace is coming in fast and hard, right beneath them.

CENTRAL BRAHUI MOUNTAIN RANGE
BALUCHISTAN, WESTERN PAKISTAN
03:22:03 PKT 10 APR

Mike Brown grabs dirt. He's lying prone in some sort of scrubby ditch. Not doing anything. Not breathing. Nothing.

They've already been on the ground for twenty minutes – but not moving, not making a sound. Just lying prone and still and, as Mike was instructed, "tuning in" to the night, and the new environment. It's nearly half an hour before the operators begin to trust their senses, their intuition that they are really alone in this lonely hollow in the mountains.

The other members of the team are probably no more than twenty yards away from Mike, and the closest is nearly at his elbow. But they might as well be on separate planets; Mike can see nothing. He's in the blackest blackness he's ever experienced. The night is completely overcast and there's probably not a street light for three hundred miles in any direction.

And NVDs, night vision devices, are not one of the toys he's been given to play with yet. He doesn't know whether it's an oversight, or they just think it's safer with him holding someone's coattails.

Instead of thinking about what might be out there beyond the black cloak of the night, Mike mentally reviews the last shouted instructions from the helicopter. With the final seconds ticking down before insertion, Rheinhardt huddled the team up in the back of the bird.

"Last points," he barked. "One – since this is the source of their biggest attack, we assume it's their headquarters element. That means well-defended. So unless OPFOR have the courtesy to count off, always assume there's one more somewhere. And even if there isn't, they'll have sympathetic neighbors – every fourth person in this town is some flavor of Islamist militant; and three out of four will be armed.

"Two – we need live ones, for interrogation. Particularly anyone we find working on a computer. Less-than-lethal force is harder – but that's why you assholes get paid the big bucks.

"Finally – there's no backup or QRF this morning. There's no air, or artillery. And local police and military can be counted on only to capture us if we're lucky, or shoot us if we're not. Also, there's only one secondary exfil plan, and it sucks. So either we get to our extraction point – or we don't. And if we get in trouble along the way… well, don't fucking get in trouble."

"Two-point-five," Mike said aloud. Everyone turned to look at him – and he paused, sort of stunned by the sound of his own voice speaking up. "A second and a half point: if any of them is on a machine logged into AfterWar – *we need that session*. Don't let them log out, and don't let the machine get blown up."

"You heard the man," Rheinhardt says. "Anything else? Okay. From here on out, throat mics only. And NVDs and infrareds or thermals. Positions."

* * *

Thus far, Mike hasn't had to try very hard to avoid having amorous thoughts about Aaliyah Khamsi. He's had a hundred other things on his mind at any given moment, most of them matters of life and death. Nonetheless, any live, heterosexual man – any human being, for that matter – could not entirely fail to notice her poise, easy confidence, and striking physical beauty.

Now, with the team finally in motion, and with his arms wrapped around her waist and his front pressed against her back, Mike is, for the very first time, having to try very hard not to have amorous thoughts about Aaliyah Khamsi. He is the only member of the group without his own ATV – except Mac, who rides with Javier. Ali is the lightest of the others, so Mike is her passenger. Just Mike and the dog.

The ATVs are small four-wheeled off-road bikes, like the spawn of a motocross motorcycle and a golf cart. And, like virtually all other Delta equipment, they are custom jobs. In addition to reinforced suspension and sturdier components, they have dual-use internal combustion/electric engines. The electric mode is totally quiet, allowing silent insertions. But the engine, when running, recharges the battery, providing for longer range and higher speed.

All of this was explained to Mike somewhere along the line. He's learned more in the last four days than in the previous four years. His brain hurts.

Also, his nuts hurt. The ATV, while moving slowly and nearly silently, has been bucking consistently for nearly a half hour. He figures it's best that he can't see a damned thing. Seeing the path, the passes, the cliff edges, would only terrify him. Nonetheless, he finds himself hoping they continue for a while longer. What's at the end of the path is even scarier.

Soon, though, a faint glow appears on the horizon. The night is so dark that even the weak lights of the town put a dent in it. In the ambient orangeness, Mike can see the vehicles ahead pull off onto a side trail, and maneuver behind an outcropping of rock. Ali steers to follow. All the machines shut down together.

And then, without a word, without sound, without hesitation, they begin moving in single file through the darkness, down the lower steeps of the foothills, picking their way, pausing, pivoting, panning weapons in all directions and planes, black and silent, with mechanical, monocular protrusions from their foreheads, like an invasion of stealthy, deadly kings from the land of the blind.

THE MEDINA, KOH-I DALMACH
BALUCHISTAN, WESTERN PAKISTAN
04:02:03 PKT 10 APR

<u>Bette Noire</u>

"In position, eyes on. Sniper has targets." Aaliyah, like the others, has mastered the art of working her vocal cords so lightly that the mic pressed to her throat picks up her voice, but a person standing four steps away would not.

"Target sitrep." Rheinhardt's voice speaks deep in her ear.

"Stand by for traffic," Ali says.

"Send traffic."

"White, Alpha-One, blind." Delta's snipers, as Ali explained to Mike during their training, assign alphanumeric codes to all windows and doors of a target building. White: front side of the structure. A: first floor. 1: first window or door. "Thermal shows two to four pax, intermittent movement. White Alpha-Three, same as previous. White Alpha-Two, shut. White Bravo-One and White Bravo-Two visible, zero pax. Roof, clear. How copy?"

"Solid copy. Stand by."

Ali shifts her thighs, which are laid out behind her, facing down. She is currently wedged into the top of the tiny minaret of a run-down mosque about 250 yards from the target building. Some part of her regrets this small blasphemy. But she doesn't second-guess the decision. It was the only overwatch spot with a clear look at the whole front of the target building, plus the roof.

Using this position also necessitated a quick check of the prayer schedules for the month. Not only did she not want to be cheek-to-jowl with the loudspeaker when the muezzin issued the morning's first call to prayer. She also didn't want to have to kill the muezzin on her way out of the building.

Little Bo Peep and Uncle BJ

"Well, they're not asleep," says Rheinhardt.

"Would have been nice," Johnson says. "It is the middle of the fucking night."

"Doesn't matter. Stack it up. Another day at the office." Rheinhardt presses his throat mic. "Assault element inbound."

The two work their way forward, silently, invisibly, in a light crouch, through the maze of the medina, navigating solely from memory. Their rifle barrels and NVDs point straight and sharp ahead of them, like the prows of military spacecraft.

Bit Twiddler

"Roger that," Tim says nearly soundlessly. He pats himself down in one or two places to ensure everything's strapped down tight, then steps out from the cover of a bank of chimneys.

He crosses the smooth surface of the roof, mounts a section a half-story higher and, without hesitation, leaps a six-foot gap over the black pit of the medina below. Landing on the pads of his hands and feet, Tim gives silent thanks that the roof, which might be made of mud, holds.

He moves through shadow to a last roof edge, and this time crosses to the next rooftop with a single wide step. Now he is on top of the house which they have all crossed an ocean to assault.

He removes a bracket-shaped charge from his duty bag, assembles it, and emplaces it. In a few seconds, it will either blow a dynamic entry hole – or it will collapse the roof from under him. Pressing his throat mic, he says,

"Santa's in the chimney."

J-Dawg and Mr MacSnuggles
By pedigree and evolution, Mac moves more silently than the others. And with his black body armor and two-foot-high profile, he's that much less visible. His only disadvantage is his smell, which makes him more likely than the others to arouse the interest of local dogs.

Javier peeks around the front corner of the building, from where he can see the two members of the front-door stack, but only because of the night vision. And they are not what he's looking at.

At ground level, Mac has already sniffed, nearly silently, from one edge of the building front to the other. He pauses a second time at the front door, running his faintly shining nose from corner to corner.

Satisfied, he pads back to Javier and presses his muzzle into the waiting, outstretched, gloved hand: the front door is not rigged with explosives. Slipping backward into the shadows, Javier whispers: "The dogs are in the house."

Wile E. Coyote
Mike Brown, PhD, U.S. DHS ISD, confirmed pointy head, has finally gotten his Delta radio call sign – bequeathed in honor of the two "kinetic events" he survived in London.

Johnson initiated this meme back in Hereford, when he referred to Mike as the "incredible exploding IT guy." That proved too wordy, and too hard to abbreviate. But the image of a blackened and smoking Wile E. Coyote, blown up again in another ill-fated attempt to dynamite the Road Runner, stuck.

Mike is in the darkest corner of the most cramped alley within a thirty-second sprint of the target house. Three twists and a left-hand turn separate him from it. When the moment comes, he will have to navigate by memory. And he alone, without NVDs, will have to do it nearly by touch.

"Wiley – sitrep," a tiny voice says in his ear.

Finding the throat mic control, Mike presses it and says: "Wile E. Coyote in position. I'm ready."

"Roger," the voice, Sergeant Rheinhardt's, says. *"Hold there."*

Mike releases the mic control and exhales.

The adrenaline in his veins now is, somehow, both better and worse than it was in Michigan and London. In Michigan, he'd had no reason to think anything would go wrong. In London, he'd had no idea what was going on.

Now, here, in the far west of the Islamic Republic of Pakistan – a Pashto-, Urdu-, and Balochi-speaking region, at the edge of the trackless Brahui Mountains – without a passport, without an innocent explanation for his presence, with only a laptop and a handgun and five friends and a superdog… here, now, for the first time, Mike has some idea what he is doing. But he also has some idea of how spectacularly, and in how many directions, things might go wrong.

And he also has a sense of the stakes. The CNN images of the effects of nerve-agent poisoning on humans float before his face, out there in the darkness. He understands that this is it. Either he gets this job done… or more people will get hurt and die. Maybe a lot more.

Inexplicably, the awareness of the enormity of this… calms him. He hears the shape charge go on the roof, with a slightly muted whump.

He puts two fingers to his earpiece and waits for the call.

TARGET HOUSE, KOH-I DALMACH
BALUCHISTAN, WESTERN PAKISTAN
04:07:55 PKT 10 APR

Though Mike is not there to see it, the takedown of the medina safe house looks nearly precisely like the demonstration takedown he saw in the Shooting House at the Delta compound. That is, it doesn't look like anything – nothing that anyone, other than those conducting it, would have even a fraction of the time or attention to see or to understand.

The signal to begin is the explosion on the roof. With that, the three oblivious occupants of the ground floor of the house snap their heads irresistibly toward the ceiling, or toward the stairwell in the back corner. And it is in the air over their heads, right in their faces, that the flashbang grenade goes off.

Now they are blind and deaf, and none of them ever saw or heard the front door blast inward.

Now each takes four to six shots in the upper body, in the center of mass, with solid rubber bullets fired from submachine guns. They experience this only as a convulsion of inexplicable, primal pain – and a complete, if temporary, loss of the ability to breathe.

Now they are knocked to the floor with forearm smashes, or pulled down with crooks of elbows around their throats, and steel boot toes in the backs of their knees.

Now they are face-down and tied hands and feet with plastic flexi-cuffs, heavy electrical tape encircling their heads at mouth level.

And that is it.

Javier, last in, pulls the door shut as Mac slithers inside.

Tim radios *"Bravo clear,"* sticks his head and gun barrel down the stairwell to check things out, then goes back up to hold the upstairs. He's had nothing really to do but blow the shape charge, fall through the hole, and have a quick look around.

"Alpha clear," Rheinhardt says aloud. "Target secure."

Then, pausing from his designated corner of the room, peeking out through one of the curtained windows, he cycles the channel on his throat mic.

* * *

"Roger," the voice, Sergeant Rheinhardt's, says. *"Hold there."*

Mike releases the mic control and exhales.

He hears the shape charge go on the roof, with a muted whump.

Then he hears the flashbang go, with a sharper crack.

Sergeant Rheinhardt's voice speaks again in his ear: *"Wiley – bring it in."*

And Mike freezes, questioning his perception of what he's heard. There was almost no perceptible delay between the two transmissions. Could they have taken the whole house down in a single second? Then he flashes back to the Shooting House, remembering the supernatural speed of it. And he takes off into the darkness at a jog.

The front door swings half open for him. And now, safely inside, it is his turn to "man up" – and to get the job done.

* * *

"This is Bettie to Bo Peep with the neighborhood watch report: all quiet."

"Copy that."

Aaliyah puts her eye back to her sight – or, rather, her sights. As she explained to Mike, the primary day sight on her CheyTac sniper rifle is a 22x56mm variable magnification telescopic sight. The night vision system is a third-gen monocular night sight – which simply attaches to the back of the first one, the two stacked up front-to-back. In sniper parlance, this makes for a big gat with an even bigger glass.

And Ali is using all of this glass thoroughly. She knows that, from their positions at the center of the action, the assault team are not able to judge how much of a ruckus they are making. They probably think they were in like church mice.

But, from her vantage – higher, quieter, more in tune with the sleep rhythms of the town around her – she could hear the soft bang of the shape charge on the roof; and then, just before a sharper crack, she could see the flashbang fire off, like a lightning strike indoors.

So now she takes great care to see who else may have seen, or heard, the takedown. And who may be moving to investigate – or to counter-attack.

In addition to the day optic, and the night sight, she also has an AN/PEQ-15 Advanced Target Pointer/Illuminator/Aiming Laser. Effective out to 300 meters, the illuminator fires a wide infrared beam – basically a powerful infrared flashlight – totally invisible to the naked eye, but which broadens and improves night vision in insufficient ambient light, or for seeing into shadows.

It also has an IR laser pointer, which can be used as a laser sight in NVDs – or to paint targets for terminal guidance ordnance (smart bombs). It allows you to reach out and touch anything you can see, even when it's too dark to see it. Soldiers who have used the PEQ-15 liken it to "the Hand of God."

Now, up in the spire of the mosque, Aaliyah considers the irony of this. That she is using a tool like this to combat religious zealots who believe in a literal Hand of God, which moves all things. And who believe that God sees all things.

In reality, it is Delta sniper Aaliyah Khamsi who sees all.

And as she pans her scope, she does in fact see a spectral figure cross an alley between two buildings. And then another just behind it.

"Bettie to Bo," she says, head angled down to the scope, butt of the rifle pulled into her shoulder, index finger straight out along the receiver. "The neighbors are up."

ONBOARD A V-22 OSPREY VTL AIRCRAFT
SOMEWHERE OVER AFTERWAR
22:10:09 AUT 09 APR 2018

Mike has no complaints about the comfort of the seats on this military transport – mainly because he's not actually sitting on it. All he cares about regarding this plane is that it can take off and land vertically, by tilting its rotors to point directly upward. And that it can fly very fast with the rotors pointed forward.

The U.S. military spent the better part of two decades working on the Osprey, thwarted by endless design and production problems; and has only recently been rolling them out into the field. The Anglosphere Military, on the other hand, within AfterWar, has had a working version of the plane for years. That's because open-source programmers have had the specs on the plane for years.

And now the avatar known as "WileyC" (aka Mike Brown) has one, too. His colleague BigD is flying it, while he stares at his heads-up large-scale AfterWar map, trying to navigate. They are attempting to fly to a very particular spot on the map – an al Buraq safe house, two of whose garrison have been hijacked, and their real-world owners tied up on the floor in Pakistan. And whose avatars are now controlled by two Delta operators – namely Javier and Uncle BJ.

They bought this aircraft with an enormous slush fund of half a billion Warbucks – procured by a government accounts-payable clerk who actually went onto eBay to buy them in the middle of the night.

And it is this very expensive plane which now, to Mike's horror, has begun taking heavy anti-aircraft fire. They have just crossed the frontier and are flying over the Eurabian front lines. And they are doing it, it turns out, at too low an altitude.

"Pull up! Pull up!" WileyC shouts over the secure, in-game channel that Dharmesh has built for them. (In his copious spare time, he's been hacking the open-source AfterWar client.)

"I know, man!" BigD answers, hauling on the yoke.

WileyC watches the interior of the plane shake epileptically; and Big D watches the horizon do the same out through the cockpit window. The plane already feels as if it will shake itself apart. As they take more near misses, and

```
then direct hits, from AA flak, smoke fills
the cabin - and their climb flattens out
and becomes a dive.
   "No!" WileyC shouts. "Fuck me! No!"
```

"Hey, you better keep it down, man," Johnson says, from two machines over. He is at one of the two PCs they have captured in the target house in Koh-i Dalmach. Mike is at his laptop, which he has set up on a crate. "We've got company outside. And one RPG through this window will really fuck up everyone's day."

"And what's taking so long?" Rheinhardt hisses, striding across the room. "How long to go?" The room is now dimly lit by monitor glow, and they have all flipped their NVDs up on their heads.

Mike watches his screen go completely bright, and then completely black, as he, and his plane, and his telecommuting coworker, spiral in, explode, and die. He is shaken by this setback, but not panicked.

"We've got to fly in again," he says. "I've got to spawn, pick up more of the missiles – and get in back in the air."

"Can you get a new plane?"

"Yeah. It will take a little time."

"*How long?*"

But before Mike can answer, a heavy thump sounds against the front door. Then another, a bit fainter, against the wall just beneath one of the front windows. Rheinhardt shoulders his rifle and speaks into his throat mic. "Bettie. Sitrep."

"*You're fine,*" Ali says, from across the medina. "*That's two tangos down at the front of your location, dicks in the dirt.*"

Everyone in the room, each of whom is also on the open channel, turns to look at everyone else. Rheinhardt steps to the window, pushes aside the drapes, tilts the window out, tilts his NVDs down, and scans the area. Lying on the ground a few feet away are the potato sacks of two lifeless bodies. Two rifles lie near their outstretched and motionless hands.

Rheinhardt eases the window closed and lets the drape swing back. He presses his throat mic. "Interrogative: any *more* of those out there we should know about?"

"One or two," Ali says. *"But let me worry about them. What YOU need to worry about is the dark side of the building."*

"BT here," Tim's voice says across the channel, from upstairs. *"We've got some issues out back, boss."*

Rheinhardt shoots one look at Mike.

But Mike does not look back.

He is busy spawning.

TARGET HOUSE UPPER FLOOR, BACK ROOM
KOH-I DALMACH, BALUCHISTAN
04:16:02 PST 10 APR

Tim carries the AA12, his "twelve-gauge fire hose", slung on his back. Nestled in his arms, tucked tight into his chin, is an H&K MP5 submachine gun, SD3 version – for "*schalldampfer*" (or sound dampened). It has an integral, two-stage sound and flash suppressor. With the bolt noise absorbed by rubber buffers, and firing subsonic ammo, it cannot be heard from fifteen feet away.

And this gun is no longer loaded with rubber bullets.

Tim stands erect, a full five feet away from the window overlooking the courtyard behind the house. Moving in a side-to-side arc, he has a good field of fire, while presenting nearly no target silhouette to any shooters outside.

On top of his submachine gun he has mounted his own monocular night vision sight. Lightweight and compact, it runs on a single AA battery, provides 2.25x magnification and has a red LED aim point with windage and elevation adjustment. Most importantly, with one eye pressed to it, he can see in the dark, while keeping his night vision in his other eye.

Tim is tracking a figure who has been skulking in the shadows out back for the last minute or so. Finally, the man shows himself, revealing that he carries a weapon. This seals his fate. He manages one step out of the shadows before Tim puts a half-dozen 9mm rounds into his center of mass.

The man never hears the shots that kill him.

But someone, who was lurking behind, figures out what has happened – and realizes his peril. He too is carrying a weapon, a 7.62mm AK-47 assault rifle.

And the next shots, fired from this, large-caliber and distinctive in their guttural roar, are heard by virtually everyone in the old town of Koh-i Dalmach.

As wood splinters shoot off of the window frame before him, and two rounds plunk into the ceiling over his head, Tim realizes the game is up.

And the clock is now seriously ticking.

***

```
WileyC and BigD meet back at the Anglosphere
Command Center Airfield, inside the main
hangar. When they bought the first plane,
they didn't yet know where they would be
flying it. That would only become clear
when and if the raid in Pakistan yielded
them a live in-game session, and thus
the location of another virtual terror-
ist safe house - hopefully the main one.

  As WileyC rushes in, BigD is already
opening up the large storage unit they
rented earlier. WileyC catches him up and
grabs one from the stack of Javelin mis-
sile launchers.

  The Javelin is one of the most effec-
tive anti-armor weapons ever created - it
is what allowed a handful of U.S. Green
Berets in Iraq to stand and fight an entire
```

armored company, destroying nearly a dozen tanks and APCs. (This was referred to as "The Alamo" of Second Iraq.) The missile is fire-and-forget, locking onto armored targets via an infrared sight and then self-guiding. It is also pretty effective against buildings and fortifications.

In real life, a single Javelin missile costs about $80,000 – and they are equivalently pricey in AfterWar.

For all these reasons, they are much coveted in the game, as in life. But the Javelins which WileyC is loading into their second, frantically purchased Osprey, are very special missile launchers indeed. These versions have some non-standard code embedded in them – code inserted by Mike Brown. (In *his* copious spare time, Mike has been hacking AfterWar weapon mods.) And code that is, ultimately, going to make these weapons a lot less popular with al Buraq.

Now the two of them have got to get these hacked missiles back in the air and out to the newly discovered AQA virtual safe house – where Johnson and Javier are even then doing half-assed impressions of terrorists with their hijacked avatars, walking around slowly, looking blameless, and trying not to talk to anyone.

```
    Just as the Osprey's rotors are spin-
ning up, WileyC hears gunfire through his
headphones. He checks his health – still
at 100%. And then he realizes the gunfire
wasn't through his headphones at all. It
was around the sides of them, from the
real world outside.
```

"Fuck it, my Arabic sucks anyway," Johnson says, standing up, grabbing his rifle, and heading for the stairs. "And I shoot straighter in real life."

"Stand down," Rheinhardt says, from near one of the windows. They still haven't taken any fire from the front, though two more bodies have piled up, courtesy of the Bette Noire Neighborhood Watch. "When Tim needs help he'll ask for it."

Johnson sulkily props his rifle and sits back down.

Which is when the shatter of window glass, and clatter and skid of metal on kitchen tile, alerts them to the arrival of the first grenade.

Instantly, instinctively, Rheinhardt and Johnson crash down onto their stomachs, facing away from the entrance to the kitchen – thick rubber boot soles angled to absorb blast or shrapnel. Javier is a half-second behind, crashing down on top of Mike, who has no such instincts. The grenade explodes a second later. All of the team are shaken and deafened, none hurt.

Which is much more than can be said for the three prisoners, all of whom had been stowed away on the floor in the corner of the kitchen.

"Fuck sake," says Johnson, looking over his shoulder at the gore and moaning that manifest in there as the smoke and echoes dissipate. He grabs his medical bag and rifle and moves to the rear.

When Rheinhardt looks for Mike to ride herd on him, he finds him already upright and back at his keyboard.

```
"Is this heading right?" Big D is saying
anxiously. "Wiley?"
   "Yeah, perfect."
   "Thanks. You okay there? I lost you
for a second."
   "Fine," WileyC says, not wanting to
muddle the online op with news of fright-
ening developments in the real-world op.
"This thing go any faster?"
   The twin-rotor plane zooms over the
virtual landscape, dark gray and indis-
tinct in the darkness of this hour of the
future - now up at a safer altitude.
```

KITCHEN, REAR OF TARGET HOUSE
KOH-I DALMACH, BALUCHISTAN
04:26:02 PST 10 APR

Rheinhardt enters the kitchen behind Johnson. He sees, above the grungy sink, the shattered rear window the grenade sailed through. He leans in and smashes a second window on the left with his rifle barrel, and stands covering that flank – while Johnson silently works on the two suspects who have survived the grenade attack.

Mac sits stilly on his haunches at the entrance to the kitchen, looking back and forth, waiting for someone to give him instructions.

"Hey, guys, my bad there," Tim says, through the open radio channel. *"Everyone okay?"* It was his job to keep opponents, including grenade throwers, from slipping in their back perimeter. *"I've got the rear cleared up now."*

"Affirmative, and copy that," says Rheinhardt, pivoting now and firing twice out the left-side window, up toward the second floor of the building opposite them. More gunfire is building up now, mostly from this building to their immediate left.

"How you doin'?" Johnson asks Rheinhardt from the floor, one hand pressed on a blood-soaked gauze pad, the other removing a surgical clamp from his mouth.

"The left flank's a big flaming bag of shit," Rheinhardt says, crouching down below an incoming volley – then popping back up and driving the volleyers under cover with his own fire. "I've got an entire building of hostiles here."

"Where'd all these assholes come from so fast?" Johnson asks, ducking some incoming rounds – and then an arterial spray of blood, before clamping it tightly closed. "Hang tight, I'll be there in two jiffies and a fart…"

"*One* jiffie, motherfucker, *one* jiff—" but Rheinhardt is cut off by a crescendo of machine guns, by his own doubling up for cover – and finally by a thundering explosion outside the window, which cracks and buckles the wall. This was probably an RPG fired low – though they're all hoping it was only a grenade thrown short.

The radio channel is still open, and Tim catches all of this. Though no one would guess from the tone or reaction of any of the operators, the situation has deteriorated, in less than a minute, to become nearly insupportable.

Rheinhardt speaks levelly on the open channel: "Assault team in heavy contact from the left and rear. We might be overrun here."

He doesn't need to add that being overrun in this case will most likely also mean being wiped out.

* * *

Such a situation, Tim considers dispassionately, calls for bigger guns. Still covering the rear through the upstairs window, he slings his submachine gun around behind him – and unslings the Auto Assault 12 from the opposite side. He steps up onto the desk, hunches over, and hops smoothly out the second-story window. He lands in a patch of weeds, taking the force of the fall in a flex of leg muscles.

He knows the rear of the building is clear at this moment in time, because he's been keeping it that way. He hopes it will stay that way for another fifteen seconds, which is as long as he intends to be down there.

He side-steps out into the center of the yard to get a good look at the side of the house on their left flank, and at each of its firing positions. He brings the AA-12 to his shoulder and plants his feet wide.

"Now," he says quietly under his breath, "how's this feel?"

* * *

From Aaliyah's vantage, all of the enemy firing positions of the left-flank building are perpendicular to her. She can see muzzle flashes erupting from its windows, she can sense Rheinhardt returning fire. She can even occasionally see barrels sticking out of windows. But she cannot get a shot.

She reaches around and unholsters her sidearm, placing it on the floor beside her. With all the noise, and the violence, and the ratcheting tension – every second they spend here reduces their chances of ever leaving alive – she starts taking her eye from the scope and snatching quick glances behind and around her. She cannot afford to get snuck up on.

When she brings her eye back to the scope, it takes her a moment to process what she is seeing below.

It appears to be the left-flank building blowing up. Not precisely blowing up in a structural sense. But rather each of its rooms blasting outward, vomiting smoke, flame, debris, and body parts – starting with the upper left and finishing with the lower right. Left to right, then top to bottom. A scanning wave of total obliteration, courtesy of the Auto Assault 12.

That, she thinks, *is blunt-force trauma room-clearing.*

* * *

"Left flank is clear," Tim says across the net, while regarding the smoking, flaming, now-depopulated hulk of structure.

He stands in the rear courtyard, his gun's fat barrel angled downward, smoke pouring from its open and locked-back breach, finger to his earpiece. He feels rather jaunty and light on his feet – lighter by a score of 20mm grenades, with lock-out stabilizing fins.

He drops the empty drum magazine, replaces it with a fresh one, switches weapons, walks around the house – right past the kitchen window, where he can see Rheinhardt regaining his feet and coughing – and back in the front door.

"How we doing?" he asks, pressing the door closed behind him.

"Hold on," Javier says. "Mike's got a tricky landing. I can hear him buzzing in now."

AQA TRAINING CAMP
N.W. PROVINCE, AFTERWAR
22:42:38 AUT 09 APR 2018

BigD has gotten the two of them and the aircraft across the frontier, and is now bringing the Osprey down, this time not too low – but, alas, too close to their target. This becomes apparent when, on approach, two-inch-diameter holes begin silently flowering open in the fuselage, on opposite sides, in one and out the other.

"What the fuck is that?" BigD says. "I hear nothing."

"Rail gun, I'm guessing," WileyC says. "Just get us on the deck. And pray they don't hit a fuel line."

Their plan of action does in fact call for them getting killed. But it won't work if they die in an enormous fireball of exploding aircraft – and exploding Javelin missiles.

"Hey. I can see the guy with the rail gun," Javier says from the ground, off of game comms, aloud into the room. "I can take him."

WileyC ducks involuntarily from another shot to the plane – this one to the right rotor housing. "Can you take him out *without him seeing you do it*? If they figure out two of their avatars have been hijacked, the jig is going to be up."

"No problem," Javier says. His character is outdoors now – both he and Johnson moved outside to avoid having to talk to anyone. Edging around the side of a building, he uses his night optics to zero in on a figure on a nearby roof – one holding a bulky, light-pulsing, man-portable high-energy depleted uranium weapon. (Not, in this case, anything that has any real-world counterpart at the current time.)

"Can I help?" Tim asks, having now gotten comfortable controlling the other character.

"No, I'm good. Just hang tight."

There is now a fair volume of fire as other Buraq fighters emerge from their huts and begin taking potshots at the descending Osprey. So Javier is able to fire a half-dozen shots unnoticed, placing them expertly. The railgunner tumbles off of the rooftop.

The Osprey touches down heavily, but safely.

WileyC and BigD leap off the rear ramp before it is fully lowered. Now they've got to do two things: get off a couple of Javelin missile shots – and make sure

```
they're impressive; and then both get
killed, with the rest of the missiles
piled up behind them.
    And then the final act will be down to
Javier and Tim.
    At about a hundred yards from the center
of the compound, Mike takes a knee – and
flips opens the CLU (Command Launch Unit),
the targeting component of the Javelin.
    He's then forced to stop dead and
wait for the refrigeration unit to cool
the CLU enough for the thermal target-
ing to get a lock. He forgot this can
take up to 30 seconds. Shit.
    Something with an explosive warhead hits
nearby and rocks his vision. He checks his
health and armor. They're not what they
used to be. And, at this rate, they're not
going to be that for much longer.
```

At this point, almost nothing can wrest Mike's eyes from his screen, or his hands from his mouse and keyboard. He is now sitting in the middle of a real-life 360-degree firefight – and more than a few live rounds have come through windows and walls, and reached their final resting places where he can see them hit. But his job is not fighting the gun battle.

He is fighting the AfterWar.

But when Mac growls out loud, the organic and unfamiliar sound draws from him a sidelong glance – just in time to see the dog leap up the back stairs, powering himself with his strong hindquarters.

And, after him – Uncle BJ, with pretty damn big hindquarters of his own.

Johnson has grabbed his rifle, left a casualty report with Rheinhardt – "*KIA, imminent, stable*," pointing to each of the three bloodied prisoners in turn – and vaulted up the stairs on the heels of the dog.

An attacker has come in through the open upstairs window, perhaps from a nearby rooftop – and only Mac caught the sound of it. Johnson arrives to find the beagle in an upright wrestling match with a wiry man in a dishdasha and black vest, his dropped rifle skidding on the wooden floor around his rope sandals.

Johnson crashes through the door and directly into the flailing pair. It now becomes a three-creature wrestling match.

After his initial growl of warning, Mac has not made a sound. He holds his opponent's right arm clamped in his teeth, and digs his uncut front claws into the man's groin.

Clutching at each other, swaying, both the invader and Johnson curse aloud, one in Arabic, one in English – "*Kis em ick!*", "*Motherfucker!*" Johnson tries to regain his balance, and to overpower the other man, without stepping on Mac. Mac is holding on fiercely – and will do so until his enemy is dead, or until he is called off by one of his own teammates.

Johnson finally gets one leg solidly under him, and yanks his baby-sized knife clear of its scabbard. It goes directly from his thigh into the throat of the other man, who goes quiet mid-curse and drops like a stack of newspapers. Mac lets the dead man go, shuffles backward, and looks up alertly.

"Good dog," Johnson says, pulling out the knife, whacking it point-first into the wall, and picking up his rifle. He takes a quick look out the window, where the first glow of dawn is now painting Pakistan a murky brown – and revealing slithering, but recognizably human, movement. They're coming in from all directions. Johnson says to Mac, "Stay with me." Mac sits. Johnson speaks into his mic.

"Hey, yeah – Tim. Yeah, the rear's about as cleared up as my nutsack."

He then snaps the rifle to his shoulder and fires into the dimness of the alley at the rear of the yard. In response to the enormous volume of return fire that comes back, he ducks, flips his fire selector to full-auto, pops up again, and empties the magazine straight down the same vector.

In the echoing silence that follows, he hears Tim's response in his ear. *"Well, let me know if you need a hand – or have questions about the tac situation."*

"Yeah, I've got a question," Johnson says, peering over his sights. "Where are we going, and why are we in this handbasket?"

Then, stepping forward and standing upright at the window, peering down after his shots, orchestrating a no-look magazine change, Johnson takes a bullet square in the upper right of his chest. It spins him halfway around – after which he squares up again and looks down at the abraded and ripped surface of his body armor.

"Now look at that bullshit," he says, whacking his charging rod forward on the fresh mag. But before he can bring the rifle to his shoulder, four more rounds catch him square across the chest. The 240-pound man crashes to the floor.

He shakes his head violently to clear it, before bouncing back to his feet.

"*And the rear's at least slightly more cleared up than your nutsack, I hope…*" Tim's voice says jovially in his ear, as his hearing comes back. Across the net, Rheinhardt adds, *"Yeah – you're gonna turn up with penis cancer, BJ, you keep fuckin' them goats."*

"I hate penis cancer," Johnson mutters – and cuts off further discussion in this vein by unleashing, and also drawing, a whole new hailstorm of fire.

Before this ferocious volley and this phase of the battle are over, Johnson's body armor has stopped two more large-caliber rounds – and a third has creased his jaw and taken off the tip of his right earlobe. In and around the courtyard, at least a half-dozen of his opponents lie dead, dying, or incapacitated from wounds.

Pausing to take stock, Johnson first assesses the body armor, ignoring the wounded ear. The ear will live. But the liquid Kevlar won't take an unlimited amount of punishment before failing. And it will only stop so many bullets in one spot before they start coming through.

AQA TRAINING CAMP
N.W. PROVINCE, AFTERWAR
22:55:00 AUT 09 APR 2018

WileyC can already feel rounds coming through his own armor. He checks his stats: Armor: 0%. Health: 34%. It wouldn't be the end of the world if he died there and then, squatting in this field waiting for his Javelin launcher to cool off. The al Buraq cadre would probably take the remaining missiles, Mike's special-edition Javelins, anyway. But a display of firepower should make them irresistible. Also, Mike wouldn't at all mind taking out a building or two of this compound.

He's pretty sure he and the D-boys have stumbled on a significant AQ training facility – and any buildings or equipment they destroy here will take time and money to rebuild. Time and money they won't be spending to plan attacks.

And Mike has a funny feeling that this will not be his last raid on a terrorist safe house or training camp that doesn't exist in real life.

His thermal sight finally comes online. He takes aim at a structure rather than a vehicle, so there's not much of a heat signature – but he gets a lock on warm bodies and small arms fire. Just as he's about to let it go, he sees BigD's fire off first, right over his head.

The Javelin is a top-attack weapon – arcing high up into the sky like a firework, then coming back down on its target's head, where tank armor is generally weakest. BigD's shot lights up the sky in a graceful curve, then slams down shiveringly fast into the roof of one of the buildings.

The structure, and every jihadi avatar in, on top of, or around it, simultaneously disappear in a white flowering eruption, and then a roiling flood of black smoke.

Pausing not too long to admire this, WileyC fires his off. In order to minimize backblast – and thus make it safer for the friends of the guy firing it – the Javelin has a soft launch, ejecting from the launcher and reaching a safe distance from the operator before the main rocket motors ignite. WileyC's pops out of the tube, its tail sagging toward the ground, then blasts off and fills his vision with flame.

And another, even larger, building goes the way of all flesh.

Mike smiles as his avatar dies, victim of a mortar round, he thinks, that had already popped off from the camp. He turns from his laptop to the other two machines, to watch the chaos, the destruction – and the final act.

"Now," he says, "if we can just hang around long enough to see if they go for the bait—" at which he ducks and covers up his head from a spray of glass as the front window shatters from gunfire. Eyes pressed closed, glass shards and dust tickling his hair and skin, he hears a voice beside him intone, *"Follamé mas fuerte…"* When he opens his eyes, Javier is giving him a wide-eyed and open-mouthed look, but half smiling at the chaos – while, beside him, Tim has his eyes locked to his screen.

```
The al Buraq avatars controlled by Javier
and Tim are already sprinting across the
open field, leaping over the smoking corpses
of WileyC and BigD - and up the ramp into
the back of Osprey.
    In the cargo area they immediately
come upon the twelve crates of Javelins -
twenty-four launchers and a gross of mis-
siles in total - right where WileyC and
BigD piled them before takeoff.
    Grabbing a launcher each, Tim's and
Javier's avatars turn back down the ramp
to face the field. Approaching them at a
rapid clip are about a dozen Buraq infantry
- most or all of the players still alive in
the AQA training camp.
```

Javier takes a deep breath, clears his throat – and flips his mic control onto game comms.

"*Huma ma'it! Kanu 'andhum Javelin! Salihin rfíin! Sir nishan! Serbi! Tbarka llah 'lik! Serbi!*" He's telling them it's a kick-ass weapon, sent by God, and they should help themselves.

He then runs out and past the crowd, Tim following, gains some distance, and spares one look back. The others are pouring up the ramp of the Osprey.

"*Que bueno,*" Javier says – just before Tim fires a Javelin directly at their feet, atomizing them both.

The last thing Mike saw on the screens was Buraq fighters emerging from the plane - all visibly holding Javelins. "Kick ass," he says, smiling ear to ear.

Without further hesitation, Tim stands, draws his sidearm, and empties the magazine into the two monitors, CPUs, and keyboards.

"Al*righty*, then." The others look up to see Johnson standing on the stairs, shot to shit, and looking pissed off. "I've got to say I'm now personally up to about 9.4 on my Get-The-Fuck-Out-O-Meter."

Tim stands and slings his guns. Javier ducks as more rounds plink through a window. Mac leaps down the stairs, around Johnson's tree-trunk legs. Rheinhardt strides in from the kitchen, half-carrying the one surviving prisoner. "You heard your uncle," he says. "Let's get the fuck out while the getting the fuck out is good."

MINARET, RUSTIC MOSQUE
KOH-I DALMACH, BALUCHISTAN
05:04:00 PST 10 APR

"Roger that," Aaliyah says calmly, before taking another shot. While dropping out an empty magazine, she adds, "Exfil path is open. Proceed with caution. I have overwatch." She whacks the new mag home, chambers a round – and begins the most serious part of her job: protecting men on foot in an extremely hostile MOUT (Military Operations in Urban Terrain) environment.

As she hunkers down, the loudspeaker goes off – the muezzin's first call to prayer. A squelch of feedback precedes a deafening chant nearly right in her ear.

Son of a bitch. In all the ruckus, she forgot about that.

She focuses in and checks again for targets in the alleys, windows, and rooftops around their path out. When she sees the team on the move, under fire, but ineffective fire, she calls for their ride. Raising her voice to a shout above both the guns and the ululating din of the muezzin, she switches channels and shouts, "This is Bette Noire to Short Bus! Stand by for traffic!"

"This is Short Bus. Send it."

"We are six pax, one WIA, requesting immediate evac from secondary extraction point! Team is exfil'ing under fire. LZ likely to be hot! Repeat: LZ hot! How copy?"

"That's a solid copy, Bettie," a voice sounds in her ear, just audible over the din, but still cool and unflappable in its flat

Texas accent. *"Short Bus is inbound. ETA sixteen minutes. Have a good 'un."*

* * *

"How you guys doin'?! This is gonna suck!" Johnson is serving as tail gunner Charlie on the exfil run, and is last to reach their first strongpoint outside the target house. They are taking fire from a few too many directions – and almost all of it from inside darkened alleys, and darker windows. These are spots Ali cannot get a bead on from her aerie. If any of these shooters emerge into the open, she will enforce a very short life expectancy on them. But for the moment, it is a bad guy snipefest.

Also, this mad dash through dusty urban streets, in low light, taking fire from all directions, is reminding the operators unpleasantly of the Battle of Mogadishu, i.e. *Black Hawk Down*. Though none of them was there that day, it is an unshakeable organizational memory.

Johnson reaches the end of the line of soldiers, all crouching at the mouth of a narrow alley, pausing for breath and cover. He sees Rheinhardt half-supporting the prisoner. The man's cuffs have been removed, and he seems healthy enough to run, with help. Rheinhardt returns Johnson's judgmental gaze, over the top of his rifle, which he is aiming one-handed. They both know the prisoner's going to slow them down.

Javier catches this silent visual exchange, and says, "And thus does the victor belong to the spoils."

To which Rheinhardt responds: "We keep this man alive. Understood?"

"Okay, Eric," Johnson says, and spits, staining the dust a darker brown. He figures they've only got about a mile to get across alive, so maybe it won't matter much either way.

Their secondary extraction point, which became necessary to use when the op went noisy, is on a dusty ridge overlooking the town, in the first foothills of the mountains. It's flat enough to set down a Chinook. But the pilots won't much like the unobstructed line of sight to town, half of which is now joining the fight.

"Bounding," Javier says from the point position, taking off at a run. Mac lopes along no more than two feet from his boots. Incoming fire kicks up around all six of their feet. Tim, in the two-spot, leans around the corner and fires up toward elevated positions, plinking at muzzle flashes, first left, then right, then left again.

"*Set*," Javier's voice comes in again over the squad net – and now Tim squares up to follow. But instead he stops and shouts something Mike cannot understand. He has stopped firing and instead gestures with his hand, a sharp downward motion. Looking up and across the larger cross street, Mike can see faces in a window. They are wide-eyed children's faces, peering out through the dusty window – curious about the breaking dawn storm of gunfire outside. And not nearly enough afraid of it.

"*Ksséte!*" Tim shouts. "*Khatarnaak, kssâte!*" Whatever this means, it gets through, and the small round faces drop out of view. Tim brings his rifle back to his shoulder, says "Bounding," and then sprints out in Javier's footsteps.

"*Set*," Tim's voice reports a few seconds later.

"Mike," Rheinhardt says. "You're with me."

Ratcheting into the last concealed spot at the mouth of the alley, Rheinhardt, the captive, and Mike all draw breath – and then take off together on a mad dash through the shooting gallery.

* * *

Mike's laptop is stowed on his back.

His pistol is in his hand – for the first time since the Delta range – the safety off, hammer locked back, a fat .45-caliber round in the chamber.

And his heart is in his throat.

Inside the target house, in the firefight, in the center of the maelstrom, he'd been able to compartmentalize – to block out the death and hazard that surrounded him. That was a valuable thing to be able do. That was progress.

But this is death on a stick out here. He knows he is out in heavy weather and the firestorm is coming right down on his head. Now, Mike Brown thinks about nothing but staying alive – and not letting his friends down. Which now mainly means not getting shot and becoming an extra burden for them to carry.

The open stretch to the next bit of cover seems like an endless expanse – one with a receding horizon. And suddenly Mike is out in the middle of it, arms and lungs pumping, adrenaline turbo-charging his acceleration.

He can see Javier and Tim ahead now, firing from out of the next narrow alley, both corners of it, covering their run. Sparing one look over his shoulder, he sees Johnson firing out of the last alley, covering their rear.

When he looks forward again, a rock has snuck up on him in the dimness – he feels the pressure on his boot, and sprawls headlong into the dust.

Sliding to a painful stop, but his gun still in his hand, his bag still on his back, he looks up and sees Rheinhardt and the captive ahead, still running flat out. In a second they reach the cover of the next alley, slipping into enveloping darkness.

Mike shakes his head, and goes up on hands and knees, into a sprinter's start, preparing to take off again. But a glancing pressure in the small of his back knocks him back into the dirt, face-first. It feels like some rat-bastard has taken a full-arm swing at his back with a ball-peen hammer. It shocks more than it hurts. He can't believe some son of a bitch actually just shot him.

Face back down in the dirt, he can see dust kicking up around him, near misses all over. He can hear the firing, in a distant, mediated kind of way. He now really understands that there are people trying to kill him. And that he is lying dead in the middle of the road, which he cannot do long and live.

Before he can get up again, he feels an arm hook into his, elbow in elbow, pulling him to his feet in one powerful motion. Then Johnson shoves him forward like a ragdoll, Mike almost going over on his face again – but then he straightens and comes up running. And in another second he is safe in the alley.

As he tumbles in one end, the others are already at the far end, facing the next run across open ground.

"*Bounding,*" Javier's voice says, and the others cover him by fire.

"Set." And then Tim is out and running.

Rheinhardt and the prisoner square up. But Mike is looking back the way he came – where Johnson is just now angling in on the alley, slightly from the left, at a trot, his weapon held just below level, his eyes squinted and scanning.

Johnson's head swivels on his neck, his eyes widening and locking onto something off to one side. Mike hears just the tail end of the whoosh, one eighth of a second ahead of the incoming RPG. It explodes outside of his field of view, to the right of the mouth of the alley.

And he sees Master Sergeant "Uncle BJ" Johnson lift off the ground and rocket out of sight to the left.

IN THE MEDINA
KOH-I DALMACH, BALUCHISTAN
05:12:32 PST 10 APR

Mike's hands automatically go to his face, and his knees buckle, as the pressure wave and debris of the explosion swirl around him and pull at his clothing and gear. When he opens his eyes again, he can see nothing through the billowing dust.

Turning back into the alley, he also sees nothing. The others have gone. It's only him now.

Only him and Uncle BJ – who is still out in the street somewhere. Alive, dead, or ground beef, Mike has no way to know. And there is no one there to help but him.

Mike edges back toward the street, where the firing has actually intensified. He knows what he has to do and hesitates only one second before doing it. Ducking into a firing stance, he swings out of the alley and faces down the main street to the left. He steps out wide, leaving the false safety of the wall.

The dust is settling and through it he can see Sergeant Johnson – nearly thirty feet away, a distance Mike finds it hard to imagine anyone being thrown by an explosion and still surviving.

But BJ is already raising himself up on hands and knees, shaking dust from his helmet and goggles. Mike advances toward him, pistol held forward in both hands, scanning for targets. And he finds one – sooner than he's ready to deal with it.

Out of the nightmare opacity of the dust cloud, a man appears above and behind Johnson. He wears baggy black trousers and tunic, and a roughly tied black turban, and carries an AK. With this he fires a single shot into Johnson's back, knocking the big man back into the dirt, like a dog.

Mike feels his blood draining out of the bottom of his feet. His body goes cold. He freezes in his spot.

The gunman tries to fire again, into Johnson's inert body. But his weapon has jammed. He begins to pull on the bolt – then suddenly becomes aware of Mike. He freezes and looks up, locking eyes with the young American.

Drenched in horror, Mike suddenly remembers Johnson's body armor – remembers that he might be, probably is, still alive. Then he remembers what he needs to do. He raises his gun, sights in on the man's torso, and fires twice. While he is doing all this, the man is dropping into a crouch.

Mike's first round creases the man's shoulder; and the second misses high.

I was looking at my fucking sights, Mike thinks.

Before either can react further, a piercing scream, palpably female, erupts from their left. Both Mike and the man with the AK spin their heads to the side.

In an inset doorway to the left, a young woman in a burqa and headscarf is shrieking pitiably – her outstretched hand pointing in a line between the two men in the street. Both turn and look in the opposite direction. Against the far wall, a small girl, perhaps three years old, stands covering her ears and looking at the ground. When she hears her mother, she darts out through the middle of the gun battle, toward home.

As she runs by, the man in the tunic scoops her up with his free arm, and pulls her up and into him… taking cover behind her small body. With his other hand, he pushes and pulls on his rifle bolt, trying to clear the jam.

The air is nearly free of dust now, and the firing and ricochets have receded to whispers. Across the open air, Mike can see the other man's black eyes, locked onto his, the whites shining in the blanching air.

And as he looks into these eyes, and as a bent shell casing ejects from the breach of the man's rifle and a good round cycles into the chamber, and as Mike feels the weight of the pistol in his hand, suddenly it all becomes clear to him.

Looking into this man's eyes, into the face of the tiger, it is suddenly the most obvious thing in the world. There are no grievances. There is nothing there to negotiate with. There is only evil, and it must be opposed.

He brings the gun back up to level in a smooth motion. Calmly, eyes locked on his target over the sights, he feels the rhythm of his own movement, and that of the swaying figure – who raises his rifle up alongside the little girl. And Mike slaps at his trigger twice, at just the right time. The man's right eye socket turns to deep black and he tumbles over backward, the rifle in the dirt, the girl on his chest.

"Doubletap," Mike whispers to himself.

IN THE MEDINA
KOH-I DALMACH, BALUCHISTAN
05:16:32 PST 10 APR

The little girl starts wailing now, as Johnson pulls his massive frame to his feet, and Mike fast-walks toward him, gun held stiffly forward. The volume of fire around them redoubles. Worse, the effectiveness of that fire, the nearness of the misses, is increasing. All of this is happening at once.

Mike can see blood running freely from Johnson's nose. But he doesn't look groggy, and appears to clock the situation at once. He pulls his rifle from under a pile of dirt and debris with one hand, picks up the girl with the other, and waves Mike off.

"Get under cover," he shouts – and when Mike hesitates – "Fuck off!"

Mike retreats to the mouth of the alley, takes a knee, and starts putting out rounds. He sends covering fire in both directions down the street, shooting at everything and nothing. He changes magazines and shoots some more.

Then he begins to doubt his assessment of Johnson's mental state.

He sees the man curl his body, and his body armor, around the tiny girl, shielding her from fire. And he walks toward the doorway with the mother crying inside. But he exhibits no hurry in doing any of this, and seems oblivious to the heavy weight of fire coming in all around him. Mike clenches his teeth for the long seconds of this slow-motion rescue.

He sees Johnson's torso jerk as he hands the girl off inside. He doesn't appear to be hurt, but he must have been shot again. And he is still not coming back. Instead, he remonstrates with the mother, wagging a finger at her. Finally he pulls their door closed and walks calmly back to the alleyway.

As he reaches it, he staggers and pitches face forward, body half in the road and half in the alley. He groans and rolls onto his side. And Mike can see now. He has been shot through the upper right side of his chest. A round has punched through where the armor was worn down by the hits he took in the upstairs of the target house. Blood is flowing and painting the black Nomex a slick crimson. And Johnson is making scary wheezing noises with each intake of breath.

Mike holsters his weapon and grabs a tree-branch-sized forearm with both hands. And he starts pulling for all he's worth.

* * *

"Where?" Rheinhardt says.

"Unknown," Tim says. "They've dropped off the back. I'll go."

"Negative. Keep trying the radio."

Tim nods and touches his mic, "BJ, sitrep. BJ, send location. Wile E. Coyote. Mike, come in."

The three operators and the prisoner now crouch inside some kind of storage room, having crashed through the door to get off the street and out of the kill zone, and to try to locate their lost teammates. The edge of the sun has breached the horizon and sunlight now slants through the cracks of the ramshackle door.

They don't know that BJ is not responding because he is only half-conscious; and that Mike is not responding because he was shot in his radio, out in the street fight, though he never felt it.

Rheinhardt switches channels and says, "Bettie. Interrogative: have you got eyes on BJ or Wiley?"

"Negative. They were crossing an open field of fire when an RPG hit nearby. This was about a minute ago. Visibility is still extremely low."

"Roger. Interrogative: anyone down?"

"Unknown."

"Keep looking."

"Roger that. But, boss, I'm going to have to displace in about 120 seconds to make the extraction."

"Roger that. Do not miss the bus. Hey – where's Mac going?" Rheinhardt never knew the dog could open doors like that.

***

Mike never hears anything behind him. He simply sees Mac's jaws clamp onto BJ's other arm. It happens too fast to startle him. The dog is just there, and digging his paws into the dirt, as Mike does his boots. And the two of them drag the enormous, wounded man into the safety of the alley.

Somewhere along the line, Javier told Mike that they *never* leave their dead behind. And that, because of this rule, everyone learns sooner or later that a dead body is just about the heaviest thing in the world. Mike figures BJ is pretty damned heavy alive or dead. He prays it is the former.

Standing again – he fell on his ass at the conclusion of the Johnson drag – Mike clocks the dog's posture. Mac is baring his teeth, facing toward the dangerous end of the alley, head extended over Johnson's shallowly rising and falling chest. He doesn't take his eyes off the street. Totally vigilant.

Mike keeps his pistol trained toward the street as well – then realizes the gun must be nearly empty. He reaches for his last mag, then thinks better of it, holsters the pistol, and picks up Johnson's dropped SCAR. He drops and checks the mag, then pulls the charging rod, and brings it to his shoulder. Rounds are chipping the lip of the alley, further and further inside, at a less oblique angle. Probing.

Mike spares a quick look behind him. No one there. Then he remembers to press his mic control, cursing himself for getting to first things last. "This is Wile E. Coyote. Man down. BJ is down. We need some help here." When he releases the control, he doesn't hear the expected static squelch. He locates the radio pouch on his chest harness – but with no radio in it. He pulls the end of the severed wire out of the ripped fabric and regards it with dull amazement.

Mac barks once, ferociously, stirring Mike from his reverie. He sees two gunmen, just visible out in the dust of the road. They've been creeping out wide for a look down the alley – but are as startled by Mac's bark as Mike is.

Mike fires ten times, the recoil nearly knocking him over, as he's never fired the 7.62mm SCAR before. He drops to his belly and fires some more. When he stops and scans, the two men are gone. He has no idea whether he hit either.

He reaches across BJ's chest to rummage through his pouches, looking for a new mag. And a working radio.

IN THE MEDINA
KOH-I DALMACH, BALUCHISTAN
05:18:00 PST 10 APR

"Top," Ali says across the net, *"unless you're planning to try and drop me a rope ladder up here, I've got to motate. Now."*

"Do it. Go," Rheinhardt says. He turns to Tim and Javier. "Still nothing?"

Tim is shaking his head when Mike's voice breaks the open channel.

"Wile E. Coyote to team. Man down. Anyone there? Need some help. Man down."

"Interrogative: what's your location?"

"I don't know. An alley. Wherever you guys were three minutes ago."

"We're going," Rheinhardt says to the others. "Throw some smoke first." As the three of them slither out into the expanding white cloud outside, Rheinhardt says, "We should have brought Land Warrior units. I hate these scavenger hunts."

"Yeah," Javier says, "but you look like Buck Rogers with that helmet-mounted eyepiece and shit."

Rheinhardt doesn't bother telling him to shut up and move faster. He can see Javier is already doing both.

* * *

When the group is reunited, they find Johnson conscious again. Rheinhardt squats and pulls open a medical bag. Javier and Tim both take a knee at the corners of the alley, rifles raised. At Rheinhardt's instruction, Mike lies down and covers the back end of the alley. Mac sits at attention behind Javier.

Johnson is not only conscious, but also back on belligerent form.

"Where have you assholes been?" he says.

"I was cuttin' the rug," Rheinhardt answers flatly, pulling out and arranging drugs and surgical tools on a cloth. "Down at a place called The Jug."

Johnson grunts as Rheinhardt pulls his assault suit down from around his upper torso. "With a girl named Linda Lu?"

Javier briefly looks back over his shoulder. "When in walked a man? With a gun in his hand?" He turns back to the street, leans out, and triggers off a half-dozen rounds. He ducks again as withering return fire comes back in.

"And he was lookin' for you know who," Johnson says, finishing the quatrain. His voice is strong, but breathy.

"Listen," Rheinhardt says. "You've got fluid in your lungs. I've got to drain and stopper it."

"Just jam some goddamn Kerlix in there and let's get the hell out of here."

"That'll work for about a half hour, after which you'll drown."

"Fine. But I can put my own IV in. Fuck off."

While Johnson stabs and drips himself, squeezing on a bag of plasma, Rheinhardt runs a length of clear plastic tubing into his wound – straight into his lung. He plays with the pressure until a half liter of blood and mucus runs the length of the tube and spills out in the dirt. He then shoves super-absorbent gauze in and around the wound and tapes it in place, tight around the enormous upper body.

"Now we can get the hell out of here," he says. He punctuates this with a jab of full-spectrum antibiotics, straight into Johnson's sweaty and bulging bicep.

"Great," Johnson says. "I was wondering how long you were going to keep us in this alley with our faces hanging out."

Javier and Tim are still firing steadily – and effectively, as the pressure on their position lets up some – when Rheinhardt hauls Johnson to his feet.

"Hey," BJ says. "Where's that guy I patched up? Our exploding detainee."

"Don't worry," Rheinhardt says. "He's safe in a closet. Pick him up now."

Ali's voice comes in over the channel. *"Overwatch on station at secondary extraction point. You can bring it in."*

"God, she moves fast," Rheinhardt says. "Solid copy. Team is inbound. ETA eight minutes. We have an additional WIA, walking. Go!"

As the group makes good their escape, they all sing the chorus together. Even Mike knows this one. Up on the ridge, on her belly again, with her rifle emplaced on a rocky outcrop, Aaliyah is amused, but deeply unsurprised, to hear Lynard Skynard's "Gimme Three Steps" in exuberant five-part disharmony coming in over the radio, providing the soundtrack to what's turned into an ugly, dangerous, and bloody dawn in Baluchistan.

Somehow it seems the perfect closing song for this mission. They're all getting out alive – barely – and with a little luck would never be seen no more.

For sure.

U.S. DEPARTMENT OF HOMELAND SECURITY
ARLINGTON, VIRGINIA
18:00:02 EST 09 APR

Dharmesh is not in the CWOC, which is a circus at all hours of every day, but rather back at his desk. In this wing of the building, on a Saturday, he has the place to himself. He's doing some quick code clean-up.

Normally, he has neither the time nor the inclination to make his programs pretty. However, he figures the application he is writing now is going to end up in the hands of geeks in several agencies. And if they can't deconstruct what he has done, so they can rewrite it to better suit themselves, word will get around.

He takes a hand towel from the desk by one of his keyboards and pushes it across his forehead and scalp, letting it hang around his neck. He's still sweating from the frantic AfterWar incursion he and Mike have just pulled off. It doesn't occur to him how Mike would laugh to hear that *he* was sweating.

His desk phone rings. He eyes the handset, doesn't recognize the number, answers anyway. He has a gut feeling.

"Oh, good," says Jim Niewendyke. "You're in."

"Where are you calling from?"

"Hospital bed. Can't use my cell phone here. Update me."

"We're good. Extremely good. Mike's raid in Pakistan with the D-boys got exactly what we hoped for – a live, in-game session, at what we believe is their new center of operations in AfterWar."

"How about your software hack?"

"Supreme. We let them 'capture' two dozen of the Javelins. By the time we bugged out, the guns were being passed around like Creamsicles in August."

"Are they working?"

"They kick ass. I've already got data streaming in. Client and server stats. In-game video. Grid references of the players, in some cases. *I've even tapped into one guy's webcam.* I'm looking at his bedroom right now."

"Excellent. And Mike's okay?"

"As far as I know. There was a lot of shooting going on – real shooting. But Mike was still breathing when he rang off."

"And your software for monitoring the exploit?"

"Done. I'm commenting it now. Those NSA coders can be a little braindead. Hey – how are *you*, by the way? You sound better."

"I'm fine, thanks. Have you briefed Colonel Havering at Bragg?"

"No, not yet."

"Call him now. Nice work, Patel."

"Cheers, boss."

* * *

"Anything now?" Havering is pacing his TOC, headset seated, his sharp features creased and unsmiling.

"Hang on, Colonel." Lisa tilts her head, listening to a voice from the other side of the world. "Ops Room on the *Roosevelt* is reporting our team called for extraction at oh-five-oh-five local. They were under fire at the time, with one casualty – status unknown. And they were successfully extracted at oh-five-twenty-four."

"The whole team?"

"That's the report."

"Rick and his bird pull 'em out?"

"Yes. They're flying straight into Bagram, because of the wounded. It's a shorter flight time."

Havering nods and exhales in relief – then looks vexed again. "So why the hell doesn't Rheinhardt call? We don't pay to put those satellites up there because they're pretty in the night-time sky."

"Colonel, you sound like my mother. Wait – you've got an incoming call from DHS. It's Dharmesh Patel."

"Video?"

"Capable."

"Well, put it up there. Seems he's the only sumbitch who'll talk to us at the moment."

Dharmesh's face appears on one of the smaller screens on a wall of video displays. "Hi, Colonel. My boss asked me to call and brief you."

"Niewendyke. Your man okay?"

"He seems to be," Dharmesh answers. "He's okay enough to be up micromanaging me from his hospital bed. On the weekend."

"That's good, then. What have you got?"

Dharmesh fires a glance off at another screen, but catches himself, looks back and focuses. "As you know, our plan was to try and infect our opposition with our own virus, also built around a modified game weapon. One that would allow us to track them – and hopefully roll up all the cells in their network. Wherever in the world they are."

"Yeah. And?"

"It's working. We're in like Flynn. When your team took down their safe house, catching two of them live and in-game, that allowed us to hijack their characters, and Mike and I to fly to their in-game location. We then made sure the cache of modified weapons was 'captured.' As of this moment, eleven AQA players have picked up the missile launchers – and, with it, our virus code in the weapon mod. There may be more, actually, just not logged on right now."

Havering raises one eyebrow. "*AQA?*"

"Al Qaeda in AfterWar."

"Jesus. Okay, so what information can you get on these assholes?"

"Basically? Everything. The code we've slipped into the gun gives us full-spectrum surveillance. It sends us the IP address of their computers, which gets us, more or less, their physical locations. We get the address of the AfterWar server they're connected to, which might be helpful. Also, their AfterWar username and password, and their exact location, by grid coordinate, inside the game. If they've actually got the gun out and in use, we get real-time video of whatever they're seeing in AfterWar. And – you're going to love this – I can tap into a webcam if they've got one hooked up. I can look right in their faces, and get screenshots. Mugshots."

"No kidding."

"I've got one tapped now. Wanna see?" Dharmesh turns his videoconferencing camera toward one of his own monitors. On a crowded screen, in a tiny video window, a young man stares intently ahead. He is dark-skinned, unshaven, muss-haired, and his eyes dart from side to side.

"Well. Isn't that just about the greatest thing since sliced anything."

"Yes, sir. We own these guys. And it's reasonable to hope we'll get led to any we don't already own by the ones we do. It's mainly just a question of how much surveilling we want to do before we go in and take them. I've written some pretty easy-to-use software tools for watching live, and capturing all this intel."

Lisa touches Havering's elbow. "General Buster for you, sir."

"What chan—" But he catches himself, and looks instead over his shoulder, where the General himself is once again staring at him from behind glass. "Good lord. Does the man ever go home? Gotta run, Dharmesh. Great work." Dharmesh nods and disappears from the screen.

As Havering turns at the waist and pulls off his headset, Lisa stops him again – this time *grabbing* his elbow. She speaks intently. "We have a situation."

Havering shows an outstretched palm to General Dilbeck and leans over Lisa, where she is flipping through radio channels and speaking, and listening, with grim intensity. A video feed from the TF145 ready room at Bagram AFB flickers to life on the wall, showing a man in a cluttered and dingy room wearing a dusty flight suit. He is not wearing a happy expression.

"Oh, lord," Havering says quietly. "Tell me this isn't what I think it is."

ONBOARD "THE SHORT BUS"
3.5 MILES FROM THE AFGHANISTAN BORDER
05:42:26 PST 09 APR

Mike comes to after blacking out again – once again as a result of the radical deceleration of an aircraft. The helicopter has come to a stop now. But there is still movement everywhere.

The interior walls are buzzing and zinging. Blasted, shredded insulation fills the air of the dim cabin with white drifting material, like snowfall on a stormy night. Burning hot, slick liquids from burst hydraulic lines spray the interior, scalding exposed flesh.

As Mike's vision and hearing both dial back up, the first thing he becomes aware of is something heavy peppering the skin of the Chinook from the outside – a sound like a hundred smithy hammers on warping sheets of metal. The same hammers are slicing through the exposed bundles of live electrical wires that run along the walls, lancing the darkness with angry blue sparks.

A small object, moving too fast to track, zips through the right cabin window and explodes against the left interior wall. It strikes a high-altitude oxygen bottle, spraying shrapnel. A fire in the insulation starts to burn its way along the wall. Mike hears Johnson say, from his position strapped to a stretcher on the floor beside him, "Hey, man, you gotta put that fire out."

Mike nods, unable to speak. He crawls toward an extinguisher strapped to the wall behind the cockpit, through thick and acrid smoke. He somehow hears Johnson mumble behind him, "*Goddamned fucking helicopters.*"

* * *

When the CH-47 Chinook, the Short Bus, took off again from the ridge overlooking Koh-i Dalmach, with all hands aboard, and everyone still breathing, Mike had never felt such relief in his life. He allowed Javier to strap him into his harness; safetied Johnson's SCAR and laid it on the deck; and felt the ground go away with a total lack of sentimentality. As far as he was concerned, the Taleban and al Qaeda could have this rat hole, and he'd be happy never to lay eyes on it again. He'd be happy never to get shot at again in his life.

A few potshots from down in the town plinked into and around the helo as they loaded up. But, otherwise, the extraction went like a drill.

Delta operators spend an enormous amount of time in the air, much of it on long-haul flights – and so have an amazing ability to rack out in seconds. So, while Rheinhardt and one of the crew chiefs tended to Johnson, the others got flat on their backs with eye patches and earplugs. Which, flat on the deck, proved to be a fairly good place to be when the first RPG hit.

Those who were on their feet all went down together, in a single violent motion. The flight was well clear of the town by then, and climbing into the mountains, staying tight with the terrain. So the rocket-gunner was somebody out in the hills somewhere – somebody with the dumb good luck to have the fat, slow, ungainly Chinook fly nearly directly over his position.

Like Javier said – one lucky shot is all it takes to ruin your afternoon.

The rocket-propelled grenade punched through the aircraft's electrical pod a few feet below and behind the pilot, Rick – and only inches from the gas tank. An RPG-7 has a shaped charge with the penetrating power of an artillery shell. It went clear through the left minigun ammo can before exploding in the interior. The blast stunned the right-door minigunner and knocked the other crew chief to the deck.

Much more critically, it took out all three electrical generators – and thus all AC power. The miniguns spun down, rendering the flight nearly defenseless. In the cockpit, the LCD screens – the multi-function displays that supply the pilots with engine data – faded to black. Also out were the nav systems with GPS, the radios, and the automatic flight control system. Without these, only a few top pilots can even *taxi* a Chinook.

With no power to the flight controls, the helo was barely flyable. But it was flying. Rick started pulling power – no rotor droop, he noted, saying a silent prayer of thanks – then banked hard right and dove down, as an evasive maneuver.

When Mike realized something very, very bad was happening to them up there in the sky, he grabbed the metal rail his safety harness was clipped into and held on with both hands. Which was just as well, as the G-forces and motion of the bird for the next few seconds made any movement or positive action nearly impossible.

The terrain was overwhelmingly forested – but Rick spotted a small bare hilltop only a few hundred yards out. He angled toward it, staying close to the spur – trying to stay out of the line of fire of whoever had tagged them. He executed a swift "pop at the top", just before reaching the crest. At 90mph, he flared, leveled, and brought the bird straight down, like dropping onto the deck of a ship.

And that was when the first bullets crashed through the chin bubble. In the right seat, he watched as holes blossomed in the windshield glass. Two hit his helmet and whiplashed his head; another half-dozen hit him in the chest, one lodging in his Kevlar, the others flecking off.

With a cold shock that dwarfed that of being shot, Rick suddenly realized he'd brought the aircraft, his whole flight crew, and the entire insertion team, straight into the hornets' nest – right into the position of those who had fired the RPG in the first place. And, in addition to rockets, they had small arms and an emplaced DShK – a large-caliber Soviet anti-aircraft gun, which was specifically designed to blast helicopters out of the sky.

Pummeled, but lucid, now only twenty feet off the ground, Rick increased speed, trying to abort the landing. He was nosing the bird up when he heard the agonized shredding of the right engine's turbine blades. The left engine surged to pick up the load. He gripped the controls bloodlessly with both hands, praying for airspeed.

"Not gonna make it," he said to his co-pilot. "Gotta bring it down." He threw it into a flare, trying to bleed off inertia in the blades. "Oh shit, this is going to hurt," he said, this time to no one in particular. The 40,000-pound aircraft went into the dirt at 500 feet per minute.

With the sinking knowledge that this bird was done flying, probably forever, Rick reached up and shut down the engines. He looked over to his co-pilot – and saw he hadn't been so lucky in the initial enfilade. His chest was pulped by large-caliber rounds from the DShK - his chest cavity a real, visible cavity. His body armor might as well have been cling film.

Clenching his teeth, he unbuckled his seatbelt and turned to exit through the companionway, but immediately stumbled into fire and smoke – plus gunfire from multiple directions, cutting the airframe to cheese. Bullets were also shredding the cockpit's plastic and metal, glass and insulation. An electrical fire burst from the cockpit's right side panels. He could not stay there long and live.

Steeling himself for a few last puckering seconds, he pulled the handle for the rear ramp, saw that ICS was still up (it ran on DC power), and shouted into it, "Fire in the cabin! Go, go, go! You are ramp-clear down!" He then ripped off the headset, grabbed his right door handle, jettisoned the door, pulled his rifle from its mount, and rolled out – hitting the ground from a height of more than six feet.

No one else, that he could see, had yet made it out of the aircraft alive.

HILLTOP, CENTRAL BRAHUI FOOTHILLS
3.5 MILES FROM THE AFGHAN BORDER
05:42:26 PST 10 APR

"Contact, two o'clock! Engaging!" The right-side minigunner was one of the first back on his feet. With his minigun down, he has brought his M4 rifle up and propped it on the lip of the window. He now fires steadily.

As the Delta operators unhook their safety harnesses from the floor, they quickly realize they are targets in a large, unprotected shooting gallery. Bullets are coming through the cabin from at least three directions.

Mike, after putting out the fire, has pressed himself face-down on the deck. The helicopter's right-side self-sealing gas tank absorbs most of the rounds from that direction. Behind it, Mike feels marginally safe.

Swiveling his head, he sees the tied-up prisoner has taken cover beside him. He is swarthy, young, maybe Mike's age – handsome, with a wispy black beard, but some ugly abrasions around his temple. They are nose to nose. Mike nods. The man nods back, then tries to burrow his head into the steel deck.

Mike looks around when he feels something jabbing into his shoulder. It is Johnson's SCAR, and Javier is pressing it on him. "Shoot anyone who comes up that ramp and isn't us," he says. "And good luck." And just like that, with no further preparation or preamble, Javier, Rheinhardt, Tim, Aaliyah, and Mac slither down the back ramp into the deadly storm on the buzzing hilltop.

They are, Mike knows somehow, assaulting. Assaulting through the ambush.

Mike looks across at Johnson. Once they were in the air, he had allowed himself a quarter grain of morphine sulphate – not a hell of a lot of anesthetic for a huge man with a sucking chest wound – but he now seems fully awake again. He has unbuckled his own stretcher straps and holds a .45 in his good left hand.

The volume of fire outside doubles, then redoubles. The hillside roars, sounding as if it wants to *eat* the helicopter, before spitting it out. But the bird itself is taking fewer direct hits.

Looking at Johnson dully, Mike says, "Aren't you right-handed? Oh, I guess you can probably shoot with either hand."

Something explodes outside – a grenade. Then another.

"Yeah," Johnson says. "We all have to be pretty good at shooting left-handed. Sometimes, you're shooting around left-hand corners." He pauses and looks thoughtful. "About half the time, in fact."

The crew chief firing from the window yelps and jumps back. He's clutching and staring in disbelief at his smoking, burning glove. It takes Mike a second to understand he's been hit in the hand by a tracer – a round covered with burning phosphorous. Mike looks to the other side of the cabin, and realizes the other crew chief has never gotten up off the deck. He starts to crawl toward him, but Johnson shakes his head. "He's dead, man. Already checked."

The unceasing firing, and regular explosions, are sending Mike into a near-panic, and it occurs to him to fish out a radio to see what's going on. While he does this, Johnson slathers salve on the surviving crew chief's hand, slaps a pressure bandage on it, wraps it up, and sends him back to his firing position. Mike slips the earpiece on and tunes in.

"—inned down. Suppressing fire, east ridge line."

"Roger, I've got you."

"Fire ineffective on bunker. Flanking now."

"Wheel on flank. Wheel on me."

"Roger that."

"Bounding, covering fire."

"I have base of fire."

"Bounding."

"Bounding."

"Set."

"Set."

"Loading."

"Loading."

"Heavy SAFIRE still coming from east ridge. Frags up." This last is punctuated with another pair of whumping explosions.

All of this is criss-crossed and undercut and overlaid by the staccato percussion of ferocious small-arms fire. And, throughout, all of the voices – Rheinhardt's, Javier's, Tim's, Ali's – speak in the calmest tones, perfectly businesslike. They might be maneuvering a large sofa through a doorway.

"Get some 40 on that gun emplacement."

"Roger. Zeroed, firing for effect." A whump, another explosion.

"This fire lane is open. Advancing and rolling up. One tango down… two… five… clear."

And, just like that, it's over – or very nearly. There is still intermittent firing, short bursts, as if from a single light machine gun.

"Short Bus. You receiving? BJ or Wiley – come in." Mike startles, as if caught eavesdropping. It's Tim's voice.

"Wiley here."

"Can you bring me my ruck, please?"

"What – out there?"

"Yeah. Go down the ramp and come around the left side of the aircraft. You'll be under defilade. And you'll see me from there. I'll direct you in."

Mike rummages around until he finds Tim's big bag, then looks blankly at Johnson. "Um – I'll be back." He shoulders the ruck, hefts his rifle, and hightails it down the ramp.

Edging around the left side of the shredded helicopter, he hears the machine gun is still firing, but evidently not toward him. He sees Tim waving from a nearby treeline, beneath a large earthen berm. Mike puts his head down and runs at full speed. He crashes into the berm, turns around, and hands Tim the bag.

"Thanks," Tim says. "C'mon." The two crouch-walk toward the sound of the machine gun. A few yards along, Tim points toward the top of the berm. "Bit of a bunker system."

The two round a bend – and run straight into Ali, accompanied by Mac. She's holding an M4/M203, rather than her sniper rifle. The machine gun is firing from nearly over their heads. She says, "Can't get 40 mil up there. Bad angle. And the roof of the bunker's stopping grenades."

"I've got it," Tim says. Ali takes cover.

Tim pulls a satchel from his backpack – a satchel *charge*, Mike realizes – primes it, and gives it a mighty hurl over the top. He then covers Mike with his body.

The explosion shakes the entire hilltop.

And there is no more firing. Only silence.

Both in his earpiece, and from six inches away, Mike can hear Tim say, *"This hill is secure. RV at the crash site."*

Ali climbs up the berm with her rifle to her shoulder, Mac leaping up behind her. "Don't jump the gun, Tim." A few seconds after she disappears over the top, Mike hears single shots, at intervals of a few seconds. Finishing shots.

Now the hill is secure.

1ST SFOD-D TACTICAL OPERATIONS CENTER
NEAR FT. BRAGG, NORTH CAROLINA
18:33:54 EST 09 APR

"Oh, sure, *now* you pick up the phone." Colonel Havering has his hand flat on a console, hip jutting John Wayne style. He's talking to Rheinhardt in Central Asia again – and the whole TOC, plus a two-star general, are listening in. He affects a whiny voice. "Colonel, get me a CSAR bird. Colonel, send us some para-jumpers. Colonel, get me air."

"Yeah, that's pretty much it." Once again, Rheinhardt's voice is projecting out into the TOC like he's standing there with a megaphone – no static, no delay.

Havering softens now. "Okay. What's your status, Bo Peep?"

"We are down hard on the deck – and will not be taking off again. We've got one crew chief and the co-pilot KIA. We have, let's call it, two or three walking wounded. We have one litter casualty – who may be litter-urgent by nightfall. Oh, and we've got a package – a nice young fellow we met at the target house."

"What's the security situation?"

"Stabilized. Poor Rick picked us a good-looking emergency LZ – which must have also looked real defensible to a platoon-sized element of AQT. We've suppressed that. But I'm worried about who else might come by, with all the noise."

"Okay, Bo. We're going to get you out of there most ricky tick. I'm working to scramble some C Squadron boys and hopefully a CSAR team from Bagram to dart over the border and pick you up. We're also tasking a couple of nearby

UAVs, to get some eyes up there for you. ETA six minutes on the drones."

"Solid copy, thanks. Right now, we need to displace and find an appropriate LUP. We won't go too far if we can avoid it. And will keep you updated."

"Okay, son. You keep those transponders on. And good luck."

As Havering rings off, he turns and sees that General Dilbeck has stepped out of the room, behind glass, and is talking with his hand cupped over his phone.

* * *

Rheinhardt stows his satphone and walks back to the helicopter wreckage. He motions to Aaliyah, Javier, and Mac, out on perimeter security, to bring it in.

"Saddle up," he says, standing now on the bent back ramp. "We need to get down off this mountain, before we have to fight our way off it. The terrain's pretty rough and we'll need four to carry BJ."

"I'll tell you what," Johnson says, ripping out his IV and rising to his feet like a stone idol. "You fuck off, and I'll… no, actually, that's the whole deal. You fuck off."

"Jesus," Rheinhardt says, shaking his head. "Fine, but if you overdo it and die, we're leaving you for the dingoes. You're too goddamned heavy to drag around, and not worth the effort dead."

Rick, the pilot, steps forward, his upper body heavily taped and bandaged from the bludgeoning he took through his body armor. He leans in close to Rheinhardt's ear. "What about my guys, Eric? I can't leave Bill and Aaron."

Rheinhardt looks into the cabin at the two covered bodies lying parallel. "We'll get them home, Rick. But we can't strongpoint this position. And I don't have enough healthy shooters both to carry them, and to defend the patrol." The two men stare at each other from a few inches distant, both with unyielding expressions.

"We'll seal up the helo," Rheinhardt says. "We can even booby-trap the doors if you want. And as soon as the rescue force shows up, we'll pull 'em out." Rick still doesn't speak. "Look, we'll almost certainly have to extract from this hilltop anyway. We'll be back. Probably within the hour."

"Alright, Eric."

Rheinhardt turns back to the group. "Pack it up," he says. "Here's your combat load priority: water, ammo, radios, food. And more water. And more ammo. We go in ten. Now, who's got a map of this godforsaken mountain… Oh, yeah, I do," he says, walking off and thumbing through menus on his palmtop.

Mike retrieves his gear from the devastated cabin. Stepping outside again, he moves to stay close to Javier, who has produced and puts on a floppy boonie hat.

"Nice look," Mike says.

"Hey, at this altitude, the sun's a killer. Don't want to end up looking like Robert Redford… Well, okay, maybe you do want to end up looking like Robert Redford. But you get my point. Come on, let's move."

* * *

General Dilbeck has taken Havering all the way back to the Colonel's office, and closed the door.

"It's like this, Dick," he says. His expression is grave. "The Pakistani Air Force is up now, and headed to the area."

"Are they."

"They are. Your bird was underneath radar – until it started blowing up. Now they've registered it, somebody's woken up a couple of staff officers, and their birds are buzzing around the mountains hunting for it."

Havering doesn't change expression. He pauses before answering. "Well… tell them we're coming in for our people. Or shoot them down. I don't care which."

Dilbeck sighs. "It's like this, Dick. When Petraeus took over CENTCOM, he promised Zardari – he personally *promised* him – that there would be no more cross-border stuff without prior."

"Goddamnit, Buster."

"I know. I know." Dilbeck slumps in his chair. "Drones are fine. They expect to see those. But a full-blown CSAR extraction, with a couple of birds… it's going to cause a diplomatic incident. I can all but promise you somebody will wake up Hilary. There's even a risk of blue-on-blue. Look, all I'm saying is: your boys are only a couple of miles from the border."

"*In the fucking mountains*. Under fire."

"They're not under fire now. Only a couple of miles, Dick."

"Jesus, Buster."

"I know. I know."

CAVE SYSTEM, CENTRAL BRAHUI MOUNTAINS
3.5 MILES FROM THE AFGHAN BORDER
08:02:11 PST 10 APR

"Well, the good thing about a cave," Rheinhardt said, before making the decision to lay up in it, "is there's only one way in. And the bad thing is there's only one way out." In the end, he decided the boulder-strewn entrance provided good protection from rockets and mortars – the most lethal threats to a fixed position like this. And that the value of getting out of sight outweighed the danger of getting trapped inside.

He'd initially vectored the team off the mountain using real-time video from a Predator drone overhead, fed directly to his PDA screen. From this, he was able to identify an insurgent patrol heading their way, and steer away from it; as well as the major tributaries of the local trail system, to stay well off them. They found the cave complex after about an hour of tough scrambling.

Now that they have established themselves inside, they sit and wait for the rescue. Mike and Javier are on first watch, lying prone with their rifles just inside the cave mouth. Javier keeps one eye on the airborne video from the palmtop. The same feed is being watched by half a headquarters element across the border at Bagram.

The rest of the group has racked out, lying against bags, nursing and treating injuries, at the back of the cave. And Mac is on station just outside the lip of the cave, flattened to the cold stone, muzzle jutting out over his paws. He sniffs silently, ears pricked up, tirelessly scanning.

Watching this, Mike whispers to Javier, "Before, you said something about dogs helping humans to survive in prehistoric times."

Javier smiles. "Yeah, there are some interesting theories about man-dog co-evolution. Ten thousand years ago, dogs were just sort of a minor breed of wolf. But then they started nosing around human settlements. And the ones that were nice to us, that learned what we wanted them to do, and could remember it, we kept around – and fed. The others we kicked out, probably literally, to fend for themselves. So learning from man, taking instructions, is very likely an evolved trait for canines. The ones who could do it out-survived the ones who couldn't."

Mac suddenly looks back over his shoulder at Mike and Javier. Mike would swear the dog knows he is being talked about.

"God," Mike says. "That dog's practically human."

Javier says, "I think so. Socialization may actually be the key to personhood. If you took a human baby and put it in a closet for eighteen years, how much of a person would you have at the end? Probably not much. On the other hand, if you take a less intelligent animal like a dog, but put it in a very social situation – and a family dog is a *very* socialized creature – you get something awfully like one of us."

"A family dog, or a squadron dog. Did you have dogs growing up?"

"No," Javier says. "My family moved around too much."

"What, for work? Business travel?"

Javier pauses slightly. "Sort of. They were migrant farm workers."

Mike tries not to sound too shocked. "No kidding."

"They came over the border from Mexico. Yes, illegally."

"But you were born in the U.S.?"

"No. I was one year old, carried in a sling, when they crossed the Rio Grande."

Mike furrows his brow. "So you're not a U.S. citizen?"

"I absolutely am. I took my citizenship test, and oath of citizenship, at a forward operating base near Gardez, in 2002."

"Wait a second. You're saying you were fighting for the U.S., after 9/11 – off fighting in Afghanistan – *and you weren't even a citizen of the country*?"

"There are thousands of men and women in the military who are resident aliens, waiting and working for citizenship. But, in any case, believe me – I feel every bit as American as you do."

Mike pauses and gathers himself before answering carefully. "Hey, Javier. You're *a hell of a lot more* American than I am. You, and all those other immigrants in uniform. You've earned it. I just had it handed to me."

Javier doesn't answer, but just stares ahead in neutral silence.

"And anyway America has always been an immigrant country. It was built by people like you and like your parents – people who came looking for a better life. And who were willing to work hard for it." Mike shakes his head. "And now the country is being defended by those same kind of people. Man."

Javier nods. "I suppose so. Thanks for saying it."

Mike pauses, gulping dryly, before continuing. "Listen, there's something I need to tell you. Something I've got to confess. I was in ROTC in college. That's how I paid for undergrad. I had a six-year Army Reserve commitment afterward. But then 9/11 happened. And I figured I was going to be called up."

Javier looks across at him in the cool dimness.

"But I weaseled out. I went back to grad school, to avoid service. And when I got out of grad school I weaseled out again – I cut a deal to do computer security work at DHS. Instead of going into the Army."

Javier takes all this in thoughtfully before responding. "I'd say you did your bit. You've been serving. Homeland Security is important work." Javier sees now that Mike is struggling to maintain his composure.

"It's not so much what I *did*," he says. "It's what I was *thinking*." He pauses to keep his voice from catching. "I was thinking that guys like me, guys as smart as me just didn't go into the military. I thought that was for a totally different class of people… God, how completely full of shit I was. How full of myself."

Javier puts his hand on Mike's shoulder. "Hey, man. Hey." Mike looks up and Javier says to his face, "You're here now. You're here, and you're doing the job. At extreme risk of death or grievous bodily harm. So you can look *anyone* in the eye. Look, there are always more chances, and more choices. And it's always about what you choose to do *now*."

Mike looks away, nods, and wipes at the corners of his eyes. He raises his head again, looking out into the wilds of the mountain. "Back in England, you said I was going to see some things that would change my views. Well… I looked into a man's face this morning. And then I killed him. And I knew it had to be done. It was a bad situation to be in. But doing nothing would have been worse. The war simply has to be won, doesn't it?"

Javier takes this in thoughtfully. "Yes. But it's important to remember that it's also an ideological war, a war of ideas – their very bad ones versus our better ones, we hope. For instance, we didn't win in Iraq when we pummeled al Qaeda. Sure, that helped. But the real victory came when the Iraqi people got sick of being brutalized by al Qaeda – and rejected their whole crappy, murderous ideology. And we need to make sure that we have something better to offer, that we have higher ideals. And that we live up to them."

"I hope winning the war of ideas puts an end to the war of blowing things up."

"*In'shallah.*"

"Don't you mean *Ojalá?*"

"It's all the same. And speaking of which – another thing you have to keep a close eye on in this job is your humanity. Particularly when you start having to take lives, as you did today. It gets really hard to remember that the guys on the other side are people, just like we are. They're people with really bad ideas in their heads, and who are dangerous, and who have to be stopped. But they also get up in the morning and put their socks on and love their mothers and weep at the beauty of a sunset. And if you forget that, if you lose the ability to regard your enemy's essential humanity, then you risk losing something very important.

"C'mon. It's somebody else's turn to get piles sitting on these cold rocks."

* * *

In the back of the cave, after Tim and Ali have gone forward to take watch, Javier notes an extremely unamused expression on Rheinhardt's face. He says, "Uh… what's the good word, top?" Not sounding very hopeful, he adds, "PJs inbound?"

Rheinhardt looks up from a color map display on his PDA. "I have been informed that the Chairman and the Joint Chiefs of Staff," he says, with gravel in his voice, "would appreciate it very much if we could manage to get over the border under our own power. On foot."

"Those fucking ass-clowns," Johnson adds, flat on his back on his folding stretcher, eyes locked on the blackness at the top of the cave.

CAVE SYSTEM, CENTRAL BRAHUI MOUNTAINS
3.5 MILES FROM THE AFGHAN BORDER
08:42:11 PST 10 APR

"Well," Javier says, reviewing the map and satellite imagery himself, "the border is less than four miles out. That's something."

"So's your mother," Johnson says. "Naked, down on all fours." Javier gives him a pained look.

"It's not the mileage," Rheinhardt says. "It's the terrain. We can't risk moving during the day for risk of being spotted. And we're a little too dinged up to tackle terrain this murderous at night."

Javier switches to a topographical view on the PDA, then checks the almanac. "We've got about ten good hours of darkness tonight. We could pick the least dicey path from the maps. Use the NVDs. And take it slowly."

"Well… it's a thought," Rheinhardt says.

"So's 'I've got to take a shit'," Johnson says. He extracts a plastic baggy from his pack and clambers heavily toward the back of the cave.

"You know something," Javier says, after him. "You turn into a real dickhead when you get shot."

After Johnson is out of earshot, Rheinhardt says, "It's hard on him. Being out of action."

"He just doesn't like having to think of himself as stoppable." Javier stares down at the map again. But he's not really looking at it. "Hey, top. The problem is with U.S. personnel, and U.S. aircraft, crossing the border. Right?"

"Yeah."

"Okay. How about indig personnel? And mules?"

Rheinhardt's eyes go wide and he nearly smiles. "Hajji Nasir. Is he still operating from out of Quetta?"

"Yes. And still crossing the border in both directions, with total impunity, last I heard."

"Ha! Pure genius." Rheinhardt begins jabbing at his phone.

Johnson returns, stepping carefully. He looks paler now. "Man," he says, "I hate wiping with leaves. Damn dingleberries…"

"Maybe," Javier says, "you should try waxing that hairy ass of yours."

"You like my ass the way it is. Or you wouldn't be checking it out all the time."

* * *

Mike has returned to the front of the cave to ask Tim what he usually does about spare laptop batteries. But, incongruously, he finds him sitting with a spiral-bound sketch pad and a stick of charcoal – sketching a section of cave mouth, some lichen, and a slender, flowering tree in the background. The likeness is excellent, and the composition seems to Mike to have real feeling.

"There's a surprise," Mike says. "I was going to ask about laptops."

"Some technologies stand the test of time," Tim says, not taking his eye from the notepad, brushing the edge of the charcoal lightly across the rough paper.

"Have you done this long? And do you always take art supplies out on missions?"

Aaliyah is smiling at this conversation, but doesn't speak; nor does she take her eye from the approaches to the cave.

"Well…" Tim says, meeting Mike's gaze briefly. "To be alive, I think, is to destroy. So it seems to me that it's a good idea to do some creating, as well."

"Particularly in your job," Mike says, probably stating the obvious. "Was that sketch pad in your rucksack when I brought it out to you in that firefight?"

Tim smiles, lines creasing the corners of his eyes and mouth. "Yes."

* * *

"This is Little Bo Peep. I'm sorry I'm not available to take your call right now. Please leave your name, number, and a brief message—"

"Okay," Havering says, speaking loudly to the entire TOC. "Who's the sonofabitching smart-ass who put voicemail on the goddamned satphones?" All of the heads around the room remain deeply immersed in their screens and notebooks. Havering makes a guttural noise. "Huh. And why the hell doesn't Rheinhardt tell me what the hell's going on up there?"

* * *

The team is packing up again, and the sun has just disappeared behind the mountains, when a half-dozen robed men and a half-dozen pack animals appear, ascending the ragged slope. Javier and Rheinhardt slip out to greet them.

As Mike warily steps out into the dusk of the open air, he sees both Javier and Rheinhardt exchanging warm embraces with a number of men in what looks like tribal garb, all carrying weapons.

"*Ssalumu 'lekum!*"

"*Wa'leikum salaam!*"

"*Labas?*"

"*Labas, barak. Ssehha labas? L'a'ila labas?*"

"*Labas, labas.*"

Rheinhardt clasps and holds the hand of the apparent leader. Solemnly, he says, "*'lla yrhem waldik, Hajji.*"

"You are welcome, friends," the other says in clear English. "You are most welcome."

* * *

Mike returns to the back of the cave to grab his gear. Ali is there suiting up. The three surviving members of the helo crew, all hurt, are helping each other up. And the prisoner is sitting propped up against the cave wall, where he's been left, watching with a wide-eyed but neutral expression. While Mike is strapping on his combat harness, he sees Javier return.

"Was that Arabic you were speaking?"

"Yes."

Mike frowns slightly. "I thought Afghans spoke Pashto and Farsi?"

"That's true," Javier says. "But these guys are Hazara, and speak a dialect of Farsi that's a little hard to get a handle on. And virtually all Muslims share some basic greetings and blessings in Arabic."

Mike frowns a bit more. "So these guys are Muslim?"

"Yeah, Shia Muslim," Javier says, looking up now. "Why?"

Mike turns partially away. "I don't know," he says quietly. "What was it you told me earlier about not trusting the locals?"

"That was not trusting the Pakistani security forces. But, for starters, these guys are Afghani. As I said, Hazara. Their tribes have been kicked around Afghanistan since the eighteenth century – by Pashtuns, by the Emirs, and finally by the Taleban. They've had their villages looted, their lands confiscated, their people sold into slavery. They were one of the founding tribes of the Northern Alliance after Kabul fell to the Taleban in '96. Which is the other thing – these guys fought with us, against the Taleban and al Qaeda in the invasion in 2001."

"*Literally* with us," says Johnson from the floor. He's staying on his stretcher, now that he knows he's getting a mule ride to the border. "With me. I met Hajji Nasir on my first hour in the Hindu Kush. I've shared a trench with him in a mortar barrage. I've danced with his daughters." Johnson snorts. "You don't like the Haj, you can go out into the mountains and play hide and go fuck yourself."

"Okay, okay," Mike says. "I'm sorry. It's just…I don't know, it's confusing – fighting Islamic guys to the death in the morning and hugging them in the evening. I don't know."

"You're having an atomic dumb-ass attack," Ali says, standing up with her sniper rifle slung in a padded bag on her back. "Who do you think we're fighting and dying to help in Iraq? Thirty million Muslims. In Afghanistan? Twenty-five million Muslims. The Kosovo intervention? Somalia?"

Mike shrinks down in the bottom of his hole, but he keeps digging anyway. "But you said yourself that Islam was incompatible with modernity…"

Ali shrugs. "That's just ideology. These are people. Real people. Don't fall into the brain-dead trap of judging individuals by their group membership."

Mike takes a breath and nods. "You're right. I'm being stupid – just in the opposite direction. Before I was thinking everyone had to be reasonable like we are… now here I am thinking everyone Islamic is crazy like the jihadis."

"He's had a rough day," Javier says. "Shot in the back, his first helicopter crash… first time having to kill someone."

Ali softens. "I know. It is hard – to find that middle ground, regarding other groups of people, and to stay on it. Of course things like racism don't come from no place. It's easy to be anti-racism – until a bunch of guys from one particular race burn down your village and kill your family. That's where it takes a little more backbone – to transcend your killer ape impulses. And listen to your reason instead. But the thing is, most people, of all races and tribes, are cool. Most Muslims are cool. So be cool." She walks out of the cave and into the last light.

Mike follows behind, mumbling, "Why do I spend all my time with you guys feeling completely humbled…?"

Walking alongside, Javier says, "Yeah, I know how you feel. *Domine, non sum dignus…*"

1ST SFOD-D COMPOUND
NEAR FORT BRAGG, NORTH CAROLINA
19:41:51 EST 12 APR

"It took us the whole night to hump over the mountains to the border. At a couple of points, I didn't think I was going to go the distance. But when we finally made it, there were four new Delta guys, plus an entire squad of Rangers, a couple of Air Force special forces medics, and two Black Hawks with aircrews. All sitting there waiting for us – six inches from their side of the border."

"Nice," Dharmesh says.

"Yeah, it was. Really nice. So was the flight home. It was the same Gulfstream jet. But somehow the upholstery, the food, the AC… they were all about a hundred times sweeter on the *back* side of the mission. *After* all the shooting, and mayhem, and crashes. And the fear of failing."

Mike is lying on his single bed, in his tiny room, hair shower-slick again – talking to Dharmesh on his quad-band phone. Back at the Ranch.

"Well, you did great, man," Dharmesh says. "We've got eyes on a whole bunch of these cyber-dickweeds. And I've got even better news."

"Yeah?"

"Your detainee. The guy you grabbed. I think he's our guy. One of them, at any rate. I can't be totally sure. He's not really talking. But he knows his shit. That much I can tell. He's not muscle – he's brains. I'm pretty sure he's one of the authors of the hacks we saw."

"You've questioned him?"

"Yeah. He's undergone interrogation by guys with at least a half-dozen three-letter acronyms on their IDs. And that's after the military intel people. But, as you'll recall, one of the first things the President did after taking office was sign an executive order explicitly outlawing any interrogation technique that might make anybody slightly uncomfortable."

"I remember. And that's probably a good thing. But, if this guy's not talking, how do you know he's our guy?"

"He's not *talking* talking. But he's dropping hints. Basically, he's bragging. You know how hackers are. They can't keep their big brains to themselves."

"That's usually why they get caught."

"Yep. He's also made some ominous claims about attacks to come. But I figure we're so deep into their network, the one in AfterWar, that whatever they've got lined up we'll see coming – and be able to head off."

"Most excellent."

"Yep. And it's all down to you. Mike the cyber commando."

There's a knock at Mike's door. He reaches over and opens it – it's Javier, also with wet hair again.

"Gotta jam," Mike says.

"Word. Talk soon." Dharmesh rings off.

* * *

Mike and Javier sit on their old bench, outside the Shooting House – drinking bottled beer now, which Javier has retrieved from a lesser-known fridge, at the back of the F Squadron Ready Room. The muted sound of gunfire, from the bullet- and explosion-proof but only partially soundproof rooms, pulses behind them.

"So, listen," Javier says. "This might sound crazy to you. But I think we need to do some more training."

Mike laughs sardonically. "Man. We've only been on the ground two hours. Do you guys ever take a break?"

"Yeah. I took a break one time. In 2005, I think. But Rheinhardt saw me and gave me a swift kick to the jimmy and I got back to work."

Mike laughs. "Okay. What do you want to teach me now?"

"Nope. Other way around this time. I want you to put together some training for the team."

"On what?"

"First-person shooters – specifically, AfterWar." He lets that float for a second. "Small-unit tactics. Infantry skills. Fire and movement. Use of the weapons. And hacks – how can we get an unfair advantage in the game."

"Are you serious?"

"Completely. Look, as so often happens, on this one we were absolutely, perfectly prepared for one year ago. We pulled it out of the fire in the end. And we did it by a clever combination of direct action – that is, taking down physical locations and shooting people; and information warfare, that is you hacking the game and infecting our opponents online. But I've been thinking about what Dharmesh said at that last briefing before the lights went out. He said that with a distributed, open-source, uncontrolled virtual world… there may be no way to go after bad guys there other than operating *inside the membrane*. Within the rules of the system itself."

"You think we may have to do more fighting inside the game."

"Maybe, maybe not. But if we do, and we fight like we did trying to take that gun store…we're in big trouble."

Mike pauses, thinking this through. "Do you really think it's likely to come up again?"

Javier pauses in turn. "Okay, look. After Saddam Hussein invaded Kuwait, he captured the U.S. Embassy in Kuwait City – including everyone working in it at the time. We thought we were going to have to go in and take it down. So B Squadron flew to Eglin AFB in Florida. And they built an entire, perfect, full-scale mockup of the embassy building, from the architectural schematics. And then they practiced assaulting it, over and over and over. Until they had it absolutely nailed.

"In the end, Saddam got wisdom and released the hostages. So we never did the assault. We never even went there."

Mike sips his beer. "But you were completely prepared to do it."

"Exactly. And *our* squadron was formed precisely to fight in new electronic battlespaces. It's past time we got really prepared to fight in them."

"Okay," Mike says. "I'll put together a training plan. I'll start right away."

Javier smiles and clinks bottles with him. "You can finish your beer first."

1ST SFOD-D COMPOUND
NEAR FORT BRAGG, NORTH CAROLINA
22:01:30 EST 12 APR

A knock sounds on the outside of Tim McDonough's door.

"Come," Tim says. "It's open."

The door swings in, revealing Mike standing beyond it. He's wearing a new set of creased ACUs, tan with chocolate-chip camouflage. This is technically because he didn't bring a lot of clothing with him from D.C. – and a lot of what he did bring has been destroyed, or dirtied beyond reclamation, in combat. But there seems to Tim more to it than a change of clothes.

Mike's uniform proclaims his allegiance.

Tim smiles and waves him in. "Sit."

Mike takes one of the two chairs. "I was worried it was a little late to be dropping by. What are you doing?" On Tim's bed are arrayed a variety of thick notebook binders, a laptop, one of the HDS sights Johnson showed Mike, and a strange headset thingy.

"Cramming," he says. "I'm being sent out on a training gig."

"Where to?"

"Southern California. ICT, the Institute for Creative Technologies, at UCLA. They're partnered with our video game guys at TRADOC, the Army Training and Doctrine Command. They've built something called the Immersive Infantry Trainer – IIT. It's sort of a series of very large, rear-projection screens that get mixed up with real terrain, and project interactive combat situations. Very good for training on the kind of shoot-no-shoot situations that crop up in urban combat and counter-insurgency."

"So – more video game warfare?"

"Exactly. But the trick is the video game has to keep up with the warfare. So I'm going out to do some training on our new version of Land Warrior. Training the trainers – plus their developers."

"What's Land Warrior? I heard it mentioned before."

"A relatively new battlespace information system. Basically everyone down to squad leaders gets one of these—" and he holds up the headset, which Mike can see has some kind of miniature eyepiece attached – "which provides real-time mapping of an operational area. Every friendly has an FOFI chip – friend or foe identification – with GPS, so every friendly appears on the map, location updated in real time. Enemy locations can be plotted as they're identified. Saves a lot of headaches, not to mention friendly fire, when everyone on the board knows where all the pieces are. It started rolling out to infantry units in Iraq last year."

"Have you done a lot of this kind of training?"

"None, actually. But, unfortunately for me, our gun-smiths and techs here have done some clever hacking of the system. This custom holographic diffraction sight displays both target ranging and GPS coords in heads-up view. And with Bluetooth the HDS now talks to Land Warrior – and Land Warrior can send the data straight to the command net. So, basically, anything being shot at by any friendly node on the net can automatically be added to the map as a possible enemy node. Everything's getting integrated, in alignment with our doctrine of network-centric warfare. And all the new functionality needs to get built into the video trainer."

"Very cool. Why doesn't Delta use Land Warrior?"

"We do, sometimes. But with anything smaller than a platoon-sized element, for instance the five or six of us that went out last time, we try to keep everyone at elbow's distance anyway. So we already know where we are. Sometimes, at a certain level of operation, more tech is just a bigger encumbrance."

Mike nods. "When do you leave?"

"Two days."

"For how long?"

"Depends. If the powers that be can arrange it, I may go on from there to Camp Pendleton. The Marines, 1st MEF, have a Battle Simulation Center there, where they've implemented IIT. Why do you ask?"

"Javier has tasked me with putting together some AfterWar training. The idea is that the team needs to get a lot better, and a lot smarter, faster, on fighting in AfterWar."

"Seriously?"

"Yeah. Seriously."

"Okay. I guess that makes sense. We had to fight our way into that gun shop, before we could get to Pakistan. And once we fought our way into the target house in Pakistan, we had to conduct an air assault in AfterWar. Or, rather, you did."

"Exactly. I think you said something on that flight to London about needing more IT to figure out where to go to do the shooting, and then to make sense of what you find when you get there. But, then again, AfterWar may be the battlefield, going forward. Hence, this training. I hope we can do it while you're around."

"I hope so, too. By the way, you can just schedule me, as well as the rest of the team, on the group calendar on the

Intranet. In fact, you'll have to. The request will get routed for approval to Rheinhardt and Havering."

"I know. Javier showed me. But I wanted to drop by and give you a heads-up in person. And get your reaction."

"I appreciate that."

"No probs. I guess I'll let you get back to cramming."

But as Mike turns toward the door, he sees a stack of canvases propped up against the wall. The one in front is a landscape painting done in dark, warm oils. "May I?" he asks. Tim gestures broadly.

Mike flips through the dozen or so paintings – mostly landscapes and structural studies, one still life. At the very back, though, is a striking portrait of a young and beautiful woman. Great care and effort has obviously gone into its execution. Mike holds it up to the light.

"Who is this?"

Tim's expression stays neutral. "Cath. Cathy."

"Girlfriend?"

"Sometimes."

Mike looks at him sympathetically. "Sort of an on-again-off-again thing?"

"That captures it fairly well," Tim says.

"Does she live here?"

"Yes. She works in town. She manages a bar and restaurant there."

Mike looks slightly wry. "Why don't you two get married? Seems to work for Uncle BJ."

Tim pauses and looks thoughtful. "I'd like to," he says at last. "But it's difficult. I can't tell her what I really do for a living. She only knows that it's dangerous. And that makes her scared." He lowers his head. "I can hardly blame her."

"I hope it works out for you," Mike says, replacing the canvas.

"Thanks. I hope so, too."

* * *

"It's open."

Mike hesitates behind this door for a moment, because he hears multiple voices inside – not just Aaliyah's. Finally he turns the handle, cracks the door, and sticks his head in.

"Hey, Mike." Ali is sitting up at her desk, back lean and straight, in front of a laptop. It is actually the laptop that is doing the talking – in a strange language.

"Catch you at a bad time?"

"Not at all. Just doing some work on my Urdu. I'm a little behind, I'm afraid." She presses a key to pause the program.

Mike steps in and looks at her screen – there are four pictures of old and young men and women skipping rope, talking on a phone, milking a goat, etc.

"Next best thing to an immersion course," Ali says. "Teaches you the same way a two-year-old learns language. No grammar rules. Just scenes and situations – as you go, the subjects, verbs, and objects change around, and it all builds up. Anyway. What brings you by?"

"I wanted to talk to you about some training I'm putting on myself. Actually, maybe I can adapt the technique – try and teach you the way a fourteen-year-old learns video games…"

"Uh oh… is this going to be what I think it is?"

* * *

Rheinhardt actually comes to the door himself. He's wearing narrow, rectangular reading glasses, which throws Mike slightly. When Mike enters, he can see that the bed sheets are slightly rumpled (unmade beds are unheard of in the military). A steepled copy of *Thermopylae – The Battle that Changed the World* sits on the bed table, beneath an angled reading lamp.

"What's up, Mike," Rheinhardt says, offering him a seat.

* * *

Morning, very beginning of visiting hours at the Army Medical Center at Fort Bragg, and the spring sunlight streams into the private room. Master Sergeant Johnson only the day before underwent some relatively straightforward but delicate surgery, to close up his lung and repair tissue damage. Mike didn't imagine he'd find the man sitting upright, much less receiving guests, the day after being operated on. But that was the word on the street. And here he sits.

"Hey. Wile E. Coyote." Johnson's voice is husky – but he seems genuinely pleased to see him. In one hand he's working a springy hand-grip exerciser and in the other holding a dog-eared copy of *The Portable Nietzsche*. He puts the former down and takes a big pull of water from a bedside bottle. Mike eyes the book.

"Javier turned me on to it," Johnson says, somewhat evasively. "I'm worried I may like it a little too much. Hey," he says, putting the book aside. "I'm sorry I was kind of a dick at the end of that mission. Getting shot always gives me a sour disposition. But I'll be out of here tomorrow, and we can get back to fun stuff. Hey – are you gonna hang around, or what?"

"Yeah," Mike says, looking up brightly. "For a week or two, anyway. Will you be on duty?"

"Light duty. They won't promote me to fully operational for a couple of weeks, however much I bitch about it."

"Well, then – I've got just the training op for you. We're going to be doing some work on our AfterWar capability. War in a chair."

"Kick ass," Uncle BJ says. "I love that game."

Mike smiles. "Great. I'll definitely keep you in the loop. Meantime, I'll let you get back to recuperating."

"Too late for that," BJ mumbles, looking around Mike toward the door.

Before Mike can even swivel, he is overrun and swarmed by a fast-moving two-person assault force – a blond little boy, and a lanky, somewhat less small girl with long sandy hair. They rush their father – stopping just short of jumping up on him on the bed. Johnson wraps the excited pair of tiny bodies in his enormous arms, mussing hair and kissing foreheads.

Last in the door is an attractive woman in her thirties, wearing jeans, running shoes, and a grey ARMY sweatshirt. She's smiling not-quite-tolerantly at the children's assault of their father's prone position.

But her smile quickly warms and she puts out her hand. "You must be Mike Brown," she says. "I'm Kim Johnson."

"Hi," Mike says, slightly off balance, but also instantly liking this warm and confident woman. He pauses, tilts his head and considers. "I guess I should tell you that your husband saved my life." He pauses further and his eyes dart to the floor. "I should also tell you that's about when he got shot."

Kim continues to hold his hand in hers, and also grasps his elbow. "Mike, my husband saves people's lives on most days. And I'm afraid he gets shot with some regularity. Luckily, it doesn't seem to affect him like it does other people."

Mike bursts out laughing despite himself. He turns to be introduced to Nathan and Marissa.

* * *

Mike finally runs down Javier again in the weight room. He's sitting upright, doing quad extensions on the leg machine. Mike lopes up and says, "I thought you said you don't get much gym time?"

"I get in here when I can. And that hump we did over the mountains was a wake-up call about leg strength. Man, I was aching. I should be wise to that by now, with the amount of time we spend up in various mountain ranges these days."

"Then I guess your Selection process, with that 45-mile mountain hike, is just the right kind of test."

"Yeah – but by accident. They came up with it mainly to be sadistic. I don't think that in 1977 anyone predicted the Soviets would be out of Afghanistan and we'd be in. So – how'd it go? You manage to track everyone down?"

"Yep. They're all onboard."

"Excellent. It's your project, so it's best that you sell it to them." Javier finishes his set and lets his straining legs relax.

"And I've now sold it to the Colonel. He's going to authorize the training time."

Mike puts an arm on the weight machine and considers. "You know," he says, "when I asked if you ever took a break, I was joking. But you never really do."

"Eh. We're busy. But there are a few days off here and there."

"It's not so much that you're working all the time. It's that you're *working on yourselves* all the time."

Javier shrugs, beneath a well-worn cloak of modesty.

Mike ploughs on. "There's the learning – the technology, the languages, the reading. And the combat training, the physical conditioning. And it occurred to me there's something beautiful all these things have in common: being in shape, being multilingual, being technical, being well-read…you can't *buy* any of them, no matter how much money you have. All you can do is put in the time. You just have to do the work."

Mike lets it rest there. But he is thinking, and has been thinking, that these D-boys he has met are a lot more than the insanely well-trained infiltrating and killing machines he'd expected. They are also *mensches*. They are *Übermenschen* – enormously high-quality human beings in more ways than he can keep track of.

Javier gets up and towels off the seat. "Yeah, I suppose it comes down to what you put into it. Like I said, everything we do here is all about the people. And Delta does mean change." He and Mike lock eyes.

"*Become more than you were*," Mike says.

"I'll see if I can get that put on the Unit crest."

D-BOY TRAINING CAMP
FAR S.E. PROVINCE, AFTERWAR
12:00:00 AUT 15 APR 2018

"We are locked, cocked, and ready to rock."

"Roger that. I have control. One… two… *three*."

"Bounding. Contact three o'clock. I'm hit."

"Me, too. I'm down - laying suppressing fire."

"Shit, I'm out. Spawning."

"Everyone left standing – rally point A. Rally on me."

"Bounding. Loading."

"Bounding."

"Shooters on the roof. I am taking effective fire."

"Okay, displace. Try falling back to FAPs."

"Ah, shit – more OPFOR coming over the hill."

"Okay, let's try to strongpoint here. Inflect on me."

"Shit – I'm out."

"Me, too."

"Well, that pretty much sucked an entire bag of dicks." UncleBJ, the only surviving member of Blue Team, limps over

```
to the base of the five-story wood-frame
tower where WileyC perches with his bin-
oculars. "Who the hell are these guys,
anyway?"
```

"Didn't I tell you?" Mike says, pulling his headset off. "Hang on a sec." He leans over his keyboard to type a broadcast message to Red Team – the designated opposition force, or OPFOR, in this training scenario – to reset their positions and wait. Mike spins back around in his chair to face Johnson, and the rest of the team.

"They're good old all-American video gamers – ones who've been playing AfterWar regularly for at least three years. And other shooters for longer."

"And how, actually," Rheinhardt asks, eyebrow raised, "did you find and recruit these guys?"

"They were all players we found to be infected with that AQA zombie virus."

"Are you serious?"

"Don't worry. We had the Bureau do background checks on them. Once we had a pool of promising candidates, we threatened some of them with prosecution for being accessories to electronic crime. But for most, all we really had to do was explain that they'd inadvertently helped al Qaeda hack a government/military system – and ask for their help in getting our own back. What sixteen-year-old gamer kid wouldn't want the chance to fight for his country – to play AfterWar for real stakes?"

Johnson grunts. "You're joking. You're telling me here we are, the most elite military unit in the history of the world – and we're training against high school kids?"

"Ahem." Mike half hides his mouth with his hand. "Some of them are in junior high, actually. But, anyway, it won't have passed your notice that they just handed you your asses in there. How many kills did you get on them, BJ?"

Johnson looks away.

"Anybody else? Anybody get any confirmed kills?" No one says anything. "Okay, then. It might be time we started considering American video game culture to be a strategic resource."

"You're late to the party," says Javier. "They're already putting Playstation controllers on the bomb disposal robots in Iraq – for the 18- and 19-year-old enlisted guys who already have centuries of aggregate experience using them."

The door to the new computer lab – where Mike has had installed a dozen high-end gaming machines, with dual graphics cards and large-screen LCDs – opens, and Lisa pops in.

"Excuse me, Dr. Brown," she says. "I've got your purchase req here. You said it was priority highest, so I've walked it down for your sign-off."

"Take fifteen," he says to the team. "Replay your video from that last round. When I get back, see if you can tell me why OPFOR knew to hit you from the flank, from over that hill – and why you didn't see them coming."

Mike steps out into the hall with Lisa and takes the sheaf of papers. He begins reading the line items aloud.

"One dozen SCAR rifles… two million rounds 7.62mm ammunition…sixteen crates grenades in various flavors… half a dozen multi-grenade launchers… two depleted uranium rail guns, with a thousand slugs… one tactical nuclear mortar, a hundred low-yield shells… the upgraded, powered body armor… fencing, construction materials, contractors…

the robot air-defense batteries… two all-terrain trucks… two Osprey VTLs… and the turboprop transport plane. Looks great. I think that's everything for now."

"Excellent," she says.

"I really appreciate you expediting this," Mike says.

"It's not a problem. Most of this stuff is basically free. The only thing I even needed approval on was the jet. Though, I should warn you – we're buying so many Warbucks on the open market that we're driving up the exchange rate. But it will have to go up an awful lot before any of this is a significant line item in our budget."

"Nice," Mike says. "It looks like not all of our advantages transfer to the virtual world – but the economic ones do. We can buy all the best stuff for our guys. And keep blowing theirs up. When do you think we'll see these?"

"The weapons and ordnance right away. But the trucks and aircraft are going to need a little procuring. There are only so many in the game, so we have to find someone willing to sell. Hopefully in a day or two. I'll keep you updated."

"Thanks, Lisa."

"No problem," she says, turning to leave. "And have a good 'un."

Mike steps back into the lab. "Alright, let's look like we're doing this on purpose. Everybody respawn? Good. Now run it again…"

* * *

"How you doing on that command console?" Dharmesh asks. He is sitting at his desk, in Arlington, talking to Mike, who is sitting at his desk at the Ranch – he's recently gotten issued one, as he could no longer work out of his miniature bedroom. They are talking about the hacking and rewriting of the AfterWar client that they have planned, and the development on which they are now supposed to be tag-teaming.

"I'm a little behind," Mike admits. "I've pretty much got it all designed, and I've written a few of the major classes."

"Hey, it was you who kept going on about how important this shit is. *I'm* on schedule." The hacks they have come up with are designed to give the D-boys enormous and deeply unfair advantages over opponents in AfterWar.

"I know. It is important. It's just that I've been spending an awful lot of my time building this training facility. And it's stopped being just a training facility, and is turning into a garrison – a full-blown FOB."

"FOB?"

"Forward Operating Base."

"Oh. Is that a good use of your time?"

"Well, it's gotta be done. When I started buying equipment for the team to train with, I pretty quickly realized we were going to need a place to *keep* it all. And if we keep it someplace, we also have to *defend* that place. Basically, if JSOC is going to operate in AfterWar, it's going to need a permanent presence there. A footprint. We can't run around buying aircraft and missile launchers every time there's an emergency. We've got to have equipment, and transport, and a staging point – and be ready to go."

"Okay. That makes sense. You're turning into the MacArthur of cyberspace."

"Pretty much. You say you're on schedule. What modules have you got done?"

"*Superman*, *Armor of God*, and *Un-Silencer*."

"Kick ass. Are they kick-ass?"

"They kick total ass. I'm leaving the serious testing to you guys, but I took them out for a test drive. And I counted much crow. Anyway, the latest build is in CVS. Grab it when you get a chance and tell me what you think."

"I think you're going to be the Gatling of cyberspace."

"Heh. Technology has been providing crushing advantages since the longbow. Gotta jam. Got real work to do."

"And back out in the field for me. Well, 'the field.' Laters."

D-BOY TRAINING CAMP
FAR S.E. PROVINCE, AFTERWAR
00:00:00 AUT 16 APR 2018

"I have control. One… two… *three*."

With that, BetteNoire drops the sentry in the near guard tower – and UncleBJ begins laying down a base of fire with an M-240 light machine gun. J-Dawg, BitTwiddler, and BoPeep sprint out toward the front gate. They plant breaching charges and take cover.

The gate blows wide.

The team is assaulting their own base – both to assess its defensibility and, moreover, to practice assaulting AfterWar-type camps, and taking down the buildings and personnel inside. This has been deemed likely to come up again.

"Assault team moving," BoPeep says. UncleBJ lays down a continuous stream of lead over their heads. BetteNoire has already dropped the sentry in the other tower – despite his having taken cover, or thinking he had – and now begins sniping targets of opportunity in the compound.

Ninety seconds later, the assault team has cleared the four buildings, killed or incapacitated everyone inside, and announced the target secure. They have

```
taken only moderate damage, though BoPeep
may yet bleed to death from a nasty sev-
ered femoral artery.
    "Shall we bring it in?" BetteNoire
asks, from up in her tree.
    "Negative," BoPeep says, lying down
so BitTwiddler can practice applying a
med kit to his wound. "Hold position."
    "I would have expected more of them,"
J-Dawg says standing just outside the
door of the largest structure, scanning
the compound.
    And that's when the counter-attack
comes – right back through the open front
gate. The counter-assaulters kill J-Dawg,
BitTwiddler, and BoPeep, before getting
picked off from afar by BetteNoire and
UncleBJ.
```

"God, I hate those fucking kids," Rheinhardt says, pulling his earbuds out.

"Uh, oh," Johnson says, his character still alive and unhurt on his belly on a nearby hilltop. "Sounds like somebody's got a case of *the sandy vaginas*."

"Yeah," says Aaliyah, letting her sniper avatar lounge languorously in her aerie. "You know, they've got creams for that."

"Children pipe down," Colonel Havering says from the doorway, behind the rows of machines. No one saw him appear, nor knows how long he has been observing. "Those goddamn H/P machines cost a fortune – and you won't let anybody else use 'em. Keep fucking around and I'll give 'em to someone else."

Mike taps a stylus to his tablet, which has his training notes on it. "Colonel, the big processors and dual video cards allow us to run at full resolution with no drag or loss of frame rate. You'll be glad for the superior vision in an engagement. When it counts."

"And are you getting them ready for when it counts?" Havering says. He adds, slightly under his breath, "If it ever does?"

"Yes, sir," Mike says. "They're making good progress. I started them on basic two-on-two skirmishes. They needed to get more proficient at controlling the characters with the keyboard and mouse. Then we moved on to small unit tactics. Along the way, we've covered a lot of stuff that's particular to the game: strafing, position and vision, triangulating with audio, the capabilities of the weapons – including ones that don't exist in real life. And in-game comms."

"So. They totally hopeless?"

"Not totally. Javier had plenty of chops to start with – and Aaliyah has some strange preternatural ability. The others have got a lot of aptitude. It's mainly a matter of transferring the skills to the virtual space. Learning to think, and feel, and act *as* one's avatar. Like learning to drive – eventually you can just feel where the back bumper is when you're reversing. And they're starting to gel. To become, um, what's the phrase? Operationally effective."

Havering leans over the closest console, which is Tim's. Him being dead, his screen shows his stats – a sort of waiting area for going back in the game.

"What's this?" Havering asks abruptly. "You're calling your unit *D-Boys*? That's not real clandestine, is it?"

"Hiding in plain sight, sir," Tim says. He flips to a registry of AfterWar teams, scrolling to D. There's *Delta*, *Delta Force*, *Delta Snipers*. "Also," Tim adds, flipping around, "*1st SFOD-D*, *5th Special Forces Group*, and *Special Ops Command*. Every little boy wants to grow up to be us."

"Well, good for you," Havering says, not seeming impressed. "Carry on." He walks out without another word.

"I've gotta hit it, too," Tim says. "I'm on the red-eye to LAX."

"When you get back," Mike says, "I'll have the first version of the hacked clients ready for you. I think you're going to like the new capabilities."

"Okay. Let's call it a day on this," Rheinhardt says. "Team training schedule for tomorrow: muster here at 8am, civvies."

"Thanks, boss", "G'night", and "Have a good 'un", the others say variously, getting up and moving toward the door.

"Hold on," Rheinhardt says. "*Six* am, parade field – sweats and running shoes." The others pause in their previously happy exodus. "I won't have you turning into a bunch of lard-asses sitting around playing video games all day."

"Have a good 'un," Mike says, pushing by, smiling.

"Not so fast," Rheinhardt says. "You, too. Until and unless somebody assures me you're never going to be along for another running firefight in bandit country, you train with us."

"Two-way street, *muchacho*," Javier says, smiling himself now.

"… Roger that, top," Mike says.

1ST SFOD-D COMPOUND
NEAR FORT BRAGG, NORTH CAROLINA
01:52:40 EST 16 APR

"Mike, wake up. *Mike*. Gotta move."

Mike tries to push away the hand shaking his shoulder. But it yanks him roughly to his feet. He can see nothing in the blackness – but he hears gunfire, and explosions, somewhere close by.

He pushes his arms out in front of him, looking for the light switch, or something to hang onto. Instead, a rifle is thrust into his hand.

"Shoot anyone who doesn't glow in your NVDs." He recognizes Javier's voice. Mike touches his own face and remembers he is wearing a pair of the night vision goggles. Infrared reflective tape on Javier's uniform glows a bright silver in the green, ghostly view. With that, Javier turns and runs out the way he came in.

Outside, Mike can hear shouting now – and then a yelp of pain, too high-pitched. "I'm hit!" With a lurch of horror, like a physical punch to the gut, Mike recognizes Aaliyah's voice. "I'm bleeding out fast," she says, her voice fading.

Mike puts his rifle to his shoulder and runs outside. He begins firing, dropping ghostly opponents – one, two, three. But more appear, spawning in the place of the fallen. They are rushing at him, firing and shouting. As they approach, Mike can see the green headbands they wear, in the nearly undifferentiated green field of his view.

He presses his throat mic and, voice weak and reedy, says, "I need help. Guys, I'm going down." He feels the floor spinning beneath him, and realizes he is in fact dropping. He looks down – and all around him are the other members of the team: Rheinhardt, Johnson, Tim, Javier, Ali, and Mac. They are all wounded, lying upon one another, writhing and moaning.

As they plummet downward, spinning faster and faster, Javier smiles at him and says, "It's okay, Mike. It's just God's will." Javier pulls his phone from his webbing and hands it to Mike. The phone is ringing. Mike knows who is calling. But he is too terrified to answer.

He knows it's the man in the black trousers, with the roughly-tied turban – and the black, oozing cavity where he should have an eye socket. He is calling to tell Mike that he is a person, too. That he loves his mother. The ground rushes up now, filling the oversized screen of his monitor, eclipsing his health and armor readout. He hears "*Wahed shwiyya*" beneath the scream of the engines.

"Mike Brown."

"*… What's going on, Mike?*"

Mike battles to control his breathing. He is drenched in sweat, sitting up in bed in the near-dark. Somehow he has answered his phone before fully waking up.

"Who… who is this?" he says, sucking air.

"Jim Niewendyke," Jim says. "Take it easy. Are you okay?"

Mike pulls the phone away from his head and wipes his face with the sheet. Only now is he fully aware of where he is. He fumbles for his watch on the bed table. The glowing face tells him it's not quite two in the morning.

"I'm fine," he says, breathing deeply through his nose and out through his mouth. "Just startled. Having a bad dream. What is it?"

"Another bad dream. We may have another breach of a nuclear facility."

"DOE?"

"No. Pakistani, Ministry of Defense. And not an electronic intrusion."

"Oh, shit."

"That captures it. Can you have your team in telepresence in twenty minutes? I want to brief you all at once."

"Yeah." Mike hits the lights, pulls on his ACUs, grabs his phone and laptop, and fast-walks out the door in his socks, still squinting. He's thinking he's glad he knows where everyone lives now. But when he gets to Javier's room, and wakes him, a single key press on Javier's phone buzzes everyone on the team.

DELTA TELEPRESENCE FACILITY
NEAR FORT BRAGG, NORTH CAROLINA
02:06:20 EST 16 APR

Havering is first in the room – he was already up, showered, dressed, and pacing around the TOC when the call came. He's put the TOC night crew on alert, woken up more support staff, and answered the incoming video call from DHS by the time the others arrive. Dharmesh and Jim are back on the screen on the wall, also waiting.

"Glad to see you back on your feet," Havering says to Niewendyke, as the others take their seats.

"Respectfully, Colonel, no time for pleasantries."

"Right. Go."

"As you'll know, we've had about a dozen AQA – al Qaeda in AfterWar - suspects under surveillance since your Pakistan operation got us tabs on them. Everything we have, intel, surveillance tools, got passed off to FBI, CIA, DIA, and NSA. They've all been working it. Honestly, no one quite knows whose job this is."

"Know how you feel."

"Also, people are only figuring out how to do it as they go along. Though we know where most of them are in real life, a decision was made not to take any of the targets down for the moment. We figured that having a view directly into their in-game activities was a lot like having undercover agents inside their cell. So we, or rather guys at these agencies, have been watching, and collecting intel.

"Earlier tonight, a CIA analyst was reviewing video footage previously taken by one of the Javelin missile cams. This is the surveillance tool Dharmesh and Mike built. And this analyst saw what looked a lot like a training operation. About fifty players were repeatedly assaulting a very elaborate and well-defended complex. They ran through the assault several times. This raised some interest."

"What precisely were they practicing assaulting?" Havering asks.

"Exactly," Jim says. "Our initial answer was – who the hell knows? It was a big, walled, guarded complex of about two dozen buildings. But so this analyst takes some screenshots of this virtual compound and starts passing them around. Copies made their way to, among a lot of other places, NNSA, the National Nuclear Security Administration, at DOE. So these NNSA guys generally take a very keen interest in nuclear materials and weapons storage facilities – in every country in the world that has any. Well, one of their guys thinks he recognizes this complex in the game."

"Ah, shit," Havering says.

Niewendyke frowns at the camera in response. "Yeah. If he's right, it's POF – Pakistan Ordnance Facilities, at their Ordnance Complex in Wah Cantonment."

"Did you ring those guys up to warn them?"

"Yes. First thing. But remember, this footage is a couple of days old."

"And?"

"And the Pakistanis sounded extremely surprised, and more than a little uneasy, to hear from us. They admitted there had been an insurgent 'incident' early yesterday morning. But that it had been handled, headed off, defended against. They claimed. And, mainly, that there was no danger of any loss of nuclear materials."

"Yeah, well. They would say that, wouldn't they."

"They have to."

"And the real story?"

"CIA has some well-placed assets in the Pakistani Air Force, including at the base at Kamra. This is very close to their weaponization activities. Somebody managed to get him on the line for five minutes. This asset says their whole base went into lockdown yesterday morning. And nobody knows anything for sure. But the word on the local street is: they lost one."

A beat of silence follows, where they can almost hear everyone in the room suddenly breathing faster. "Jesus Christ on a pogo stick," Havering says. "Those fucking people couldn't empty water out of a boot, with instructions on the heel."

"Look," Jim says, pausing and looking a little rattled. (This rattles Mike. He's never seen Jim rattled.) "Look, I've got to get to the White House. Can you scramble everybody you've got – I mean, pretty much everyone – brief them, and wait on station for me to get back to you?"

"Doing it now," Havering says. The screen goes black.

"Okay," Havering says. "The briefing on this one is gonna be by me. *And you're all gonna take notes.*" He pulls his phone from his pocket, presses one key, then waits one second. "*Bowstring load-out,*" he says to the answering voice. "Briefing in the hangar at 0230. And Lisa – everyone else, too. Everyone operational we can get in the building. Everyone not deployed or on life support."

"What's Bowstring?" Mike asks Javier, on their way out the door.

"The squadron that stays on call, ready to deploy – anywhere, at all times. We can do a load-out, that is, get everything an entire squadron needs to operate, and the operators themselves, onto transport and in the air within sixty minutes. Generally more like forty-seven."

"How many operators are there in a squadron?" Mike asks, following Javier around a corner. A low-volume klaxon is now singing out of the ceiling speakers, and the lights are pulsing slightly. Also, lanky human figures, in various states of undress, are emerging efficiently from the walls around them and falling in with their march.

"Seventy-five to eighty-five," Javier says. "Plus signals, support, and a headquarters element."

DELTA LOAD-OUT HANGAR
NEAR FORT BRAGG, NORTH CAROLINA
02:30:00 EST 16 APR

Mike feels like he's in a *Star Wars* movie, or some bizarre cloning experiment. He is standing on the bare, cold, concrete floor of a cavernous hangar. Several large vehicles are parked around the periphery, and just outside. The enormous doors are open to the cool North Carolina night. Pallets of equipment, much of it plastic-wrapped, are rolling up on motorized carts and forklifts.

And all around him stand well over a hundred Delta operators, with more streaming in, in ones twos and fours, every minute. Individual vehicles – predominately, but not exclusively, pickup trucks and motorcycles – drive up, park as close to the hangar as they can maneuver, and are abandoned.

The men wear fatigues, civvies, or bits of sleeping attire. A minority are already partially or wholly in their assault suits. They crowd in, pushing toward a raised doorway in one wall, at the top of a half-flight of stairs, where Havering stands with a couple of TOC staff around him, talking on two phones.

For the past ten days, Mike has been working, very intimately, with five supermen, and one superdog. And now, suddenly, he is surrounded by an entire race of these superbeings. Their confidence, power, calm, and effortless radiation of lethality roll over him in heavy swells. They talk in low voices, buckling things, chambering weapons, and checking messages on phones and tablets. Mainly, they greet one another quietly, and wait.

On the way to the hangar, Javier tried to give Mike some deeper background that he was unlikely to get at the briefing. "Eight countries officially in the nuclear club," he said. "The U.S., Britain, France, Russia, China, India, Pakistan, North Korea. And Israel unofficially – but definitely. By 1996, the ex-Soviet Republics with nukes – Belarus, Ukraine, and Kazakhstan – had all verifiably returned their warheads to Russian control."

At this point, they'd reached the hangar and taken their places. Javier carried on, in hushed tones, as the bodies pressed around them, and Mike ogled.

"Okay. That left North Korea and Pakistan as our two big problems. North Korea on purpose – they've been badly starved for cash, and don't care about the rules, and are perfectly likely to sell warheads, or fissile material, to the highest bidder. We've been on the verge of a naval blockade for a couple of years. It's a huge problem – but at least a predictable one.

"Pakistan, on the other hand, may become the nightmare by accident. It is not exactly the most stable society on Earth. And, as we've discussed, there are strong Islamist elements still in the military and the government. The most plausible catastrophe scenario there is a coup. And, by that, I mean *another* coup – that's how Musharraf himself came to power, and he wasn't the first. Anyway, if the wrong group of generals put one in the back of Zardari's head, and seized the controls of power, their entire nuclear arsenal could effectively be in Islamist hands overnight. That is, in the hands of close buddies of the Taleban and AQ.

"Contingency planning for this scenario has involved, essentially, a U.S. counter-coup – to go in and seize control of the nuclear arsenal ourselves. Bat-shit crazy, but slightly less bat-shit crazy than the alternative. And, as bad as that sounds, it's worse. Because this U.S. contingency plan is not a secret, Zardari *cannot afford to admit* to losing control of any nuclear material. Whether it's happened or not. Because, if he does—"

Javier stops speaking when Havering starts.

"Good morning," Havering says, which is obviously all the attention-getting he is going to do. He speaks without amplification, his voice filling the cavernous space of the hangar. Shuffling and conversation instantly cease.

"Thanks to an operation by Sergeant Major Rheinhardt's team in our usual favorite place, and in partnership with one of our OGAs, we now have a pretty good eye on the planners of the WMD attacks.

"That's the good news.

"The bad news is that SIGINT from, let's call it about five minutes ago, indicates that this same group – which are AQ, or AQ-affiliated – have pulled off some kind of raid on the Wah Cantonment Ordnance Complex in Pakistan."

A low-amplitude wave of reaction rolls across the assembled men.

"The first thing we know is: we don't know a goddamned thing. And we're not going to find out a goddamned thing, not officially. As you know, the loss of a warhead – or even, probably, significant fissile material – will mean the fall of the Zardari regime. There are operational plans in place for the 101st, with supporting JSOC elements, to go in and take control of the main weapons storage facilities, the minute it looks like the government might go down.

"Anyway, whatever the hell did happen, they cannot afford to admit to it. So the official line from the Pakistan regime is worthless. From what we can figure out on our own, the best picture of what actually happened is as follows.

"According to most reliable intel, their main storage and maintenance site for nuclear weapons, particularly at a screwdriver level, is the ordnance complex at Wah. Now it's not the weapons we've been most concerned about. We know the Pakistanis store them in component form – and the detonation codes, kept elsewhere, would make it difficult in the extreme for anyone to make one of these go bang, even if they got hold of one. And designing a relatively simple gun-barrel design atomic device isn't rocket surgery. We've found schematics for these type of weapons on captured AQ laptops in Afghanistan and NWFP.

"It is the weapons-grade material which requires large-scale industrial facilities. Everybody understands this. Now the Pakistanis have always claimed that both the weapons and the materials are accorded the same level of security. No one ever really believed that, and current events have given it the lie.

"As of last year, the Wah Complex has a very new, very pretty building designated the Gadwal Uranium Enrichment Plant. And, as of this morning, our HUMINT assets there indicate with moderate certainty that 40 kilograms of highly enriched uranium just went missing – or rather, were seized. That's enough for something a tad bigger than Hiroshima."

This statement leaves the hangar in grim silence.

Havering goes on. "There's every reason to think that AQ could easily have a device already waiting for it. Built to spec, needing only the uranium. So they could be in a position to produce a positive yield by… well, just about any minute now.

"And that is what we know. All of it. NEST of course has been scrambled, like crazy sons of bitches. They are in the air and all over the ground – in major cities, at airports, and particularly sea ports. National Guard is on alert nationwide. And intelligence and operational assets are working in theater, and everywhere else, to try to track both the materials and the bad guys.

"As soon as they give us something to go after, you're all going off the leash. Right now, I want ops personnel pitching in to finish the load-out – and then you sit your asses down on that aircraft. Bring something to read. Because you're not going back to bed until you retrieve these materials, or until someone beats you to it.

"Sergeant Rheinhardt – I want your team in the TOC with me. And bring Mike Brown." Havering turns on his heel and exits.

Mike can practically hear a hundred-plus Delta Force operators thinking to themselves, *Who the hell's Mike Brown?*

DELTA TACTICAL OPERATIONS CENTER
NEAR FORT BRAGG, NORTH CAROLINA
02:49:33 EST 16 APR

The TOC has room for special guests, but not much. Mike gets an unoccupied corner of desk, where he sets up his laptop and props up his phone. He arrives before the others, who have run for assault suits and go-bags. They file in a few minutes later, pulling on items of kit.

The room is a buzz of grim activity, while two-way video screens on the wall display live feeds from various military and government installations. Most of the scenes are static – men and women in uniform working intently at their stations, or stepping in and out of frame. Another of the screens shows CNN Headline News, as it does round the clock, every minute of the year.

"We don't wait for a call from Washington," Javier says to Mike, in answer to his question about the news channel. "If something gets hijacked, or attacked, or destabilized, we'll go ahead and run a full load-out. Often, by the time we get the order, we're already on the tarmac with the engines running. If it's a false alarm, then we've had a good practice load-out."

Even as he's explaining this, one of the top stories of the half-hour loop gets pre-empted by a suited and coiffed presenter.

"Breaking news… we are just getting word of some sort of a large-scale power outage on the West Coast," the woman says in her flat and precise presenter's voice. "We're going to try and go live to downtown Los Angeles, where apparently the lights are completely out across the city… We want to stress that, despite any similarity to the recent attacks, at this time we have *no* indication that this is any kind of terrorist activity. We urge our viewers not to jump to any conclusions, and not to panic in any way. We're going live now to Los Angeles…"

At she speaks, phones on desks begin to ring around the TOC. So do mobiles on a variety of belts. So does Mike's.

"Mike, it's Jim. You getting this?"

"Yeah. Is it an intrusion?"

"Don't know. Why don't you get your ass in there and you tell me? Meantime, I'm not betting against it. Look, I've got the DCI in the next room over. CIA has more intel coming in, in real time. Stand by there."

"I'm going nowhere." Mike rings off.

Havering grips Mike by the shoulder. "Same as before?"

"I honestly don't know yet. Looks the same. Gonna find out now."

Mike clicks on five regions of his laptop screen in rapid succession, then begins typing at speed. He is already into the DHS VPN, and now logs into a separate highly secure area. Here he can retrieve emergency tokens and one-time credentials that allow him unrestricted access to a variety of critical national systems.

While he is doing this, the corner of Mike's screen shows a ticker for the DHS CWOC Situation Board, where internal updates spool out in real time. "It's not the entire Western Interconnect," Mike says to Havering, still typing blazingly. "That would be bad, implausibly bad – lights out in all or parts of eleven states, all the way to the border of Texas. Almost to the Mississippi. Looks like it's just the California ISO… which is plenty bad enough."

"How bad?" Havering is grimacing up a storm. "How long?"

"Hold on." Logging into the internals of the California ISO network, Mike can see that their engineers are already in there, working frantically. Mike is not a domain expert on their systems. But he's done security auditing work for them. And he's a lot more familiar with how these types of systems can be fucked up, after the East Coast intrusion and outage.

Backing out again, he calls up their internal systems status board; then dives back in and pokes around in the guts further. Finally, he sends a broadcast message to the root account on their linked systems – identifying himself to their engineers, and asking for their team's assessment. Skimming the response, he says to Havering,

"Looks about as ugly as last time. Remarkably similar to last time, in fact. And it may take as long, or even longer, to repair it. The lights in California are *off* – for the foreseeable."

"Okay," Havering says. "Then we assume this is going the same direction as before. That the power outage is a cover for an attack – probably an unconventional attack." He hangs up on whoever was on the line on his cell, then presses a speed dial button. Mike listens in, as do Rheinhardt, Javier, Aaliyah, and Johnson, all of whom stand or sit nearby.

"Sergeant McDonough. Yeah. Where are you. Okay, we're diverting you. Yes, mid-air. Yes, I know it's a commercial flight. No, not Pendleton – to Coronado. Yes. They'll be scrambled when you get there. Give me your flight number. Delta Lima one one four five. Roger. Stand by."

He puts the phone on a desk without closing it. "Lisa. Get a line to both FAA and Delta Airlines, on the red phone.

DL1145 is no longer going to LAX. It's going to San Diego. Can you wrangle the authority for that?"

"No problem," she says, typing with one hand and picking up a phone handset with the other.

"You – Corporal. Wake up Admiral Roberts at Coronado Naval Base."

"Sir."

"You're sending Tim to Coronado," Rheinhardt says.

"Yeah. Some substantial chunk of SEAL Teams One, Three, Five and Seven will either be on standby or in a training cycle. He'll rendezvous with them there."

"Why SEALs?" Mike asks, from his sitting position.

"Because," Havering says, putting his palm on Mike's desk, and sinking his weight down onto it, "three of the four busiest container ports in the U.S. – Los Angeles, Long Beach, and Oakland – are all on the West Coast. LA is the biggest in the country."

"And you have a feeling," Rheinhardt says, "that we're going to have to do a ship takedown. A *big* ship takedown."

"No," Havering says tiredly. "If we're lucky… *really* lucky… *maybe* we'll get to do a ship takedown."

"And if we're not?"

"Doesn't bear thinking about."

DELTA TACTICAL OPERATIONS CENTER
NEAR FORT BRAGG, NORTH CAROLINA
03:11:33 EST 16 APR

"You hear that a lot around DHS," Mike whispers to Javier, who are both now hunched over his machine. "That the shipping ports are the most vulnerable. But I'm not sure anyone really believes a nuclear device could get smuggled in. Not even the guys responsible for preventing it. Maybe especially not us."

Javier nods. "Like the Colonel said in the briefing, the device is the easy part. It's the fissile material that's the tough ticket. But there's a hell of a lot of it out there these days – most, but not all, in Russia. And it's starting to get around. In '94, Czech police seized fifty-some kilograms of contraband HEU. The Germans got 400 grams of plutonium the same year. And in 2001, the Russian Defense Ministry admitted to repulsing two heavy attacks on weapons storage facilities. And then there's Pakistan. There are currently three Pakistani nuclear engineers – *that we know of* – who are under government house arrest for making too many visits to Taleban and AQ strongholds. It's been a disaster waiting to happen for a long time."

"And if terrorists built a device, you think they could sneak it into a port?"

Javier sighs. "Only about ten percent of all ship-borne cargo is inspected before being offloaded. Something like six million containers enter U.S. ports each year. The Coast Guard, Customs and Border Service, Sea Marshals… they're all improving their capabilities – but it still just amounts to spot-checks. They say that inspecting every single shipment would choke the global economy."

"Jesus," Mike says. "And what exactly would a hundred-kiloton device going off in downtown Los Angeles do to the global economy?"

"Good point. I've actually seen the projected scenarios – for low-yield nuclear blasts in Manhattan, in Detroit, in San Francisco. It's the most horrifying thing you've ever heard, when they start describing it and putting numbers to it."

"Don't tell me." Mike stares at the wall for a few seconds. "Okay, tell me."

"For something Hiroshima-sized, call it 12.5 kilotons, detonated at ground level, in lower Manhattan, during a workday… you're looking at about 100,000 dead instantly. This assumes a firestorm area of about a mile and a half square, with 100% fatalities inside of it. Then another quarter million with direct radiation exposure, with maybe 10% of those lethal doses. With prevailing winds, you're looking at a 70-mile fallout footprint to the northeast – a million and a half exposed to fallout. Two hundred thousand of those will die in the short term, with several hundred thousand more sick."

"My God. It really is unthinkable."

"It is – but the unthinkable has already happened once this week. Hell, 9/11 was unthinkable until it actually occurred. And, believe me – even an extremely low-yield nuke would make 9/11 look like a house fire. Almost more horrible is that the medical facilities in the region would be completely overwhelmed – many of the injured and sick would die from lack of attention. And of course much of Manhattan would be a wasteland for decades. New York would never really recover."

"And L.A.? Or San Francisco?"

"Similar."

"How do you know all this?"

"I told you – we work with NEST, the Nuclear Emergency Search Teams. They've got a couple thousand people, mostly scientists, engineers, and technicians, on call. They're divided into Eastern U.S., headquartered at Andrews AFB, and Western at Nellis in Nevada. They've got unmarked vans, a fleet of small aircraft, and gamma and neutron detectors from briefcase-sized to truck-sized. They've got very good tools for defusing and dismantling nuclear devices: X-ray scanners, high-pressure water cutting tools, robotic arms. Their techs work with military EOD teams, including JSOC. Tim has cross-trained with them. Tim can actually defuse atomic weapons, which is a pretty scary skill to have."

"Tim told me the trick is to cut the blue wire."

"Yeah, well, it's a little more complicated when there's plutonium or highly enriched uranium involved."

"You hear NEST talked about at DHS. But I've never worked with them. I've never been asked to look at their systems for security holes. Which is weird."

"They're very secretive. Though you never hear about it, they've been called out something like sixty times since 1975 for nuclear threats – running around suspected areas scanning for radiation. Luckily, it's been false alarms every time so far. They also drill constantly. And since 9/11, they've been roaming around urban areas and ports at random, doing radiation spot-checks. Problem is, a lot of things emit background radiation – like construction equipment, and the earth. And there are lots of ways to shield radiation, if you don't want it to be found. Hell, U-235 is so low-emission, you can mask it with tin foil."

Mike is staring at the wall in stunned horror, when Jim Niewendyke pops up on one of the two-way screens. He is looking down into what would seem to be his video phone. Swatches of elegant decor show in the background. When Havering has seen the call and stepped in front of the camera, Jim begins to speak. "Okay. Here's what we now think happened, based on latest greatest. First of all, the raiders of the facility at Wah had inside help."

Havering grunts, clearly conveying, *Big surprise there*.

"They also hacked the security systems in some way before they assaulted. They did this remotely, and it seems that greased their path. We don't have details on this. But we're told the Pakistanis were caught by surprise, most of their electronic defenses down. The complex was then assaulted by fifty to a hundred personnel, AQT types. The attack went off like clockwork. And they got away clean."

"Practice makes perfect," Johnson says, alluding to the AfterWar training on the mockup of the complex.

"Too true," Havering says. "And it all came together for them – the in-game training, the electronic attack, and then the assault."

Jim shakes his head. "And now it's coming together for them on our end. With the power out, our ability to respond is severely degraded." On the screen, someone physically grabs Niewendyke and turns him around. While the team in the TOC listens in, the ambient mic on Niewendyke's phone picks up the speech of the man off camera.

"Jim, listen. We just got a report from NEST West, at Nellis. Their comms and responder systems are all fucked up."

"What?" Niewendyke says dully, the back of his head filling the screen.

"Their NSC liaison called the White House switchboard from a goddamned payphone."

"You are fucking shitting me."

"No. Their mobile search and response teams are already scrambled, all over the goddamned country, everywhere west of the Mississippi. But they can't talk to any of them, or coordinate. It's a complete goat fuck."

"Andrews?"

"Andrews is fine. Their teams in New York, D.C., Philly, all fine – all on the grid and online. But the goddamned lights aren't off in the East this time, are they?"

Niewendyke spits out something low and indecipherable.

After two heavy beats, he turns back to his phone, which is now pretty clearly resting on a coffee table. "You get that?" he says to the camera, and the Delta TOC.

"Yeah, we got it," Havering says.

DELTA TACTICAL OPERATIONS CENTER
NEAR FORT BRAGG, NORTH CAROLINA
03:34:22 EST 16 APR

"Has anyone in your command got *anything* remotely useful or actionable at this point?" Niewendyke asks. He is visibly ashen.

There's another beat of grim silence, at both locations, before Mike says: "The AQA hacker. The one we nabbed in Baluchistan. Dharmesh said he was making vague noises about some kind of attack. If anyone knows what is happening, it's him."

"What's the status of his interrogation?" Havering asks.

Jim sighs audibly. "He's with CIA now. Presumably in some sub-sub-basement. If he's coughed up anything new, I've gotten no word of it."

Mike grips the table edge. "We need that guy. Get him for us."

Jim nods. "Normally, I'd say no chance – intra-agency bullshit. But I'm in the right place to do an end-run. Stand by there. Oh, and get Patel v-linked in." He lowers his phone, maintaining the connection, but restricting the view. The view is mainly of the carpet, as Niewendyke palms it and carries it down the hall.

He stops at an entryway, where the screen shows two sets of highly polished shoes on either side of a heavy door. "Gotta see him," Jim says, sounding thin and muted. "Go in, sir," a voice says and the camera and its owner enter.

"Bob, listen—" Jim's voice says, then pulls up short and adds, "Mr. Secretary."

"Jim."

"Listen, Bob. I need that HVT back – the one my analyst captured in Pakistan with the CAG team. Dick Havering's team."

"He's Agency property now, Jim. Then Gitmo-bound."

"Gotta have him. My guys are the only ones who know the right questions to ask him. And there is no time on this clock."

There's a brief pause. "Do it, Bob," says the third voice, the one Niewendyke greeted as "Mr Secretary."

"Okay. I can't give him to you. But I'll get you in there with him."

* * *

Fifteen minutes after this, Jim is back in the original anteroom, with his phone back on the table. This time the screen on the TOC wall has been split, with Dharmesh sitting on the other half, the chaos of the CWOC surging behind him.

"We're going to do a two-way with Langley," Niewendyke says to the assembled group. "I got us ten minutes of face time with this guy. But I've got to warn you – after this, I do not think any of us are going to be allowed a look into that room. Not us, not ICRC, nobody. You know what I'm saying? Stand by." He rings off.

"What does that mean?" Mike asks, addressing no one in particular. "The Red Cross won't get to see him…?"

"He means," Havering says, "that the interrogation is going to get messy after this."

"Messy? I thought we didn't do that." Mike looks to Javier.

"If ever there were a 'ticking bomb' scenario, this is it," Javier says. "Look, in ethical discussions about the acceptability of torture, the classic case that's always tossed around is having a ticking bomb somewhere, and a proven terrorist in your custody who definitely knows where it is. Is torture justified in that case? When you know you can save many innocent lives by doing it?"

"Is it?"

Javier looks away. "No one ever really has to answer the question – because it's never actually that clear-cut. In real life, it's always a question of torturing somebody who is a suspect, and who may be a bad guy, but who may also be totally innocent. And the information you get out of him may save lives, or it may be totally worthless. A situation where you either torture a known terrorist, or innocent people definitely die, is unlikely to ever come up."

"All kinds of firsts this week," Havering says, towering over Mike in the dimness and multiple monitor glow.

* * *

After a few more minutes of delay, another two-way screen lights up, displaying a bare and ill-lit room, presumably at Langley. It is overflowing with interrogators. But for the next ten minutes they move aside and out of frame. And the screen is filled with the same face that Mike last encountered from a few inches away in a crashing helicopter.

When the four-way link is confirmed, Dharmesh says – from within the TOC seeming to speak from one wall screen to another – "Okay. Who did this? Who orchestrated the California power grid hack?"

The young man laughs thinly. His face is dripping with sweat, and it falls in beads as his head bounces. "It doesn't matter. Because it is already too late."

"Is it the same people who programmed the Southeastern grid exploit? And who have hacked into NEST?"

The man grunts again. His presentation of bravado is a little thin – he is obviously frightened underneath it. "'Same people'," he says, smirking. "Yes, it was the same people – *me*."

Mike and Dharmesh trade glances across the wire at each other. Big-brained hackers, with big egos…

"Me," the man continues thinly. "And my two warrior brothers, each now a shaheed, since you cowards murdered them in the house in Koh-i Dalmach."

"Hey," Johnson says, leaning in, "it was your asshole friends who killed them. Tell 'em to check who's inside first before chucking grenades through windows." Havering pops him on the back of the head.

On the screen, the young man blinks heavily. He may not yet have been *coercively interrogated*, but he looks like he might not have slept in a few days. "It doesn't matter," he mutters, his head beginning to droop. "They are in Paradise now. And we had all of the exploits programmed before you even came there. It was all in place. All our brothers have had to do is execute it."

He finds some strength and raises his head again. "And soon we will have a great victory for God. The greatest victory. Soon you will see. A million infidels will die. Infidels and fornicators… and homosexuals. The homosexuals, soon they will feel the fire of God's wrath…"

The young man nods forward again, seeming on the verge of losing consciousness.

A man in a suit steps out of the shadows with a hypodermic needle in his hand – but the view is obscured by another, in a white shirt and loosened tie, who steps in front of the camera, very close.

"Hope you got what you needed," he says. The feed cuts out.

DELTA TACTICAL OPERATIONS CENTER
NEAR FORT BRAGG, NORTH CAROLINA
03:48:22 EST 16 APR

"Well?" Havering says. "Did you? Get anything?"

"Homosexuals," Aaliyah says. "He said homosexuals would burn."

"He said fornicators and homosexuals," Havering says.

"Yes. But he stressed the latter. Believe me, Islamists have a special horror of gays. I've got to think the target is San Francisco."

Havering's squint battles with his frown. "Lisa. Read that list of California deep-water ports. The container ports."

She taps a key. "Hueneme, in Oxnard. Long Beach. Los Angeles. Oakland. Redwood City. Sacramento. San Diego. San Francisco. Stockton."

"Aren't Sacramento and Stockton landlocked?" Mike asks.

"Deep-water ship channels," Lisa says. "Cut inland from the coast."

"That's not all of them, though, is it?" Rheinhardt asks. "Surely there are more ports than that. Smaller ones."

"Yeah," Havering says. "A lot more. Too many to cover. But the device has got to be fairly sizeable. A twenty- or forty-foot shipboard iso-container is the most likely package. And we're to the point of having to place our bets."

"Fine. I say our bet has to be San Francisco," Ali says.

"You got a channel open to Coronado?" Havering asks Lisa. "Can you get Admiral Roberts on video? Okay, speaker phone then."

A half a minute later, a gruff voice booms out into the TOC. *"Roberts."*

"Jimbo. Dick Havering. What can you tell me about your deployment plan?"

"Yeah. We're gonna have frogmen swimming up and down the entire goddamned California coast, at ten-meter intervals. Okay, sorry. This is all a little FUBAR." He clears his throat.

"We've scrambled everyone we've got, including all the boat teams. Training units included. We're massing them here, in LA/Long Beach, in San Fran, and a smaller team in Stockton. That gives us strike capability at every deep-water port, with about twenty minutes lead time. And we're keeping an additional QRF in the air. What have you got for me?"

"Maybe nothing. But we're now thinking Bay Area."

"Why?"

"Intel from a prisoner interrogation. Something about incinerating the gays. Vague. But it's what we've got."

"SF, Oakland, or Redwood City? Or Stockton?"

"Can't say. But I'd deprecate Stockton. And, hell, I'd put someone on the Golden Gate Bridge – and take a good hard look at anything sailing into the Bay."

"Roger that. I think we're just about to the point of halting and trying to interdict every incoming ship in deep water. We've got the Coast Guard falling over themselves now. Where's your man, by the way? The one who's NEST EOD-trained. Still inbound?"

"He's inbound. Question's where to."

"I think you're going to have to put your money on the table," the Admiral says. *"The wheel's spinning down."*

Havering takes a big breath before speaking. "Lisa. Divert Sergeant McDonough's flight again. SFO. Or Oakland, if they can't do that." He adds under his breath: "The other people on that flight are just going to *love* us."

"Roger that, Colonel," Lisa says. Mike starts to wonder what would happen to this command if Lisa quit.

Admiral Roberts rings off – "I wouldn't hang up on you, but it's the Secretary of the Navy on the other line" – and Havering turns back to his team.

"Okay. What do you guys want to do? Do you want to get in the air? I'm gonna put the squadron up now. But I've got a feeling this whole thing will be over before you get there."

While Rheinhardt confers with Johnson, Javier, and Aaliyah, Havering gives the squadron's orders to Lisa. "Their destination is a San Francisco area airport, military or civilian. Work that out. Wheels up RFN."

Mike is looking down at his laptop, when his eye is caught by Dharmesh stepping back into the frame of his camera.

Dharmesh taps his mic. "Hey," he says. When he's sure he's got some attention on the other end, including Mike's, he says, "Hey. They dumped us."

"What do you mean, they dumped us?" Mike says. "Who?"

"AQA. In the fucking game. They dumped us. All our surveillance."

Mike's mouth goes round-shaped. "The missiles? The Javelins?"

"Yeah. They all got put on trains heading back to the Eurabian marshalling point. And then the code itself was deleted from their machines entirely. The grid is entirely black."

DELTA TACTICAL OPERATIONS CENTER
NEAR FORT BRAGG, NORTH CAROLINA
03:55:49 EST 16 APR

"Okay," Mike says, as the others gather around. "How the hell did that happen?"

"Not sure," Dharmesh says. "It looks like some CIA guy went fucking around in the game, following AQA players around on foot. I don't know if he knew what the hell he was doing. But it looks like he was trying to tail them, gathering HUMINT. Virtual HUMINT, I guess. Avatar-INT. AVINT."

"Okay, I get it. Who the hell let him go in there?"

"It's an open game, Mike. That's the problem. Anyone can register to play. I guess this guy decided to show some initiative. Or who knows, the CIA never tells us before they do things. Anyway, according to a very terse report from my Agency liaison, this guy got made by the suspects."

"How does he know he got made?"

"He was skulking around an AQA safe house in an urban area – and out of nowhere, six players in Buraq uniform surround him. They shoot him in the legs until he's down to 5% health, lying on the ground in a puddle of himself. Then they start interrogating him. Who are you? What are you doing here? Who sent you? – that kind of thing. Finally, this bozo simply logs out of the game entirely, in despair and shame. As you can imagine, he wasn't real keen to advertise this episode to other agencies."

"CIA," Johnson sniffs, from behind. "God, those people are so much worse than useless."

Havering waves this off. "What happened then?"

"No one knows for sure. My guess? A few of the guys he was trailing put their heads together and said, Hey, how'd we get made? What do we all have in common here? Oh, this fancy missile launcher. Then one of their programmers dug into the code for the Javelin weapon patch and deconstructed it. And he found the surveillance code we put in there. These guys are not idiots."

"Didn't you disguise the code?" Rheinhardt asks from behind.

"Yes and no," Mike says, exhaling. "We only had a few hours to work with, putting it together. It's disguised about as well as their zombie code was. We found theirs; they found ours."

"Okay, doesn't matter now," Havering says. "How long ago did they dump the surveillance?"

Dharmesh's eyes dart to another screen. "Twenty-four minutes ago."

Havering nods. "Roughly the same time as the power outage, and the NEST disaster. Whatever's going to happen, it's gonna happen soon. And California's got a lot of goddamned coastline."

"And," Javier adds, "it's got three large container ports close to San Francisco. Which would make a very iconic image with a mushroom cloud rising over it."

Havering grimaces. "At the end of the day, our only chance of stopping this thing is to figure out exactly where the attack is going to happen. And where it's coming in from."

Johnson snorts. "Yeah, but at the end of the day… the goddamn day is over."

Mike's brow is furrowed, and he's staring a long way off. Finally looking up at Dharmesh again, he says, demands really, "*Where?*"

Dharmesh startles. "I don't know. I don't have any better guess than you."

"No, no, *no. Where was the AQA safe house where the CIA guy got made?*"

AQA SAFE HOUSE
FALLUJAGRAD, AFTERWAR
08:50:22 AUT 16 APR 2018

"I have control. One… two… *three*."

The shoulder-fired missile zips across the street and blows open the double front doors of the fifteen-story building. The assault team races across the street into the settling debris, trampling the body parts of the outside guards.

However, they take heavy fire just crossing the broad boulevard, where the explosion is already drawing interest. Fallujagrad is, well, a war zone. Situated at the intersection of all three combatant territories – Eurabia, ChiCom, and the Anglosphere – the city is utterly war-torn, and constantly in play. Occasionally one side or another will gain control – but will soon be driven out by the other two in tandem. This is by design. Fallujagrad is, and is intended to be, the Beirut of AfterWar.

Bleeding lightly, the members of the team gain the interior and begin mounting the stairs in two-by-two cover formation. As they ascend in pairs, a rain of grenades begins to fall on their heads from above, detonating at a variety of heights.

"Shit! Health down past fifty percent."

"We can't afford to get killed – it'll take too long to spawn and then get back here."

"Back down the stairs! Pull back!"

The team leaps down flights of stairs and rushes straight back out the door they came in – and then back across the street to their original cover, behind a pair of burnt-out cars. Before they even reach this spot, they start taking fire from one or more of the upper-story windows on the building face.

"I'm hit! I'm out."

"Me, too."

"Who, goddammit? Use your call signs."

"Alpha Romeo One-Niner. Down."

"Alpha Romeo Four. Down."

"Alpha Romeo One-Zero – I'm out, too."

The team leader, AR_01, tries to rally his squad there, at their final assault point. But things are not looking good for team Antagonist_Redress.

* * *

"Hey. Where's that sniper shooting at you from, dude?"

AR_01 spins on his mouse. The avatar speaking to him is crouched down in a blown-out window in the structure behind him. He is speaking in a laid-back voice, almost like a surfer dude.

"Who the hell are you?" He moves his pointer over the character and his heads-up displays *UncleBJ - Team D-Boys*.

"Master Sergeant, Fifth Special Forces," UncleBJ says, identifying himself in the way that Delta operators often do (not as Delta operators). "How's Langley treating you?" he adds.

"How the fuck do you know who I am?"

"Because if there's one thing the Agency can't keep - though there's not only one thing - it's a secret."

Antagonist_Redress is, to Johnson, a fairly obvious opaque name for an ad hoc spec-ops or Agency task force. Anyway, he already pretty much knew the Agency guys would be there.

"Up there," AR_01 finally says, turning to face the street. "Fourth floor from the top. Fifth window from the right."

From the deep shadows of the gutted building, UncleBJ ranges the window, then adjusts his EGLM for range and elevation. There's a *whump*, a puff of smoke, a delay of not quite two seconds – and the window in question explodes outward. Johnson has dropped a 40mm HE round in it, on the first shot.

"Jesus," AR_01 says. "Nice shot."

"Yeah, it was. What else ya got?"

"Um. The firing seems to have tailed off."

"This is BetteNoire," UncleBJ hears on his internal squad net. *"Twelve tangos now down in target structure. Sniper no longer has targets. Assault team is clear to go. I retain overwatch."*

"Stay here, man," UncleBJ says, emerging into the street in a crouch. "Maybe you guys can guard the front door or something."

Six minutes later, the D-Boys have completely cleared out the two upper floors with the mass of Buraq bad guys in it.

"*IP addresses*," Rheinhardt says, from across the lab. "What did you get?" Their hope, in conducting this in-game op, has been to pull the same trick that got them the location in Pakistan – learning additional IP addresses, and thus locations, of AQA guys, from peer-to-peer communication in a battle.

Mike doesn't answer right away. He curses under his breath. "*Nothing*," he says finally. "Well, one. Just a single IP address – only one, going in or out. Fuck."

"So the peer-to-peer comms didn't kick in," Aaliyah says. "It all went through the AfterWar server."

"No," Mike says, shaking his head – either in despair or wonder. "It's not an AfterWar server they're talking to. I'm looking at it now."

"Okay, what is it?"

"DOE. It's a fucking server at the Department of Energy, in D.C."

"What the hell?"

"Remember how they proxied all their hacks through the safe house in London? So, if we found them, we'd go there, instead of where they really were? Well, they must have figured out how to proxy all their AfterWar traffic now. And they're proxying it right through our back yard. A government server. DOE."

"Nervy bastards."

"Yeah. And still learning at least as fast as we are."

```
In the fighting in the building, Team
D-Boys succeeded in keeping four of their
Buraq opponents alive – by shooting them
down to minimal health and then disarm-
ing them. But within a few seconds, each
of the wounded logged out, their avatars
fuzzing into nothing where they lay on
the floor.
  So interrogation of survivors is out.
But they can still search the building,
and the bodies of those they killed.
  "Okay, what are we looking for?"
UncleBJ asks, stepping back from the
window, where he has been covering the
street.
  "Three possibilities," WileyC says.
"If we're really lucky, we may find a com-
puter – or a PDA, or memory stick."
  "They have computers in the game?"
  "Yeah. We haven't covered this yet.
But in-game comms and intel are a part
of game play. There's a whole in-game
```

Internet. And people move data around on handhelds and memory sticks."

"What kind of data?"

"Orders, battle plans, building schematics, maps, that kind of thing. It'd be another way for AQ to move data, safe from snooping."

"Okay," BoPeep says. "Sweep it. We start on this floor, then clear the building. Point Mike toward anything you find that's remotely interesting."

"Hey," WileyC says, "another thing – we need an inventory of every piece of equipment on everyone we killed."

"Why?"

"I don't know. Maybe it will tell us something."

"Everyone haul ass. The clock doesn't stop."

***

Ten minutes later, the team has cleared the building, with help from a couple of surviving Agency guys who have wandered in. No computers, no handhelds, no memory sticks – but they have begun piling up the equipment looted from the corpses, all in one room.

"Anything?" BoPeep asks.

"I don't know," WileyC says. "There's some cool gear, but it's pretty standard. Basic weapons, more advanced weapons, armor…"

At that moment, BetteNoire enters from the hallway. "I found these," she says, "on two guys downstairs." She presses her drop key, and plops two piles of something on the larger pile. They look like some kind of suit – but with a bulbous tank on the back.

WileyC steps closer. "Scuba gear…" he says.

"What would they be using scuba gear for?" BoPeep asks.

The group stands in a circle, regarding it.

"Shit, shit, shit…" WileyC says.

"God, there's no time for this," BetteNoire says.

"Wait," WileyC says. "If these guys trained on a mockup before taking down the weapons complex… wouldn't they do the same before taking control of a ship? A *container ship?*"

"Is there water in AfterWar?" J-Dawg asks.

"I know there's at least some playable coastline," WileyC says.

BoPeep turns to one of the CIA guys, RA_14. "The Agency has been following these guys. Have you tracked any AQA activity on water – or on the coast?"

RA_14 says, "Hang on." His avatar goes still, suggesting that he's stepped away from his desk, presumably to confer with someone. "Yeah," he says, coming back to life. "There's not only a port town with a dockside – it's called Margiers - but it's got a large dry dock facility. We saw a lot of their guys going in and out."

"Don't you motherfuckers ever pass anything on?" UncleBJ says. "Jesus Christ, it's like the fucking 9/11 intel debacle, deja vu all over again."

"Look, we've got some very smart people working on this."

"Who cares how powerful your equipment is if you can't safely operate it?"

"Enough," BoPeep says. "What's inside the dry dock?"

"Hold on… I'm putting my partner on now. They want to know what's inside the dry dock. Yeah," he says in a lower voice, "we called Bragg. They're who they say they are."

RA_14 then resumes speaking, but in a whole different voice. "We don't know what's inside the dry dock. None of the suspects ever used the Javelin missile launcher in there, so we never got any video from inside."

"Didn't you *follow* them in? Have you ever heard of infiltration?"

"Look, fuck off. It's incredibly heavily guarded. We had it under surveillance, and we were planning an op to take it down."

"Oh. Were you now?"

DELTA AFTERWAR OPS LAB
NEAR FORT BRAGG, NORTH CAROLINA
04:19:51 EST 16 APR

"If there's a ship inside that dry dock," Colonel Havering says, standing behind the row of computers and players, " – or, rather, an imaginary ship inside that imaginary dry dock – I'm betting it looks just like whatever real ship has got our nuke on it."

He speaks into his headset now, over to the TOC. "Lisa. You got that list? The one with every vessel docked at every West Coast port, and every one en route now?" There's a pause while he listens to the response.

"Well?" Rheinhardt asks.

"Yeah. We've got the list. But it's a huge list. Our focus has gotta be on the ships that have docked in the last twenty-four hours – and, most especially, the ones that are heading into port now, docking in the next few hours. Before dawn."

"Are there reports of any ships having been hijacked?"

"No. But we're calling every shipping company, to make sure they are in positive contact with their vessels."

Mike looks up. "Can't you just interdict all the ships that are headed toward U.S. West Coast ports?"

"In a word? No. We're in the process of trying to put a hold on all incoming ocean traffic. But there's no central way to do it. And then there are all the ships already docked – we're in the process of boarding and searching them. But that would take three weeks under the best of circumstances. And with

NEST trying to rope in all their teams from hell and back, using, I don't know, smoke signals… our radiation detection capabilities are, let's call it, degraded. And, hell, we don't even know for sure that it's a ship. It still might be a plane, train, automobile – or some guy riding across the Mexican border on a goddamned donkey."

"But if you knew for sure that it was a ship? And, moreover, if you knew *what kind* of ship it was?"

Havering nods. "Exactly. So get your asses in there and take down that goddamned dry dock."

* * *

"Okay," Mike says, finishing the last client install. "We've hacked the client about as much as we dare."

"Why as much as you dare?" Javier asks, from his station.

"Because we're not the first people to think of cheating by reprogramming the game. Your system has to know the location and trajectory of everything in your area, even if it's not supposed to tell you. So if you insert some code to aim for you, you'll hardly ever miss."

"So everyone does this?"

"No. Quite the opposite. Most online games actively look for things like aimbots. If they find them, they boot you out of the game. If they find you repeatedly, they ban you."

"I thought," Johnson says, "no one runs this game anymore."

"We don't have time for this right now," Ali says.

"Sorry. Okay, so first cheat: *Un-silencer*. You've now got hacked radar that tracks all incoming fire – sounding an alarm, and showing you exactly where it's coming from. So no one can shoot at you undetected. Next, *Superman*. Press F1 and you can see through a wall. Hold it down, and the range of X-ray vision zooms out, until you hit the edge of the board."

"Nice," Javier says.

"*Holy Spirit*. By tabbing F2, you can cycle through the viewpoints of every member of the squad, ending up back as yourself. Good for situational awareness. *God*. Hit F3, and you cut loose from your body and go into fly-through mode: you can zoom around at any altitude, over any part of the map – any part your client has information about – without your avatar actually going anywhere."

"Schweet," Johnson says.

"*Armor of God*. Press F4 and the module takes control of your movement, jigging you out of the way of any incoming fire. To turn it off, press F4 again. It's also got a panic 'take cover' mode. If you get in real trouble, press and hold F4, and the client will haul your ass to the best closest cover from whatever's shooting at you.

"Okay – *Yellow Brick Road*. I can't magically give you armor or ammo, as that's tracked centrally by the server. However, whenever you need some… hit F5, and your heads-up will show you a menu of every pickupable item on the board – in order of proximity. Select what you want, and a fluorescent trail on the ground will light up indicating the shortest path there."

"*Lethal Weapon*. It's an auto-target function, an aimbot. It toggles on caps-lock. Turn it on, and every shot you take will be auto-aimed until you untoggle it. It will always hit, unless your target is moving – *and* changes direction or speed while your round is in flight. But *use this sparingly*. It's really for emergency use only – when you're faced with a shot that really counts."

"So we're basically in *The Matrix* now," Aaliyah says. "We can flout the laws of physics."

"Yeah, basically. Except if you die in the game you don't die in real life."

"No," Javier says. "But a million other people die."

Mike presses his lips together. "Look. I know we haven't trained with these tools. But we're going to need every advantage we can get. You'll just have to learn fast."

Johnson grins. "Hell. We didn't get where we are by learning slow."

"One last thing," Mike says. "I've arranged for Red Team, our OPFOR from training, to join Alpha team for this op. Well, the ones who were awake and logged in."

"What," Johnson says. "The junior high kids?"

"Yeah. But if what the CIA guy said is accurate, and this place is a fortress… we're going to need all the help we can round up."

"Hmm," Rheinhardt says. "Maybe we should have the CIA team with us."

"Shit," Johnson says. "I'd rather have the junior high squad."

"Yeah," Mike says. "You would."

"Our ride's here," Javier says, pointing at his screen, where his avatar is pointing out the window. An Osprey VTL is setting down in the street outside. While the team has been briefing, BigD has been flying in from their training camp to pick them up.

Next stop: the port city.

"Let's do it," Javier says, as he and the others move back to their consoles.

ON THE DOCKSIDE
MARGIERS, AFTERWAR
09:44:56 AUT 16 APR 2018

<u>BetteNoire</u>

"Sniper has targets," BetteNoire says across the net. *"Twenty-seven of them,"* she adds under her breath. Though completely virtual, this scenario is more challenging – impossible, really – than any tactical situation she has ever faced before.

"Roger," WileyC says in response. *"Can you clear the walls and both the north and west guard towers – between when the Javelin launches, and when we reach the gate? Call it fifteen seconds?"*

She takes a breath. "No," she says finally. "But I'll tell you what. If you rocket one of those guard towers, I can take the rest."

"Good idea. We've got two launchers. Stand by."

Once again, BetteNoire is up in a high place, a long way off – the roof of a warehouse nearly a mile from the dry dock complex. And this time she doesn't have her CheyTac. Instead, she's rocking an AS50 from Accuracy International. It's a new .50 cal auto sniper rifle developed by a British firm for USSOCOM, specifically for the Navy SEALs. It is not her first choice of weapon; but it is the best sniper rifle available in AfterWar. She almost went with the McMillan TAC-50 – which in real life holds the record for longest range ever for a documented kill (Afghanistan, 2002, 2430m, a sniper from Princess Patricia's Light Canadian Infantry.) But the McMillan is bolt action – and one thing she's not going to have time for is manually chambering rounds.

She also doesn't know whether she's even going to have time to reload the AS50. She's tested this – and the gun in the game will not reload as quickly as she can do it in real life. But it will have to do – she has many more targets than bullets in the magazine. And that is if her hit rate is 100%. Which it will have to be.

Because there will be no time for a second attempt on this objective.

BoPeep and UncleBJ…
…are underwater. They are breathing through the scuba gear they captured in Fallujagrad, and swimming along the sandy bottom toward the seaward side of the dry dock. Their amphibious heroics may all come to nothing; but aerial

reconnaissance has indicated that the seaward side, and the ship-launching ramp, are lightly defended.

And they definitely won't have to surmount the fifteen-foot wall, studded with guard towers, and mounted with heavy machine guns, which surrounds the rest of the complex.

They do have to hope their air holds out – and that they can make it out of the water without being shot down.

They swim on, watching the clock, and looking over their real shoulders to monitor the progress of the rest of the team.

<u>J-Dawg…</u>

…is hovering, at about a hundred feet, just out of view of the dry dock complex. He is in the Osprey, piloted by BigD. He stands in the back, with the sliding side hatch cracked – and surrounded by several large wooden crates.

He is carrying a 7.62mm SCAR, with an underslung EGLM; as well as an enormous quantity of extra ammunition. He wears heavy powered armor, which will slow him down, and will stop being useful when its power cell runs dry. But which will allow him to drop from height without damaging himself. Plus take a lot of hits.

He already has a 40mm thermite grenade loaded up in his launcher.

He is also wearing an ICS (Inter-crew Communication System) headset that allows him to communicate with BigD. Otherwise, the heavy rotor wash and engine noise make it difficult to hear much.

He, too, waits for the go signal.

<u>WileyC and Red Team</u>

WileyC has received a field promotion from private first class to buck sergeant. This allows him to manage the comms and coordination of the squad that has been put under his control: Red Team, of the D-Boys Company - the designated OPFOR in their training exercises. The junior high-schoolers. The all-American kids.

He and these eight recruits are currently massed underneath a wooden pier, standing in sucking muck, just out of view of the front gate of the complex, about 300 yards out.

WileyC has a Javelin missile queued up, as does one of his protégés. The two edge out from under the pier, to gain a line of sight to the front gate and the west guard tower. They are slightly exposed. But they have to let their thermals cool and acquire targets.

>   As soon as they do so, WileyC will
> give the signal - and BetteNoire will
> begin dismantling the guard force, from
> a mile out. And then WileyC and Red Team
> will begin dismantling their firing plat-
> forms out from under them.
>   "WileyC and Red Team in final assault
> position," he says. "All elements
> sitrep."
>   "*BetteNoire at FAP.*"
>   "*BigD at FAP.*"
>   "*J-Dawg, FAP.*"
>   "*BoPeep and UncleBJ. FAP.*"
>   "Roger that," WileyC says. "All ele-
> ments ready. Sniper, you are cleared to
> engage."

At Javier's feet, in real life, under the computer table, sits one Mr MacSnuggles. He lies flat with his real, fleshy, droopy muzzle upon his outstretched paws. He watches the others in the lab, uncomprehending, vaguely hurt. Because he knows that something important is going on, and that he is not being asked to help.

Javier, for his part, wishes that there were some interface to allow Mac into their virtual ops. God knows he is missed. He gives Mac a little nudge with his foot.

And then his vision, his perspective, his sense of place, are all instantly sucked back into the monitor—

>   —as the Osprey begins to climb and bank,
> as the rotors swivel to generate forward

momentum, as the engine and wind noise ramp up in his ears, and as the first firing and explosions ring out in the distance.

AQA DRY DOCK COMPLEX
MARGIERS, AFTERWAR
10:00:00 AUT 16 APR 2018

The enormous double front gates of the complex erupt in a fireball. Bodies, in ones and twos, heads turned into canoes by .50cal sniper rounds, fall from their positions on the wall into the blossoming inferno. One of the two guard towers on the front of the complex also erupts into hot metal slivers and expanding gases. From there, only body parts float to earth below.

Before the fireball has dissipated, before the cloud-sized bloom of black smoke has reached its full volume, and while guards up top are still taking clockwork headshots and tumbling out into space, WileyC and Red Team launch their balls-out charge across the open expanse.

They've got a lot of open ground to clear. But they've also got a lot of lethal chaos going on to cover their advance. And so they swoop through the wall of smoke and into the compound without taking casualties.

The dry dock complex consists of a single enormous, warehouse-like structure, surrounded on three sides by the fifteen foot wall, and the four guard towers - and on the fourth side by water. The only entrances to the building are far around the sides, near the ramp and the water – making a lengthy gauntlet that any invaders must run from the front gate. And one which is covered on all sides by elevated firing positions.

WileyC urges his Red Team forward, left into the compound. But Buraq fighters have begun regrouping from the initial assault, and mass together to oppose them.

And WileyC is learning that there are upsides and downsides to virtual combat, versus the real thing. On the upside, he doesn't have to worry about being actually hurt or killed. On the downside, neither does his enemy. Virtual explosions, virtual dead and wounded, virtual gore and screams, do not produce the shock and chaos that real ones do.

Dozens of Buraq fighters now spill around the corners of the hulking structure, coming at Red Team from both sides. And Red Team are now in range of shooters on the wall – ones not visible to BetteNoire in her hide. WileyC and his team drop to the ground and begin firing to defend themselves. But they are immediately pinned down – in a wide open area with no cover.

***

J-Dawg is kind of amazed at the similarities between a rotary-wing air assault in the game, and one in real life. Video game designers use and abuse every quirk of human perception, just as illusionists do, to trick the brain into seeing things that are not there. Virtual spaces seem real to the players of these games – and many remember game levels they've played, years later, just as vividly as they remember their childhood homes.

The roar of the engines… the ground blasting by below… the wind trying to pull him out the door. Even the adrenaline. All similar. And when the Osprey starts taking ground fire, J-Dawg even feels the old traditional dread of getting shot down and turned into charred meat waffles.

And, just as in real life, he pushes that fear aside and gets on with his job.

The Osprey clears the wall, rounds from elevated shooters plunking into its airframe. The rotors begin to swivel, bringing the bird into a hover – directly over the largest mass of Buraq, about thirty players, who are engaging Red Team from their left. Many of them are only just beginning to shift their fire to the threat overhead, when J-Dawg kicks the first wooden crate out the door.

It falls into their midst and spills open – dozens of small metal cylinders rolling in all directions. Before the Buraq can react, the second, third, and fourth crates follow, crashing open in nearly the same spot. And, finally, there's the single 40mm thermite grenade from J-Dawg's launcher - taking no perceptible time to rocket the forty feet from the Osprey straight down to the ground.

The grenade explodes in a spray of white hot burning thermite embers, nearly instantly setting off the 192 grenade canisters all around it on the ground - high explosive, fragmentation, airburst, HEDP, more thermite, even illumination and smoke. These have tumbled out in a wide and uneven pattern, and cook off in accelerating secondary explosions. In about a second, the forty Buraq fighters have been turned into meat vapor.

When the smoke begins to clear, there is nothing left on the ground but scorch marks, blackened entrails, and the twisted metal shards of blooming gun barrels.

"*Move it out,*" WileyC hollers to his team, getting to his feet and raising his rifle to his shoulder.

By the time they have crossed over the blood and soot, J-Dawg – who pushed himself out of the Osprey only a few seconds behind the crates of grenades – has caught WileyC up and fallen into formation.

And the other force of Buraq – the other forty or so who came around from the right side – have begun to give chase.

BigD's Osprey rises, banks, and accelerates back out over the walls of the complex.

REAR OF AQA DRY DOCK COMPLEX
MARGIERS, AFTERWAR
10:08:22 AUT 16 APR 2018

BoPeep and UncleBJ breach the surface of the water an inch at a time. As they peer over the edge, they see no movement, and no opposition. They lever themselves up, roll onto the ramp, and shed the scuba gear – then clear their weapons.

A few seconds later, they duck into the lee of the building. The enormous boat launch doors are closed. To the left, there is a human-sized door – reinforced steel, and locked. They plant breaching charges and clear out. The explosive goes with a throaty whump, and the door remains hanging from its hinges.

BoPeep enters from the left, angling right; and UncleBJ the reverse. They are somewhere in the rear of the huge building, in a claustrophobic complex of storerooms. They clear the area, follow a short hallway, open the door at its end – and are immediately confronted with three things: the dizzy space of the main dry dock area; a huge section of ship hull, rising to the ceiling; and an uncountable number of Buraq guys, who

```
are running to and fro, and who quickly
detect the intrusion.
     Bo and BJ drop to their knees and
open up. They take out five or six of the
Buraq before their rifles run dry – and
before attracting a ferocious counter-
assault. They have no choice but retreat
back down the hall. They reload, take
opposite doorways, and cover the end of
the hall. Two opponents burst through.
They drop them both.
     And BoPeep shouts, into his other
radio,
```

"Bo to TOC. Did you see that? Did you see it?"

"Yeah," Havering says. "We saw a big-ass section of ship hull." He looks up at one of the two-ways on the wall. A man in a white uniform fills that screen, his face intently watching a monitor in his own command center. He is a Captain from the U.S. Coast Guard, District 11 (West Coast), a specialist in container shipping. And he is watching a video feed piped directly from the back of Rheinhardt's machine into the TOC – and from there over the wire to the Coast Guard station in California.

The man shakes his head. "No," he says. "No vessel name, no IMO number, no port of registry or call sign. And impossible to tell the shipping line – or even the class, or dimensions. I have to see more."

Havering speaks back into his headset. "All we can tell is it's a goddamn container ship. Ya gotta get back in there and give us a decent look at it."

"*Roger that,*" Rheinhardt says, the sound of in-game gunfire leaking out into his other comms.

* * *

```
BetteNoire takes a last couple of shots,
emptying her mag. But there are very few
living Buraq on the walls on this side of
the complex, or in the guard tower. Those
that are alive have stayed that way by
keeping their heads down. And down behind
something very solid – a .50cal round
will go through six inches of concrete.
    She stands, cradles the rifle, and
dashes up a metal stairwell to the upper
part of the roof, where the Osprey is
angling in. She throws herself aboard,
through the side hatch, before it touches
down. BigD throttles it back up and pulls
the bird up and away – back toward the
dry dock.
```

* * *

```
Just for grins, J-Dawg tries to Superman
through the wall of the building. The
wall disappears, but behind it is void.
This is because he's never been inside,
so the server never sent his client any
information about what is in there.
```

Less for grins than for a team-wide sitrep, WileyC Holy Spirits through the views of the other members of the team. He finds BoPeep and UncleBJ pinned down in a back area of the dry dock, taking extremely heavy small-arms and grenade fire. He looks out from the side of the Osprey through BetteNoire's eyes, as the bird zooms in toward one of the guard towers, slowing into a hover. He sees himself, out of J-Dawg's eyes, from a few feet away. Then he gets the big surprise – tabbing back to his own view, where he sees a heavy tank rolling around from the back of the dry dock.

Their advance intel did not say anything about armor.

***

BetteNoire leaps the last ten feet to the stretch of wall outside the guard tower. Storming the door, she finds one remaining defender inside, looking away. She drops him with three twelve-gauge slugs to the back, fired from her close-range weapon. She slings this behind her again, pulls the AS50, and emplaces it on the window ledge – facing in toward the courtyard.

She puts her eye to the scope to begin picking out targets, when an explosion fills her vision. She pulls back wide and pans around. There's a main battle tank coming around from the left. And it is firing its main gun, right into WileyC and J-Dawg's Red Team. Bodies from one side of the group fly into the air as the shell explodes in their midst. The team is stopped dead, unable to advance into this onslaught.

At the same time, the other half of the Buraq ground force is bearing into them from behind. Red Team is fighting valiantly – moving and shooting well. But they are getting cut up. BetteNoire starts taking shots into the advancing mass of Buraq: headshot, torso shot, miss, another headshot.

But she already knows cannot take down enough of them. And soon the ground assault force will be crushed between these millstones.

FIFTY FEET ABOVE THE AQA DRY DOCK COMPLEX
MARGIERS, AFTERWAR
10:14:54 AUT 16 APR 2018

BigD grips the controls of the aircraft. By this point, after two close passes over the battlefield, he's been severely shot up. He can feel a crescendoing tremor in the rotors and controls. And he doesn't know how much longer he can keep it in the air. But it doesn't matter, because keeping it in the air is no longer part of the plan.

BigD flies out over the walls a last time – working to gain a little altitude and a lot of airspeed. Once he has both, he swings it back around, puts the flaps down, and points the nose straight at the building, right at the juncture of wall and ground. And at a spot between Red Team and the attacking tank.

He begins taking heavy fire – and the hatch gunner of the tank swivels his dual .50-cal machine gun upward. Gaining speed rapidly, the Osprey starts to pull apart at the seams. But it only needs to hold together for another few seconds.

***

The thermals cool again on WileyC's Javelin launcher, and he acquires the tank. He lets the missile go. It's a perfect shot, arcing upward and slamming down again on the soft upper skin. The tank bends in two at the waist, at the same time as it lifts up off the ground. Incredibly amusingly, even in the serious circumstances, the .50 gunner launches out of his hatch and shoots two hundred feet into the air. WileyC cannot help panning up and tracking the man's superhero-like flight, then watching him fall to earth and disappear behind the wall to the west.

When he looks around him again, confirming that the tank is a charred hulk, two things happen nearly instantly. First, the Osprey slams into the wall of the warehouse at ground level, creating a massive explosion. And, secondly, two more tanks roll around from the backside of the warehouse.

***

BigD smiles as the building and ground race in at him at hyperspeed, the wall growing to become, for an instant, his whole world. He never hears the explosion. His screen merely goes black, and his headphones go dead.

"Over to you guys," he says, pushing back in his chair.

* * *

"Move!" WileyC shouts, leading the remnants of his team directly into the flaming miasma of wreckage. He climbs over some twisted rebar, through a rising wall of flame – and comes upon yet more wreckage. He checks his armor and health: not great, and getting worse fast. He's taking heat damage from the fire.

He tries left, then right; then finally retreats and moves all the way around to one side, then the other. The rest of the team is doing likewise. He curses aloud. The wall is well and truly demolished, in a twenty-foot-wide and ten-foot-high section. But the hole has effectively been plugged with destroyed aircraft and rubble. There is no way through.

The two new tanks begin firing their main guns on their position.

* * *

BetteNoire reloads, willing the computer to go faster. She's seen the two tanks begin their assault. There's nothing she can do about that. All she can do is continue to try to stem the tide of infantry coming at the team's rear. She's already got at least 40 kills on the day. But there are still too many of them.

As her gun comes back online, and she sights in to acquire another target, an explosion rips through the ranks of the Buraq fighters, sending several flying. Then full-auto gunfire rings out, cutting into bodies and dropping several more. The Buraq turn to face some unknown threat from behind them.

BetteNoire pulls back from her scope. And she can now see something like sixty newcomers screaming through the front gate – shouting, and firing, and cutting down and scattering the Buraq before them. They are moving fast, and coordinating well. The newcomers are all dressed in Anglosphere uniform.

But they are all wear identical sand-colored berets. Zooming in, BetteNoire can see winged dagger patches upon them.

Aaliyah smiles and shakes her head at the screen.

AQA DRY DOCK COMPLEX
MARGIERS, AFTERWAR
10:28:01 AUT 16 APR 2018

For a few seconds, WileyC doesn't know which way to face to get killed. Either direction should work. He does know that his seconds are numbered. The assault is faltering – and the mission failing. Enormous shells are coming in, more and more accurately, from the two tanks. And the force to his rear is pressing home their attack. The remains of his team are down on the ground again, firing in all directions.

And then he hears a sudden increase in firing volume behind him, sees explosions amongst the Buraq - and, just like that, the force to the rear is cut down, overrun. And coming through their ranks, and closing fast, are strange avatars in beige berets.

WileyC stands. The avatar at the fore of the newcomers approaches. He takes a bead but doesn't fire. "What?" the player says. "You're not hard enough to take on a bunch of wankers like that lot?" And he makes a gesture – a custom, obscene gesture, obviously programmed or downloaded from somewhere – putting thumb and forefinger together, his other fingers in a circle, fist pumping up and down.

"Jesus fucking Christ," WileyC finally says. *"Nigel?"*

"Yeah, mate. At your service. Don't think we can help you with that armor. But the other way's open now. You with us?"

"Jesus Christ. I mean, affirmative. Let's do it."

He, and J-Dawg, and his handful of surviving Red Force kids, take off at a run, just ahead of the SAS players - an entire Sabre Squadron of SAS, consisting of four 16-man troops (minus a few casualties now).

"Oi, wait for us!" Nigel says, running to catch up. "It's not a bloody race…" Nigel seems to reconsider, remembering the tanks behind them, while running full out. "Okay, maybe it is a race…"

***

"Friendlies! Coming in!" J-Dawg shouts, before stepping into the hallway in the rear of the complex. BoPeep and UncleBJ check their firing, then step out into the cavernous dry dock. The ship comes fully into view now. It is nearly a hundred feet in height – and too long to estimate, in their foreshortened monitor view.

Bodies litter the concrete floor, lying in pools of blood. The combined Red Team/SAS force has cleared the interior in only a few minutes, with moderate losses.

"Who the hell are all *these* people?" BoPeep asks. UncleBJ steps around for a look at the newcomers – allowing Nigel to mouse over him and see his screen name.

"Would have been here sooner," he says. "But we lost track of time over at your mum's house." Now Nigel's avatar is holding his hands before him at waist height, and pumping his pelvis back and forth. Then he slaps from side to side with his right hand. (*Someone,* WileyC thinks to himself, *has been spending way too much time customizing his avatar.*)

"*Nigel!*" UncleBJ shouts. "Heya, mate! What the fuck are you guys doing here?"

"Bit of a story, that. Let's just say you're not the only ones operating in new battlespaces."

"Oh, yeah. And I always forget that your boss and my boss stay in such close contact."

"You also always forget," Nigel quips, "that you blokes are always copying us. Have been from the start. We do everything first."

"Yeah," BJ says dismissively. "'Who dares, whinge.'"

"Enough," BoPeep says, taking off and running in a wide circle around the ship, panning his view up and down. "TOC. Are you getting this?"

DELTA TACTICAL OPERATIONS CENTER
NEAR FORT BRAGG, NORTH CAROLINA
05:32:04 EST 16 APR

"Affirmative, Bo," Havering says. "Vision is good. Captain?" he asks, looking severely at the screen on the wall.

"Okay," the man in white says. "From those dimensions, I'd say it's either a Panamax or Panamax II class container ship. Can you get some human figures in the frame? Right up next to the hull?"

"You got that, Bo Peep?"

"Roger. How's this?"

"Those figures are man-size?" the Coast Guard man asks. "Okay. Hang on. I'm taking some screenshots… Yeah, if I'm reading this right, it looks to be about 1000 feet in length, with about 40 feet of draft. That's Panamax. The problem is that's an extremely common class of ship – it's the largest size that will get through the Panama Canal. There are literally thousands of them."

"Lisa?" Havering asks.

"Sir," she says, tabbing through screens. "On the West Coast… we've got fourteen Panamax class ships inbound. We've got four docked at Long Beach… two at San Diego… six at Oakland…"

"Okay," Havering says. "Not good enough, Sergeant."

The Coast Guard guys pipes up again. "It *looks* like a Maersk line ship to me. But without markings, I can't be sure. I mean, it's a computer sim."

"Colonel, stand by," Rheinhardt says.

* * *

"Okay, what?" BoPeep says. The others are crowding into the back room where WileyC has summoned them. But BoPeep is losing his patience. He's not sure the whole video game, simulated-ship gambit hasn't been a total waste of time – time they didn't have. "Christ," he mutters in frustration, "this is stupid…"

"Stupid like a fox," UncleBJ says. He points around WileyC's shoulder, where the latter sits at a desk – and at the console of an in-game computer.

"*Jackpot,*" WileyC says.

Just visible on the tiny virtual screen (upon the larger real screen) are complex blue-and-white schematics – evidently the full design and layout of the container ship. From WileyC's position at the computer, he can both see details and operate the machine (from his machine). He tabs through screens of graphics and data.

"What else? *What else?*" The group jostles around.

"Hold on…" WileyC says. "Yeah. Here. Does this look like a registry number? 'IMO' followed by seven digits?"

"*Fuckin'* A," UncleBJ says. "International Maritime Organization code. Money."

ONBOARD THE "MIKE MURPHY", MAKO SPEC-OPS CRAFT
ON SAN FRANCISCO BAY
02:12:54 PST 16 APR

"Taking control of something as big as a container ship is a lot easier than you think," the Navy SEAL Lieutenant is telling Tim McDonough, seemingly casually. "These huge craft are so automated these days they practically have skeleton crews – maybe a dozen sailors, something like 300 containers per crewman. Pirates roll up in speedboats, with a few AKs and maybe an RPG, they throw a pipe ladder up on the deck, and they climb onboard. The captain knows he can't outrun them – and he'd rather stop than risk being fired upon.

"The pirates can't do anything with the cargo, of course. Usually, the goal is hostage-taking and ransom. The pirates are actually looking for the big vessels – ideally American, British, Japanese, or Korean. That way they know shipping lines can pay. Hell, you can go on the web sites of these companies and get the cruising schedules and ports of call of all their vessels. It's as easy as getting flight info. The most dangerous spots at the moment are Indonesia and the East African coast."

"This one is sailing out of Hong Kong," Tim says. "And it's not about robbery or ransom. You've been briefed, right?"

"Yes. And don't think we haven't been preparing for this kind of thing, either. In 2003, pirates boarded a supertanker in the Malacca Straits. But all they did was practice steering the ship. And all they stole were manuals and technical information. We figured then it was practice for something like this – using a tanker as a weapon."

Swabbies, Tim is thinking to himself. But he can't quite bring himself to be really irked – both because he needs to be very cool right now, and because he's not easily irked by nature. And also because he's tired. It's been a long night – cross-country red-eye flight, two changes of destination, landing at SFO, pickup off the tarmac by a Navy Sea Stallion helo, and now insertion, in the pitch dark, onto an 82-foot Mk V Special Operations Craft. Zipping across the great black mass of San Francisco Bay at a sizzling 50 knots.

Onboard the boat are a variety of mounted weapons – M240 and M60 machine guns, a GAU-17 minigun, a Mk 19 40mm grenade launcher – as well as 16 Navy SEALS, all of them decked out in full amphibious assault kit. There are also four inflatable Combat Rubber Raiding Craft with outboard motors, used for stealthy insertion. But there's simply no time for stealth tonight.

At their current vector, they will intercept the target ship within a half mile of the Golden Gate Bridge – *on one side or the other*. This is far enough out, command has surmised, that the tangos will not be planning to detonate their weapon yet. They will almost certainly want to get in tight with one of the big cities in the Bay, either SF or Oakland. But it *is* close enough that a 15-kiloton detonation there will still cause an enormous amount of ugliness. Some death. A fair bit of destruction. And a hell of a lot of fallout.

The SEAL team's plan is to hit the vessel hard and fast from fore and aft – and hope they can take it down before anything goes boom. Destroying the ship with air or artillery was seriously discussed. But with a crude gun-barrel atomic device of the type they expect to find, there would be a significant chance of an explosion setting it off. The advanced nukes of state actors are very stable. The improvised devices of terrorists are not. The only way to be sure of not inadvertently creating positive yield is to take control of the ship.

Which is what the SEALs are unrivaled experts at. They practice ship takedowns day and night. And which is also why Delta Staff Sergeant Tim McDonough is less annoyed than he might otherwise be at the team leader's digressions on the subject of piracy. There is really no assault plan that needs discussing – these operators, and the sixteen others in the MAKO craft behind them, have practiced taking down exactly this kind of ship many times.

All Tim has to do is follow them onboard.

And then defuse and dismantle an atomic bomb.

Assuming of course it hasn't already gone off by then. At which point, it won't be his problem anymore.

And which is, in a way, another reason why he is so relaxed about the random piracy lecture from NAVSPECWARCOM's finest. It is a small matter, in the scheme of things – nothing worth getting upset about. And, moreover, it could easily be the last lecture he ever hears.

One of the team of combat-craft crewmen manning the boat throws up an index finger: one minute.

DELTA TACTICAL OPERATIONS CENTER
NEAR FORT BRAGG, NORTH CAROLINA
07:24:04 EST 16 APR

The whole of Alpha team is now back in the TOC – Rheinhardt, Johnson, Aaliyah, Javier, Mr MacSnuggles, and Mike. The whole team minus Tim. They are listening to him check in with the Colonel for a final brief before hitting the ship. The conversation is amplified throughout the dim, glowing, spectacularly tense room.

"Sergeant, you know what national policy is on this, as well as standard counter-terrorism doctrine."

"Yes, sir."

"Operational casualties, civilian casualties, collateral damage – none of it matters now. Scuttle the ship if you have to. Blow up sailboats in your way. Drown puppies. With a nuclear device in play, everything else is secondary. *Everything*. Including those SEALs, and including you. As Churchill said to the garrison at Malta: 'No surrender, no retreat. Senior officers should die with their men.'"

"Roger that, sir."

"That said… you defuse that bomb and bring your ass home. You got me, Sergeant?"

"Yes, Colonel."

"What's your ETA?"

"Right now. Gotta go."

"Godspeed, son."

Not a word is spoken in the TOC now. Eighteen men and women sit in silence amidst the dim pulsing lights, and wait for the next sitrep.

They know it will probably all be over in a minute or two.

* * *

The first booby trap catches the mass of the initial SEAL team element, call sign "Juliet", as they try to enter the wheelhouse. Tim is still hanging on the rope ladder, halfway down the hull of the hulking ship, thirty feet above the water, when the massive explosion rocks the boat.

The SEAL's demo guy found and disabled the first charge, placed behind the wheelhouse door. But it was merely a dodge for the bigger bomb – which was essentially the whole wheelhouse itself. The thick glass windows of the structure exploded out into the darkness, and black-clad bodies hit the deck all around it.

"Man down," the word comes over the command net immediately, calmly, no sign of panic. The SEALs have been hit hard – but they are pros, and do not rattle.

"Roger, Juliet," their commander responds from the MAKO. "What's your casualty's status?"

But that's when the small arms fire opens up – cutting into the already decimated sixteen-man team, causing more casualties, and pinning them down in and around the wheelhouse. They are immobilized within seconds, and unable to respond or maneuver. Tim hangs from his ladder and waits to be called forward, listening to the gunfire and shouts of pain.

He is not afraid of going in and fighting – but he knows that, because of his skills, he is indispensable to the mission, and cannot risk himself that way. If Juliet is doomed, he must not die with them. At least not yet.

By now, the second element, call sign "K-Bar", has begun sweeping the rear deck of the ship, from the stern forward. The second group can see the flashes of firing at the fore of the vessel – but that is still nearly a quarter of a mile away.

When the second booby trap goes – igniting a large oil fire amidships, cutting off the rescue force, and prompting another flurry of grim squad-net communication – that is when Tim realizes things are well and truly going south.

He climbs the remaining section of rope ladder and looks over the gunwale. A few feet away, he can see the Juliet team members firing in all directions, tending to wounded, and dragging prone figures behind the smoking wheelhouse. Looking down the length of the vessel, he can see a sheet of fire burning across its midsection. Backlit by the flames, a group of several men are maneuvering something bulky up to the edge of the boat.

Tim realizes it is some kind of a crew-served weapon, only a second before it fires – destroying, in a single shot, the command boat where it sits in the water, two hundred feet to starboard. The little metal craft turns into a fireball, and secondary explosions cook off from munitions onboard – but only for a few seconds, after which the boat is swallowed whole by the Bay.

Frantic updates continue going out over comms. But there is no voice of command or control coming back.

Tim levers himself up onto the deck and slithers to the left, toward the stern, to avoid the melee around the wheelhouse. He unslings his rifle, an HK416 – a version of the M4 redesigned by Delta gunsmiths and Heckler & Koch to solve the jamming problems of the standard M4. It is new and sleeker, with much greater reliability and accuracy. It also has "over-the-beach" capability, meaning it can safely be fired after being submerged in water, without even being completely drained first.

Tim brings the weapon to his shoulder and cheek, flips the fire selector to full-auto, sights in down the length of the ship – and kills the entire gun crew, before they can fire on the other MAKO. He drops to the deck to reload, and to plan his next move. He now has a significant dilemma.

The assault plan was to kill the hijackers, secure the ship – and then simultaneously get it steaming in the opposite direction, while locating and defusing the atomic device. But this plan has gone to hell from the start. The tangos are killing *them*, and the ship is nowhere near secure. And that doesn't look like changing very soon.

That still leaves the critical third and fourth tasks: turning the ship around, away from inhabited areas; and finding and defusing the bomb. The trouble is that if Tim pursues the former, he will have to cross the firefight to reach the wheelhouse and the pilot controls. And this could easily leave him dead or badly wounded, and no good for bomb disposal. So instead he gets on the horn.

"Juliet team leader – this is Delta element. Acknowledge."

A voice rises above the frantic shouts that criss-cross the squad net: *"Delta, switch to secondary frequency."*

Tim punches his radio and signs in. The voice comes back again. *"Delta, Juliet team lead is down. This is the 2IC."*

"Stand by for traffic," Tim says, speaking over the roar of gunfire. "Objective is *not* secure."

"Yeah, no shit, D-boy," the man says; and this is followed by a long rolling peal of gunfire – both from across the deck and right in Tim's ear, through the radio.

"Juliet, you need to get this boat turned around. I will locate the device. Interrogative: can you gain steering control?"

"Affirmative," the SEAL says, sounding breathless, and perhaps wounded. *"Ship is being remote-piloted. But we've located the radio control, and are disabling. Now if we can just keep this position from being overrun…"*

And with this, Tim feels the ship underneath him not turning, but slowing. Quicker than turning around a vessel of this size is stopping it and reversing. The SEALS seem to be making that happen. Tim unslings his backpack and pulls out a handheld gamma- and neutron-detector. It's while powering this device up that he feels the bullet hit.

Damn, he thinks, lying on the deck, and bringing his weapon to bear, sighting in on the man who's sighted him. *Decent-sounding plan. Got shot anyway…*

DELTA TACTICAL OPERATIONS CENTER
NEAR FORT BRAGG, NORTH CAROLINA
07:31:04 EST 16 APR

"TOC, this is Bit Twiddler. How copy?"

The voice, speaking out into the silence and tension of the TOC, is thin and labored. It makes everyone in the room tense their shoulder muscles.

"Solid copy, BT," Havering says into his headset. "We are right here. Coronado indicates they have lost contact with their team. Advise status."

For a few seconds there is only labored breathing in response. *"SEALs have lost their command element,"* Tim finally says. *"Both teams pinned down on the deck…Interrogative: where are we?"*

"Where are you? You mean where's the ship?" Havering checks his screen. "We have you moving at about one-eighth speed back out of the Bay. Out to sea. You have reversed course. What's your mission status?"

More breathing. *"I'm down in one of the holds. Have located the device."*

Another group intake of breath around the TOC.

"It's on a timer. And tamper-proofed. I can defeat that. I'm just having a little trouble focusing."

"Are you hit, BT?"

"Yeah, a little bit."

Johnson starts shoving people until someone gives him a headset, which is not very long. "Tim. Where you hit, buddy?"

"Neck," Tim says. *"Just bad luck. I've got it wrapped up okay."*

"Listen to me, man. How much blood have you lost? You'll need help."

"Negative. No time, Uncle."

Havering uses his hand to cover up his mouthpiece. "Coronado says they've lost contact with *both their teams* on the ship. They still see some firing going on. But there's no comms… Everyone may be dead up there."

"Tim, listen," BJ says. "You gotta keep yourself conscious."

"Roger that. I've got the tamper-proofing defeated. Stand by."

"Tim," Havering says. "Interrogative: how much time on the timer?"

"Thirteen thirty-four," Tim says.

"Thirteen minutes?"

"There's also a radio control. I've got that pulled out. Stand by… Power supply to the detonator's disconnected now…Conventional explosive removed. Just gotta separate the U-235 halves…"

"Tim. The device is safe now. Listen. The quick reaction force is inbound. There are helos landing on the deck right now. Just hang on and wait for those personnel. The device is safe."

There is a lengthy pause, just static. Finally, Tim speaks again. He sounds serene, almost carefree. *"Device safe now. Uranium's out. Safe. Just gonna sit here and take it easy for a while."*

"That's it, Tim. You stay with us, Sergeant. The QRF is coming to you now. Just hold on. You hold on."

"Roger that, Colonel."

There's another long silence.

"Tim."

"Safe."

"Tim."

GREEN BERET PARACHUTE CLUB
FORT BRAGG, NORTH CAROLINA
20:04:00 EST 23 APR

There are at least a hundred people in the bar, filling it to above capacity – probably above the fire marshal's safety limit. But there is not much noise, and none of the boisterousness one expects in packed bars. Just quiet conversation, a buzz of solemn men and women speaking respectfully. Speaking to, and of, close friends.

Mike says to Javier, "This isn't your first one of these, is it?"

"No. Not nearly."

"And you're the baby of the group."

"Yes."

The two of them stand at the far end of the bar, in a line with Eric, Aaliyah, and BJ. They are like the immediate family, as if they are in the receiving line. Mac lies at their feet, up against the brass foot rail of the bar. He has his chin on his paws again. Before him sits a whole bowl of pork chops. But they lie untouched. He has been through this routine before. And Mike feels very sure the dog knows exactly who is missing tonight.

"He looks so young there," Mike says.

Propped up on the bar, in the middle of the group, is an 11x13 photo of Staff Sergeant Tim McDonough in his Class A dress uniform – dark green, creased, with necktie and all his citations. No eyeglasses. No pens in his pocket.

"Do you think Tim will get the Medal of Honor?" Mike asks. "Like the two operators who died in Somalia?"

Rheinhardt shakes his head slowly. "No. You can't get a medal for an operation that never happened."

"And this one definitely never happened," BJ says. "Hell, it could never be allowed to happen. Much less go as badly as it did."

"We did let that one get pretty close to the brink," Mike says.

They all sort of spontaneously turn their heads inward, back toward the photo on the bar; and then up over it. Behind Tim's image, hanging on the back wall of the bar, is one of his pictures. It is a large oil painting of the front of the Delta complex, the Ranch. It shows the rose garden by the front gates in full bloom.

"And it's probably going to happen again," Ali says, finally. "Things are going to get worse before they get better."

"Better get another round in that case," BJ says.

Mike puts his empty glass on the bar. "Why is no one paying for drinks?"

"Tonight's on Tim," Javier says. "It's traditional to leave a thousand dollars in your will for an open bar here. For your friends."

Mike shakes his head. "Man. It just shouldn't have happened. He was… God, he was such a completely nice guy. This sucks."

Javier sips from his beer bottle. "Military life is all about give and take. We give our all. And the Army takes. Sometimes everything."

"You don't really feel that way."

"No. I don't. Tim did his duty. No one ever made a nobler, or more important, sacrifice. No one ever died a more meaningful death. And Tim knew, and completely accepted, the risks, from the very first day. I've never been prouder of anyone." He sets his bottle down on the bar. "But none of that changes the fact that our friend is dead. And, you're right, it sucks."

Colonel Havering approaches the group. He addresses each member of the team in turn, squeezing arms and patting shoulders. When he comes to Mike, he turns businesslike and asks, "You take care of that botnet of zombie machines for us?"

Mike pauses to pull himself together. "Yes, sir."

"How?"

"I wrote a modification of their AA12 shotgun weapon mod. Now it shoots 20mm grenades with pop-out stabilizing fins. We're distributing it for free – out of the same shop where they originally sold theirs. It's turning out to be a popular mod. And everyone who downloads it also downloads a virus that eats the original AQA zombie virus. Their whole botnet is getting scrubbed."

"Nice job. Listen." Havering pulls him off to one side. "If I recall correctly, your Reserve commitment began in the summer of 2001. Right?"

"Yes, sir."

"So that means your *inactive* reserve commitment still has a few months left on it." Mike looks into the Colonel's pale blue eyes. "How'd you like to get activated?"

Mike blinks. "You're not inviting me to join the Unit."

"Not as an operator, obviously. But as signals and support personnel. Senior support personnel. You've proven your value. And with Tim gone, we need your skills more than ever. I've talked it over with Sergeant Rheinhardt. He and his team are in agreement. They'd like to keep you around."

Mike shakes his head to clear it. "I don't know… that would be… a really big step."

"Well, you know, if I need to, I can simply have you called up and then stop-loss you for a few years."

Mike's eyes go wide.

"Just kidding, son. This only happens if you want it to. But the job is yours if you want it. You take some time and have a think about it. It's a pretty special opportunity to do some serious good in the world." He pauses to clock the down-turned corners of Mike's mouth. "Mike, I'm sorry about Tim. I know he liked you. He only had good things to say about you, and your work."

Mike nods. "I'm sorry, too."

"You take it easy." Havering departs.

* * *

Mike starts to feel claustrophobic in the heavy press of bodies, and steps outside for air. He walks a few yards out into the last light of the pretty North Carolina spring evening, the terrain flat and green and wide around him. He puts his hands in his pockets and breathes deeply of the clean air. A few vehicles, mostly pickup trucks and motorcycles, whiz by on the road out front.

"Well," he says quietly, to himself, "I guess I'm not gonna get anywhere standing in this parking lot with my face hanging out."

The front door bangs open and a small knot of men and women, three couples, spill out, swaying slightly with drink. The men look sturdy and swarthy – obviously part of the special operations community, if one has eyes to see. Which Mike does now.

One of the men catches Mike's eye as he walks in front of him toward the parked vehicles. He smiles from under his thick moustache, eyes crinkling in a friendly way. "You have a good 'un," he says, touching his hat.

"Yeah," Mike says, nodding back to the man. "Have a good 'un."

Love this book? Share the love, support independent authors, and make me your best friend forever, by posting a quick review on Amazon. Thanks! - Michael

Want to be alerted when the next D-BOYS book or other title from MSF is released? Sign up for e-mail alerts at michaelstephenfuchs.com/alerts and I'll keep you updated. (And I'll never share your address or use it for anything else.)

And you can follow Michael on Facebook (facebook.com/michaelstephenfuchs), Twitter (@michaelstephenf), or by email (www.michaelstephenfuchs.com/alerts).

They are the most capable, committed, and indispensable counter-terrorist operators in the world. They have no rivals for skill, speed, ferocity, intelligence, flexibility, and sheer resolve.
Now one of them is the enemy.

Alpha team leader Sergeant Major Eric Rheinhardt is retiring from the Unit – hanging up his guns and taking up a desk at the Pentagon. But now a ghost, and a lost love, have emerged from his past, dredging up a secret shame and past-due debt. Much worse, his old mentor and now nemesis has turned up on the payroll of the Iranian mullahs – training their proxy fighters in Hamas and Hizbullah, purchasing cyberwar talent and fissile material from the Chinese… and laying the groundwork for the fall of the Third Temple, the modern state of Israel.

The explosive collision of these two legendary operators will ultimately embroil Israeli special forces, Chinese hackers, squadrons of D-boys, Tier-1 SEAL teams, CIA paras, Iraqi spec-ops teams, Kurdish Peshmerga fighters, hyper-skilled jihadis, and Iranian Revolutionary Guards – all in a no-holds-barred street fight for survival. Before it's over, the battlespace will be littered with armed robots, stealth drones, a nuclear-cruise-missile-armed submarine, a hijacked Soviet warship, shrieking helicopter crashes, radiological rocket attacks, hacker duels to the death, vendettas, betrayals, reversals, feints, diversions, doublecrosses, disasters, dognapping, assassination attempts, one-in-a-million shots at victory, and unstoppable kill-crazy rampages.

Get ready for **COUNTER-ASSAULT** – where the action, tactics, high stakes, and blasts of sheer adrenaline assault off the page and do not relent.

> *The D-Boys will return in 2016 in* ***CLOSE QUARTERS BATTLE***

The book in your hand is a work of imaginative fiction. The author would like to stress that – in another illustration of how fiction cannot hold a candle to real life – the imagined exploits of the fictional characters in this novel are a dull shadow of the real-life exploits of our real SOF operators, who train like professional athletes, perform like minor gods, and lay it all on the line every day in the defense of freedom and decency. In a tiny gesture of thanks to them, a portion of the earnings from sales of this book will be donated to the Special Operations Warrior Foundation – which provides college scholarships to the children of SOF personnel who are killed in operational missions or training accidents. Tax-deductible donations to this foundation can be made at www.specialops.org, or to Special Operations Warrior Foundation, P.O. Box 13483, Tampa FL 33681-3483, USA.

ACKNOWLEDGEMENTS

A number of extremely excellent books were indispensable in the creation of this one. Foremost of these is *Inside Delta Force, The Real Story of America's Elite Military Unit*, by Eric L. Haney, Command Sergeant Major, USA (ret). It was from this single (and singular) book that the author learned 80% of what he knows about the make-up, operations, and life of the operators of the 1st Special Forces Operational Detachment-Delta. (You should go buy a copy for yourself right this minute – it's one of the best and coolest and most inspiring and entertaining books of all time.) A lot of the other 20% came, in the form of dramatic and visual illustration, from the television series *The Unit*, co-created by Eric L. Haney, David Mamet, and Shawn Ryan. (Go buy these DVDs, too – they also rock.)

Most of the really big ideas about the nexus of virtual worlds and terrorism came straight from *Synthetic Worlds, The Business And Culture Of Online Games*, by Edward Castranova, to whom the author owes another enormous debt. (Though, the author did at least come up with the basic concept – terrorists using a FPS-MMORPG as a platform for terror attacks, and the good guys having to go in and fight them there – before reading Castranova. But most of the implications came straight from him.)

Ayaan Hirsi Ali's *Infidel, My Life* informed many of the political themes of this book (as well as a certain character).

Finally, everything in this book about crashing, and shot-up, Chinook helicopters came straight from *Roberts Ridge, A Story of Courage and Sacrifice on Takur Ghar Mountain Afghanistan*, by Malcolm MacPherson – in which he relates the harrowing real-life tale of elite American forces in a life-or-death struggle at 8000 feet.

BIBLIOGRAPHY

In addition to the essential works mentioned above (and mentioned again below), the following books were helpful in the research for this book. All are commended to anyone who would like to learn more about the amazing world of SOF.

Inside Delta Force, The Real Story of America's Elite Military Unit, by Eric L. Haney, Command Sergeant Major, USA (ret)

Roberts Ridge, A Story of Courage and Sacrifice on Takur Ghar Mountain Afghanistan, by Malcolm MacPherson

Black Hawk Down, by Mark Bowden [another stunning, heart-stopping read]

Delta, America's Elite Counterterrorist Force, by Terry Griswold and D.M. Giangreco

Weapons of Delta Force, by Fred J. Pushies

Night Stalkers, 160th Special Operations Aviation Regiment (Airborne), by Fred J. Pushies

The Battle of Mogadishu, Firsthand Accounts from the Men of Task Force Ranger, edited by Matt Eversmann and Dan Schilling [who were both there]

Warrior Soul, The Memoir of a Navy SEAL, by Chuck Pfarrer [the Eric L. Haney of SEAL Team Six]

Not A Good Day to Die, The Untold Story of Operation Anaconda, by Sean Naylor

Lone Survivor, The Eyewitness Account of Operation Redwing and the Lost Heroes of SEAL Team 10, by Marcus Luttrell with Patrick Robinson

Bravo Two Zero, The True Story of an SAS Patrol Behind Enemy Lines in Iraq, by Andy McNab

Roughneck Nine-One, The Extraordinary Story of a Special Forces A-Team at War, by Sgt. 1st Class Frank Antenori, U.S. Army (retired) and Hans Halberstadt

Killer Elite, The Inside Story of America's Most Secret Special Operations Team, by Michael Smith

The Operators, Inside the World's Special Forces, by Mike Ryan

Shadow Wars, Special Forces in the New Battle Against Terrorism, by David Pugliese

Down Range, Navy SEALs in the War on Terrorism, by Dick Couch

Synthetic Worlds, The Business And Culture Of Online Games, by Edward Castranova

Infidel, My Life, by Ayaan Hirsi Ali

GLOSSARY

1st SFOD-D - U.S. Special Forces Operational Detachment-Delta, also known as Delta Force

ACU - Army Combat Uniform

AO - Area of Operations

AQ - Al Qaeda

AQA - Al Qaeda in AfterWar

AQO - Al Qaeda Online

AQT - Al Qaeda and Taleban

ATV - All Terrain Vehicle

CAG - Combat Applications Group, also known as Delta Force

CENTCOM - Central Command of the U.S. military, responsible for the Middle East

CIA - Central Intelligence Agency

CO - Commanding Officer

CQB - Close Quarters Battle

CSAR - Combat Search and Rescue

CT - Counter Terrorism

CWOC - CyberWar Operations Center

D-DOS - Distributed Denial of Service Attack

DA - Direct Action, combat operations

DCI - Director of Central Intelligence

DEVGRU - U.S. Naval Special Warfare Development Group, aka SEAL Team 6

DHS - U.S. Department of Homeland Security

DNS - Domain Name System

DOE - Department of Energy

DWEP - Dynamic Wired Equivalent Privacy
EGLM - Enhanced Grenade Launcher Module
EOD - Explosive Ordnance Disposal
FAP - Final Assault Position
FATA - Federally Administrated Tribal Areas, areas of Pakistan bordering Afghanistan
FBI - Federal Bureau of Investigation
FOB - Forward Operating Base
FUBAR - Messed Up Beyond All Recognition
GWOT - Global War on Terror
H&K USP - Heckler & Koch Universal Service Pistol
HDS - Holographic Diffraction Sight
HE - High Explosive
HEDP - High Explosive Dual Purpose
HEU - Highly Enriched Uranium
HRT - The FBI's Hostage Rescue Team
HUMINT - Human Intelligence
HVT - High-Value Target
ICRC - International Committee of the Red Cross
ICS - Inter-crew Communication System
IMO - International Maritime Organization
IR - Infrared
ISD - Information Security Directorate (DHS)
Indig - Indigenous, local personnel
Info-sec - Information security
JSOC - Joint Special Operations Command
LUP - Laying Up Point
M203 - A grenade launcher, typically mounted underneath an M4 assault rifle
M9 - The U.S. Army's standard service pistol, a 9mm Beretta.
MEF - Marine Expeditionary Force
NII - National Information Infrastructure

NSC - National Security Council
NVD - Night Vision Device
NWFP - Northwest Frontier Province of Pakistan
OGA - Other Government Agency, usually meaning the CIA
OPFOR - Opposition Force
P2P - Peer-to-peer, a many-to-many networking model
PJ - Para-jumpers, air force personnel who rescue downed pilots and crews
PKI - Public Key Infrastructure
QRF - Quick Reaction Force, a unit kept on standby for rescues
RFN - Right Now, a time designation
ROTC - Reserve Officer Training Corps
SAD - Special Activities Division, the paramilitaries of the CIA
SATCOM - satellite communications
SAW - Squad Automatic Weapon, a light machine gun
SCAR - SOF Combat Assault Rifle
SEAL - U.S. Navy's SEa, Air, and Land Teams
SMG - Submachine Gun
SOF - Special Operations Forces
SOPMOD - Special Operations Peculiar Modification
SSB - Strategic Support Branch
SIGINT - Signals Intelligence
TF145 - Task Force 145, a mixed team of SOF tasked with capturing HVTs
TOC - Tactical Operations Center
TRADOC - U.S. Army Training and Doctrine Command
UAV - Unmanned Aerial Vehicle
USSOCOM - United States Special Operations Command
VPN - Virtual Private Network
VTL - Vertical Takeoff and Landing

ARISEN
Hope Never Dies.

Fans of the bestselling ARISEN series call it "**Staggeringly**

good - the most consistently excellent franchise in zombie literature"…"Wall to wall adrenaline - edge of your seat unputdownable until the very last page"…"totally stunning in its originality"…"jaw dropping"…"moves like an avalanche"…"You can smell the smoke, feel the explosions, and hear the rounds headed down range"…"edge of the seat, nail biting, page turning mayhem"…"had me holding my breath more times than I could count"…"a knock down drag out kick ass read - the best ZA book series around, period"…"rolls along like an out of control freight train"…"Left me shaking at the last page…"

Alpha team will return – but so will Spetsnaz Alfa Group – in
ARISEN, BOOK ELEVEN – DEATHMATCH

They are the most capable, committed, and indispensable counter-terrorist operators in the world.

They have no rivals for skill, speed, ferocity, intelligence, flexibility, and sheer resolve.

Somewhere in the world, things are going horrifyingly wrong...

Readers call the D-BOYS series "**a high-octane adrenaline-fueled action thrill-ride**", "one of the best action thrillers of the year (or any year for that matter)", "a riveting, fast paced classic!!", "pure action", "The Best Techno Military Thriller I have read!", "Awesome!", "Gripping", "Edge of your seat action", "Kick butt in the most serious of ways and a thrill to read", "What a wild ride!!! I simply could not put this book down", "has a real humanity and philosophical side as well", "a truly fast action, high octane book", "Up there with Clancy and W.E.B. Griffin", "one of the best Spec Ops reads I have run into", and "**hi-tech and action in one well-rounded explosive thriller.**"

ABOUT THE AUTHOR

MICHAEL STEPHEN FUCHS, in addition to co-authoring the first eight books of the bestselling ARISEN series with Glynn James, wrote the bestselling prequels ARISEN : GENESIS and ARISEN : NEMESIS (an Amazon #1 bestseller in Post-Apocalyptic Science Fiction and #1 in Dystopian), as well as Book Nine (#1 bestseller in War, #1 in Military Science Fiction) and Book Ten (an Amazon overall Top 100 bestseller). The series as a whole has sold nearly a quarter million copies. He is also author of the D-BOYS series of high-tech special-operations military adventure novels, which include D-BOYS, COUNTER-ASSAULT, and CLOSE QUARTERS BATTLE (coming in 2016); as well as the acclaimed existential cyberthrillers THE MANUSCRIPT and PANDORA'S SISTERS, both published worldwide by Macmillan in hardback, paperback and all e-book formats (and in translation). He lives in London and at www.michaelstephenfuchs.com, and blogs at www.michaelfuchs.org/razorsedge. You can also follow him on Facebook (facebook.com/michaelstephenfuchs), Twitter (@michaelstephenf), or by email (www.michaelstephenfuchs.com/alerts).

Printed in Great Britain
by Amazon